Richard Gill is a well-known and respected music educator and conductor. He has been Artistic Director of OzOpera, Artistic Director and Chief Conductor of the Canberra Symphony Orchestra, and the Adviser for the Musica Viva in Schools program. He is currently Music Director of Victorian Opera and Artistic Director of the Sydney Symphony Education program.

Richard Gill is a well-known and respected music educator and conductor. He has been Artistic Director of OzOpera, Music Director and Chief Conductor of the Canberra Symphony Orchestra and the Adviser for the Musica Viva in Schools program. He is currently Music Director of Victorian Opera and Artistic Director of the Sydney Symphony Education program.

RICHARD GILL
Give me excess of it

{A MEMOIR}

Some of the people in this book have had their names changed
to protect their identities.

First published 2012 in Macmillan by Pan Macmillan Australia Pty Limited
This Pan edition published in 2013 by Pan Macmillan Australia Pty Limited
1 Market Street, Sydney

National Library of Australia
Cataloguing-in-Publication data:

Gill, Richard (Richard James), author.

Give me excess of it: a memoir / Richard Gill

9781742613642
(paperback)

Gill, Richard, 1942-
Conductors (Music)—Australia—Biography.
Music teachers—Australia—Biography.

784.2092

Typeset in Bembo by Kirby Jones
Printed by IVE

This memoir is dedicated to
Maureen Gill, without whom there
would have been no memories

Contents

I

A Short Overture

(In Which My Theme is Set)

I CANNOT REMEMBER A TIME WHEN MUSIC WASN'T present. My allotted three score years and ten have well and truly passed, and for at least sixty-seven of them I have been singing or playing or conducting something. Music will remain my life until I die (something I do not intend to do for at least another seventy years). Which is not to say that it has been a bed of roses – more like an enormous struggle and a never-ending quest for knowledge, understanding and wisdom.

Working as a musician, teacher, conductor and music director has provided me with some of the lowest points in my life, as well as some of the highest. I have experienced devastating failures, as well as uplifting success. In the process, I have learned a great deal about myself, about others, and about life. My failures showed me that I was inadequately prepared, or had not done enough of the right sort of work. In my successes I see a combination of factors: the right people at the right time, and the right preparation. Hardly rocket surgery, as a violinist once said to me.

Music is, in part, about people. Through my calling I have met some of the most wonderful people in the world and some of the nastiest. In a profession where jealousy, fear, suspicion and good old-fashioned hate intermingle with compassion, love, support and integrity, it is easy to sort out the sheep from the goats, the lovers from the haters. For me, there has been a fortunate abundance of people with whom I have forged strong and enjoyable working relationships. I count myself privileged to have met and worked with a few of the gigantic talents of twentieth-century music: composer Carl Orff, and conductors Otto Klemperer, Carlo Maria Giulini, Georg Tintner and Carlo Felice Cillario. These men were astonishing in many ways, and all have been a great inspiration to me. At the other end of time's scale, I have met young artists whose great talents I have been able to recognise early, and to whom I have been able to offer opportunities and assistance that were not available in my student days.

I did not begin formal music lessons until the age of thirteen. As a late starter, I had the distinct advantage of having enormous amounts to learn and enormous amounts to do. I say this in all sincerity. In the early part of my life, when I wanted to learn music above everything else but family circumstances meant that it simply wasn't possible, the good, the wise and the clever reminded me constantly that all the great musicians started very early, and that I had probably missed the boat. Mozart was a child prodigy, Beethoven began composing very young, Chopin was a genius as a teenager, and so on. I was to learn that discouragement could be almost as effective as encouragement (just as false encouragement is potentially very dangerous indeed).

One of my mother's friends, for example, had received her cap and gown for the piano at the age of seven. Another said that young Betty Bucket, who had been learning piano since she was three, had just got her cap and gown at the age of nine, and was going to a place they called 'The Con' for special lessons!

What a cap and gown meant, and what was required to earn them, were concepts totally unclear to me. But the idea that they were the measure of success was drummed into my brain very early. As a young child I developed the notion that music was all about caps and gowns – which probably explains why I don't have any now. My letters for music consist of two honorary doctorates, neither of which was directly my doing.

Other words I often heard as a child were, 'You have to catch up; you will need to catch up; you will never catch up if you don't start soon.' The warning was never exactly clear. Catch up with what? And to whom? When I started at the New South Wales Conservatorium of Music in 1959, these words came back to haunt me. I was suddenly acutely aware of how far my musical knowledge lagged behind that of my contemporaries.

So much of what happens in our early lives is entirely out of our control. Music was never really part of my early childhood in a formal way; nor was ours an overly musical home. Nonetheless, I owe my parents, Stephen and Lydia, a massive debt, which I never fully acknowledged while they were alive. I regret it but there is nothing I can do now other than acknowledge it here. My parents instilled in me a love of words, of reading, of literature. Above all, my mother instilled in me a love of learning for its own sake. It was enough to learn something because it was there. It is to her, principally, that I owe my love of poetry.

My father was a great reader, especially of encyclopaedias and dictionaries. He left school at the age of twelve and went to work for the Sydney firm of William Brooks, a publisher of school texts and reference books. Although he had received a very limited formal education, at Holy Cross College, Ryde, he was widely read, deeply interested in learning, and a person with a genuine sense of inquiry.

That he was such a devoted reader was due, partly, to his deafness, first diagnosed when he was a child of ten or eleven. Reading led him into worlds about which others around him had no idea, or could never share with him. Within this silent world, my father could hear. The pages of the books spoke to him, and he conveyed something of them to me, albeit obliquely.

To my father I owe also the notion of being independent or, at least, having a sense of independence and not being in anyone's debt. 'Stand on your own two feet and don't expect anyone to do anything for you,' my brothers and I were told, almost on a daily basis. Dad was self-employed, delivering paper bags and wrapping materials to shops all over Sydney. He kept and supported a family of three boys, educating us at Catholic schools because of his firm beliefs about God and the church.

My mother did the books for his business, running the household from a swivel chair positioned at the end of our dining-room table, where she held court for all the women of the neighbourhood, for whom she was a sort of oracle and problem-solver. There were more cups of tea and sympathy shared in that dining room than one could ever hope to count. The drinking of tea sustained my seriously overweight mother in the same way that air sustains the rest of humanity. A cup of tea would solve every problem, ease every heart, and soothe every condition.

Our first family home was at 229 Clovelly Road, Clovelly; a semi-detached cottage in a beachside suburb, south-east of the city. The wireless set provided the only music in the house, and it was usually switched on. My mother was a keen listener to Radio 2FC – Radio National, as it is known today – a station run by the Australian Broadcasting Commission. The announcers had quasi-English accents, and the programs carried no advertising of any kind. Among many people around us, the ABC was considered a little bit snooty and very North Shore indeed. But my mother, who lived in Clovelly, which was *definitely not* the North Shore, listened to the ABC all day.

I have vivid memories from very early childhood of the wireless emitting a wonderful sound, high-pitched, strong, sweet and multi-layered, which I learned later was that of violins. There were regular programs of classical music including an opera hour each day at 11 am, the sounds of which went right through my body. I found the sounds of operatic voices – half-singing, half-crying – extraordinary and I tried to imitate them.

Also in my memory, courtesy of the ABC, are the musical themes of its children's programs: *Kindergarten of the Air* – 'Boys and girls, come out to play' – and *The Argonauts* – 'come with a hop, a skip and a run'. You could join the Argonauts club by writing in for membership. Via return post, you received an Argonaut badge and an identifying ship name. Mr Melody Man, the pianist and composer Lindley Evans, would encourage us Argonauts to write music and send it in to be played on air: 'Hellas 36 of Nambucca Heads writes a tune for flute, and here it is.' To be an Argonaut was very sophisticated; it gave one just a slight edge over everyone else in the playground.

The other musical sound that is still vivid in my memory is that of plainchant associated with the Roman Catholic mass. In 1946, at the tender age of four, I began school at St Anthony's, Clovelly, a convent school run by the Sisters of St Joseph. For years, I puzzled over these frightening women, but what I can thank them for is the fact that they cared about singing the mass, and made sure we learned it. I can still recite all the responses from the old Latin mass, as well as the entire Benediction, including all the hymns. It was the most amazing form of memory training.

Singing was not the only memorable thing about church. The mass was pure theatre. The altar was the stage, the priest was the principal actor, the altar boys were the extras, and the choir in the gallery was a heavenly chorus. To this scene add swinging thuribles belching frankincense, bells ringing at the altar, the priest holding up a monstrance, allegedly containing the body and blood of Christ, and the choir roaring away, and you have a scene rivalling the 'Triumphal March' from *Aida*.

My favourite musical times were Easter, the Forty Hours Devotion and Christmas, in that order. Lent, the period preceding Easter, was a time for fasting and self-denial. As a five-year-old, I gave up eating sugar of any description; a huge sacrifice for me. I was devoted to sweets of all kinds, including cakes and biscuits, but God, our Father in Heaven, would know if I had eaten a sweet and would punish me accordingly when I died.

During Easter, all the statues in the church were covered in purple. The altar was stripped bare. The priest wore purple vestments, and the 'Gloria' was not sung. The organ was silent. Once we started to practise the music for Easter, my world changed and I entered paradise. Come Passion Sunday, and then Holy Thursday, a musical feast would unfold, with chanting, anthems, motets and the like, and incredibly long litanies of the saints, to which one responded with the chant '*ora pro nobis*' – 'pray for us'. All this with incense, and the lighting of the Pascal candle from a flame produced by a flint struck outside the door of the church. And the altar! What an extraordinary transformation! From a plain marble surface to one featuring a luxuriant floral display on Easter Sunday. But best of all, the fast was over and we could eat sweets to our hearts' content without offending God or the Sisters of St Joseph – well, God, anyway.

It was one of those inspirational Easter rituals that encouraged me to build an altar in our backyard at home. I made a spectacular structure out of bricks, boards and corrugated iron, which included a wooden altar with a tabernacle in the form of a large tin can. I filled jam-jar lids with mud, and stuck sprigs of lantana into them for the altar flowers. My vestments were a sheet and a towel.

The girl who lived next door, Wilma Moore, was asked to join my sacred order of the backyard, in the capacity of a chorister. As women were not allowed to serve at the altar in those days, I relegated her to the back of it, and set her up with a small sheet of corrugated iron, which she banged with a stick for the instrumental music. At first, my parents were unconcerned. They decided to remove the altar the day my maiden aunt Josephine was seen kneeling in the dirt, while I heard her confession and forgave her sins.

Forty Hours Devotion, while not as special for me as Easter, still had all the trappings of a major theatrical event. There were two solemn High Masses and the Exposition of the Blessed Sacrament. If you stood in front of the Blessed Sacrament you had to genuflect on both knees, accompanied by a deep bowing of the head. There were endless litanies of the saints, a favourite musical pastime of mine because of the repetitive and trancelike nature of the music. Best of all, I was chosen one Forty Hours weekend to be a flower strewer!

The nuns dressed me in white silk pantaloons, a white silk shirt and a half-cape in red and gold, and gave me a large basket of rose petals to strew before the priest who carried the Blessed Sacrament. I kissed each petal before it hit the floor, and sang '*ora pro nobis*' in response to the litany ('*orate pro nobis*' if two saints were mentioned). My great joy was to count the number of times people sang the wrong response, which I noticed happened often. This was clearly the first sign of the obsessive-compulsive strain that has remained with me to this day.

There was nothing that matched the excitement I felt when we sang something in church, whether a litany, Gregorian chant, or one of the hymns I then believed to be examples of the most beautiful music ever written – 'Hail, Queen of Heaven, the Ocean Star' or 'Hail, glorious Saint Patrick, dear saint of our Isle'. Even the jingoistic, brain-washing hymns written for schoolchildren – 'I am a little Catholic, I love my holy faith' – worked for me. All my troubles would vanish as the music began. It has been the pattern of my life.

Quite late in my career, I was asked to become founding music director of Victorian Opera. I didn't jump at the chance, I flew at it. How often is one asked the question 'Would you like to start an opera company from scratch?' An opportunity to commission new work, an opportunity to do work on a small scale, an opportunity to present work that would not normally see the light of day, and an opportunity to engage young people in this work in a very special way. I did not share the view of many Melburnians that, at last, there was once again a company to perform *La Bohème* and *La traviata* on alternate nights. I knew I would disappoint such people. I have a broader view of the repertoire than most of my colleagues, and have used this view to direct the company as I see fit. I was not commissioned to maintain a status quo, for by the time of my appointment, in 2005, there was none.

It was high-stakes poker. The funding, much as it was appreciated, was undoubtedly tiny. The company had no proper home. Friends and foes alike told me that it had been set up to fail – no opera company could survive on such a modest portion. It was grist to the mill for me. All my life I'd been told what I couldn't do, and this was no different.

Even my career as a musician has had its share of controversy. As far as conducting goes I've certainly been told, from the day I started, that I'd never make a conductor. I remember the first review I received for a professional conducting engagement. It appeared in the *Sydney Morning Herald*, and was written by the music critic Fred Blanks. The performance organised by an enlightened patron of music, Dr Vincent Shepherd. I conducted a Bach cantata – and here I use the word 'conducted' in its loosest sense – with a very good professional orchestra and a cast of great professional singers.

The review when it finally appeared contained this wonderful smack in the eye: 'Under Richard Gill's conducting, there was no gainsaying the professionalism of the rest of the ensemble.' In other words, everyone else was very good but the conductor was rubbish. This has been a theme with some reviewers, though in my own defence I should add that I have also had my share of very good reviews, even when, I felt, I didn't deserve them.

It's not only reviewers who've caused me grief over the years. I've been told by string players and wind players and brass players that I would never be a conductor because I'm not a string player or a wind player or a brass player. I have also been informed by musical authorities in the business of employing conductors that I'm no good at all. On one occasion I was actually told 'I'd heard you were a bad conductor, but that's not really accurate'. That was a conversation stopper, though I'm sure it was meant as encouragement.

I figure that with such a track record the only way is up, and therefore I have everything to gain by keeping on conducting. I can only improve, and effect this improvement by being involved, and listening to what players and singers have to say, especially in rehearsals. I will often ask particular players to give me feedback if they can be bothered, and many do, for which I am truly grateful.

That is also pretty much my approach to music generally. I know no other way! Which is not to say that the experience has been painless, or that skin has not been left under fingernails. Often in the writing of this memoir, I've had to relive that pain. When I say that it has been a form of purgatory, I am only half-joking. Yet, I hope that readers, particularly the young and musically inclined, will find something of worth here. For this book is about the musician's journey as I have experienced it: the sublime and the ridiculous; the happy chances and the rude awakenings; the life-changing encounters with true genius; the strong friendships with other singers and players who, like myself, were merely mortal; the providential announcements; the miscommunications; the artistic differences; and – rarely – the invidious enmities, that all somehow combine to form a life in music.

2

'Hail Mary, Full of Grapes . . .'

I WAS BORN ON THE FIRST TUESDAY IN NOVEMBER: Melbourne Cup Day. It was 4 November 1941, to be precise, and Skipton, ridden by W. Cook, won the race that stops the nation. I arrived rather more tardily at the Waverley War Memorial Hospital in Sydney, and was promptly named Richard James Gill, after Richard Honner, the doctor who delivered my poor mother from thirty-six hours of labour. Apparently my head was too big. According to close personal friends and enemies, nothing has changed!

Five weeks later, I was christened at St Anthony's Catholic Church, Clovelly, where my parents had married. It was Sunday 7 December, the date Pearl Harbor was attacked and war began in the Pacific. What a beginning! World War II was already in its third year, and Japan's attack on the US naval base left the Americans no choice as to their position.

'Fence-sitters and cowards,' my parents were fond of saying about the Yanks, as the Americans were known. The Yanks were nearly as bad as the Nips . . . couldn't be trusted. I was to learn fairly quickly that the world was divided into those who were trustworthy and those who were not. The chief division was between Catholics (trustworthy) and anti-Catholics (obviously not). Within the anti-Catholics, there was a sub-genus known as non-Catholic. The fate of these non-true believers, whether Protestant, agnostic or atheist, would be the same . . . Hell!

Somewhat inconsistently, the British, though officially Anglican, were to be trusted, adored and idolised. My mother frequently referred to England as home, even though we were three-quarters Irish. Lydia was a royalist of the first order and remained so until her death. She corresponded regularly with Buckingham Palace, and had a large collection of official replies. The Windsors enjoyed her regard to a degree to which that other influential family (Jesus, Mary and Joseph) could only hope to aspire.

At school, on the other hand, the holy family reigned. Each day began with catechism. It came from a book known as the Blue Catechism and it had to be memorised before we could make our First Holy Communion.

'Who made the world?' screamed Sister Mary Rita. 'God made the world,' we answered. 'Who is God?' she screamed again. 'God is our Father in Heaven,' we chorused. 'What is Heaven?' 'Heaven is a place of eternal rest.' 'What is Hell?'

Each day at school was a trip into Hell. We were shouted at incessantly and told that we were all sinners.

Sister Mary Rita, may she have her own special oven in Lucifer's kitchen, would then bang a hand bell on her desk and announce in a voice filled with such threatening tones that none would dare disobey: 'Change over for spelling.' Banging the bell on her desk was her way of gaining our attention, and changing over was the procedure of moving from subject to subject. I dreaded the sound and hated the changing.

'Spell "be",' she screamed at the class. I had no idea how you spelled 'be': for me it was the letter 'b' and what was there to spell?

'Who can spell it?' she yelled, her teeth bared like a tiger about to kill.

I shot my hand up and said 'b'.

'Come out here, smartypants, and we'll see how well you spell after this,' said this nun, who had missed her true vocation as a prison warder. One cut of the cane later and I was back in my seat, wondering how I got that word wrong; and I still didn't know how to spell 'be'.

'So that's what happens to smartypants, everyone,' Sister Mary Rita had announced to the class, as I walked shamefacedly back to my seat. She was an incredibly awful human being, and, on mature reflection, I have had no cause to revise that opinion. While I can forgive, I can't forget. She was a vile, nasty person who loved girls and hated boys.

'Smartypants' was a form of insult reserved for boys. Obviously, one mustn't be smart. As the English writer Charles Kingsley had put it: 'Be good, sweet maid, and let who will be clever.' We were reminded frequently that children should be seen and not heard, and had to respect their elders and their betters! Anything to do with being smart had to be eschewed in favour of being good: being smart was seen as getting above one's station. At the age of four, I hadn't worked out that the concept of cleverness versus goodness was inherently stupid.

There was an approved Catholic way of thinking, and anyone thinking outside that approved way was damned. If you doubt me, then read Frank Hardy's *Power Without Glory*. I have come to see the Catholic Church, and indeed all organised religion, as inherently problematic and fraught with fear of ultimate damnation. I don't doubt for one minute that there are branches of the Catholic Church that do incredible work, or that within all religions there are people who are inherently good. However, as I went through the Catholic education system it became very obvious to me that the church's interest in our minds was governed by the way in which any information we might gather could be used to help us save our souls in the next life. In fact, there was no present life. One's reason for being on Earth was to die and go to Heaven! That was what I had worked out as I approached my fifth birthday.

The next life was more important than this one. Everything had to be forsaken so you could save your immortal soul. What did it profit a man if he gained the whole world and lost his soul? I didn't know and still don't. Thinking could be construed as dangerous, and could lead one to entertain thoughts that had nothing to do with Catholicism. So well brainwashed was I that it took me years to find my feet intellectually, and the guilt with which I was tainted as a result of those early years remains with me.

Bang went the bell a second time as Sister Mary Rita yelled at us to change over again, this time for arithmetic. My blood pressure would rise, I would begin to sweat, and my mouth would go dry. Arithmetic – especially mental arithmetic, as it was called – put the fear of God into me. Mental arithmetic was very clearly designed for the express purpose of making me look like the only five-year-old idiot in the class.

'Four plus three take away two,' yelled Sister Mary Rita.

My game plan at this tender age was to think of any number between one and ten and blurt it out, get the cane and then it would be all over for the morning. I would stick to this plan all through primary school, and it worked very well, in spite of the pain and humiliation of being caned for ignorance every day of one's school life.

'Six,' I'd yell, feeling that this answer had a certain ring of veracity about it. Caning over, I could relax and daydream, looking out the window at the back of the classroom, which had a view to the ocean.

My seat in Sister Mary Rita's classroom was at the end of the last row of desks in the room. There were four children to a desk and four rows of desks in a block. The three blocks had a label on the front desk of each row. The labels had on them, in large capitals, VG, G and H, standing for, respectively, Very Good, Good and Hopeless. I had earned the rare distinction of being classified as hopeless at the age of five and, indeed, was in the last seat of the back row of the hopeless.

My mother was as formidable a woman as one could wish to meet, having the warrior spirit of Joan of Arc, and the ferocity of a lioness whose cubs had been attacked, with just a touch of Lady Bracknell in the mix.

She visited the convent, and afterwards I spent the rest of my short stay at St Anthony's relatively untouched, apart from a few significant instances that I will relate, as they contributed greatly to my mental state at that time, and set me on the path of confusion and guilt to which I have already alluded. Such powerful feelings when instilled in a young child evoked sensations of confusion, bewilderment and terror. I had weird and terrifying dreams, about which I told no one, and imagined that the gates of Hell were ever open and ready to bid me welcome.

The first instance of real significance was discovering the notion of sin. There was a difference between mortal and venial sins, and what they did to your immortal soul. A mortal sin was a grievous offence against God and a venial sin was a lesser offence against God. Missing mass on Sunday or on a holy day of obligation, or saying 'bugger' or 'bloody' to someone, were examples of mortal sins; or that was how I understood it. I felt guilty about everything. In preparation for confession, I tried to keep count of the number of sins I committed and their relative gravity. I was developing a very powerful neurosis about the way one learns.

I had decided that the state of mortal sin was actually a geographical place, rather like New South Wales or Victoria. It was called 'Kingdom Come', and lay somewhere outside Clovelly, visible from our backyard. This concept of literal associations was reinforced in the prayers we had to learn from memory and probably helped slow down my grasp of genuinely abstract concepts.

All the prayers we said had literal significance for me, in that I tried to associate something I knew about the area in which we lived with the text of the prayer. Kingdom Come, as I have just explained, was stationed on the other side of Clovelly Road. 'Thy will be done' was to me something that was going to happen one day just beyond the tram terminus at Clovelly Beach. 'Our daily bread' was always sliced and wrapped in wax wrappers, and 'our trespasses', which we asked to have forgiven, were seen on fences and other places where notices appeared to the effect that trespassers would be prosecuted. Outside our school there was a sign, 'Pedestrian Crossing', which I believed was only for Protestants who needed to cross, Catholics being forbidden to use that part of the road.

Prayers to the BVM (Blessed Virgin Mary, to the uninitiated) were a goldmine of inspiration for spectacular imagery and literal associations. For years I believed the prayer was: 'Hail Mary, full of grapes, the Lord is with thee. Blessed art thou amongst women and blessed is the fruit of thy womb, Jesus.'

Because the state of venial sin was not as important as mortal sin, it lacked a geographical location. It was nonetheless a type of sin, and we children used to discuss what we had done during the day and whether we had committed venial or mortal sins. Any Vatican theologian would have been thrilled to overhear these relatively recently emerged organisms discussing the complexities of sin.

For example: eating meat on Friday – probably venial. Not doing homework – again, probably venial, but when in doubt, the safest thing to believe was that all sins were mortal and that way you knew exactly where you stood in God's sight. A mortal sin caused your soul to be black. You knew this, and that if you died in the state of mortal sin you would go to Hell.

My soul, I firmly believed, sat somewhere in my stomach, situated just above the navel. It was round and white like the moon and fully visible to God, who saw everything. When I sinned in a mortal way – for example, by saying 'bloody' or 'bugger' – a black blob would descend onto my soul. The blob was a source of huge and constant worry because I didn't know how to get rid of it. Not only did it blacken my soul but God knew about it. God knew I had done wrong and he was watching. In fact, God knew everything and there was no hiding from Him: Sister Mary Rita had told us that if you tried to hide from God on the Last Day of the world, he would find you, even if you hid under a rock or in a cave!

Sister Mary Rita, fortunately, had the answer that could relieve me of all my worries. We were all about to make our First Holy Communion, the initial step towards being accepted wholly and fully into the one true Catholic Church. To do this we needed to love the Lord much more than we already did.

Sister Mary Rita was forever telling us that we didn't love the Lord enough and that, if we were to make our First Holy Communion as planned, we would need to be very certain that we were not in the state of mortal sin, thereby showing our love for the Lord.

There was a girl in my class called Margaret. The two of us decided that we would show Sister Mary Rita just how much we loved the Lord. We knew the Lord lived in the tabernacle on the altar and stayed there for most of the week until Sunday, when he came out in the form of communion wafers. One afternoon, we made our way into the church, ostensibly to pay a visit. In fact, we had decided to climb up onto the altar and throw our arms around the tabernacle in a positive declaration of our love for The Lord.

We scaled the altar easily, by means of climbing up at the end, where we could get some purchase on the railing. We then crawled along the altar and threw our arms around the tabernacle in a fervent embrace. At that precise moment, the parish priest, Father Kelly, entered the church, mistook our holy intentions for vandalism and reported us to Sister Mary Rita. At no stage were we questioned about our intentions. It was assumed we were perpetrating a highly sinful act and had to be punished.

Sister Mary Rita had just the weapon: a piece of dowelling she used on our knuckles. It had been taken from a broken window frame, and still had the tacks in it. When she drew blood, she stopped. We had descended into the very pit of evil and deserved the most terrible of punishments. This punishment was a public display in front of the class and a lesson to all not to climb onto the altar.

To rid ourselves of sin, and by now I was a walking catalogue of both the mortal and venial variety, we were to go to confession and tell our sins to Father Kelly. To tell your sins to a complete stranger was a nightmare! To tell them to the priest who had seen you vandalising his tabernacle could only be the ultimate form of humiliation.

Although we had been told that the confessional was secret and that the priest would forgive us all our sins without saying a word to anyone, my worries began to increase. Sin, with special emphasis on the mortal variety, was always in the forefront of my mind, together with the warning that to leave a sin out, to fail to confess a sin, was to make a bad confession. To make a bad confession was in itself a mortal sin. 'If you die in the state of mortal sin, you will go to Hell,' said Sister Mary

Rita with distinct pleasure, looking at the boys in the class. My worries flooded back in a huge way. The concept of Hell was terrifying.

Hell was illustrated in a spectacular manner in junior bible history, with a picture of fire engulfing numbers of human beings, all of whom had their hands outstretched for help as the flames licked around their bodies. Purgatory was less gruesomely illustrated, with the flames not as high as for Hell. Limbo was a collection of souls living on a cloud. Limbo got my vote!

'The pain of Hell,' said Sister Mary Rita, 'is worse than sticking a pin into the middle of your hand.' I could hardly wait to test this thesis. On arriving home I went straight to my father's roll-top desk, took out a pin and drove it into my palm. It stung briefly and then the pain stopped. Hell was going to be OK: a bit of a sting at the beginning, and then it goes away! What didn't make sense to me was the flames. I knew what sunburn was and how it hurt. How could a flame be less potent than a pinprick?

The worries of the state of my soul returned in a spectacular way as we prepared for our First Holy Communion. How in the name of everything that is sacred could I possibly tell Father Kelly that I had said 'bum' to one of my friends and had used the expression 'bloody bugger' about a kid up the road; a Protestant kid, to boot! My mother had overheard this remark and had washed my mouth out with soap. The soap of choice was called Lifebuoy, pinkish-red and containing carbolic acid. It didn't work. I swear profusely to this day. My mother used to say that people who swore had no vocabulary and couldn't think of anything nice to say about anyone. She was wrong!

The day of our First Confession arrived. Sister Mary Rita's class was led over to the church of St Anthony, patron saint of lost articles and missing things. I was by now a mature five-year-old with a firm grasp of sin and associated theologies, but secretly trembling in fear of having to say 'bloody bugger' and 'bum' to a priest.

I had plenty of sins in reserve, such as 'I didn't say my morning and night prayers', 'I disobeyed my mother and father', or 'I didn't do my homework'; sins that were to stand me in good stead in the confessional for the next twelve years. My turn came and I repeated the words we had learned by heart: 'Bless me, Father, for I have sinned, this is my first confession.' It was a bad confession: no 'bloody', 'bugger' or 'bum' passed my lips. The black blob on my soul grew larger until it covered it entirely. Bad confession equals bad First Communion equals mortal sin – next stop Hell! This five-year-old was doomed, beyond redemption.

After confession the rest of the class chatted in the playground about their sins and who had said what, who had left out sins, who had made up sins. I couldn't join in. Not only was I shocked about the state of my immortal soul and my failure to speak to the priest about my swearing, but I knew that I was on the verge of making a bad First Communion.

The mass took place and all I can remember is the music and the communion breakfast. '*Kyrie, eleison, Christe, eleison,*' chanted the choir from its loft: sounds I can still hear in my head today. Everything vanished with music. Hell, Sister Mary Rita, mortal sins, venial sins, bloody, bugger, bum – they all disappeared, while a new world was beginning to develop in my head.

The guilt would return later, and remain with me throughout my school years. It is very interesting to me that at the age of seventy years I can recall these episodes as though they happened yesterday. Yet the music touched me and stayed with me throughout the hideous years of my schooling. The sound of the singing, especially the chanting, formed me musically and set in me the desire to be involved with music at some level.

At no stage did I feel sorry for myself or feel that anything was especially unfair: life was as life was. My mother used to say, 'Be thankful for small mercies.' It was not a sentiment I entirely shared. Sister Mary Rita was small! How could I possibly thank this cruel, though vertically-challenged, Sister of St Joseph?

My time at St Anthony's, Clovelly was drawing to a close. By now I had two younger brothers, Terence and Christopher, and my mother had decided we needed space.

We were moving to Epping, even though, according to all my parents' friends, this was tantamount to moving to another state. In late 1946, the outer suburbs of Sydney, especially the Epping–Marsfield district, were still essentially farmland surrounded by houses that had plenty of space in the front and back yards. There was room to grow.

Home decoration, home improvement and renovation occupied my mother's thoughts on a daily basis. That was somewhat paradoxical, given that, on a good day, our home looked like a cyclone had been through it; and on others, like Pearl Harbor after the attack. Nothing deflected Lydia's yearning for the ideal home or her dream to turn the ideal home, once attained, into an even more glorious place.

'A glorious home' was her mantra. She boasted that she had every copy of *Australian Home Beautiful*, dating back to the magazine's inception. I can only guess that it was the source of the idea of decorating with decals, a type of stick-on transfer.

Decals were the poor man's decoupage. They came in themes or pattern clusters: floral sprays for kitchenware, dining room and lounge-room ornaments; animals for laundry and bathroom objects, and so on. You bought a sheet of them, soaked the adhesive on the back, and pressed the decal to any undecorated surface, be it china, glass or wood.

The family's removal to our 'ideal home' at Epping occasioned a decal frenzy. The bathroom was a festival of ducks in various bathing positions: scrubbing their backs with brushes; cleaning their teeth (even I knew that ducks and hens didn't have teeth); showering with their shower caps on. In the kitchen, floral decals adorned the condiment jars, while decal labels made a joyous display on the flour, rice, sugar, tea and coffee. Even our new school exercise books were not exempt, splattered with teddy bears or goldfish.

The Mercy nuns in Epping had obviously been to the same training college as those at Clovelly, although my new classroom teacher, Sister Mary Ligouri, had a little more compassion than Sister Mary Rita. My brother Terry was not similarly blessed. A fiery nun called Sister Mary Coleman developed a special hate for him. One day, in the playground, she made the mistake of observing to my mother that 'there must be some good somewhere inside that boy'. Lydia dressed her down spectacularly, embarrassing us all. I remember Sister Mary Coleman turned a violent shade of red, faced with the gift of my parent's invective.

Mother had a spectacular vocabulary and the voice of an ABC announcer. She could make her presence felt in most circumstances, none more so than at Sunday mass at Our Lady of the Immaculate Conception. When the parish priest, Father Heffernan, announced from the pulpit that the first and second collections were filling up with pennies and ha'pennies, and if that continued to happen he would throw them in the corner of the church, Lydia's response could have been heard within a five-mile radius: 'Well, I'll be there to pick them up.' My father, being fairly deaf, was spared this embarrassment, but we kids just slid slowly into our seats and wanted to die.

She had ways of disciplining us that were far cleverer than the nuns', as I found out when a friend of mine, Bob Dunnicliff, invited me to join a junior lodge. I had no idea what this meant but imagined it was rather like Boy Scouts. The Boy Scout movement was frowned upon by Father Heffernan, who informed us that such associations were Anglican in origin, and therefore not for Catholics. Sister Mary Ligouri said that the Church of England had Union Jacks all over the altar, and to visit an Anglican church was a sin. How did she know? I had to find out for myself and visited St Alban's C of E church opposite the home of a friend of mine, Johnny Smith. The nun was right. There were flags and the Union Jack was there. It was worth the sin to find that out.

Joining the junior lodge was discussed at home, and as there was money involved the answer was a firm 'no'. I was devastated. For some reason, I had become obsessed with the idea. My parents' refusal shocked me, and I decided to run away from home. On Friday night, the night I should have been going to lodge after tea, I packed my schoolbag with my school coat and a toothbrush, and headed out the front door. I marched defiantly down the drive and turned in the direction of the park. You had to walk through a very narrow lane between two houses and then, hey presto, Epping Park!

There were excellent swings and a very special wooden contraption. It was made of two parallel boards attached to a centrepiece suspended from a huge metal frame. As the centrepiece swung backwards and forwards, the boards gained height and momentum and were incredibly dangerous. Many a lip was cut severely and many a tooth was prematurely lost as the machine made contact with the faces of the unwise and uninitiated children in its path. I spent at least an hour alone on this device and had a wonderful time.

Gradually it grew dark and I began to wonder where I might sleep. Running away from home was fine in principle but there was the small matter of a bed, food and the other necessities of life. I returned home. As I walked in the back door (there were no keys in our house and no door was ever locked) my mother said, 'Who are you?' When I told her, she replied, 'No, you couldn't be Richard – he has run away from home. You can go into his bedroom if you like, to see if he's come back.' I went into my room and went to bed. In the morning, the entire household sent me to Coventry. I was in disgrace. As the ice slowly melted and I began to offer contributions to the household, my mother used an expression she favoured whenever I was getting a little perky: 'You are not out of the woods yet, sonny Jim, not by a long chalk.' 'Out of the woods' and 'not by a long chalk' have stayed with me and I use them frequently.

3

Fluck is a Five-Letter Word

THE CHOIR AT THE CHURCH OF OUR LADY OF THE Immaculate Conception was led by the local piano teacher, Miss Kathleen Gardoll, who sang the soprano solos when required. I thought her voice incredibly beautiful – my mother told me that she could hit a high C, whatever that was. There was also a spectacular bass soloist called Mr Dalton. At least, I thought he was spectacular. He had a voice like the voices you heard on the radio. What was even more important was that he lived next door to us. We lived at 42 Essex Street, Epping, and he lived at number 44 and, joy of joys, I could hear him practising!

Members of the congregation spoke reverently and quietly about the abundance of musical gifts in our parish. When the choir sang, you could hear Mr Dalton and Miss Gardoll cutting through loud and clear. The concept of blend, an idea with which I still have trouble, was obviously not a consideration. But when they were on, they were on! It was thrilling to this musical tadpole, who had no idea about music other than the glorious sound it could make, to hear these two voices shatter the airwaves.

Loud and strong was good. I also sensed a thrilling element of competition between them – anything you can sing, I can sing louder. I still find such contests exciting. When I'm in the pit, conducting the accompaniment to a duet, and sense that the singers above me both know that one of them is doing better than the other, the effects can be electrifying.

Christmas at Immaculate Conception was very special. Miss Gardoll sang an especially high part in 'Adeste Fideles', which I learned was called the descant. I secretly sang along with her and learned the part by heart, until I could sing it through at home in the backyard. I was desperate to learn about music in a more formal way.

I thought about it all the time, especially in relationship to performance. I wanted to be a performer. This feeling was confirmed – indeed, cemented – in my mind when I attended my first pantomime: *Jack and the Beanstalk*, at the Tivoli theatre in Sydney. Here was theatre outside the confines of the church, performed in English, with stories one could follow and music one could sing. I immediately wanted to perform on stage.

I asked my mother whether we could have a pantomime at home. When she said yes, I led a musical press-gang, co-opting a tribe of local kids into rehearsing and performing *Cinderella*. My mother wrote a version of the story in rhyming couplets; my father, who was a very gifted illustrator, drew a backdrop in coloured chalk on a black holland blind. I scored the role of Prince Charming. This was living!

Rehearsals began in earnest, and costumes were cobbled together. We had make-up – lipstick and powder – and props covered in silver paper, including a wand for the fairy godmother. Dad constructed a stage curtain, which could open and close in one movement. It was made of green cotton material, suspended by brass curtain rings on a piece of clothesline, and was operated by someone hiding behind the curtain itself, moving with the curtain to open and close it. Operating it was a high-powered job that was coveted among the kids in the neighbourhood. Serious theatre.

Parents and friends were invited to our backyard premiere. Towards the end of a speech about my constancy and total devotion to Cinderella, I dried up. In the middle of a line. It was a hideous experience. As I stood there, gaping at the audience like a dope, Dianne O'Toole, the girl next door who was playing Cinderella, smiled sweetly. No assistance there!

At the end, we were greeted with generous and warm applause by the audience (a huge afternoon tea awaited them in our dining room). The afternoon was a triumph. In my mind, the next stop was the Tivoli, notwithstanding my massive lapse of memory.

The most annoying thing about this lapse was the fact that I knew the entire play by heart; every line, every move, every inflection and nuance. I could prompt everyone else whenever a line or move was forgotten, and didn't hesitate to do so. It is a quality that is highly developed in me; one that I still bring to the opera rehearsal room today. I refer to this dubious trait as being an IOC or Interfering Old Cow. The point is that if I refer to myself in that way, it brings out the same quality of being an IOC in all the singers in the room, and frequently elicits fresh and wonderful responses from performers and directors alike.

The thing missing from our pantomime was music. No singing! Not one sound of a musical note. This was all to change the following year, when I went to Marist Brothers' High School, Eastwood, which offered three years of primary education followed by five years of secondary school. I started there in 1950, in fourth class, the third-last year of primary school.

In my experience, Catholic education in Sydney in the post-war period was very hit and miss: if you missed the answer to a question, you were hit. The nuns and the brothers implemented a particularly brutal style of teaching that remained the same right up until my last year of schooling, and to which I became completely accustomed. I was caned every day at Marist Brothers Eastwood.

My younger brothers and my friends all suffered under the same atrocious system, and can corroborate much of my experience. In primary school, in years four, five and six, we were in classes of eighty – unthinkable these days, but standard practice then. I still have report cards detailing where I came in the class over those years, and it was way down towards the bottom!

I understand, from a reasonably thorough examination of the internet, that the school I attended is now called Marist College Eastwood. Judging from its very detailed and very attractive website, full of elevating information, it is a far cry from the borstal it was in the period between 1950 and 1957.

In my first few years there, choir was my reason for going to school. It was under the charge of Brother Ignatius, who taught every song by rote, music and words. Not a note of music was ever handed out in choir. Words were either written on a blackboard or recited by 'Iggy', and we repeated them. The tunes were learned through individual lines being played on a piano.

We sang music in two, three and four parts, and performed in Marist Brothers eisteddfodau, competing against other Marist schools such as Mosman; Manly; St Joseph's, Hunters Hill; Marçellin College, Randwick and so on. I passionately loved eisteddfod time. We had to sing a hymn in unison, a two-part song (prescribed), and a free choice in four-part harmony. To me, this was truly heaven. We heard such ravishing music as 'The Dream of Olwen' by Charles Williams (better known to Australians as the composer of the ABC's signature tune); a huge collection of Irish tunes such 'The Kerry Dance' and 'Come Back to Erin'; and – best of all – selections from musicals by Ivor Novello, Sigmund Romberg and from the hugely gifted pens of Rodgers and Hammerstein.

We also sang endless hymns, mainly from the St Basil Hymnal, which I considered to be a treasury of beautiful music. If music can be likened to alcohol, then I was a one-hymn wonder and a cheap musical drunk! I loved it all, indiscriminately, and couldn't get enough. Connoisseurs considered the St Basil Hymnal to be a collection of sentimental junk compiled by distressed Mercy nuns – for this thrillseeker it was a joy.

The greatest of my musical pleasures was the plainchant we sang at Benediction. I can still sing the entire thing from go to whoa, starting with '*O salutaris hostia*', followed by '*Tantum ergo*', and so on. Our chant was inauthentic inasmuch as much as Brother Jack provided an organ accompaniment.

Brother Ignatius made the assumption that all boys could sing. In hindsight, that was enlightened thinking on his part. As far as I can recall, we were never taught about breathing or tone production. We simply did it.

Choir taught me that there were types of voices: good voices, very good voices, and unbelievably beautiful voices. A young treble called Guy Nucifora could sing ''O sole mio' like nobody else on earth. I admired him hugely. I tried to copy his full-throated Italianate sound, to no avail. He even had a sort of sob in the voice, a slight crack, that was, to my untrained ear, just like a genuine Italian singer's. Peter Contemprée, another treble, had the most extraordinary voice and could be heard above the whole choir. Indeed, he was encouraged to sing out.

This was the true beginning of my music education, although there were no formal classes in music.

The rest of my time at school was ghastly. In my first year, I became so neurotic about the mental arithmetic, with which we began each day, that my mother took me to the doctor. I was pale and grey. A specialist tested me for leukaemia. But when a second opinion was sought, an astute general practitioner asked about school, then pronounced that I was allergic to arithmetic. A medical first and one for the books: allergy to numbers.

Each wrong answer was punished with one cut of the cane. I was in the front row because I couldn't see the board properly and therefore would receive the first question of the day. I could learn tables by rote, and can still quote reams of formulae to do with weight, height, distance and the like. In secondary school I could remember more formulae than any other boy. What I couldn't do was apply that knowledge on the trot.

Convert two yards to inches! I would proffer an answer and, knowing it was wrong, would automatically head out to the front to be caned. One day I gave a correct answer – a complete fluke. The trouble was, I didn't know it was correct. As I headed towards the front, Brother Palladius, our teacher, said: 'Well, Gill, that was the right answer but, seeing as you're here, stick your hand out.' Bang! Damned if you're right and damned if you're wrong. Palladius was actually a kind person, in spite of the fact that he caned some of us every day.

Caning was seen as strengthening the moral fibre. If you winced, flinched or cried, you were deemed a sissy or a coward. I never cried, not once in eight years, and I never flinched. If you flinched, the brothers would frequently bring the cane back onto your knuckles and that was worse than being caned on the hand. Often a teacher would miss, and you'd be hit on the heel of the hand or the wrist. That was terribly painful, and some boys who received the cane less often than I did would weep inconsolably if hit that way. I was a veteran of corporal punishment and took it like a man!

One of the most savage of these Christian men who had been called to the vocation of a religious life was someone I will call Brother Tom. He was built like the proverbial brick shithouse, and had a vile and uncontrollable temper. His favourite trick was to hold a boy by his heels out of a second-storey window, then throw the boy physically onto the stack of suitcases that were kept on the veranda. The screams of the suspended victim could be heard all over the neighbourhood.

This brother also liked to take the pupils swimming in the cesspond misleadingly referred to as a swimming pool, and impose a series of conditions. No duck-diving; no running; no jumping in from the side; no bombing from the high diving board; no ducking and no cock-fighting. (Lest you wonder, cock-fighting referred to one boy carrying another on his shoulders and attacking a similar pair of boys until one of the pair fell into the drink.)

These events happened on a Thursday afternoon, a period laughingly referred to as 'sport'. The reverend gentleman with the special vocation for teaching would stand at a vantage point overlooking the whole pool, and write boys' names in a book. He watched the boys without ever saying anything to anyone during the commission of an offence. My best friend, Errol Cranney, and I broke rules as a matter of course and with certain pride.

On Friday, immediately after Benediction, when we were filled with the joy of the Holy Ghost and had genuflected ourselves into a frenzy, we would stand in the yard and listen to the names being called of those boys who had transgressed Brother Tom's rules. Cranney and Gill featured frequently, and for every entry you received a cut of the cane.

Each brother had his own style of caning. Tom kept his canes in linseed oil and polished them often. He would raise the cane as high as he could and crash it down with all his strength. My pain was bottled up, and transmogrified to hate. How dare these so-called Christian men call themselves teachers! How dare they flog us in that way! One of the things we had belted into us was to rise every time a brother entered the room and say, 'Good Morning, Brother, and may God bless you.' I learned very quickly to add, under my breath, 'and may your life be short'.

Brother Tom was the closest thing to a sadist I ever encountered, although, at the age of eight, I was unfamiliar with the term. If he detected in a boy the slightest modicum of sensitivity, he took even greater pleasure in delivering corporal punishment. I recall that I was tinkering on the piano at the back of our classroom one day when Tom walked by. He came into the room, thundered down the back to the piano, collared me and gave me four cuts of the cane for interfering with other people's property. Thank you for fostering any desire I might have had to improve myself, especially musically!

We were supposed to say thank you after any form of punishment. We had to be grateful to these men for bashing us, and thank them after each cut of the cane. Now, so many years later, I look back in wonder. Was the Catholic system in serious disarray? How was this allowed to happen, and why did our parents not intervene?

IN PRIMARY SCHOOL WE HAD THE OPPORTUNITY TO BE treble soloists, and I was hoping above hope that such an opportunity would be afforded me. I sang everywhere. I sang in the yard, I sang in the shower, I sang on the toilet, and I sang walking out in the street. I especially loved to sing high. I made up tunes to nonsense syllables and memorised them. I rehashed hymns. I sang whole masses from memory and couldn't shut up. I tended to have favourite bits of songs and go into what would now be called a tape loop. One I remember vividly had the text 'Hear my song, Violetta, hear my song beneath the moon. Come to me in your gondola, come to me beneath the moon.' I would repeat the phrase ad nauseam and enjoy it more each time.

Another favourite was a song called 'Ma Bella Margarita'. It began with the words 'In September when the grapes are purple', and had a terrific chorus with a great top note for 'Ma'. Our neighbours, the O'Tooles, of Dianne O'Toole fame, could hear my singing, and suggested that I shouldn't start before six in the morning. Stopping around nine at night would probably also be a fair thing, they thought.

Often, as I repeated phrases I raised the key, until eventually I finished up shrieking. This brought my mother into the picture. She told me to mind my vocal chords or I would go hoarse. From time to time she also insinuated that I had been mentally affected by a peacock that screamed in the gardens at Waverley Hospital when I was born. Is it any wonder I'm the way I am?

Brother Kevin, a gentle and refined man of the cloth who had the most brilliantined hair in the order, auditioned boys to be soloists. My practising paid off. I was chosen. Oh frabjous day, Callooh, Callay, he chortled in his glee. I was beside myself with delight and could hardly wait to get home to tell my parents, who were as proud as Punch.

My mother, who had a rare gift with the telephone, and who actually pre-dated the concept of the telethon, could tie up a line for hours on end without drawing breath. She spent that night calling her myriad friends with the news. I'm sure they were thrilled: 'Yes, Mavis dear, Richard is a soloist at school now, Mavis . . . very talented, yes, lots of work, Mavis, you know,' and on and on!

My father was pleased, if more restrained in the expression of his pleasure. My brothers thought being a soloist was stupid and very sissy. Only girls sang. It wasn't that they weren't supportive. It was that they felt free to express their views. I didn't mind at all. I was going to be a soloist and nothing was going to stop me.

At the first practice, I was given some sheet music. A song called 'Duna' and another called 'Little White Boat'. This was the next stage of heaven. The opening line of 'Duna' confused me mightily: 'When I was a little boy with folly on my lips'. It wasn't considered proper to ask questions, and Brother Kevin didn't think it necessary to explain the meaning of the text. I assumed folly was like some sort of coating of powder, which would soon disappear as the song progressed. Indeed, it did, because the second verse began with words referring to manhood. Folly gone for good!

'Just sing it beautifully, boys, and say the words properly,' exhorted Brother Kevin, and I strained every muscle in my face and neck to sing that text and say those words, because they were real words and real music on real music paper. There was a lady called Mrs Woods who would add the accompaniment once we had learned the song; a song with its own accompaniment and one voice singing! Next stage of Heaven reached.

The lyrics of these songs were very simple and, in the main, heavily nostalgic. Longing for home, longing for love, longing for spring or, indeed, any other season, but always longing; lots and lots of longing, and it was this concept of nostalgia that appealed greatly to me. It brought out a melancholy streak in my nature and I could be easily moved to tears because of a certain chord progression or movement in the melodic line. I know this only with hindsight.

These songs were the most precious things in my life and I practised them until I was note-perfect and word-perfect. Frankly, that didn't take long. I was always hankering for more material. I was given a song called 'There's always much to love', the opening line of which was: 'I love the early morning to breathe the first fresh air; to usher in the dawning with grateful praise and prayer.' For the first time in my life I suspected the text. I didn't usher in the morning that way at all; most days, I was actually terrified, at least until sixth class.

My solo career was taking off and I was entered into the City of Sydney Eisteddfod in the boys' under-nine vocal solo set piece, the aforementioned 'Duna'. When I arrived at the auditorium, it was very obvious to me that the competition was strong, at least numerically. There were over sixty competitors in my section. The adjudicator, Dr Edgar Bainton, a former director of the NSW Conservatorium, was sitting in the middle of the hall with a woman at his side to write his notes for him. The stage manager would call out a competitor's number and a boy would proceed to the stage and wait for the woman to ring the bell on the desk, as a sign the adjudicator was ready. Visions of the dreaded Sister Mary Rita banging on her bell immediately came into my head.

My number was called, the bell rang, the accompanist played the introduction, I sang, remembering not to look the adjudicator in the eye or smile at him; I finished and, at the end of the session, I got my report. I scored well in diction, enunciation, clarity, pitch and rhythm. My scoring in characterisation and dramatisation was very poor indeed. I wasn't even sure what the latter words meant: they were terms completely unfamiliar to me. However, after this, my mother decided I should study verse speaking.

Before the eisteddfod, I had been angling to take up piano. We had no piano at home, but I knew that one could make an arrangement with the convent to organise practice time. My dreams of piano lessons persisted, but verse speaking became my mother's obsession.

The Marist Brothers had hired an elocution teacher, whom I will call Mr Dickens, who came to the school each Wednesday afternoon. He was short and rotund, with slicked-back hair that was always shiny. An elocution lesson would begin with breathing. We breathed in and stuck our chests out. Dickens would walk around the class and bang on our chests with his fist in an extremely vicious way until we collapsed.

If you were banged on the chest, the last thing you should do was collapse, as it was a sign of weakness. I collapsed every time because it hurt a great deal. Dickens yelled a lot, and called us weaklings. What this had to do with elocution, I had no idea. My mother had learned elocution and it was about poetry, verse, Shakespeare, reciting, reading out stories, and finding meaning in the lines.

The elocution lessons continued with tongue twisters such as 'the ragged boy ran round the rugged rocks'. We had to roll the letter 'r' at a spectacular rate. This was something I could do as well as anyone and better than most, and I loved the sound. Such practice had nothing to do with elocution, as I later discovered, but, at that stage, what did I know? We also learned verse speaking, with the most artificially induced way of delivering the text. The words were distorted, beyond any recognition. We delivered the text in a sing-song way with hugely exaggerated rising and falling inflections. Our plosives exploded, our fricatives created enough friction to make fire, our sibilants hissed like a nest of snakes, our vowels were so pure as to make one gasp, and our diphthongs were the envy of all who knew anything about diphthongs!

One day after school my mother asked me to recite something we had learned at elocution. As I mangled the immortal lines of Henry Kendall's *Bell Birds*, she gasped in disbelief:

Barll Buds bah Hanrah Kandall
(*Bell Birds* by Henry Kendall)
Bar charnels of karlness thah eechoes ah carlling
Arnd dahn the deeeem gorgus, ah hah thah creeeeeeerks farling.
Et leeeves in thah marntains wah morse and tha sardges . . .

(Which translates as:
By channels of coolness the echoes are calling,
And down the dim gorges I hear the creeks falling.
It lives in the mountains with moss and with sedges . . .)

While this recitation was underway, the dining room chair, my mother's self-styled chair of justice, swivelled as rapidly as I had ever seen it swivel. 'Who is teaching you this rubbish?' she asked. 'Mr Dickens,' I replied. 'Right!' Uttered in this particular way, this response was of huge concern to me. It meant, almost invariably, a phone call to the headmaster; at that stage, one Brother Terrence.

Subsequently, my mother took over my coaching, and entered me in the City of Sydney Eisteddfod in the boy's under-12 verse speaking section, restricted. 'Restricted' simply meant that prize winners in any other sections from previous years could not enter.

The set poem was 'Tom's Angel', by Walter de la Mare. I was wholly immersed in it and could visualise every scene. I practised it until I was word-perfect and had captured every nuance that my mother had tried to instil in me.

The day arrived, we went to the hall, and listened to the other boys go through their paces. My mother, who had a copy of the program, gave every child a mark out of ten as he finished performing. I was competitor number 52 in a section of about seventy children. The session took all morning, then the adjudicatrix gave her summary. She thought, as my mother repeated endlessly to anyone who would listen over the next month or so, that the standard was poor; many boys could not pronounce some of the words to her satisfaction, had poor enunciation and no sign of any expression in their delivery of the poem.

She announced in a voice only an elocution teacher could produce: 'There were, however, two exceptions; competitor 27 and competitor 52, and I have given them first and second prize respectively. Session closed.'

I felt quite numb, but nonetheless pleased. A woman who had been sitting opposite my mother came up and said: 'Your little boy should have won. The child who won I can't even remember, but I will remember your little boy until the day I die.' This excited Lydia beyond all reasoning, and that night the telephone practically melted. She was on the line for hours and hours: 'Yes, Mavis, eighty-seven marks; the winner got eighty-eight marks, Mavis, yes, ONE POINT! Yes, Betty, we're all thrilled, I was telling Mavis and Patty.'

The news travelled to school by virtue of the *Sydney Morning Herald*, which published eisteddfod results, and the school entered me into the under-13 championship at the next eisteddfod. By then, my begging for piano lessons was becoming somewhat repetitive. My parents approached the convent school at Eastwood to ask about lessons, but were told that there were no vacancies and that I couldn't practise at school. Dead end!

Meanwhile, preparations were underway for the school eisteddfod and the inter-school Marist eisteddfod. The vocal soloists were to have special coaching with none other than Miss Gardoll of high C fame, the choir mistress from the Church of Our Lady of the Immaculate Conception!

Her residence was at Epping, well over a mile from school, which meant that I had to beg, borrow or steal a bike from any boy who rode to school regularly and who was prepared to lend his bike to the likes of me for an hour or two. I found one such boy, whose name was McIntyre. He said that I could borrow his but explained it was a fixed-wheel bike. That meant nothing to me.

The road from school to Miss Gardoll's was pretty much flat, except for one very steep descent that crossed several intersections. I pedalled on the flat without expending any real effort. As I began the descent and took my feet off the pedals, the bike automatically maintained a pedalling action, which became faster and faster. I was headed downhill, accelerating at an incredible rate. For the first time in my life I knew genuine terror.

The notion of using the brakes attached to the handlebars did not occur to me, as I had only ever ridden back-pedal brakes. I started screaming out 'Help! Help!', but no one came to my assistance. How could they?

As I sped through the first intersection I thought how lucky I was. At the second intersection a car was approaching. The driver saw me coming, screaming, and accelerated rapidly out of the way. Leaning out of his window, he called out a word I hadn't heard before, and suggested that I should stick the bike in my bottom, or words to that effect. I didn't find that advice either appropriate or helpful, but my vocabulary was enriched.

At the third intersection, the road began to ascend gradually and the bike slowed down a little. As the ascent grew steeper, the bike slowed enough for me to get off it and wheel it to Miss Gardoll's.

My companion was Anthony Hunt, a close friend at school and now a Marist Brother, under the name of Brother Irenaeus Hunt. I believe he is very senior in the order. He showed no compassion for my plight, and thought my antics ridiculous. We headed into Miss Gardoll's front yard, rang the bell and went through the house to the music room.

Our job was to learn the duet 'O, lovely peace' from *Judas Maccabeus* by Handel. It was a tough call for very young boys and we had only that morning to master it. I was singing second, to Anthony's first, and loved the harmonies of this extraordinary music. Phrases such as 'Let fleecy flock the hills adorn and valleys smile with wavy corn' are still in my head, and I recall the joy of singing an independent part against another part being sung by a friend.

The misadventure on the bike ceased to occupy my mind and I devoted my full attention to Handel. As usual, the music became my reason for being. Miss Gardoll played the accompaniment, swaying backwards, forwards and side to side in the manner of one also obsessed by the music. As I watched her do this, and as I sang the beautiful lines, I knew that this was exactly what I wanted to do. I had to learn music and I had to learn the piano.

The interesting thing in hindsight is that I had not the slightest idea who Handel was, or Judas Maccabeus, or what the text was about. The meaning and context of the piece were irrelevant. It was the absolute nature of the sound that transported me and, to this day, it is a strong and essential part of my philosophy of music education that subjecting children to second-rate music implies that they do not have the capacity to be affected or moved by good music. In short, playing children rubbish means you get a rubbish response. I will never subscribe to the poison that currently permeates the curriculum of all music having the same value. If you think J.S. Bach and Britney Spears are equals, you have serious problems in perception and probably should seek counselling sooner rather than later!

I WAS APPROACHING THE END OF PRIMARY SCHOOL, AND there was still no sign of a piano. School had become a monotonous routine of mental arithmetic speed tests and endless canings. It was now that the word I had heard the gentleman call out from his car as I freewheeled down the hill came in handy. The word was 'fluck'. The exact phrase used passed me by as I was concentrating on not killing myself, but the gist of it was 'you flucking idiot'.

I asked my friend Errol if he knew what 'fluck' was. He didn't, but thought it sounded hilarious. On our way home from school we would stand on the flats, an area of run-down park situated directly below Eastwood Oval, and scream out 'fluck' at the top of our voices.

The word had a certain ring, a certain punch and a powerful directness. Yelling it out provided a distinct satisfaction. It was a type of therapy in an age when the word therapy was almost never used. We were able to use 'fluck' quite correctly in three different ways: adjectivally, as in 'the fluckin' thing'; as a past participle, as in 'this is flucked'; and as a noun, as in 'what a flucker'. It suited our needs at the time.

One morning, Brother Palladius arrived in the classroom to announce that it would be impossible for all boys to sit the Primary Final exam, so only half the class would do so. Forty boys out of the eighty would be chosen and a list of their names would go up on a noticeboard. I was so unconcerned about this test, being absolutely certain that based on my less than impressive academic record thus far I wouldn't be chosen, that I didn't go near the board. It was a friend, Peter McGinley, who told me that both our names were on the list. I was shocked. Surely some error had been made.

I sat the exam, and the results were published in the *Catholic Weekly*, an overrated publication that was called compulsory reading for entry into Heaven! My pass was pleasing but, in all honesty, I felt that I hadn't deserved my promotion to secondary school. I was much more concerned about the fact that it looked as if piano lessons were never going to happen. To add to my musical trouble, I could feel my voice was changing, even though I had yet to turn twelve. The high notes were a strain and there was a huskiness in my sound that hadn't been there before.

When school returned, I entered Year One, and was promptly moved from the trebles to the tenor section of the choir. My voice was still in the process of breaking, but that didn't deter Brother Jack from insisting that I should be soloist at a celebration dinner for the school's senior rugby league teams (beer was obviously not available – they had me instead). I could, at a squeeze, still manage the high notes, and was able to produce a shrill sort of shriek, but the low voice and middle of the voice had gone.

I begged Brother Jack not to put me through the agony of performance, but he told me not to be cowardly and ordered me to act like a man. The results were predictably ghastly: a mixture of unintentional yodelling, free-range arpeggios and death throes. An entire room of rugby players threw their heads back and laughed.

After this humiliation, my father took matters in hand. It was definitely time to learn the piano. He suggested we should try Miss Gardoll. He was impressed with the fact that attached to her front gate she had a gold plate with her name and a string of letters after it.

The great day arrived. I was sent in to see Miss Gardoll on my own, a test of standing on my own two feet, while my father waited in his delivery van.

Miss Gardoll was expecting me and ushered me into the music room, a room to which I was no stranger as a soloist but was now a room in which I was about to launch my solo career as a concert pianist! She asked me to sit at the piano and put my hands on the keyboard. My heart was racing as I prepared to strike some notes. As I raised my hands to the keyboard, she let out a shriek and said in a high-pitched scream, 'Get your hands off the piano at once.'

It was a desperate and terrifying cry. I was shocked and remember looking at her in disbelief. She stood up and asked, 'What are those things on your hands?'

'Just warts,' I replied. The backs of both my hands were covered in small warts, reddish in colour and slightly raised. They were not the big warts that sometimes appear in isolation. These were dozens of little strings of very unattractive growths, which covered the backs of my hands and made strange patterns. When I was anxious, they practically illuminated themselves.

Miss Gardoll had seen them at their best, and her response showed a distinct lack of compassion: 'Well, you'll have to go. You can't play the piano with warts.' She showed me to the front door.

I was shattered. It was the closest in my entire school life that I had ever come to crying. This pain was far worse than all the canings and name-calling! My best hope of learning the piano had rejected me. Warts were my downfall.

4

The Bad-Tempered Clavier

THE YEAR 1955 WAS A TURNING POINT FOR ME IN many ways. I had reached Intermediate, the third year of high school, and there was talk that I might leave school at the end of the year, as so many boys did. For the previous two years, I had coasted through school, doing the barest minimum.

It was the year of my worst behaviour at school as, by then, the group of boys with whom I had been classmates since 1950 had formed a close bond. As I see it, we had created a special world of our own, in order to survive the cruelty and the appalling behaviour of those who had been put in charge of us. We had our own rules and codes of behaviour. We had secret ways of describing things, special codes and rituals that we had evolved in order to take a form of revenge on the brothers.

We were a group of approximately forty boys, not without talent. Some were particularly gifted in mathematics and science. There were some forceful personalities among us, whose principal roles were as class clowns. And there were some utterly fearless boys, prepared to confront a brother head-on in full knowledge of the consequences of their actions.

It was a version of *Lord of the Flies* (about which, at that time, we knew nothing). We were all Piggies in the one class, bent on one thing. Get the teacher! Teachers were our natural enemies and had to be dealt with. Every opportunity to create a disturbance or organise misbehaviour was taken. We were intent on disrupting the routine of school.

Enrolments at Marist Brothers Eastwood were increasing – God only knows why. As the accommodation issue became pressing, the building of two laboratories and several new classrooms commenced. The brothers also acquired a house with a vacant block of land attached to it, some distance from the school, and my class was chosen to move there while the construction process went on. By then, we had the dubious reputation of being serious troublemakers. It was hoped that removing us from the main school would dilute our influence.

Because of our distance from the school, the usual arrangement of a single period of forty minutes was replaced with a triple period of one hundred and twenty minutes! For me, triple science or mathematics was hell. At lunch, we played a dangerous game of improvised hockey outside the house, using a golf ball, roughly fashioned sticks of privet bush, and suitcases as goalposts.

I was not at all happy. Choir had almost ceased to exist. The brother in charge had moved on to another school, and there was obviously no one prepared to take on the role – until the arrival of the most pompous, self-centred, arrogant, foppish Marist Brother ever, whom I will call Brother James.

Whoever created James confused the recipes very badly indeed. He was cruel and sarcastic to a degree we hadn't experienced before. He insulted the class as a matter of course, referring to us either as 'untouchables' or 'peasants'. 'Would the untouchables in the back row come and receive their due reward for stupidity?' The cane would come crashing down on our hands and never with fewer than four cuts at a time.

One of his best essays in insulting behaviour I remember very well. It was 14 July, Bastille Day, and James began a French lesson by saying, 'Today is a French holiday. But because you are peasants and because you are so stupid and lazy and you have no idea about French, you will be doing French.' As if we weren't going to be doing French anyway! His behaviour in today's educational climate would have parents asking for his immediate dismissal.

The real pity was that he could teach French and knew an enormous amount about music. His mission in life was to teach the entire school to sing at Benediction. He changed the hymns and introduced a 'Tantum ergo' by Haydn. It was the first time I had heard the composer's name and adored this melody. He taught with a hymn-book in one hand and a cane in the other.

'Sing, you vermin. Sing, you untouchables; sing, you peasants.'

I needed no encouragement, and bellowed as loudly as I could and actually enjoyed it.

James had a passion for the garden that surrounded the house, and would often leave us to our devices in the classroom while he picked camellias and other blooms, of which there was an abundant supply, wrapping them in newspaper and bringing them back into the classroom. While he was out gathering flowers, the class resumed its water-pistol battle, a continuing struggle of spectacular proportions that was waged between the boys who sat in the front half of the room and the ostensibly well-behaved group who occupied the rear.

As soon as James was out the door, it was on for anyone who was fast enough to fill a pistol and start shooting water all over the room. Boys were drenched in a matter of moments. Uniforms were soaked, books became sodden, and ink ran all over the pages. There was yelling, hysterical laughter and a full and frank exchange of filthy language, as it was referred to by those in charge of our souls. Occasional bursts of 'fuck you' and 'you poofter' were intermingled with 'you bloody bugger' and you bloody bastard'. One of our number, a little older than the rest of us, had the sophistication to coin the phrase 'you fucking bloody bugger', which thrilled and delighted us with its intensity.

One day, James spent a good half hour in the garden, and the fighting waxed particularly ferocious. He returned to the classroom laden with blooms, and announced that while he had been outside he had heard yelling, screaming, laughing and foul language. He asked any boy who had participated in this particular sortie to put up his hand and admit guilt. No one did, of course, so James caned the whole class. Class canings, probably the first type of class action, were quite common. The guilty were certain to be punished, but it was tough on the innocent.

Brother Wilfred, a colleague of James', taught us trigonometry and geometry, and was also responsible for giving us lectures on sex. Sex education was a huge problem for the brothers. As celibates, their knowledge was presumably based on their own experiences as boys or young men, and sex was highly likely to have been as perversely explained to them as it was it to us. Most things were an occasion of sin and practically everything to do with the penis was taboo. The problem was that I believed it. Was it any wonder that lots of us were screwed up in all sorts of ways?

Nevertheless, the Marist Brothers had remedies designed to help us control our sexual urges:

1. Football, first and foremost. Rugby league, the working man's game, was tough, with lots of running and good strong, friendly tackles together with cuddles and hugging in the scrums. Guaranteed to knock any thought of your penis right out of your mind, especially with some boy's head in the second row of the scrum sticking halfway up your arse. You had other things to think about.
2. Running eight times around the oval, followed by a cold shower. If you could find your penis after this exercise, it was either a miracle or your instrument was oversized.
3. Daily mass, confession and Holy Communion. The best remedy of all for any sexual urge.

I resorted to joining in hockey games with a newfound energy and zeal.

As we were about to sit a public examination, we had to attend school on Saturdays – every Saturday, it seemed, for ages.

Our glorious game of golf-hockey had been banned, thanks to complaints from the good burghers of Eastwood, so we relocated to a field directly below Eastwood Oval and resumed playing it after these extra classes. The games went on until late afternoon, and were highly enjoyable and very ferocious.

One Saturday, Brother Jack was walking briskly up the hill, on his way back to the brothers' residence, when he spied us playing our game. He called out to us to stop and go home. One of our number, quite reasonably, indicated that it was our own time and he couldn't tell us what to do. Jack was enraged at this response, and demanded that we leave immediately. A gallant but foolhardy boy called out in genuine anger, 'Fuck off, Jack.' And he did.

We continued the game, went home and thought nothing more of it. On Monday morning the headmaster, Brother Aelred, turned up for a triple period of English and history. His demeanour suggested that there was trouble brewing, which generated a highly nervous feeling in the class. Every boy knew that something very serious was about to happen.

He began asking the class in a very calm and general way: 'Stand up the boys who were playing hockey below the oval on Saturday.' To a man, those who were involved stood. It was the first time I heard the phrase 'the usual suspects'. As Aelred uttered this phrase, he drew a cane from the pocket of his cassock and asked, 'Who was the boy who called out to Brother Jack?' The boy who had called out put up his hand and was ordered out to the front. 'Put your hand out, son, for six of the best.'

We thought that was the end of it. Wrong. In turn, the rest of us were called out one by one. We were perceived to be accessories to the fact, accomplices in crime, and we too had to be punished. It was a freezing winter's day. The first cut barely registered. By the sixth cut my hand was on fire and, as I sat down, I could feel the pain in my hands as I never had before. I was unable to hold a pen for the rest of the day and had to pretend to write.

It wasn't until I left school that I discovered that other children were not treated in this manner. My friends of the non-Catholic variety were caned rarely, seemed actually to enjoy school, and thought that we were being treated very badly indeed. My one consolation was that I believed that they were going to go to Hell, for the simple reason that they weren't Catholics, as we had been told frequently by the nuns. The Catholic faith was the one true faith and our Holy Mother, the Church, was the one true church.

♪

Just when life was looking particularly grim, something wonderful happened. I know the date precisely: 28 June 1955, my brother Christopher's birthday. Such anniversaries were celebrated at home with parties, generally after school, and the fare was exactly as you would expect in Sydney in the 1950s. Sausage rolls, cocktail frankfurters generally known as LBDs (little boys' unmentionables), fairy bread, cupcakes, sandwiches and a birthday cake, all washed down with fruit cordial or lemonade and other fizzy drinks. But this time there was something more.

I arrived home from school to find a piano standing in the corner of the lounge room! I recognised it instantly as the instrument from my aunt's house in Randwick: a duo-art Steck, which meant that at one time it had had the capacity to play piano rolls. We often visited the family home in Bishops Avenue, Randwick; it was a favourite thing to do. We would all sit at the player piano and beat the hell out of it as we played the rolls backwards.

By the time this bad-tempered clavier joined us at Epping, it had lost most of its action. The bellows had perished, and the tubing, which connected the pumps to the bellows and caused the action to operate, was rotten. There was ivory missing from many of the keys, and in wet weather the humidity caused the adhesive, a silvery glue, to stick to my fingers.

The Steck had been given to my father, in circumstances he did not speak of. My mother was strongly of the view that the gift was conscience money of some sort. I couldn't have cared less. We had a piano! At last I could start lessons. I could hardly wait to take my first step towards my career as a world-famous concert pianist.

My thoughts flew immediately to Miss Gardoll. I was wart-free again, thanks to the ministrations of a brilliant GP who had cured me using the placebo effect; in those days, a very new treatment. His pink pills, which I swallowed religiously, were my introduction to the world of psychological medicine, and I remain forever in Dr Woolnough's debt.

Miss Gardoll was called forthwith, but had no vacancies. Surprise, surprise! The memory of my warts was obviously clear in her mind. She did suggest, however, that an advanced student of hers might agree to teach me. This was my introduction to a wonderful lady called Pam Salkeld, who lived just around the corner from our house, in Brucedale Avenue, Epping. I could be at her place in a matter of minutes and I watched the clock like a hawk so that I would never be late.

I had to purchase *The Magic Land of Music*, my first piano book. The first tune in the book, which I can still play and is probably the best thing I do on the keyboard, was entitled 'Middle C March'. Middle C can be found under the letter A on a Yamaha or between the I and the N on my very beautiful Steinway. The tune, which began on Middle C, had a text: 'Left, right, left, right, marching to and fro. Right, left, right, left, forward as we go.'

Going forward, even in the fifties. The Gillard government's fortune was being told when I was a child!

All the early tunes had words and there were lots of songs that, being me, I sang as well as played. I suspect that this was the source of my later responsiveness to the processes used in music education, especially in the teaching of music to young children. It became clear to me, as I progressed with piano instruction, that singing had prepared me remarkably well. Singing from a very early age, whether in the backyard or in the choir, had developed in me a memory for pitch and rhythm, and a sense of musical style. That insight is the basis of the barrow I push today.

I went to my first lesson on a Saturday afternoon in early July 1955, from which moment my life started on a new course. Music was once again the most important part of my existence. I counted the minutes between lessons, and practised incessantly. I flew through *The Magic Land of Music* in a matter of weeks. I ripped through Stephen Foster's selections, singing at the top of my voice: 'Way Down Upon the Swanee River', 'Old Black Joe', 'Camptown Races', and 'Jeannie with the Light brown Hair'. I churned through Brahms's *Lullaby*, and whisked my way through endless dances of goblins, witches, fairies, clowns and other creatures, real or imaginary. However, I drew the line at the 'Dance of the Anemones'. I felt that anything fastened to a rock had a slim-to-none chance of actually dancing.

At the back of the book were pieces by the so-called great masters: Bach, Handel, Haydn, Mozart, Beethoven, Chopin, Brahms, Schumann, Schubert and Tchaikovsky. I say so-called not because they are not great. I have learned, however, that we don't create converts to music by telling people that Brahms is good for them or that an understanding of Tchaikovsky is essential to a normal life.

I played a minuet by Mozart, which he had written at the age of six, a fact that took me back hugely. How could it be? I was thirteen and had been playing the piano for at least three months! What was more, there was a wrong note in the second-last bar. There was a clashing sound, a discord, a hideous, ugly noise. It was the note E natural against the note F natural. A harsh clash. Two notes exactly next to each other! A semitone.

I suggested to Miss Salkeld that the child composer had made a mistake. Her benign smile indicated to me that I was about to learn something. The chord I hated was called a suspension, a discord, which finally resolves into a concord. It was the spice of music. Frankly, that didn't convince me. I felt that I had one over Mozart, and I used to correct this note every time and go straight to the F natural to avoid the clash.

Haydn, for his part, had rhythm problems as well as discord issues. The minuet from his *Military Symphony* had strangely placed rhythms and equally strange harmony. As for Bach's Minuet in G – frankly, if that was the best he could turn out, Bach had pretty well nothing to say. Chopin was a different story. He really could compose. His A Major Prelude was a masterpiece and spoke to me instantly. Beethoven, however, was the winner. His rondo 'Rage Over a Lost Penny', a highly active piece, allowed me to thump my way through it at great speed and it sounded impressive. Here was I, a thirteen-year-old, already passing judgment on the masters!

Unknown to me, I was sowing the seeds of my own musical destruction. I became a very good sight-reader, ploughing through repertoire and tackling everything I could get my hands on. The boy next door, Johnny Garret, was learning the piano at the convent in Epping. He had lots of music I could borrow and read, as did our neighbour, Jan O'Toole, who was very advanced and had Chopin waltzes, Beethoven sonatas and the durable 'Für Elise'.

As a sight-reader I had not made time to practise properly. I was catching up – reading music and learning a repertoire. Scales, arpeggios, chromatic scales and all the essential ingredients to establish a good technique for playing the piano went by the wayside as I travelled the musical highways and byways of this fabulous repertoire. I discovered that I could play things on the piano that I had heard on the radio, adding the harmonies more or less correctly. Pop songs and the tunes on the hit parade joined my ever-increasing repertoire.

I could also make up tunes and accompany them, which I happily did for hours. All sorts of well-intentioned people who seemed to know everything about music, and certainly far more than I did, told me that playing by ear was bad;

making things up was bad; the things I was making up were rubbish, and I needed to learn one or two pieces properly. The last point was certainly correct.

In one of the pieces I was playing there was a footnote, which contained some advice the great composer Robert Schumann offered to young pianists. I'm paraphrasing here, but in essence he said that it was better to play a simple piece really well than a more difficult piece indifferently well. Good advice and very sound. Nonetheless, I was hell-bent on covering repertoire and was determined to read as much music as I could.

By now, I was capable of observing how others were taught the piano. Johnny Garret had a very special system, which had been devised by his teacher. Written on his music for every piece he had learned was a series of letters: R.H. L.H. TOG. EXP. They meant that in week one, the right hand had to be practised; the left hand was practised in week two; the following week, the hands came together; and week four, the expression was added. Couldn't be simpler!

Miss Salkeld didn't work like that at all. She was very happy to listen to anything I had prepared: I can see now that she was possibly having difficulty holding me back. To an ever-growing pile of sheet music I added more and more material, given to us by people whose relations, friends and acquaintances had someone in the family, or knew of someone, who once learned the piano. This included volumes of the Beethoven sonatas for piano, and the Bach preludes and fugues.

I tried to play what I thought were the easiest pieces in all the books, plunging into the repertoire like someone possessed. My playing must have sounded hideous to anyone who had the vaguest idea about music, but the difficulty of the music didn't deter me. Nothing was really out of bounds for someone as desperate as I was to learn – apart from the pages covered in dense forests of black dots of which I could make no sense whatsoever.

The music of Bach, apart from some of the preludes, eluded me entirely. It seemed to lack real melody. Melody for me existed principally in the music of Chopin, which was full of what people referred to as 'expression and feeling', and I understood this completely. There was a boy at school named John Dowd, at least two years my senior, who played piano in an eisteddfod I attended. Hearing him so effortlessly play music that was not unlike Chopin's inspired me. It gave me new impetus to work and encouraged me to practise even harder. Another boy called Tony Murphy, whom we all called Spud, was learning the Prelude in C Sharp Minor by Rachmaninoff. This was hugely impressive. I was jealous both of Spud and Dowd, envying their technical skill.

My close musical friend at that time was a boy called Neil Slarke, a fellow sufferer at Marist Brothers Eastwood. He was learning the piano from a woman who lived next door to him in West Ryde. Neil had a highly refined mind; he was an avid reader, a genuine aesthete and a very sensitive individual for whom I had – and, indeed, still have – enormous respect. His playing was elegant, and intensely musical with a sense of reserve. My playing was ebullient, forthright, and equally as intense for a totally different set of reasons. His playing was generally mistake-free, while mine was full of passion and error. He introduced me to a piece of music called 'Norwegian Cradle Song' by a composer called Gabriel Morel, and to a group of other works in this style by a composer called Alfred Ketelby, 'In a Monastery Garden' and 'In a Persian Market'. I liked them very much.

Years later, musical colleagues were to pour scorn on this music, describing it as sentimental, cheap and poorly written. Their derision made me feel as if I had been wrong to like it; that by showing any affection for or interest in this style, I had demonstrated a lack of musical taste and maturity. It was my first taste of peer pressure and the beginning of a realisation that there was something akin to a class system in the appreciation of music. The terms 'lowbrow' and 'highbrow' entered my vocabulary. The impression given to me was that there were two musical worlds, the popular and the classical. Regrettably, this terminology is still frequently used in a pejorative way today.

Not long after I started piano lessons, two of our near neighbours, Miss Natalie Rosenwax and her companion, Miss Rene Maxwell, invited me to a concert by the Sydney Symphony Orchestra at the Town Hall. It was an all-Beethoven program, led by the orchestra's chief conductor, Eugene Goossens, who was also the head of the NSW Conservatorium. Goossens, who was respected by musicians all over the world, had had the distinct privilege of conducting the first performance of Stravinsky's *Rite of Spring* in the presence of the composer in 1921.

The SSO concert had a profound impact on me. I distinctly remember the sound of the strings as silvery and silky. Poor words to describe string sound, but they were all I could summon up at the time. Ernest Llewellyn led the orchestra, and I was mesmerised by the way in which he moved with the music. Every phrase was alive and seemed to be of utmost importance. I was still pig-ignorant at the time, but one thing about which I was absolutely certain was that music was special. It was different from everything else. It affected me in a way nothing else did, and it still does.

I am frequently moved to tears in the rehearsal room when a singer sings a particular phrase in an especially beautiful way. Even looking at a score can move me to tears. I can open the quartet from act three of *Bohème* and be moved greatly by the beauty of the writing. While it may be a perfectly reasonable thing to describe these reactions as touchy-feely or as a cheap form of sentimentality, good music, be it Beethoven, renaissance polyphony, or a good arrangement of a jazz standard, is one of the most thrilling sounds in the world.

The notion that classical music had special qualities that had an improving effect, and that liking popular music was the beginning of a slippery slope, was all-pervasive when I was a student. Old equals good and new equals bad. Even in the so-called classical music world, it was a theme: Stravinsky bad, Brahms good, modern music rubbish. Genuine musicians, I was later to discover, knew music to be either good or bad.

ALL THIS PIANO PRACTICE STILL LEFT ME TIME TO GET into trouble. One day, after school sports, four of us perpetrated a spectacular piece of bad behaviour. It created a serious public disturbance, and while it was behaviour of which I was not necessarily proud, I considered it brilliantly inventive at the time.

Each Thursday afternoon, years one to three played football at Meadowbank, a short train ride away. This weekly excursion, under the guise of sport, was a form of day release for us, and a nightmare for the supervising brothers. At 3 pm, the final whistle blew. After changing out of our filthy shorts and mud-filled guernseys, we were marched back to the station, free to go to our homes and travel in any direction we wished.

Four of us – Errol Cranney, Robert Dunnicliff and his cousin Colin, and I – decided that once the crocodile march set off for the station we would make a dive for the canal that bordered the field, and wait there until the group was out of sight. Our cunning plan worked brilliantly. Once the rest of the school was gone, we headed off down the canal with our schoolbags filled with dirty sports gear and books, and walked out onto the mud flats. The tide was low, and the flats were alive with thousands of small crabs that we decided to catch.

How and why we decided to indulge in what was blatant animal cruelty is no longer in my memory, but we spent at least a good hour and a half stuffing our school bags with crabs. Between the four of us, we must have had hundreds of the poor creatures in our cases by the time we decided that we should head home as it was getting dark.

What were we going to do with the crabs? On the way to the station, we agreed that we would release them in the train. Like commandos, each of us had a particular area, or carriage, to deal with. We planned that when we arrived at West Ryde we would all get out and wait for the next train to take us home to Epping, protecting our identities and preserving our anonymity. The train would be crowded, because it was peak hour, and we figured we could slip into the crowded carriages, weaving our way slyly through the standing passengers and releasing our catch undetected.

The results were even more spectacular than we had imagined. The screaming and yelling was unforgettable. Once released, the crabs went berserk. They climbed on peoples' shoes, they climbed up people's legs, they clawed their way up the seats, and ran wildly everywhere. We almost brought the train to a standstill. At West Ryde, we crab commandos alighted, compared notes, agreed we had done a good job and waited for the next train.

The only flaw in our otherwise perfect plan was that we were wearing our school uniforms with the Marist Brothers Eastwood badge visible for all to see. Our school hats also had a badge, allowing for instant identification; we were the only Catholic boys' school between Strathfield and Hornsby whose students wore a grey suit with a red badge.

It didn't help that I was tall and gangly, with horn-rimmed glasses, a face covered in pimples, and incredibly curly hair that stuck out from underneath my hat. Colin Dunnicliff was just as hard to miss, with the most wonderful head of brilliant ginger hair.

The next day at assembly, Brother Aelred stood up and announced that on the previous evening, a most serious event had taken place on a train travelling between Meadowbank and West Ryde, and four boys had been seen misbehaving in the most atrocious way. They were in school uniform, bringing disgrace on themselves, bringing disgrace on their friends and, worse than that, bringing disgrace to the school. Trifecta!

Aelred called out our names and told us to stand outside his office. No charges were laid. No questions were asked. No confirmation was sought as to whether we were the only culprits or, indeed, the culprits at all. We were presumed guilty, and all caned, with six of the best. It was a vicious and savage caning. I distinctly remember, as with after the 'Fuck off, Jack' incident, not being able to hold a pen for the entire day. Afterwards, we were ordered to go to detention and each write out one thousand times: 'I must not make a nuisance of myself on public transport or disturb the peace.'

Anyone who has ever had to write lines knows that this sentence will not fit on one line of an ordinary exercise book. This punishment turned out to be two thousand lines, by virtue of the length of the sentence. We sat in detention from 3.30 until nearly six o'clock, by which time none of us had finished. We were ordered to complete them that night and, before we went home, we were each caned another four times.

The one consolation in all our trouble was to hear the headmaster say that the school telephone had rung until the wee small hours of Friday morning, keeping him awake all night, such was the magnitude of our misbehaviour. I was thrilled to learn that his sleep had been disturbed. It was the one shining moment in an otherwise hideous misadventure.

Why did we do this? I have no idea. Was it stupid? Undoubtedly. The older I get, the sorrier I feel for the crabs.

One thing was certain. I was living in cloud cuckoo land. My adolescent dream had to end soon, and it did. I arrived at school one day to discover, to my shock, that the public examination known as the Intermediate Certificate was about to begin. The English paper was upon us.

5

God Helps Those Who Help Themselves

THE EXAMINATIONS CAME AND WENT, AND I MANAGED to pass. Actually, I passed quite well, even scraping through physics. I knew that my results in no way, shape or form reflected a study plan or any organised work. The combination of a good memory and good luck had got me through.

To celebrate I went on holiday in the Blue Mountains with Aunt Pauline, my father's sister, and her husband, Uncle Edward. Pauline, whom my father idolised, was a linguist who spoke fluent French and German, and had lectured in languages at Oxford University. Eddie was what was known in those days as a man of parts. He had been a mining engineer and a captain in the British Army, and had served as British high commissioner to Nigeria. They had travelled the world, and were great raconteurs.

My cousin, Tony Skewes, my best friend within the family, came along, and Pauline and Eddie took us on trips all over the countryside, Eddie talking endlessly. He didn't actually drive in the conventional sense of the word. Rather, he aimed his car at the road and yelled at those in front of him, 'Out of my way, you foxy beetle.' He would also use the word 'bloody' in splendid ways such as, 'Look at that driver! What a perfectly bloody driver he is.' Pauline: 'Edward, please. Not in front of the children.' Eddie: 'Of course, Pauline, you are quite bloody right.' I loved this banter between adults. It had never really occurred to me that serious grown-ups who had done and been *something* could talk to each other this way. What joy!

BACK IN SYDNEY, THERE WERE SERIOUS DECISIONS TO be made. I was fourteen, but legally allowed to leave school. Did I have the intellectual ability to stay on and secure the Leaving Certificate, or should I seek gainful employment? The decision was made by my parents, as it often was in those days. They wanted me to apply for a cadetship in radio. There was one vacancy with the ABC, as a trainee presenter for Kindergarten of the Air; another at radio station 2CH. We sent off my applications and I managed to secure interviews for both. For the ABC I had to present a prepared reading of a folktale. I read in (what I believed to be) the approved ABC voice, and could tell from the faces of the recording engineer and the producer that they thought I was a prat!

The people at 2CH were extremely kind, and I had two interviews. One of the questions on the application form was: 'Do you have any dependants?' I answered: 'Two, my mother and father', completely misunderstanding the question. The folk at 2CH were so concerned about my apparent plight that they telephoned my mother and father to ascertain the truth. I didn't get the job, so back I went to school.

The old gang was breaking up. Errol had started work. My friend Neil Slarke had left school and was studying independently for his Leaving Certificate. My other musical friend, Anthony Hunt, had gone into the novitiate to train as a Marist brother, as had another of the boys, Leo Fry.

With less company to keep, I hurled myself into practising piano every spare hour of the day. When I say practising, I actually mean playing. I doubt if I've ever really and truly practised over an extensive period of time in my life. My real problem was that I was a reasonably good sight-reader and that was my downfall. Near enough was good enough. But I did amass a fairly good knowledge of the standard keyboard repertoire, and Miss Salkeld decided that I should move on to another teacher. I was sent to a Miss Gladys Hart, who taught in the city at Palings' Studios, Ash Street, Angel Place, down the lane from Palings' sheet music shop (now the Angel Place City Recital Hall).

Catching the train all the way into town on Monday nights was an adventure in itself for a fourteen-year-old. Miss Hart was a very thorough piano teacher. She thought, quite correctly, that I was undisciplined and had no technique. She saw through me in a minute. She did, however, tell me that if

I were to practise seriously, I could be quite good. A ringing endorsement!

She decided that, in September, I should sit an examination in piano, at grade five level in the series of national examinations known as the Australian Music Examination Board. At the same time, I should sit the grade three theory of music exam. I played a study in D major by Loeschhorn; a courante from the G major Partita, No. 5 of J.S. Bach, a mazurka in B*b* by Chopin, and Debussy's 'The Little Shepherd'. There were also other pieces that you had to study and play just as well as these if they asked you to. I had buckets of material for the extra lists and wasn't worried about repertoire.

The examination was broken down into sections, which consisted of technical work such as scales, arpeggios, broken chords, chromatic scales and the like, followed by the four chosen pieces.

Aural tests followed the playing of the chosen repertoire. These tests dealt with the identification of rhythm and pitch patterns; the singing and naming of intervals, as played by the examiner; the singing and naming of chords; and then some sight-reading. There was a slight nod to general knowledge, 'Who was Chopin?' and so on, and then the extra lists.

A week before this examination, I was at school playing cricket in the nets. The bats were pickaxe handles and the wickets were wide steel plates. I was not known for my sporting prowess at the best of times. The boy who was bowling to me took an almighty run up and sent down the ball at a scorching pace. I made no stroke, but placed the pickaxe where it would stop the progress of the ball. There was so much power in the delivery that it shied off the handle and went through a closed window in the brothers' residence nearby. The whistle blew. This was the signal for the entire school to freeze.

A brother, whom I shall call Brother Toby, called out at the top of his voice, 'All right, Gill, you smart alec, get out here.' Everyone knew how unfair this was, but could do nothing about it. This Christian gentleman was known for his particular brand of cruelty with the cane. He marched me behind his second-year class at the end of lunch, and then proceeded to break every rule in the book by caning me eight times: four cuts on each hand, three of which fell on my wrist, and two on the heel of my right hand. It was a special kind of sadistic cruelty and I felt genuine hatred for the first time in my life. My hands were locked in pain and I couldn't move the fingers of my right hand for three days. I told my parents that I needed to concentrate on general knowledge and ear training, which was why I wasn't practising as much.

It would be too easy to say that my performance in the examination was directly related to the fact that I had been caned. There is no doubt that the pain and injuries from the caning prevented me doing any practice for that week. However, I knew that the section in the exam that would cause me the greatest difficulties was the technical work. Because I had avoided scales and arpeggios ever since I started learning the piano, in favour of playing pieces, my technique was, in a word, poor.

The examination was at the NSW Conservatorium, where my examiner, Dr Alex Burnard, was a professor of harmony and composition. (He would later become one of my favourite teachers at the Con.) Dr Burnard offered to carry my suitcase to the exam. He told me that I would need both hands to pray!

He smoked a pipe, had a walking stick and, to my immature and highly impressionable fourteen-year-old mind, seemed fairly ancient.

We walked up a spiral staircase inside one of the northern turrets of the old Con. As we entered the room I could see the upright piano I was to play, and a blackboard that had music written all over it. Dr Burnard began with the scales. The first was Bb major. Shocking! I managed to muck it up in a spectacular way. On and on it went: scale after scale, arpeggio after arpeggio, and all fairly disastrous. I played a chromatic scale with considerable flair, and thought that would impress him mightily. It didn't.

I scored full marks for aural, sight-reading, extra lists and general knowledge, but my technical work let me down. I received 75 marks in total, with the comment that 'there was some evidence of musicality'. Miss Hart believed that I had had my just reward. Becoming a WFCP (World Famous Concert Pianist) was a rapidly fading dream.

In truth it was inconceivable that I would ever become a concert pianist. Although I adored music I did not have the discipline, the single-mindedness or unwavering sense of purpose that marks such an artist. Even more than that, I didn't have the talent. I wasn't talent-free, but when I heard others play I knew where I sat in the ranks, and it was most certainly not at the top.

Furthermore, along with the piano I had been developing my skills as an impromptu speechmaker and reciter of verse. In my fourth year at school I won the open verse speaking championship and the open speechmaking championship but came second in the open piano section. Was I being given a message?

This didn't deter me from continuing with piano. My mother was an avid purchaser of volumes of tunes from musicals, and I sang and played them as soon as she brought them home. I also learned to read the chord symbols, which can be found on top of most sheet music of this sort, from which I improvised simple arrangements to go with these songs. I was a bit like the advertising slogan for a popular household soap: 'Sunlight Soap – useful for most occasions.' I was becoming a handy pianist without any specific or considered focus. That didn't worry me: I was simply hungry for music.

By now my dilapidated old Steck was in serious need of repair. A solution presented itself. Just down the road from us in Essex Street, Epping, lived the Kent family. Ernie Kent, father of three, was a compositor and typesetter for the Fairfax press. On Saturday afternoons, he worked as a sportswriter for Fairfax's afternoon newspaper, the *Sun*. He called my parents to ask if I would act as his runner one afternoon, as the boy who usually did it had cancelled at the last minute. Initially I resisted. My mother and father said that it was a good chance to make some pocket money and that I would be doing Ernie Kent a really big favour. I felt I had no choice but to accede to their requests. I left home that Saturday afternoon feeling that I faced a huge challenge.

The *Sun* published several editions on a Saturday, starting with the midday edition. Throughout the course of the afternoon at least four others appeared, the last being the late final extra. The paper's sportswriters were distributed about various Sydney grounds, covering club rugby league or rugby union in winter, and grade cricket and tennis in summer. My job was to take the reporter's hand-written copy to a nearby phone especially installed for use, and phone the story through to a copy-typist, who took it down and passed it on to a sub-editor.

By the time a game was over, we could buy an evening copy of the *Sun* and check what we had sent through. The rapidity of the process was awe-inspiring and I loved the elaborate rituals of filing. My first job of the day was to call the paper and find out the catchline for our copy, and the times at which the paper expected updates. The typist at the other end would rattle off a series of intervals: 3.10, 3.33, 3.40, half-time, 4.05 and so on, which I would take back to my reporter.

As each deadline approached, the reporter would say 'Run,' and I would go like the clappers to the phone, which was usually at the back of the grandstand or near the dressing rooms. I would either turn the handle on the phone, if the line were connected directly to the paper, or dial B0944, the main number of the *Sun*, then ask for the sports desk. I would lead off: 'Catchline NORTHS. After a messy kick-off deep into East's territory, Smith was brought down just outside the twenty-five, FULL POINT NEW PAR' – which was our way of saying full stop, new paragraph – 'A melee ensued and referee Duncan awarded Easts a free kick after Jones landed an unprovoked punch on Smith's jaw.'

Ernie Kent said I was a natural. I took the job on permanently, and did it every Saturday afternoon thereafter until I had saved enough money to have the piano fixed. It cost me £75 for the repairs, and took me one and a half years to save the funds.

After some months, Ernie became extremely ill and asked me to cover for him. We had to ring in every Thursday afternoon to find out what game we were covering. I told the

Chief, a gentleman named Mr Albert McKeown, that I was ringing for Ernie, as he was busy, and I'd pass the message on. In fact I was writing and running. I knew Ernie's style very well, and was able to use his language. I managed to pull this off for a long time, and looked forward to reading my copy, under the name of E.K. Kent, each Saturday night.

In the end I was dobbed in, probably by a reporter from the rival *Telegraph*, who was suspicious of the fact that a kid aged sixteen was writing and running. I was too naive to deflect his questions indefinitely. One day I confessed that Ernie was very sick but didn't want to lose his job. Done like a dinner. I was called in to the *Sun*'s head office on Broadway, and fired. It was a terrible shock and I couldn't tell my parents for some time. I honestly believed that I was doing the right thing by covering for Ernie and honouring the code of silence. In any case, it was a fantastic adventure.

I COULD HARDLY WAIT FOR SCHOOL TO FINISH. IT WAS not a matter of wishing my life away – I simply wanted to arrive at a circumstance where music was the main focus of my everyday activities. The Leaving Certificate was approaching, Saturday school was in full swing, and we were given dozens of past exam papers to plough through for practice. The brothers emphasised that we needed to do as many as possible, and we usually got through five each week.

Exams started on 5 November 1957, the day after my sixteenth birthday. I went to mass that morning, hypocritically, and prayed for all the questions I needed. In English I needed two poetry questions, one from the Elizabethans and one from the Romantics. In history, I needed the second section of the paper to start with the Congress of Vienna, answers about which I had prepared. In ancient history I needed a question on the Mycenaean civilisation, separately from the Minoan Cretan civilisation, and a good question on Solon or the Gracchi.

French was not going to be a problem. In fact, the French paper was remarkably easy, and I know I would have scored close to full marks. I couldn't believe how straightforward it was, especially as I was also to sit for French honours, an extra examination to increase one's chances of gaining marks. The French honours syllabus was very tough, with a heavy emphasis on complete knowledge of all aspects of grammar.

Every candidate for the Leaving Certificate had an examination number in place of his or her name, for all the obvious reasons. My number was 26293. The French honours examination was held at Homebush Boys' High School. A quarter of an hour after it had started, a school secretary came into the room to tell me that the Department of Education had contacted Marist Brothers Eastwood, informing them that I had been using the wrong number throughout the exam period, and that, as a result, my papers would be cancelled. Just the news I wanted to hear fifteen minutes into the one exam in which I actually thought I had a vague chance of scoring second-class honours, or even a first, with a push and a shove. I wasn't brilliant at French, but I was pretty damned good!

I remember the blood draining out of my face. I sat there for the next three hours, wondering what would happen. Time was called, and I handed in a blank booklet. On the way out of the school I went to the office and was told that the circumstance surrounding my number had been sorted out and that I had, indeed, used the correct number after all. They had my number confused with a boy from another Marist school! I went back to Eastwood to talk to the brothers, who already knew of the affair in great detail, and who had been in a flap trying to sort it out. They apologised and said that everything was going to be fine. Sure! I would need every mark I could get to scrape a pass of any kind, now that the hope of extra marks in the honours had completely disappeared.

The Leaving Certificate results for our year were especially (if unsurprisingly) shocking. In the *Sydney Morning Herald*, under Marist Brothers Eastwood, my surname was the first on the list. Out of the twenty-two boys who had sat for the examination, a significant percentage had failed outright. I passed, with three Bs and one A. The Bs were in English, Modern History and Ancient History, and the A was in French!

During the 1950s in Australia, tertiary education was free, so entrance to university was the provenance of the academically brilliant and the intellectually gifted. Based on Leaving Certificate results, you were awarded either a Commonwealth scholarship or a teachers' college scholarship. With my results, there was no guarantee of either.

So that was that. At least I was out of the clutches of the Catholic education system. Over the years, I have done all the reflecting that I am prepared to do about the One True

Church and the Holy Catholic faith, and say simply that it isn't for me. I am not a little Catholic anymore and if I have been excommunicated, which I'm sure I have been, then I feel as if a cancer has been removed from my body. The guilt still remains – the Catholic Church did a good job in that regard – but the the fear of Hell has gone. Heaven and Hell are here on earth. My family is my Heaven. My Hell is within me. Hell is not a place. Limbo is a dance and Purgatory is writing your memoirs!

I remember that I first began to question the concept of faith when a brother told us that the soul did not leave the body for fifteen minutes after death, which allowed your family time to fetch a priest to administer extreme unction and the Last Rites! Over a very long period of time, I have gradually erased the sense of worthlessness that was relentlessly instilled into us as children, and have tried to assess my place in the world. I hope I am perceived as someone whose fundamental role in life is to attempt to find the true worth in others and develop that worth wherever possible.

It is one thing to be told that man is master of his own fate, but what about a child? How does a four-year-old master his own fate with the fear of death, Hell and punishment looming over him? If you are told all your school life that you are stupid, silly, dumb and worthless, it stands to reason that, after a while, you will begin to behave that way. I believe that the hideous incident with the crabs in the train was a direct attempt to demonstrate that we were stupid. We proved it in spades and paid the price.

Sometimes I think it is a wonder that I am not in therapy or psychiatric counselling! But the truth is that I believe I have been made stronger because of my early experience. I feel I have, in a perverse way, come through reasonably well. I don't hold grudges against the Marist Brothers, but I don't have any affection for them either, with the exception of Brother Palladius, who involved me in the choir, and Brother Joseph, who one day asked me if I'd like to stand in front of his class and try to teach them something. There is no doubt that a seed was planted in my mind then and there, and to Brother Joseph, whether he is alive or not, a debt is owed.

The shame of sin, the impurity of my thoughts, my failure to approach the so-called Blessed Sacraments successfully, have developed in me an understanding of the nature of hypocrisy. The good people I know who are Catholics are good in spite of, and not because of, Catholicism, I believe. They may disagree.

While hypocrisy exists in every walk of life, one tends to expect that institutions such as churches and religious organisations, which are preaching and teaching the doctrine of Christ, would be able to set a consistently good example. That is wrong. Religious teachers, priests, brothers and nuns are human and capable of error. I understand this only too well, as I have done things of which I am not proud, and am well aware of my own particular foibles. The Delphic Oracle and I are very close friends!

What religion has done for me is, by default, made me aware of the great works of art in architecture, painting, sculpture, literature and, of course, music.

Credo in Unum Deum. I believe in one god. The god in whom I believe is Johann Sebastian Bach. I can believe in him implicitly, absolutely and wholly. I know he existed.

I know he wrote music of a divine nature because I sense, feel and know its divinity. Every note of Bach's I play teaches me that he is truly great, truly good, truly omnipotent and truly omnipresent. He is infallible. His notes tell the truth. His truth is great and feeds me daily. In the quest to reach my God and know his perfection, I know I am dealing with the unattainable and therefore make the greater effort to attain him. I know my God through his deeds, words and actions, and he is good.

My saints are all the other composers, poets, painters, architects, writers and philosophers who live in my mind and challenge me on a daily basis. They give me my daily bread and forgive me my trespasses. They are my One True Church. Here again is another Heaven for me. One can have many heavens and hells.

The Edward FitzGerald translation of the *Rubaiyat of Omar Khayyam* has a quatrain that reads:

I sent my soul into the invisible,
Some letter of that after life to spell.
And by and by my soul returned to me
And answered, I myself am Heaven and Hell.

What I am getting at is that while I feel that many members of the Catholic Church behaved in a terrible way towards us, their students, I don't necessarily blame them. They were victims of their own circumstances, who had no genuine grasp on life or reality, and behaved in the only way they knew how. It is easy to forgive, and I do. It isn't so easy to forget, and I don't.

I don't need an apology or any financial settlement for the damage and mental pain. Nevertheless, it is immeasurable, and will always be part of me. As Tennyson's *Ulysses* says:

I am a part of all that I have met;
Yet all experience is an arch wherethro'
Gleams that untravell'd world, whose margin fades
For ever and for ever when I move.

I frequently quote this poem when talking to students about the concept of giving in or giving up on something, especially the last lines, which read:

but strong in will
to strive, to seek, to find, and not to yield.

Bad and all as my schooling was, at least I committed an enormous amount of information to memory. I had a sense of the world, from the point of view of geography; I had a good knowledge of the British version of Australian history, from the arrival of Captain Cook, through to the settlements of the penal colonies, the gold rushes, the Eureka Stockade, and so on.

I adored ancient history. The Greco-Roman world appealed to me greatly, especially the benevolent despots of ancient Greece. The European world was taught from the time of William the Conqueror, through to the events causing World War I. There was an intense concentration on European history, from the late Bourbons through to the Congress of Vienna in 1815, the European revolutions, the

Franco-Prussian War, the Russian revolutions and the emergence of modern China and Japan.

I knew who Shakespeare was and what he'd written. I knew a great deal of poetry by Milton, Keats, Byron, Shelley, Wordsworth, Browning, Elizabeth Barrett Browning, Longfellow, Tennyson, Coleridge and Arnold, with a special concentration on Australian poets from an anthology entitled *The Wide Brown Land.* I still have all my poetry books from those days, and can recite many poems from memory, as, I suspect, many other older Australians can.

I had a reasonable smattering of French, which proved useful when I finally went to France. I knew something of English and French grammar, and was at least aware of the sciences and the branches of mathematics. And, after all that, I was considered by Aunt Pauline, the lecturer in languages, to be under-educated by her standards! 'If you get into university, you will have to work very hard indeed, especially to catch up.' That phrase again – to catch up!

Make no mistake. The getting of this education was far from ideal. Far from ideal in its delivery and far from inspirationally taught. The things for which I am grateful are the memory training, the constant repetition, and the notion that writing things out is a good way to learn or remember them, especially for the drudgery of learning formulae, theorems and so on.

Also, while it was far from perfect, the education system itself was completely free from the tomfoolery and pretentious rubbish that pervades the current state curricula. No more so than in Victoria, where the Department of Education has inscribed over one of its doors, 'Failure is not an option'.

What a shocking thing to have in any way associated with learning! It plays with the idea of education. It is patent nonsense, insulting and cheap populism. It is the touchy-feely gobbledygook that breeds insecurity, nurtures uncertainty, and strips children of their capacity to develop resilience and tolerance.

Sometimes it is only through failing that we learn. To fail at something, as my wife constantly says to children, is not to be a failure. Failure at something is a sure-fire way of assessing a process, re-evaluating a circumstance and starting again, with a view to establishing a path to potential success. The soft, dumbed-down pap being fed to children these days is a damned disgrace and a national embarrassment.

I was certainly at risk at school in all sorts of ways, but the danger was in no way comparable to that which children face today. University lecturers frequently complain about the quality of the courses they deliver, and the academic achievement of the students they teach. Even as I write this chapter, a report commissioned by the federal government, dealing with the thorny issue of school funding, has just been released. Its overriding observation is that educational standards in Australia are slipping.

I have watched music education move out of the hands of the genuine musician into the hands of the bureaucrats and curriculum writers, who know little of education and nothing of music. I have watched school education descend from a serious study of identifiable disciplines to the random and meaninglessness of NAPLAN and standardised testing. I have watched the profession of teaching descend into an abyss of fear where teachers are reluctant to speak out against what they know as iniquitous practices, such as standardised testing, in case they lose their jobs or are perceived to be bucking the system.

I worry that our benighted leaders have completely lost their grip on education.

6

In Which the Door Opens, But Just a Crack

In January 1958, I applied for a scholarship to the New South Wales Conservatorium of Music. Offered in conjunction with four years' training at the Sydney Teachers College, it prepared the successful applicants to become specialist music teachers at secondary-school level. I saw this as a way to receive conservatorium training on a scholarship – in other words, to receive free tuition to do what I had always wanted to do! Teaching wasn't high on my list of priorities at the time.

All applicants for teachers' college scholarships had to undergo a fairly rigorous medical examination, a spelling test, comprehension test, and an extra written examination that included questions about their vocation to teach. I scored fifty out of fifty for spelling, and also scored very well in oral comprehension.

The examiner who interviewed me for the scholarship informed me that I was the youngest candidate in the state (I had recently turned sixteen). He added that competition would be very strong. He kindly encouraged me by saying that, although I was very young, I was clearly not completely stupid, and that he would recommend me for a pass. I didn't know whether he was being humorous or sarcastic, and was just glad of the recommendation.

The next step was to undertake a musical aptitude test, known as the Wing standardised test of musical intelligence, which was supposed to measure your musical age, as well as your aptitude and capacity for studying music. I presented myself at Sydney Teachers College for the first part of the aptitude test. There were about thirty other candidates in the classroom, which had a blackboard at the front on which the words 'absolute music' were written.

I seated myself in the front row and, pen poised, felt a tap on my shoulder from the girl sitting behind me, who asked: 'Hey mate, what's absolute music mean?' In a fairly pompous voice I replied that I thought it was music that was essentially non-programmatic, such as the music of Mozart, Haydn, Beethoven and the like. She said 'Shit. Thanks', and the test began.

We then had to present ourselves for a practical examination, which included a performance from memory of a work of our choice on our principal instrument, some sight-reading and the singing of a song we had prepared.

I had chosen to play Chopin's 'Polonaise Militaire in A major' which I thought was guaranteed to blow them away, and to follow that with a dazzling performance of my pièce de résistance, 'The Gendarmes' Duet' by Offenbach, for which I planned to play the accompaniment and sing both parts.

While the candidates waited outside the audition room, it was very easy to hear those inside going through their paces. The girl before me, Wendy Denham (RIP), brilliantly played another polonaise by Chopin. I knew just how hard the work was, having attempted to play it myself, very unsuccessfully. Her performance was flawless and she flew through the most difficult passage, which requires that the left hand play very fast octaves while the right hand moves in a completely different way.

It was a first-class act. Oddly, I wasn't as fazed as I should have been, believing in my ability to do equally as well in my own way with the same style of work. I was welcomed cordially to the room, in which there was a group of examiners led by the inspector-in-charge of music, Terence Hunt, and his girl Friday, Barbara Mettam. I played the Chopin, and noticed that they didn't exactly fall off their seats in wonder. I then played the sight-reading, making sure that I spent little time looking at it first, as I wanted to convince them of my capacity in this field. I just ploughed in, and again there was a lack of appreciative sighs or gasps.

They asked me what was I going to sing, and laughed uproariously when I said I would accompany myself and sing both parts to 'The Gendarmes' Duet'. Terry Hunt said that I wouldn't be able to do it and I assured him I could. He stood up, came over to the piano, invited Barbara Mettam to play the accompaniment and we proceeded to sing the duet together.

In the general discussion that followed, I learned my Wing tests result was unusually high. I had no idea what that meant, so made no comment. Questions followed, such as: 'How long have you been playing the piano?' Two and a half years! 'Have you done any examinations beyond third grade theory and fifth grade piano?' No. 'Very well then, we can't give you a scholarship now, but if you can manage to do sixth-grade theory and sixth-grade piano before the end of this year, we will give you a scholarship for the 1959 intake. Try to complete all the exams by May. Goodbye!'

When the next round of scholarship offers was published, I was offered a place at Wagga Wagga Teachers College. This was not part of my grand plan! It was hardly the feast of music at the Con that I had imagined. I declined, and deferred the scholarship until September, when another round of offers would be made.

I needed to find a job and start earning money. On the southern corner of George and Park streets, in the centre of Sydney, was a store called Waltons-Sears. It was a type of franchise of the American Sears-Roebuck chain, a very successful mail-order company with a massive catalogue of everything the human heart could desire, and then some. I applied for a job as a trainee buyer. Thinking back on this makes me shudder, but my parents had suggested that retail was an appropriate path to follow while I prepared for my piano exam.

I was chosen for an interview, part of which was a session with the in-house psychologist, who asked a series of very strange questions about my past. He told me that I was young for such a position but a job with the company was not entirely out of the question. The letter of acceptance finally arrived and I duly turned up at Waltons-Sears' head office, in

Reservoir Street, Sydney, not far from Central Station. I was assigned to the buyer in charge of floor coverings, a Mr Albert Cooksey.

Mr Cooksey was a very nice man. He encouraged me to go on 'executive thought walks', as he called them, whenever I had to mull over a problem; I went on executive thought walks often. Waltons-Sears was never going to be my real place of employment. I did, however, learn a whole series of new words. Words that fell, essentially, into the category of filthy language or foul talk, as our elders and betters referred to it.

I had not previously encountered the expression 'Christ on a crutch!', a term reserved for the office manager's appearance. I also learned any number of declensions and conjugations for any number of nouns and verbs, essentially to do with bodily functions. I was introduced to the concept of crawling to senior staff, something I did not do in any circumstance. At school, the kid who crawled to a teacher was despised. None of this education did me any lasting harm. (I did, however, regrettably start to smoke and drink.) In the end, I hated going to work in what was essentially an unimaginative environment, which seemed to have a stultifying effect on everyone.

I continued piano lessons with Miss Hart, and studied theory with Miss Dorothy Fountain, who introduced me to the concept of four-part harmony, a style of writing music in which three more parts could be added to produce a fairly bland and uninteresting piece of music. None of the music I had previously played was in this style and I thought that the closest music one could find to it would be hymn tunes.

At that stage, it seemed to me dull and unimaginative stuff, like solving a jigsaw puzzle. Had we been introduced to the extraordinary four-part chorales of J.S. Bach from day one, the sense of four vocal parts would immediately have become clear. It would have at least provided a goal. Nonetheless, I had to learn all about this style, as it was going to be a big factor in the examination. Miss Hart said that Miss Fountain was a whiz and that I would develop in leaps and bounds if I took her tuition seriously. She was right. I practised what Miss Fountain preached, and managed, under her wizardry, to score a very high mark in sixth-grade theory.

Sixth-grade piano came and went. I was examined by a lady called Winifred Burston, who found it in her heart to pass me, and pass me well. I had taken the precaution of practising my technical work to a much higher standard than I had achieved for fifth grade.

Thus emboldened, I telephoned the music branch of the education department. I asked to speak to Mr Hunt, and, when I was finally put through, reminded him of what he had said at the end of my audition in January. He responded with devastating news: I would have to wait until the end of the year to hear if an offer were to be made for the Con. Furthermore, if I were offered a teachers' college place in the September round, it would be advisable for me to take it.

I was crushed. I had been pinning my hopes on these examinations and on the doors that they potentially would open. As far as I was concerned, it had been a done deal, promised and finalised. Wrong!

The September offers came, and I was offered a place at the brand-new Alexander Mackie Teachers College at Paddington. Along with a couple of hundred young hopefuls, I walked through the gates of this institution one bright September morning in 1958. We were told at the first assembly of students on that memorable day that we would be expected to go and work in schools in mid- to late October, to undertake a four-week practice session. So, after just six weeks of tuition the chips would be down, and we would all have our first indication of whether we would make the grade as teachers.

Our course covered a huge range of subjects, including English, mathematics, biology, art, craft, physical education, music, psychology, philosophy, sociology and all the related teaching methods. We were encouraged to keep detailed notes and meticulous records of every lecture we attended. We were also required to visit those institutions designated as demonstration schools, with the express purpose of watching teachers teach and writing evaluations of what we had seen.

We were advised not to write blow-by-blow reports of the teaching we had witnessed, but instead to assess how the lesson had taken place, and what techniques the teacher had used to convey information. I loved 'dem' lessons, as they were known, because the experience of watching someone else teach encouraged me to think that I could do at least as well and, in some cases, probably better. In this, I was genuine. I really believed I could do exactly what I was witnessing, and was already thinking of ways to lead my own classes.

For the first time in my life I was exposed to the methodical study of philosophy. Until that time, I had believed that you were either Catholic or you weren't: that was how life was, and you didn't ask questions. When I started at Alexander Mackie, I really had no idea what philosophy was, let alone the ways in which thought could be brought to bear on circumstances, to solve problems of existence, to provoke argument or to stimulate questioning.

We were expected to familiarise ourselves with the writings of Plato, Aristotle, Socrates, Hume, Dewey, Hobbes, Montessori and Steiner, a task I found thrilling. I didn't understand very much about philosophy but adored hearing about the ideas of these thinkers and was particularly impressed by John Dewey's experiential approach to learning. We were also told that there were two types of teaching: inductive and deductive, that is, either *giving* children information to repeat and learn; or *asking* them to deduce the information themselves through a set of questions that would lead them towards the right answer. I had no preference for either method. All I knew was that I could hardly wait to get into a school and start teaching.

At college, music was taught by a wonderful musician called John Cassim. He introduced me to musical concepts that I had never dreamed of, and music that generated fresh thought in me about music and its myriad styles. He opened my eyes to the world beyond the piano. The live symphony orchestra and its special sound, which I had experienced only once, were reintroduced to me through recordings, along with other forms such as chamber music and electronic music. It was the age of the development of the Moog synthesiser and John Cassim had early recordings of its synthesised sounds.

After a period of time, we were allocated to schools for practice-teaching. I was sent with four others to Eastwood Public School. Its headmaster, Mr Wood, suggested that the most difficult class, a group of grade-five boys, should be avoided by anyone who felt that discipline would be a problem for them. As if any of us knew! I certainly had no teaching experience beyond the one class Brother Joseph had given me to oversee for a short period of time in my final year of school.

Guess what – I finished up with this particular group. The classroom teacher was called Peter Black and had a wondrous accent, which I took to be Irish. He was sometimes very savage with the class, calling his pupils all sorts of hideous names while simultaneously randomly lashing out with a cane. When he wasn't banging it into the sides of his leg like a riding crop, he banged it on the desktops to great effect, causing the boys to flinch and duck in terror. Perhaps because of my own exposure to the cane at school, it took me some time to appreciate that this behaviour was a spectacular form of bluff. Mr Black knew exactly how to handle these boys and got some good work out of them.

I was not frightened of teaching this class, but I was nervous. However, I learned the names of these potentially troublesome boys very quickly, which helped enormously with discipline; my nervousness turned quickly to confidence. Learning the names of people even in large groups is something I can still do. It is a freakish attribute in some ways: I have no system and no idea how I do it, and the names stay with me for a very long time. Even fifty-four years after I first stood in front of the class at Eastwood, I can recall many of the names of children I taught.

For a leader, knowing the names of those under your direction is a very positive thing. Making the effort to learn someone's name says very clearly that you really want to be able to speak to them personally, and care about what they can do or what they have to say. I am always careful when working with youth opera groups to learn names quickly, and usually know them all by the end of day one of a rehearsal.

I was sixteen, and the children I was teaching were eleven and twelve. They thought I was old. Our supervisor was a wonderful woman called Mrs Holder, who gave us ways and means by which to introduce ourselves to the class. I still use her method today if I am working with children. She told me to stand in front of the class, write my name on the blackboard and say, 'My name is Mr Gill – good morning, everybody!' It works like a charm every time. She also said, 'If you are going to tell a class a joke, then you must say to them, "This is a joke", and then they will laugh at the right place!'

As student teachers, we had to present lesson notes for every single lesson, set out in a particular style. The supervising teacher signed the notes, as did the supervisor from the Alexander Mackie College. At the end of the lesson, we had to write a summary of our efforts and present a critical evaluation of how we believed the lesson had been received, and what we thought had been achieved. At the end of my time at Eastwood Public School, my supervising classroom teacher wrote in my notes: 'Mr Gill, I believe, will make a strong and compassionate teacher.'

I MAY CREDITABLY HAVE GOT THROUGH MY FIRST experience of teaching, but in my personal life, I was still dreadfully immature – well, I was only sixteen!

At college, smoking, drinking and gambling on the premises were absolutely forbidden. We had to wear coats and ties; the lecturers referred to us as Mr or Miss, and there was a section representative, elected from the students, who dobbed in anyone who wasn't present at a lecture without a reason. The absent student's name was recorded on a card and handed in to the office for filing.

In breaks between lectures we went to the Bat and Ball Hotel, played snooker, drank beer and smoked cigarettes. Every day we found an excuse to play poker illegally, in the student common room. The game was known as 'browns in' – a brown being a penny. The poker game was led by a student named Max Dewes, whom I admired hugely. He was a big, blond-headed guy, who more or less took me under his wing. After my mates from school, he was my first close friend. There was a genuine bond among this friendship group. We made our presence felt simply by the fact we were inseparable. We were noisy without being overtly brash, funny without being overtly vulgar, and enjoyed one another's company in every circumstance.

When one of our number became engaged, it was decided, unanimously and spontaneously, to celebrate by doing a pub crawl, from Circular Quay to Central Railway Station and along Castlereagh Street, with occasional deviations into Pitt and George Streets. I am not necessarily proud of what happened next, but it taught me a great deal about myself, and the power of alcohol.

We had agreed to cut morning classes, and started drinking at 10 am. When we got to a pub called the Royal Bognor (long demolished), one of our number, a young man given to voicing his views in direct proportion to the number of glasses he had consumed, suggested that one of the barmaids was sufficiently well endowed that one could get lost for days looking around in there. He further suggested that other parts of her anatomy would probably give up their secrets if you asked her politely. His own version of asking politely was limited to the phrase 'I suppose you wouldn't be up for a root?' The barmaid shot back: 'You wouldn't know what to do with it once you got your nappy off.' The manager of the hotel was called and we were asked to leave.

I remember this exchange between the barmaid and the boy as if it were yesterday. It was embarrassing and, of course, stupid, but at the time we found it very funny to watch our smart-arsed friend receive his just desserts. He had attended a prominent private school, and believed he was certainly as good as everyone else and probably better than most. I had been brought up to believe that I was essentially worthless, as far as the Marist Brothers were concerned, and at home we were taught to respect our elders and betters. At the age of sixteen, almost everyone was older and, by definition, better. My friend's display was an interesting lesson in the expectations bred by class.

We left the pub and piled into taxis to head back to afternoon lectures. That we were drunk was not the point – we were paralytic. I remember falling out of a cab onto the footpath outside college. A group of girls standing at the gate laughed and pointed at us, and one of them said very loudly to her friends, 'They're pissed.' It was a little bit like saying, 'It's Monday'.

We stumbled off to a maths lecture and, at this point, I will just cut to the chase: it is alleged that, during said lecture, I yelled out an impertinent and inappropriate comment on everything the lecturer said. I can't recall this myself, but friends told me later that these comments were very funny and caused considerable mirth. That's one way of looking at it. My mother would have said that I was being a fool to myself, and a burden and a bother to others.

I was duly reported to the deputy principal, Dr Campbell, a mild and compassionate man, who explained to me that my behaviour was sufficiently bad to earn expulsion and cancellation of my scholarship. It was, he intoned in a very distressed voice, a serious offence in the eyes of the college to insult lecturers with rude and unseemly comments while they were lecturing. By my behaviour I had let the college down, let my friends and colleagues down, and 'third, and worst of all, you have let yourself down'. (I cannot begin to count the number of times I have heard teachers refer to unfortunate consequences in threes.) He suggested gently that I should take a long hard look at myself.

I left his office 'duly chastened', as they say, and went to the common room, where a poker game was in full swing. Max Dewes asked me how it had gone with 'the Doc'. I said that I had almost been tossed out. No one really cared, and the game went on. Next day we all went to the beach, where we discussed the possibility of three or four of us flatting together somewhere in Bondi.

When I went home and told my parents I was considering moving out, they were deeply offended. They went on at length about how much they had sacrificed to make a home for us boys, and that I had shown a singular lack of appreciation for all they had done for me. I was an ingrate, I was selfish and, above all, I was thoughtless. Their displeasure was not short-lived. I was sent to Coventry in much the same manner as when I had first attempted to leave home at the age of seven. (Their attitude was understandable. In those days, unless you came from what was known as a 'broken home', you didn't leave the family nest until you married – not unless you joined the seminary!)

Could I redeem myself by winning a scholarship to the NSW Conservatorium? I sweated on the hope that Terence Hunt would remember what he had said to me at my audition. As the year wore on, I was increasingly concerned that nothing would happen, and resigned myself to becoming a primary school teacher.

I arrived at college one morning just before term ended and was summoned urgently to Dr Campbell's office. I entered it somewhat trepidatiously: I was certain that I was going to be reprimanded because of my recent outburst. But the deputy principal informed me that he had received a telephone call from the Music Branch that morning, and its substance was that I had been offered a four-year scholarship to the Con. Was I going to accept it? he asked.

I was completely stunned.

Of course I would accept it. I could hardly wait. I felt as if I had been given a miraculous reprieve.

It was almost the end of the year. My studies at the Con wouldn't start until mid-February. I went to Eastwood Public School and asked if I could do an unpaid, unsupervised practice session for two weeks in the early part of February. Mr Wood remembered and welcomed me. I was assigned to another fifth-grade class, under the supervision of a Mr Smith, a terrific teacher who was able to guide me while I was teaching, and not make me feel like an idiot when I made stupid mistakes, preached heresy, or stated errors of fact.

There was a piano at the back of his classroom. 'Do you want to play the piano to my class,' he asked, 'or would you like just to give them a music lesson about one of your favourite pieces?' I decided I could do both.

Chopin's A major Polonaise had become my party piece and I was preparing to play it at my first lesson at the Con, which was to take place very soon. I had a recording of Tchaikovsky's *Capriccio Italien*, which I listened to at every opportunity. Playing the polonaise and giving a lesson on the Tchaikovsky would be a good thing to do, I thought, and give me practice delivering a music lesson.

I didn't really have the faintest idea about how to teach music. I told the class the story, such as it was, of the Tchaikovsky, and banged on for ages about how beautiful it was and how they really all should like it enormously because it was a good thing to like his sort of music. I was becoming a crusader for classical music and was not yet mature enough to realise that crusading was actually destructive. As I would discover a few years later, as a qualified teacher, crusading was likely to turn people off the very thing to which you hoped to convert them, simply because the fundamental idea behind any crusade relies heavily on one party persuading another that their way of thinking is not only better but preferable in every sense.

It also occurred to me eventually that I was teaching the way I had been taught at Marist Brothers Eastwood. Didactic, inductive teaching masquerading as a modified form of preaching, followed by questions at the end of the lesson, which were essentially designed to assess how strongly I had been able to persuade the children of my views and how many of my views they had been persuaded to remember. Hideous rubbish; impossible to defend.

In pondering this circumstance now, after almost fifty years of working in music and music education, my blood runs cold at the idea that I could have become a crusader responsible for killing young minds. I thought I was simply sharing my enthusiasm for music – a benign thing to do, surely? It was not until I was a young high school teacher that I was put right about that.

7

'So You Think You Can Play the Piano?'

THE GREAT DAY ARRIVED, AND AT LAST I WALKED through the front doors of the NSW Conservatorium as a student. In 1959, when you entered the Con you were immediately surrounded by music. There were studios to the left and right of the main entrance, and it was always a thrill to walk into this field of sound, in which voices and instruments mixed in a strange and wonderful confection. Even before you entered the building, you were greeted with the sounds of piano and voice. The windows of the studios opened onto the road – no air-conditioning in those days.

While the new Conservatorium certainly has much to offer (and I refer chiefly to its facilities, of course), the fact that you never hear a sound as you walk by is very disconcerting to me. The music was the lifeblood of the institution, and hearing it everywhere was an indication that there was a living, breathing heart inside this fortress, which had been built in colonial times. It was an outward manifestation of an inward miracle, taking place on a daily basis.

In those days, it seemed to me the Con was a place where dozens of like minds were gathered in one arena, arguing passionately about music and loving the extraordinary privilege of being part of a vital fraternity and sorority. It gave the Con a distinctive style, unlike that of any institution I have known since. Unfortunately, those days are well and truly over, and the Con has forever lost its very special style. It has been subsumed by the University of Sydney, in the process becoming simply another segment of a giant educational factory – that, at least, is my view, which I will enlarge upon in a later chapter.

Back to that day in late February 1959. I had my first piano lesson, with Dallas Haslam, a graduate of the Juilliard School of Music, who had recently arrived from the United States and was very much flavour of the month. I had not chosen him, nor him me. I had asked especially for Alexander Sverjensky, considered by many the top teacher at the Con, but it didn't take me long to work out that Sver, as he was generally and affectionately known, took only the crème de la crème.

I was quite nervous before my lesson, so while I waited outside Haslam's studio, on the ground floor near the entrance to the Con, I smoked a couple of cigarettes, in the mistaken hope that they would calm me down. Graham Russell, a young baritone, was also waiting there, to meet the fabulous Raymond Beatty, one of the Con's most charismatic voice teachers. I introduced myself by offering him a cigarette:

'Would you care for an Albany, with the new wonder filter made from aylon?' He laughed, took a cigarette and we smoked the brand devotedly together for years. Graham became a lifelong friend.

When the time of my appointment with Dallas Haslam arrived, I knocked, entered and was asked to sit at the grand piano. I had never before played such an instrument. It was a Welmar five-foot six-inch grand, and the action was quite stiff in comparison with my old treasured Steck upright.

I played the A Major Polonaise, acquitting myself fairly well, I thought, and going for some extra-special loud effects and some dazzling pedalling. Haslam smoked a cigarette while I was playing (his brand being Rothmans filtered), then asked me to play some scales and arpeggios.

After he had heard me, he said, 'What do you want to do?' I replied that I wanted to become a concert pianist. He said that he had something to tell me, and that was that I couldn't actually play the piano and, indeed, had no idea about how to hold my hands or make a legato sound; no concept of pedalling or phrasing; and a generally clumsy technique, based on my inability to play evenly. Apart from that, it seemed that everything was OK.

He walked over to the piano and asked me to do a five-finger exercise similar to the very first piece I ever played, the march beginning on middle C. He took my hand and showed me how to form a hand position suitable for playing such exercises, then asked me to practise this in front of him so he could assess that I had grasped the idea. He also gave me another exercise, with the thumb passing under the first two fingers of both hands.

Humiliation! To say I was devastated would be an understatement. Dallas Haslam had abruptly brought down the curtain on my career as a concert pianist before it even got started. Now, at the ripe old age of seventy, I can see that it was an absolutely appropriate assessment of my ability. In truth, I had worked out by the end of my second lesson that there was no hope in Hades of me ever becoming a pianist of any description. A great start it was not, but I wasn't deterred.

The next activity was choir, conducted by Doctor Noel Nickson. We all filed into the auditorium known as the Small Hall, and sat in our appropriate sections. By all, I mean all the students who were in the teachers' training course, approximately eighty singers. When the music was handed out, I discovered that we were to sing Handel's *Israel in Egypt*. We were scheduled to perform with the conservatorium orchestra the plague choruses from this oratorio at the end of term. The sheet music was like nothing I had ever seen. In every choir I had ever sung in, we had simply learned the music by rote.

This notation consisted of two lines of music, joined by a brace at the left-hand side of the stave, and written in the bass clef. The upper line of the music was denoted First Bass and the lower line was denoted Second Bass. Nickson said that we should find the most comfortable part to sing, and so I called myself a first bass and sat down next to a boy called Wilfred Blencowe, who was from Leeton, in country New South Wales, and was a student of piano.

The accompanist was a girl called Wendy Swan, a second-year student who impressed me mightily with her pianistic abilities and especially her ability to sight-read. She played the introduction and the altos began to sing, which sent a shiver down my spine. On the top of our music was an empty stave with the figure **18** written in big black numerals, followed by four bars of another voice line, which was printed in very small type, and then the basses' first entry began.

I had no idea what was going on. Suddenly, Wilfred began to sing, and I wondered how on earth he had known to do that. Not only had he begun to sing but every other bass had, too. It occurred to me that I was the only one who was silent. I listened as hard as I was able to, copying what I heard, turning the page at the same time as everyone else and becoming totally involved in the beautiful sounds. Because I was listening so intently, I was singing marginally behind everyone else, but I felt that, among so many voices, hopefully only the boy next to me would know that I was a little out of step.

A *little* out of step! I had just been told that I couldn't play the piano, and now I had the embarrassing revelation that I couldn't read vocal music or sing from sight! The music of *Israel in Egypt* poured on. When we reached one of the plague choruses, which had to do with hail and rain, I finally made a connection. This particular chorus was very clearly and neatly divided into two choirs, with one choir answering the other. Its text, which I remember to this day – as, I dare say, many of my friends do – was: 'He gave them hailstones for rain, fire mingled with the hail, ran along upon the ground.'

The connection I made was that the bass line was an arpeggio (the notes of a chord, sounded in succession), which I easily recognised and could sing readily, as I had played them before. There were also scale passages I could recognise, and, as the choirs answered each other almost exactly, I was able to copy what I heard, whether arpeggios or scales, and repeat them with the relative certainty that I was going to be more or less accurate. But fudging it was not a long-term proposition. Early the next day I went to the Con's library, and asked if I could have a score of the Handel work we were learning. I took it home and started to commit the vocal lines to memory, and also played through the accompaniment in my devil-may-care sight-reading style, trying to understand the music better.

Day two, I had to present to a harmony class. The lecturer in harmony and counterpoint was Dr Nickson, our choirmaster from the previous evening. There were about eight students in the class. I sat in the front row, keen as mustard. On the blackboard were two lines of music; one a melody line and, below it, a bass line. Nickson pointed to me and said, 'You, phrase the melody.' I had not the slightest idea what he had asked me to do and I blushed the colour of a well-formed beetroot. Wilfred Blencowe – may the gods forever enfold him to their breasts – was again sitting next to me. He whispered, 'Put a line across the top of the melody.' I went to the board and did just that. Nickson breathed a sigh of disgust and said, 'How do they let people like you in here?'

I was finding out in a spectacular way that I was as free from musical knowledge as a frog from feathers, and that I had an extraordinary amount of catching up to do. All those friends of my mother had been right. I had to catch up! My new colleagues had all studied music from an early age. They had played much more repertoire than I ever had, and they certainly had a much more secure knowledge of harmony, history and related subjects.

I was not daunted by the massive weight of my own ignorance, because I actually believed that I could make up the time. Let me say right here and now – you never make up the time. It has gone! It will never come back! The earlier you start a child in music, the better.

However, the circumstance was as it was, so it was fortunate that I was determination personified. Now that I was at the Con, where I had always wanted to be, I wasn't going to let anything stop me from doing what I could to become a musician of some description. I couldn't play the piano; I had no idea about phrasing in harmony; I knew little about chords and their function; I was ignorant of Handel and Bach, and I couldn't sing from sight. When I began attending lectures in the history of music, at last I found something I understood and was good at. I loved these classes and thrived in the circumstance of devouring new information. It energised me for everything else I had to learn. On the practical side, I was constantly bowled over by the abilities of my colleagues, which only served as an inspiration for me. Very gradually, I started to make progress.

It was suggested that I should learn the oboe for my second study. Ian Wilson, then principal oboe of the Sydney Symphony Orchestra, became my teacher. He showed me how to make reeds, how to crow the reed (make it speak), and how to produce a sound from the instrument itself. As it was my second instrument, I borrowed one of the Con's oboes, and it was that fact that prematurely ended my woodwind career.

The oboe had seen better days. Its case had too. The blue felt lining had a most unsavoury smell about it and had transferred itself to the instrument. Even my teacher grimaced whenever he tried a reed and had to put the instrument to his mouth. There was always a very strange taste and odour when I inhaled to make a sound. I persevered and was finally asked to play in the Sydney Teachers College Orchestra. The only reason I was asked was that they had no one else. At the first rehearsal, we played an early Haydn symphony in D major. The oboe part was not technically difficult, but I was still struggling to produce a note that didn't sound like an animal being tortured: any part would have been difficult for me.

When I played – and I use the term loosely – the whole group burst into uncontrollable hysterical laughter. The volume of the sound I made would have penetrated a ten-foot-thick concrete wall. Was it a musical sound? No. Was it in tune? No. Was it in the right place? Mostly. Was it loud? Yes, it was deafening.

At the end of the rehearsal, John Gordon, the lecturer in charge, suggested that perhaps I might like to take the part home and practise it. He was a gentleman and a scholar, a wonderful musician and very knowledgeable. I could not find it in my heart to tell him that no amount of practice was really going to change my status as an oboist.

This much I had realised: the oboe and I were better off at a distance. Ian Wilson agreed, and I moved to singing as my second study. The day I told him I wouldn't be continuing as a second study oboist was the first time I saw him smile spontaneously, and he remained in that state for some minutes! At least I had made someone at the Con happy.

Singing was something I had been learning, more or less, since I was four. It was something musical that I could actually do. I had even taken some singing lessons from my last piano teacher, Miss Hart, after I became interested in the aria's form. I found an album containing about fifty songs from various periods, including French, German and English arias, early Italian arias, ballads and something called *lieder.* Under her tutelage I sang most of them, and accompanied myself in a dramatic and intense way. What I lacked in accuracy was more than made up for in the style and commitment of my performance.

In my usual way, I had devoured these songs as fast as I could. For me, the aim of learning any work was to establish an overall view of the music. I wanted to understand the big landscape, to see where everything was going. Detail could come later. It is not a bad general philosophy in coming to grips with most things at the beginning of a learning period. However, if the detail never appears, then one only ever has a general picture. I point this out to my students now, reflecting on the fact that I had no one shaking me by the scruff of my neck to encourage me to be self-disciplined, or to check that the solution to all my technical issues actually lay inside me. My path was a continuous struggle to cut through the undergrowth, knowing that beyond it there existed an enchanted garden, over which blue sky hung and golden sun shone perpetually.

In the end, I have no one but myself to blame for most things, but I wish now that an insightful mentor had come along and provided me with a sense of reality. I was a dreamer. Nothing sickens me more than when I hear children being told 'Follow your dreams and you can do anything you want to do, and become anything you want to be.' Rubbish! Dream by all means, but be aware that it's only a dream and that wishing things were so won't make them happen. My dreams had been rapidly brought into check at the Con, but I still imagined I had a date with destiny.

Sheer circumstance diverted me towards more realistic goals. I was now taking singing lessons with Raymond Beatty, the ebullient, superbly rotund and jocular singing teacher who already taught my friend Graham Russell. Quite by accident, Beatty opened up a new path for me, which had the most profound impact on me musically. After my first lesson, he asked if I could stay behind to play the piano for his next student. This was to be a turning point in my musical direction.

The singer, a mature-age student, was a tenor. In those days the Con offered three ways of studying music. There was a two-year diploma for the truly brilliant, and a four-year teachers' college course such as the one I was doing, which could be combined with the diploma if you were good enough. There was also a system whereby any singer could study for an hour or so a week, if a teacher at the conservatorium auditioned them and decided to take them on. The tenor was one such student.

He came into Beatty's room and put his music on the bracket of the piano. It was a song called 'Linden Lea', an arrangement of an English folk song by Ralph Vaughan Williams. Beatty began with a few exercises, using his favourite, 'the tip of the tongue and the lips and the teeth', and some 'me-may-maws' in scale patterns, then asked the tenor to sing the song. I played the accompaniment; it was recognisable as a piece of music.

I noticed that I could follow the vocal line and the piano lines, as well as keeping up with the idiosyncrasies of the singer.

When he slowed down or sped up or needed to breathe, I was able to accommodate him. Furthermore, I went for rhythm rather than pitch, and the bass line when I couldn't get all the notes, and we more or less finished together.

At the end of the song, Beatty made some suggestions and we played it again. This time I was better. I played more notes and started to feel the music along with the singer. The experience was hugely enjoyable. All those hours of reading masses of piano repertoire, as opposed to practising one piece for ever, had more or less paid off, and I found that I really could sight-read reasonably well.

I knew I wasn't as good as my dear friend Chris Henry, a superb sight-reader and an immaculate accompanist. She played brilliantly but had that extra something an accompanist should have, which was reflected in the way she listened to the singers. Nevertheless, this short episode with 'Linden Lea' led me to the discovery that accompanying people was at least as interesting as playing solos, and possibly even better, because there was another level of responsibility attached to the process of accompaniment.

Through accompanying other musicians my whole attitude to listening changed, as I learned to follow several lines at once. I became aware of the independence of the lines, and the way in which the accompaniment supported the voice or the instrument. I was a regular in Beatty's studio and began to learn the song repertoire in earnest. I also made myself available for other students who played orchestral instruments and realised that there were whole repertoires of music out there about which I knew nothing. I was anybody's who wanted an accompanist who was prepared to have a go.

I also learned about the methods singers used to produce sounds: the way they could be made long or short, legato or staccato; the way sound swelled and receded; the way it was sustained; and the seemingly endless variety of colours that instrumentalists and vocalists could produce. With singers, my appreciation for poetry was an advantage in every sense of the word, as I could sometimes help with text and, in this way, I was developing, inadvertently and fairly obliquely, into a vocal coach. Listening to singing teachers instruct their students was an eye-opener. I heard such an extraordinary amount of conflicting advice about breathing, and about the way in which the throat behaved while one was singing, that I was very confused for some time. The use of the word 'support', a common term used by wind and brass players as well as singers, varied from studio to studio, as did theories of the use and function of the diaphragm. I stopped worrying when I heard one teacher describe the way in which one approaches a high note. One simply tucks one's stomach right in, squeezes one's buttocks as tightly as one can and pushes to reach the note, assisted by the constricted fundamental orifice!

I knew after this particular lesson that quite a deal of singing teaching consisted of a mixture of mythology, folklore, a generally poor knowledge of physiology, a less-than-poor knowledge of anatomy and a great deal of 'Good, darling, that's sounding lovely. We are improving, aren't we,' as the student went into oxygen deficit and appeared to be on the verge of collapse after a particularly excruciating top note.

SOCIALLY, I TENDED TO GRAVITATE TO THE SECOND-YEAR students, the group that would have been my cohorts if I had been accepted the first time around. We considered ourselves very sophisticated, frequenting a coffee shop, The American, after choir on Monday nights. There, we drank black coffee and smoked cigarettes, and bullshitted our way through conversations about music, poetry, art, and the meaning of life and religion (or, at least, I did). We had strong opinions about everything, even if they were based on the scantiest knowledge.

What distresses me about this now is that at school, we had never been taught how to think or how to argue, so all my arguments and discussions tended to descend into emotional outbursts or shouting matches that became personal. I had no mechanism for arguing dispassionately about anything. The only argument I ever remember winning convincingly was about the statement 'There's nothing new under the sun'. The student sitting opposite me scratched a mark on the table with a pencil and said, 'That scratch is new.' To which I replied, 'You have simply rearranged the varnish on the table and exposed the wood. They were already there.' Conversation stopper!

My children, Claire and Anthony, and my wife, Maureen, are much clearer thinkers than I am, and are much more logical in thinking about how to solve problems or present a case. This lack in me causes me more frustration, more heartache and more pain than any numbers of canings ever did. I was the product of a system that was driven entirely by fundamentalist principles of the worst possible kind, based exclusively on fear and intimidation. I know I am not alone in thinking this.

As I have matured, albeit slowly and sometimes very painfully, I have come to know the condition of my mind and have been able to take steps to do something about its singularly impoverished state. I have closed massive gaps in my reading, by becoming a little more familiar with the ancient Greek philosophers and dramatists, and with as much contemporary philosophy as I can lay my hands on. I have also read bleeding chunks of Aquinas and St Augustine, approved Catholic philosophers, and especially enjoy the *Pensées* of Blaise Pascal, my copy of which is heavily annotated.

I discovered Aquinas in the strangest way. One day at teachers college, I passed a table stacked with bundles of textbooks that were being thrown out. I picked one up and opened it at a passage on Neo-Thomism, the modern revival of Aquinas's thought. It made more sense to me than anything I had ever learned about God at school. In essence, it said that religion was a personal matter between God and oneself. In one short sentence the church had been obliterated. I could go to God directly, if I wished.

This chance encounter with Neo-Thomism, and my own, probably highly imperfect, interpretation of it, provided me with more hope and more comfort than I had ever had in my life. As a seventeen-year-old who was deeply confused about all sorts of matters, from sex, love, religion, music, art, philosophy and politics, right down to what sort of clothes to wear, the concept of a God who was available via a direct line of communication was exhilarating, and provided me with all sorts of renewed hopes. I had a similar experience when I discovered the work of Bertrand Russell, a philosopher we had been warned off at school because he was, they said, an atheist. We were told that his writing was dangerous for us and could lead us away from the faith.

Halfway through my first year at the Con, I had all but stopped going to mass and confession, knowing that my now perpetually black soul was beyond redemption. Not one of my newfound friends was Catholic. I was fraternising with the enemy! I began attending services at Protestant churches where my friends sang as members of the choir. Often, I was invited along to sing and make up the numbers. The services were strange to me: there was no Latin, the hymns didn't have the same quality as the Gregorian chant or the motets I had sung, and the anthems were all by English composers I gradually came to love, but whose names were then unknown to me: Byrd, Gibbons, Tallis, Purcell.

My parents, especially my father, were scandalised by my behaviour. As a devout Catholic, he feared that I was turning towards Protestantism. I wasn't turning towards anything. I was simply moving away from the Catholic Church and increasing my knowledge of the ways of other faiths and the music of other religious persuasions.

With my new friends, I also discovered art movies. There was a cinema in Sydney, the Savoy, which offered movies that were radically different from those at the local picture house: Ingmar Bergman's *Wild Strawberries*, John Cassavetes' *Shadows*, Nicholas Hytner's *The Crucible*, and Federico Fellini's *Juliet of the Spirits* and *8½*. These films offered up a heady diet of thought-provoking views of life, relationships, love, sex and marriage, as well as intrigue. The Savoy also brewed fresh coffee in the theatre during the show: it was full of its aroma during the first feature.

People who attended 'continental fillums' and went to concerts, visited art galleries, and read books that weren't comics or light romance, were perceived as being pretentious or 'up themselves'. There was a prevailing attitude in Australia at that time that meant any effort made by the average person towards the improvement of their intellectual life, or the enrichment of their everyday life through cultural pursuits, would earn the scorn of family and friends. This pursuit of higher things was seen as trying to climb out of your class, the one to which you rightly belonged by virtue of your birth. If it was good enough for your parents and grandparents, it was good enough for you.

My friends and I wondered why we couldn't have it all. Why did one have to have such unreasonably fierce allegiances to the traditional things, to the exclusion of every other thing, thus reducing the chances of a truly rich life? It is a question that still exercises my mind.

I find this attitude – the devotion to a narrow existence, the dedicating of one's life to a limited range of activity – a very common trait, deeply ingrained in the Australian psyche, especially in Melbourne, where sporting tribalism generates a feverish activity in the newspapers, on the television and radio – and, indeed, in the public. For about eight months of the year, the media is obsessed with Australian Rules football, feeding the tribalism frenetically and fervently as Grand Final weekend approaches.

Similarly, the Grand Prix, a car race held in the middle of one of Melbourne's parks, effectively shuts down large chunks of the city for four days in March. The annual cost of this extravagant event is well over $50 million. Imagine if all the taxpayer funds expended on this race since its inception in 1996 had been spent on public education, including repairing and maintaining government schools! We won't really have come of age as a country until we fix up our dilapidated education system, introduce a sense of equity in the way schools are funded and examine how teachers are rewarded for their work.

There is nothing intrinsically wrong with football or car racing, except for the deadening conformity of them, and the group-think about what matters. If I sound resentful, in truth I am. I have always been surprised by how hard it is to persuade people to look at alternative ways of thinking and acting. Perhaps this is partly the perspective of a musician.

UNDER DALLAS HASLAM'S TUITION, I MOVED ON FROM five-finger exercises to proper repertoire. He introduced me to the *French Suites* of Bach, collections of dance movements originally written for harpsichord or clavichord, and to the piano music of Shostakovich and Brahms, which I found very strange at first but ultimately hugely satisfying. My party piece was a Beethoven Sonata Opus 10 no. 3 in C minor, which I loved to play but, frankly, never mastered to my satisfaction.

My teacher had a pupil who played the Beethoven Sonata Opus 2 no. 3 in C major, which had a brilliant third movement. I used to hide in between the soundproof door and the studio door so I could hear her rehearse. She was a tough act to follow; I'm sure Haslam learned a great deal about tolerance and patience when I entered his studio.

My vocal sight-reading was improving, my piano sight-reading was developing at a really good rate, and I was gradually gathering a reasonable knowledge of the instrumental repertoire along with the vocal repertoire.

In the course of playing for students I met my very dear friend the violinist James Stewart, who introduced me, through his teacher, to the Mozart violin concertos and the Beethoven sonatas for piano and violin. This was some of the toughest music I had ever encountered, but at the same time some of the most rewarding I had ever played.

A new vista was opening up for me in the form of orchestral music, as many of my friends played in the Con's orchestra, and I became desperate to join them. The senior orchestra rehearsed on Tuesday evenings, and I frequently went to listen, secreting myself in the back of Verbrugghen Hall.

One of my friends, Beverley Liebermann, a violinist and violist, suggested that I should learn the viola; she thought that after one lesson on the viola, I'd be ready to join in at the back of the section. This, I did. I joined the orchestra completely uninvited, seated myself at the back of the violas and pretended I could play. It was without doubt one of the most thrilling, and at the same time, frightening things I have ever done. Sir Bernard Heinze was rehearsing the orchestra in the *Capriccio Espagnol* of Rimsky-Korsakov.

From my position, I had a good view of the whole orchestra. The sound of the instruments around me was exhilarating. It was as if I were travelling in a music machine. Gary Andrews, later leader of the Sydney Symphony Orchestra's second violins, played the solos brilliantly. The music made me feel intoxicated, as if I had lost control of my senses and was caught up in a massive web of sound that surrounded me entirely.

It was an especially formative experience. I had been introduced to a brand-new world of sound, which gave me a very special appreciation of the way in which an orchestra worked. Even as a raw, pig-ignorant student, I could work out that this group of musicians was a complex, highly evolved musical entity capable of producing the most exquisite sounds imaginable.

There was a break in the rehearsal, after which the orchestra reassembled to read through the Beethoven Symphony No. 5 in C minor. Beverley asked me how I was going, as if she needed to, and we sat down to await the arrival of Sir Bernard Heinze to lead us through the symphony. What happened next was one of the most terrifying musical experiences I had ever had, resulting in a near nervous collapse on stage. I could barely hold the viola, let alone play it, and simultaneously read the clef in which my part was written, which was different from any music I had previously read.

Heinze was unhappy with the way the orchestra performed the opening motif, the so-called fate motif, which consists of four notes played by the strings and clarinets, more or less in unison; in my case, definitely less.

'I'm going to ask all the strings to play it desk by desk, starting with the violins and working our way through to the double basses,' announced Sir Bernard.

My stomach turned; I could feel my bowels turning also. The first desk of violins played the theme perfectly. As the theme travelled from desk to desk, the quality of the playing deteriorated in direct proportion to the distance of the players from the front. Heinze was in a mild state of despair and the orchestra was in shock. He immediately moved from the violins to the cellos, and went desk by desk through the section with the same intensity, muttering comments about standards, bad students, intonation, rhythm, stupid students, rhythm, intonation, hopeless students and so on.

He turned to the violas and announced that, instead of starting with the front desk of the violas, he would start at the back of the section and work his way down to the front. He called out, 'Back desk.' I had been listening like a madman to everyone else and by now had worked out that I could use an open string and keep my finger on the Eb on the lowest string. That would get me through the first two bars. There was no way known to mankind that I could play the next three bars.

Everyone in the orchestra knew that I had no business being there. There was a slightly festive atmosphere by now, with them looking forward to what was clearly going to be a public execution. I grabbed the bow like it was a weapon, decided that the louder and stronger I played, the better it would be, and simply went for it. After the first three bars, Heinze called out, 'Next desk'. I couldn't work out whether he had decided that what I had done was so appalling that there was no point in saying anything at all or whether I had actually pulled off the bluff of the century. After this experience, Beverley and I agreed that it might be better if I were to have a few more lessons before embarking on further assaults on the orchestral repertoire.

Heinze and I were to cross paths several times while I was a student, and each time they did there was some type of musical drama played out. One day, I happened to be walking along the corridor near his studio when his door opened. He saw me and said, 'Do you play the piano?' I responded with a quavering affirmative. He then insisted that I come into his studio and play an accompaniment for a singer he was auditioning.

The singer was a tenor named Desmond Taylor, and he was preparing to sing the aria 'Celeste Aida', from Verdi's *Aida.* It was in the time signature of 6/8 and the key of Bb, neither of which was a real problem until I arrived at a passage of very rapid music, which, unbeknown to me, would have been played by flutes in the orchestra. It was written in the score in a very special form of reduction I didn't know. Somehow, we made it to the end, I stayed with the tenor and we finished together. When I got into trouble I simply played his line and guessed at what the bass line might have been. At the conclusion, Heinze turned to me and said, 'Were you sight-reading that music?'

'Yes,' I answered proudly.

'Well, it certainly sounded like it. Out you go!'

Out I went.

8

To the Dark Side and Back

SHORTLY AFTER THAT, I HAPPENED TO BE HEADING towards Verbrugghen Hall to listen to an orchestral rehearsal when Heinze again stopped me and asked if I played piano. He had no idea who I was, and indeed why should he? Heinze tended to remember only the very brilliant students, and referred to us all as 'Darling girl!' or 'Darling boy!' He asked me to attend the rehearsal and play the piano part in the Bach B minor Orchestral Suite, a work for solo flute and strings.

Playing with the orchestra as a pianist was a special privilege, and a real treat. What I didn't realise until I began was that the part I had been given contained, quite rightly, only my music. Where I wasn't required to play was indicated with bars of rests, which I had not previously encountered.

To make matters worse, I had no idea what conducting pattern Heinze was beating in, but the orchestra seemed to be able to follow him. He kept looking at me as the rehearsal progressed, and shaking his head while muttering about students and pianists who couldn't count. After some time he suggested that I be relieved of my duties as a pianist and that the rehearsal would be better served if the piano part were to be cut entirely. That is to say, shoot the pianist! I left, disappointed but still not defeated.

Thanks to Heinze, I had been introduced to the concept of a continuo line, a line of music that exists in the bass in baroque music, from which and on which the accompanist can improvise a part that blends with the rest of the players.

It is a style and technique dating back to the late sixteenth century. There is evidence that singers improvised extended figures at the closing sections of Gregorian chants, sometimes known as 'Alleluias', and included ornamentation, the decorating of a written note, by singing notes above and below the given note and by changing the length of the notes. Certainly, in most baroque operas, singers were required to add decorations whenever they sang a repetition of the first section.

The baroque aria was generally in three parts: a first section, which enunciated the nature of the feelings of the character; a second section, generally in a different key and developing a new aspect of the text; then a return to the first section, with extensive decoration including brilliant trills, passing notes, leaps, scales and arpeggios, often rendering the music unrecognisable. This type of performance from the great castrati, male singers who had given their all – or, more specifically, their balls – for art, thrilled the punters but terrified the composers, who sometimes, quite correctly, thought that their music was becoming as mutilated as the person singing it.

Bach, Handel, Haydn, Mozart, Beethoven, Chopin, Liszt and Brahms were all great improvisers, and frequently performed public concerts of improvisations, requesting themes or setting limits to the nature of the improvisation. Johann Sebastian Bach, for example, improvised on a single given hymn tune a prelude and fugue, an organ trio, a chorale prelude and a final fugue! The seventeenth-century German composer Dietrich Buxtehude and his Dutch counterpart Jan Pieterszoon Sweelinck, a composer who straddled the sixteenth and seventeenth centuries, used to attract audiences who travelled large distances to hear them improvise and invent music.

Today, within so-called classical music, the concept of improvisation has been generally lost to musicians (except, perhaps, for church organists). However, it still exists in jazz. The player's points of departure are both the melody and the chords that accompany the melody. Great improvisers in this style are able to decorate the melodic material, expand it, develop it, and give it new life and shape. There is a case to be made for jazz and its associated styles as the most vibrant and constantly developing form of music.

In my years at the Con, there was a certain snobbishness associated with so-called classical music, and those of us who crossed the border into popular music and jazz were frowned upon. There was an unwritten law that seemed to imply, very strongly, I might add, that treading outside the boundaries of the sacred and especially blessed classical arena implied slightly grubby behaviour on the part of the transgressor. Playing jazz was bad for your technique and playing the popular music of the day required you to sink into an abyss of musical slime.

Not only did I sink into the slime, I dwelled and evolved there.

A musician in the year above me, a trumpeter named Jimmy Saunders, had a dance band that played around Sydney on Friday nights and weekends. He asked me to fill in when their regular pianist was unavailable. I did. It was another baptism of fire, a fabulous lesson in the discipline needed to play with this type of instrumental ensemble, consisting of piano, drums, saxophone, trumpet and (from memory) guitar.

Jimmy was a very strong leader, with strong musical opinions about the way in which the piano contributed to the music's texture. His view was, quite correctly for this style of music, that the piano should be like an extension of the rhythm section, and should play the chords with the drums, without excessive decoration or improvisation. The moment I deviated from chords and started to add extraneous material, Jimmy would scream out, 'Stay with the bloody chords!' in an almost savage way.

As if that wasn't enough extracurricular music, three friends and I decided to form a rock 'n' roll group. It was the idea of one Peter Dunnicliff, brother of Bob Dunnicliff of fluck and crabs fame, from my days at the Marist borstal, and included my old friend Errol Cranney. Male vocal quartets in fluorescent ties, smart suits and pointy shoes were all the rage at that time. We soon assembled a quartet, which we called the Mark Fours.

Three of its four members were exceptionally good-looking, and adored by the girls who frequented our gigs. The fourth member, with thick black horn-rimmed glasses and a very dodgy crew-cut, made up for a lack of Adonis-like qualities with Adonis-like musical arrangements that sounded good from a distance, especially when accompanied by an incredibly loud band.

We formed a partnership with a band known as Phil Wilde and The Wilde Cats! This collaboration saw us working fairly regularly at Penrith Town Hall on Friday nights, Parramatta Town Hall on Thursday nights, and also performing the occasional gig at the Surreyville in City Road, Chippendale, near Sydney University; not to mention Eastwood Masonic Hall.

We were never going to topple the Delltones – or anyone else, for that matter – but we did work hard and tried to keep up with the latest and greatest in musical trends. Our biggest mistake was not to listen to my mother's advice when she said that we should all learn to play the guitar and not rely on another band. We were too young and too stupid to listen and, after all, what would a parent know?

I was the only member of our group who read music fluently, and had never worked with non-readers of music, so teaching harmonies and parts to songs had to be done by rote. Not that rock 'n' roll arrangements are hard, anyway. There were the standard four chords that became a formula for every rock band or vocal group and a standard pattern for writing a song. One started with four bars, repeated those bars, moved to the new concept of the bridge for another four bars and then repeated the opening eight bars. Easy. Pop song done.

The lyrics were simple and generally inane. The tunes were similarly simple and inane, but very catchy and very easy to learn. It is no small source of pride to me that, as a result of my industrious slumming in tin-pan alley, one of my songs was recorded as a single for the local EMI label. 'I Think of You' (R. Gill) made the local hit parade, and stayed at number 17 for about three weeks, then disappeared. It was on the flip side of a disc that contained a Paul Anka song called 'Lonely Room'.

Paul Anka was a typical teen heart-throb of the fifties: clean-cut, suit-clad, all-American; outwardly appealing and very uncomplicated, in the sense that our generation was free from opinions on anything outside of music and fashion. I was in the same condition, intellectually and emotionally, if not physically. I was essentially free of opinions on all sorts of serious world issues.

All this was about to change. In the early sixties, the beatnik generation emerged and, suddenly, young people had opinions and ideas, especially about world poverty, human rights and wars. It was the age of the teenager and of a special musical culture that swept the world. Teenagers all over the globe became interested in music, especially music that allowed them to dance. In this sense, they were behaving exactly as their counterparts behaved at the courts of medieval Europe, and later in the Baroque and Classical eras. Dance was a popular way of spreading musical ideas.

Rock music has stayed the distance as a concept, but has undergone many transformations and had many manifestations of musical style. Chuck Berry and Bill Haley and the Comets were superseded by folk music. The Beatles' star ascended into the heavens, proclaiming the birth of a new level of musical sophistication in the field of popular music. The musical world had changed forever, and teenagers and young adults changed with it. Bob Dylan showed great bravery in moving folk music from comfortable touchy-feely-ness to a more challenging sound that he was able to adapt to contemporary trends and concerns, showing his own rare songwriting sensibility.

My experience with pop was as far removed from the Conservatorium experience as you could imagine. I was in grave danger of embracing a life in popular music, or even jazz, which would have seen me defect permanently to the dark side.

My colleagues at the Con thought that my forays into the composition of popular music were a waste of time, and not to be taken seriously. What I learned from this experience with the commercial world and the inherent simplicity of the music scene in those times was invaluable. It also made me sharply aware of the view that if music came from the USA or the United Kingdom, then it had to be good, while Australian music was, by definition, poorer in quality, not as well-crafted and, possibly, a very cheap imitation of its northern-hemisphere counterparts. I was to learn later that this was called cultural cringe.

The cringe came in another form as well, one that looked a lot like hubris. Australia had the best of everything. Australia was a world leader in everything. Australia was, quite simply, the best place on earth. (That form is still alive and well today. Anything coming from overseas is no good, especially human beings travelling by boat. They are drains upon the economy that will end up being supported by the government while honest-to-goodness, dinky-di Aussies work their butts off for thirty-six hours a week. It's not fair in the land of the fair go!)

As a concertgoer I have witnessed genuine excellence firsthand. Yehudi Menuhin and his sister Hepzibah came to Australia and performed the complete Beethoven sonatas for pianoforte and violin. I sat on the stage at the Sydney Town Hall, having slept in the street overnight in order to procure the best seats available, on the stage, about two metres away from Hepzibah Menuhin. I saw Russian violinist David Oistrakh playing the Beethoven and Brahms violin concertos in one program, accompanied by the Sydney Symphony Orchestra. I could list more events here and overseas in which I have witnessed excellence, and I am not swayed by what is portrayed as excellence in my own country. I know excellence.

WHY STOP AT JAZZ AND ROCK, WHEN YOU CAN BE A Broadway star as well? Errol, my friend in fluck and crabs and rock 'n' roll, informed me that the Lane Cove Musical Society was holding rehearsals for the Rodgers and Hammerstein musical *Oklahoma!* Of course I was interested. I had never been in a musical, I had never danced, but why should that stop me from trying out for a part? It was suggested that I audition for the juvenile lead, Will Parker, as I was not experienced enough for the main male role, the lovelorn cowboy, Curly.

Experience? I had none. But needless to say, at the ripe old age of eighteen, I knew everything there was to be known about everything. I had an opinion on every subject related to music and its performance, and was very happy to offer it freely to anyone who would listen. My opinions were not only of earth-shattering importance, but available to all. The word for this type of behaviour is smart-arse. I was becoming a fully fledged smart-arse.

The auditions for *Oklahoma!* were open, meaning that everyone tried out in front of the entire company. We were given a song to sing and some dialogue to read. I knew I could do a passable Southern accent, and I learned 'Kansas City', Will Parker's first number, before the audition.

The list was narrowed to two contenders: a six-foot-three, tanned, blond-haired, muscle-bound hunk whom I christened Tarzan; and an eighteen-year-old boy, who was six foot one and a half, pale, skinny, pimply faced, horn-rimmed-glasses-wearing, smart-arsed weakling. Once I heard Tarzan, I knew the part had to go to me. He read like a four-year-old and sang like a drain. The disappointment on the faces of the panel when they realised that I was their man was visible for all to see.

When the casting was finalised the director announced, in a voice that one would use to inform the nation there was smallpox epidemic on the way, that the part of Will Parker was going to Richard Gill. I was thrilled, and had my lines completely memorised by the first rehearsal. Errol was in the chorus, and was a huge support to me, especially when I had to learn a fairly complex tap solo. The dance teacher was excellent and very patient. She never knew my name, and called me Sid. I practised that routine more than I had ever practised anything in my life, until I mastered it.

At the same time as rehearsing the musical, I began a part-time job as a counter-hand at the Woolworths in Eastwood.

My musical comedy career was taking off and I was overloaded to buggery, and I failed to hand in some assignments for teachers college. Miss Phyllis Bennett, our wonderful English lecturer, was not impressed when I told her that I was the juvenile lead in *Oklahoma!* and that was why I couldn't do my English assignment. She told me that she couldn't have cared less, and that I needed to get an assignment to her by the end of the week, or fail and possibly finish up in juvenile detention! Did I also mention that at the time I was again working as a runner for the *Sun*'s sportswriters?

Being a star of a musical comedy was a terrific fillip to my ego, and I received many favourable comments about my prowess as a dancer. While Fred Astaire's position was comparatively safe, I sensed a new horizon in front of me, involving a possible change of direction in my performing life. It would only be a matter of time before Broadway was calling me to star in a big musical.

One Friday night, the junior staff from Woolworths came en masse to a performance, and clapped like mad every time I appeared. The next morning at work one of the juniors affixed the program to the official Woolworths noticeboard, with the caption 'Our Star'. The general manager, a philistine of the first order with no appreciation for tap dancing and singing, ordered the program to be taken down, muttering within my earshot: 'We won't have rubbish like that on the board.'

Slightly hurt and just a little deflated, I assumed my customary post on the kitchenware counter, and served endless numbers of customers with the laundry powder special of the day: two packets of Rinso at two shillings and eleven pence halfpenny per packet, which came to five shillings and eleven pence, or one packet for three shillings and sixpence! Mad if you didn't buy the special: that was four pence in the pocket straight away!

I loved working at Woolworths because it was a type of performance. Dealing with the customers could be tricky, and we were taught that the customer was always right. We had a special way of greeting the customer and then conducted a ritual known as the mode of sale. Failure to perform the mode of sale correctly led to instant dismissal. Supervisors patrolled the shop floor regularly and one's counter had to be immaculate, with the bins on it topped up. I was good at this sort of trivia and was offered a full-time job by one of the supervisors, who encouraged me to think seriously about a career in retail. This was a genuine compliment, and I took it as such and thanked him politely and respectfully.

Not long after, I reached my nineteenth birthday and was duly sacked. At that grand old age, I was perceived to be an adult in the eyes of the employer and therefore entitled to adult pay.

I took myself off to Woolworths' head office in the city, and attempted to talk some sense into them, to no avail. I was sacked, and that was that. Unable to face my family with the news, I walked from Central Station towards Circular Quay, stopping at every shop en route and asking for part-time work. I must have gone into fifty shops only to be told there were no jobs. Finally, I arrived at a shop called City Hatters on Pitt Street, where the general manager, a Mr Hicks, took pity on me. He was interested in music and was, in my view, a cultured gentleman.

One thing about this period of my life was certain: as far as I was concerned, I had finally taken a step towards genuine independence. Although I was still living at home, I felt that through my employment, even in a part-time way, I was closer to self-sufficiency. It was a small step, but a step nonetheless. Even as a student, I was aware of the necessity of earning my keep and not relying on others, especially my parents. There was a sense of pride associated with this and a sense that one was making a contribution.

Meanwhile, back at the Con, I had persuaded my piano teacher that in my second year I should do the highest-level piano exam, known as Sessional 1. At the Con the system of examinations progressed from Sessional 10, the lowest grade, to Sessional 1, the highest, required for entry to the respected diploma class. My first attempt was a fail. No one was surprised, least of all my teacher. I had only failed by a few marks, but a miss is as good as a mile, as we were often told. My report stated in unequivocal language that I was simply not good enough and should try again in a year's time.

I was devastated, but I knew that justice had been done. I knew I wasn't good enough, that the days of wine and roses were over, and that I would have to knuckle down to some serious work if I were to achieve a pass in the third year of my course. I had been to the dark side, and now it was time to get back (as the Beatles once said).

I became very serious about singing and accompanying, and decided in my final year at the Con to sit Sessional 1 as both a singer and a pianist: in short, a double major. I accompanied my friend Jimmy Stewart when he did a brilliant recital for his examination for the Associate Diploma of Music (AmusA). He was very well prepared for the occasion. We had practised incredibly hard as a duo, and I was very aware of my responsibility. In fact, it would be completely fair to say that until that time, I had never practised so hard for anything to do with music.

When Jimmy played the violin, the sound he produced was sweet and heart-rending. His tone was a genuine cantabile – a real singing sound – and every note had a very special life. My future as a musician looked more mundane. Having decided to study singing and piano at the highest level, I more or less knuckled down to learn a program of music for both examinations, which I passed relatively comfortably. I was so thrilled with my piano result that I suggested to Dallas Haslam that I might, after all, be able to do the dip, as it was called. He replied that the only 'dip' I would get would be a sheep dip. He was right, but it hurt just a little.

♪

Academically, I performed fairly well at both the Con and teachers college, progressing to the fourth year of the course. That would take place entirely at Sydney Teachers College, a year of enforced separation from the Con that I detested. I tried to spend as much time as I could at the Conservatorium, making myself available as an accompanist for scholarship examinations for single-study students. The scholarships were open to all orchestral instruments and voices, and the examinations took place in the November/December general examination period.

For an entire week I played dozens of accompaniments, almost always from sight, as there was little or no time to rehearse. In this way I became acquainted with a huge amount of instrumental and vocal repertoire, and learned something about the idiosyncrasies of instrumentalists and their instruments. I was already well and truly conditioned to the frailties of singers and their all-consuming egos, and it was refreshing to find that most instrumentalists simply got on with the job and did not have a volume of excuses for why they weren't at their best on a particular day.

It was so stimulating just to play the music and not to have to listen to such statements as 'the top of the voice isn't quite right today' or 'the breathing is a little off today and my support is not as good as it should be, which sometimes happens on a Tuesday'. One of my favourite comments from singers, especially students, involves the *passaggio*; a godsend for them, as they can blame it for all circumstances: 'My *passaggio* isn't working well at the moment', or perhaps 'This aria lies right across the *passaggio*.' Most singing students I have encountered have no idea what or where their *passaggios* are or what they even do.

There are as many views on the way to teach *passaggio* as there are singing teachers. In the *Harvard Dictionary of Music* and *Grove's Dictionary of Music and Musicians*, *passaggio* is defined as a transition or modulation, i.e., a type of bridge or change of key. Neither source makes any mention of this word in association with the voice. *Passaggio*, as far as singing is concerned, involves the registers of the voice, the differences between head and chest registers, and how one negotiates and explores the voice's capacity to move with ease from register to register. The point is to create a seamless transition from one register to another.

Not a problem for the likes of outstanding Australian artists such as Joan Sutherland and the spectacular Lauris Elms, or the great German singers Elisabeth Schwarzkopf, Fritz Wunderlich and Dietrich Fischer-Dieskau. All these artists, some now sadly gone, knew how to breathe, how to produce sound and how to thrill audiences.

Mere mortals may struggle, partly because they have not mastered breath control. But I digress. I could only avoid the teachers college up to a point. Every Thursday for two hours we had college choir, under the direction of John Gordon, the same teacher who had had to endure my efforts to control the oboe. Gordon, a musician skilled in the art of improvisation, and hugely knowledgeable about the general repertoire, was clearly used to dealing with know-it-all youths. He had a passionate hatred for the physical education students who banged out 'Heart and Soul' on the college pianos in their abundant spare time and, according to Gordon, inflicting permanent damage on these instruments.

Choir was compulsory for all students, about eighty, training to be music teachers and we were rehearsing Felix Mendelssohn's wonderful oratorio *Elijah*, in preparation for a performance in the college's Main Hall. Rehearsals, always fun (especially for us in the back row) were intense, to say the least. As the performance drew closer, the intensity of the rehearsals increased and the pressure mounted. The choir belted out the chorus, 'Yea, and the Lord who by fire shall answer that He is God', with great enthusiasm and, at the conclusion, I yelled out 'Cha, Cha, Cha'.

Gordon looked up at me and said, 'Mr Gill, outside . . . now!' I left the rehearsal to a very warm round of applause, a splendid way to be chucked out of a rehearsal, and went to the Con.

I skipped lectures frequently, often against the advice of well-meaning friends who thought it was a risky thing to do, particularly at this late stage of the game. My absence from college had been noticed and I was given a talking-to by the principal, who said that I was in danger of failing and being conditionally certificated, which would mean a reduction in salary when I entered the workforce as a teacher.

We were all guaranteed jobs upon completion of our course; indeed, as a result of having been paid for four years to study to become teachers, we had all undertaken to enter into a bond with the Department of Education, which meant that we agreed to work for five years. If we broke the bond, we had to pay back the funds we had received during our studies.

In May 1962, we fourth-year students filed into our music method lecture with John Gordon. I had been tipped off that this was the lecture I absolutely had to attend, as it was when we would be allocated schools for practice teaching. Gordon started by saying that this would be the most important part of our work for the year. We were to be supervised by college lecturers, all of whom had complete authority to pass or fail us, and, indeed, the failing of a student by a supervisor was not unknown. Students had been given outright fails before and that was that. There was no recourse and no further discussion was ever entered into. The only option was to repeat the entire year at one's own expense.

Gordon began reading out each student's name, and the school to which they would be attached. In 1962 there were still numbers of single-sex selective high schools, all of which had outstanding academic records. A selective high school had an entrance examination and rejected children who fell below a certain standard.

I sat in this lecture and waited for my name to be read out, attached to a first-rate selective high school. After a while, as Hornsby Girls' High, North Sydney Girls' High, Sydney Girls' High, Fort St Boys' High and Canterbury Boys' High all had students allocated to them, it dawned on me that I was going to miss out.

My name was read last for some reason; possibly because my track record for attendance was not exactly Olympics-standard. It turned out that I had scored Marsden High School, Ermington. This news was greeted with shouts of amazement and even derision from some of my colleagues. I was to be shunted off to a co-educational high school in the western suburbs, one which had only opened in 1959 and, as yet, lacked a strong cohort of senior students. Co-educational high schools in Sydney were a relatively new phenomenon, even though country high schools had been co-educational since their inception.

As I tried to absorb the news, I was told by caring and concerned friends (although I must say that, in those days, we didn't care and share, thank God, we just said things straight out) that I was being punished and tested at the same time. This was the college's way, I was told, of seeing whether I could actually do anything at all!

9

'How Old Are You, Sir?'

THE SOUNDS OF A SCHOOL CHOIR GREETED ME AS I approached Marsden High. The music room had windows opening onto the driveway, and a chorus from Smetana's opera *The Bartered Bride* was the first thing I heard as I drew near. This had to be a good omen!

It was my first stint as a student teacher at secondary level, and I was, quite plainly, terrified. I was introduced to the music teacher, Joyce Walsh, who led me straight to the music room and asked me if I could play the piano part for the Smetana choruses. I read the music easily, and sang any part as required, which immediately impressed her. Joyce had done a very special job in gathering enough forces to establish a strong school choir, including a good representation of boys, and she had also established the nucleus of a school orchestra. Although, for all sorts of reasons, we later fell out, she was a force to be reckoned with, and had laid a strong foundation which, in the right circumstances, would allow for the development of a very good music department.

This period of prac-teaching at Marsden High changed my life completely. It was one of the most formative, instructive and, certainly happiest times in my life musically, educationally and socially. The school was considered a difficult one at which to teach, for reasons I have outlined. This view was, quite unreasonably, promoted by parts of Sydney's community that felt co-education in city schools was a licence for early sexual experimentation, a reputation that was deserved.

I rapidly became aware of the massive advantage that placement at Marsden had afforded me. Later, I discovered that I had been singled out, to determine whether I would be appointed to this school the following year, in the capacity of full-time music teacher.

It was 1962, the year that the recommendations of an official policy report on education in New South Wales were implemented. The Wyndham report, as it was known, would have a profound effect, in that it recommended an extra year of high school study, from five to six. It also created a mandatory public examination in fourth form, known as the School Certificate, and a similar public examination for those who stayed on into sixth form, the Higher School Certificate, or HSC. Other recommendations included the study of a wide range of languages, industrial arts, music, art and drama, which were all to be offered in the early years of high school, so that students could elect specialist subjects later.

As someone who had been educated, more or less, under a very old system based around the Leaving Certificate, the

Wyndham report sounded as if were based on solid educational principles, and formulated in order to provide a wider range of options for students so that they could make informed choices.

One thing I have learned about education is that, despite all the syllabi in the world, all the tags attached to learning, the dozens of enquiries, endless research papers and all the curriculum changes made from time to time, the old truism holds: there is no such thing as a good school, there are only good teachers. The larger the number of good teachers collected in one place, the greater the chance it will become known as a good school.

My time as a student teacher was the beginning of a realisation that I could probably teach and, even more positively, probably become quite good at it. I had a crusader's drive to disseminate knowledge about music and felt that unless everyone had some sort of music in their lives, their lives were the poorer. It was an arrogant view, but it was founded on what I felt to be a solidly based philosophical belief, details of which had not yet formulated in my mind but were slowly emerging. In other words, I did not yet know much!

I was truly ignorant in every sense of the word. Not simply ignorant in respect to content, but also in respect to method. I was, as I guess most young males were then, hugely confident, and felt that I could take on the world singlehandedly. Yet I was also well and truly aware of my position as a young teacher about to enter the workforce and my evaluation of myself.

Even though I was competent in some aspects of the technique of teaching, some of which might even have been classified as based in genuine educational theory, I had not made many connections between teaching and learning. I had yet to understand how children learn and, more importantly, why they want to learn. Add to this the fact that I could not really articulate any coherent philosophy of education and you have a recipe for a potential educational disaster. I could not have explained to parents in clear and simple terms why I thought that their child should study music or undertake private lessons in an instrument. Worse, I could not have explained to children in clear and simple terms why I thought that the study of music was good. What the hell was I doing?

Obviously, I should have attended many more philosophy and method lectures at teachers college, and paid more attention. However, I was dead certain of one thing, and unshakeable on this point: I just knew that music was innately good, and because of its innate goodness everyone should have access to it as early as possible in their lives. It was largely that belief that kept me together musically and philosophically in my early years as a teacher. I was strong on enthusiasm and passion.

There is no doubt in my mind that many of my students were carried along by this enthusiasm and did not suffer too much serious intellectual or musical damage as a result of my work. I was full of theories about music and the way in which it worked. I could make connections in a very simple way with the students, based on my reasonable knowledge of popular music, and I could play a great deal of 'their music', as they thought of it, on the piano.

My supervisor, Miss Christine Stirling, had heard of a theory of mine that Bach and jazz were closely related, especially Dixieland jazz, where lines interwove in a polyphonic way as the musicians improvised. She was very keen to see me explain this to a class of children as part of my supervised work, and demanded that I prepare a lesson in order to prove my point. To say that she was sceptical would be to underestimate her attitude. I was getting ready to be failed! During the early 1960s, to talk about jazz and Bach in the same breath was tantamount to talking about God and Joseph Stalin as equals.

I gave the lesson, and the kids, thank Jupiter, were hugely interested. It wasn't really a lesson: it was more in the nature of an impassioned sermon on the parallels between ancient and modern music; and how music has many connections, if you want to look for them.

How much Miss Stirling was convinced by my spectacular display of Bach and the comparison to the great jazz musician Graeme Bell, I will never know. Obviously, Joyce Walsh had put in a good word for me, so I passed my prac. Joyce also asked me to return to the school every Monday afternoon after classes had finished for orchestra, and to play for the school choir on the occasion of the school's speech night in December. I did it happily, though I remember that I did not play the accompaniment particularly well, a fact she commented on. The reason was simple: I hadn't practised it and had relied on my sight-reading skills. It was my first encounter with a Vaughan Williams choral arrangement and the music was tough. Some people are slow learners!

The practice-teaching session came to an end, and I returned to college to face an apparently endless line of assignments. I was missing teaching terribly and probably, if the truth be known, I was slightly depressed about this sudden separation from the strong reality of the classroom.

The end of the year was a disaster on a number of personal levels, including a broken relationship. Then there were the final examinations. My elective subject was physical education. I had attended one lecture – just the one. I turned up for the paper, which consisted of one sentence. It wasn't even a question, just an instruction: 'Draw and label a squash court.' I was playing competition squash every Sunday afternoon and knew every inch of the court. In spite of my lack of draughtsmanship, I managed a passable drawing, and labelled it within an inch of its life.

The rest of the examinations were also straightforward and almost designed to get rid of us. We'd been there for four years, and it really was time to go.

With exams finished, the world seemed grey and grim: I was clearly suffering from *Weltschmerz*, or the pains of the world. In order to feed and nourish this worldly pain, I read massive chunks of poetry by T.S. Eliot, W.H. Auden, Dylan Thomas, James Joyce, Sylvia Plath and Walt Whitman, smoked lots of cigarettes, drank black coffee and suffered from the realisation that I had probably lost the faith. I was no longer a genuine practising Catholic. It was a strange moment, which came to me on a train. As it pulled out of Strathfield station, the glass in the window of my carriage started to emit weird musical tones, as if it were singing. At the same time I had the strangest physical feeling of all the blood rushing to my feet and my stomach collapsing in on itself while the singing increased in volume. I had not smoked dope and I was not drunk. But nor did I immediately think I had had a revelation! The world simply shifted on its axis.

The exam results were finally posted on a college noticeboard. I went with my friend Graham Russell, the baritone I had met on my first day at the Con, and saw that I had a C after my name, as did he. He explained that it meant we were fully certificated, and we would be employed as graduate assistants beginning 31 January 1963.

The final step at Sydney Teachers College was to fill out a form on which you requested a posting to a school. You had to make three suggestions of areas or districts, and country service was very much on the cards. It was taboo to request a specific school by name, and was seen as very bad form and incredibly arrogant. As a lowly ex-student, what rights did I think I had to anything, other than the guarantee of a job somewhere in New South Wales?

I arrived at the part that asked for a region, district or preferred area, and reasons. Most people requested Sydney Metropolitan, and wrote that they had elderly parents who needed constant nursing. The rise in the population of those in need of care spiked suddenly every December, when former students fought to stay in the city. I wrote on my form:

First preference: Marsden High School, Ermington.
Second preference: Marsden High School, Ermington.
Third preference: Marsden High School, Ermington.

I handed it in to the appropriate office, and the worthy functionary there, whose job it was to collate all these forms, informed me in a gentle but strongly bureaucratic way, all the while looking at me as if I were a complete idiot: 'Your form is incorrect; you have nominated a school. That is not allowed.'

I said that I had also nominated a region: Ermington. He told me not to blame him if I finished up in the back of New South Wales in a one-teacher school, teaching all classes from kindergarten to year six.

♪

When I nominated Marsden High School, I had no idea that the next seven years of my life would be so totally consumed by this school, or that my future path would so much depend on experiences I had there. I was simply thrilled to be back somewhere that I was wanted. It was greatly encouraging to me to be welcomed by those students who remembered me from my time as a student teacher, and by staff members who had been so friendly and helpful to a gawky student.

My timetable included twenty-eight teaching periods a week, each being forty minutes long. It included a three-period block of sport, and playground supervision. I had been allocated an elective music class of three students, who were sitting for the Leaving Certificate in music. This class, established through the diligence and persistence of Joyce Walsh in order to give music some standing as an examination subject, was handed to me to teach from scratch. I had no experience in preparing candidates for the most important examination of their school lives, so it was a huge responsibility. I also had some general music classes to teach.

We began teaching on day one. In the dark days of 1963 there were no such things as student-free days or teacher planning days. We went straight into the trenches, so to speak.

It was a baptism of fire, but I was happy and could not wait to get to school every day. It wasn't long before vocal groups were established, orchestral rehearsals were in full swing, and all sorts of musical activities were being planned.

For some reason, the school had a significant collection of brass instruments belonging to the Royal Australian Air Force, lying idle in a storeroom outside the music room. They were obviously there to be used by boys who had enlisted in the school cadet corps, known as the Air Training Corps. The set included cornets, flugelhorns, tenor horns, baritone horns, euphoniums, trombones and tubas, and were the finest that money could buy. The RAAF had excellent taste when it came to purchasing musical instruments.

Several teachers assisted with the running of the corps, including a senior maths teacher, Mr Clarke, who was also Marsden High's special master, i.e., in charge of music, physical education and art. Mr Clarke took me aside very early in my time at Marsden and suggested that I should start a brass band. Our conversation took place in the corridor outside the storeroom where these magnificent instruments were housed, and was witnessed and overheard by a young boy whose name was Robyn Pethybridge. This young boy also happened to be in the ATC and, coincidentally, was a trombonist in a Salvation Army band. I had no knowledge of brass instruments, but this enthusiastic boy offered to teach me the trombone. By the end of the conversation it was clear to me that I had been conscripted.

We took a trombone from the storeroom, and he showed me how to buzz; that is, make a sound on the mouthpiece. He also showed me some slide positions, suggesting at the conclusion of this exercise that I now knew enough to be able to form the band!

First, though, I had to join the ATC as an officer. I had no interest in armies, guns or war. In fact, I was definitely a pacifist. But in the interests of keeping the instruments I underwent the psychological examinations and prescribed interviews. The best the RAAF could offer me was a non-commissioned rank, which made me no more senior than a senior boy cadet. They said, however, that if I wanted to train the band, they would be very pleased I agreed most enthusiastically and wholeheartedly.

And then, shock horror, at the conclusion of the interview I was informed that someone from the air force would come to the school to collect the instruments and return them to base!

A date was given for their collection, but the most unfortunate thing happened. We had a shocking burglary at the school. The music room was broken into, an easy enough thing to do, as the windows faced the street on one side and the school drive on the other. None of the doors or windows were alarmed, and the workmanship put into the manufacturing of them was such that a child could force either with comparative ease. Once in the music room, it was a simple matter for the thief to gain entry to the corridor and force the door of the internal storeroom.

Yet, as it turned out, there had been no forcing of the door. It had been left unlocked. The burglar, who clearly had an intimate knowledge of where the instruments were kept, managed to steal the entire collection and remove it to a place unknown. I imagined that the instruments had been melted down and sold for their value as scrap metal – in this case, highly valuable scrap metal – or sold off in their own right.

There was a search for the stolen instruments, and then an official enquiry, to which, regrettably, I was unable to offer any useful information. It was a terrible blow for all concerned and a shock to the whole school. The RAAF had to write them off as a loss.

Some weeks later, I arrived at school, at the usual time of 7.30 am, to find that the entire set of instruments had mysteriously reappeared in the storeroom. To this day the circumstances of their return remain unknown to all but the thief. There was no question of sending them back to the air force, as they had been written off. Mr Clarke suggested that this had been an enormous stroke of luck and we should go ahead with our plan to start a band.

It wasn't difficult to attract members to the band and soon, in spite of my total lack of knowledge, we had a more or less functioning brass band ensemble with a very small repertoire of tunes I had arranged for them, including the 'Marines' Hymn', a very suspect version of 'Colonel Bogey', and 'Anchors Aweigh'. The most interesting thing for me was learning that all these brass instruments read music in the treble clef: the actual pitch sounded miles away from the nominal pitch, especially in the case of tubas and trombones. Along with mastering a basic knowledge of trombone positions and the B-flat major scale, I managed to get my mouth around a euphonium and then a baritone horn.

The local scout troop – let's, for the sake of the narrative, call them the First Eastwood Deserters – was holding a fundraising event at which we were invited to play. It was in a park near the school, in an area known as Brush Farm, which had hideous connotations for me, as it was there that, as a primary schoolboy, I had played rugby league among the cowpats.

The fundraiser included the usual irresistible attractions: a barbeque that served, at stellar prices, sausages placed semi-cooked between two slabs of white bread and smothered in tomato sauce or mustard; a fairy-floss machine to cater for dessert; a flying-fox contraption, which broke down early in the afternoon due to excessive use; and a jumble sale that included everyone's unwanted old rubbish, which, in the interests of promoting scouting, was about to become someone else's new rubbish. The boys thought all this was terrific.

We played our marches several times over. During the fourth repetition of our cycle of gems from military land, an unkind spectator strolled over to me and asked me if we knew anything else, as he'd heard that song four bloody times! I felt that discretion was the better part of valour in this circumstance, as some of the boys had obviously heard his remark. I asked him if he'd like to conduct them in a march, given that he seemed to be very familiar with the music. He accepted, then proceeded to conduct 'Anchors Aweigh', in the sense that he waved his hands around in front of the band. We played the 'Marines' Hymn' for the fifth time and marched out on a high.

It was clear to me that we needed a brass band teacher, pronto. Enter the messiah of the brass band world, Cliff Goodchild, principal tuba with the Sydney Symphony Orchestra. He visited the school, and in half an hour turned the kids from a raggedy ensemble into a disciplined musical unit. Long live the teacher who knows things! I knew what

Cliff was going to suggest. I just needed an expert to tell the authorities at the school what I instinctively knew.

Cliff was very encouraging and, as I had hoped, suggested that we hire a teacher to come to Marsden High on a regular basis. Soon, a Mr Bill Soames became responsible for the band. We entered them in the New South Wales schools' brass band competition, an event that proved to be an eye-opener for my young bandsmen. At this competition the boys heard bands that sounded like symphony orchestras. They heard bands play marches that would wake the dead, and hymns and chorales that would cause one to seek refuge in religion.

The competition required us to play a hymn, a march and a free selection, for which I had arranged some tunes from the musical *Oliver!*. There was no way we were even going to make a dent in this competition but when our section was adjudicated, we were given a special mention for our rendition of the hymn, 'The Old Rugged Cross', and awarded the prize for the best percussion in the selection. I suspect a certain party had worded up the adjudicator, and had suggested to him that we deserved an encouragement to continue our work.

The prize was the miracle. The boy who played percussion for us had a vast range of dynamics, a colourful selection of sticks and mallets, and endless ideas on rhythm patterns for all occasions. His approach to tempo was highly individual, as was his approach to meter. He was a different drummer to whom nobody marched, but he clearly impressed the adjudicator. I would often watch him during rehearsals and wonder where he was visiting at that moment. It was obviously a place of contentment and utter serenity, and I sometimes wished that I could have gone there too. He would return to earth after one of these visits, revitalised with fresh ideas about speeds and dynamics that kept us all on our toes, until, with no small input from me, he conquered march-time and another drummer was born.

This competition was an extraordinary experience for us all, particularly for me, as learning about the brass band movement was a novel aspect of my education. The boys in the band were not, in the main, academically motivated. Nor were they driven to excel in any particular discipline at school, except the band. Some of them were like lambs, but others were regarded by the teaching staff as difficult to handle in class. The tough ones interested me because they constantly challenged and tested me.

I tried to maintain their interest in working by also entering them for public examinations in music, under the auspices of the Australian Music Examinations Board. I prepared them for the third-grade examination, including all the technical work, the main pieces, the extra lists, the general knowledge, the sight-reading and the aural tests.

One Saturday morning, we boarded a train for the NSW Conservatorium. After we checked in I took them out to the courtyard (where there was a fish pond, which I thought might help distract them) in order to remove them from the rest of the young people who were there to be examined in piano, singing or violin, and whose sense of decorum and of how to behave in public was on a higher plane than my charges.

Alan Mann, at that time principal French horn in the Sydney Symphony Orchestra, was the examiner. I went into the room with the boys one at a time, played their accompaniments, and then left him to do the rest of the examination. During one of my visits to the studio, I heard shouting and excited screams of encouragement, which I guessed, with a sinking heart, to be coming from my clutch of developing organisms in the courtyard. When I returned, I found they had invented a game called 'jump across the pond', which in itself was harmless enough. But the crux of the game lay in a jumper's capacity, while airborne, to throw a stone at one of the goldfish swimming freely in the pond.

Why they couldn't have been content to throw stones at the fish without the addition of a jump puzzled me: no matter where you stood around the pond, the fish were an easy target. I had to ask them. One of the boys explained to me, in the tone of voice that only a year-nine boy can adopt of addressing a complete imbecile, that their sense of sportsmanship prevented them from taking pot shots at easy targets.

Screams greeted each jump, and whoops of delight indicated a fish had been struck. It wasn't long before a small crowd had gathered to watch, so I brought the activity to an abrupt halt and tried to encourage them to focus on the music.

When the results came out, they had all passed. Some of them did very well, but most of the results were what you would expect from kids who would rather stone fish than worry about D major scale. I noticed they all loved playing the articulation where you tongue two notes and slur two notes. Why? I have no idea, but they would practise that particular pattern for hours.

Brass band was only a small portion of my time, and took place before and after school. There were other activities before and after school hours, including choirs and orchestra, and a huge program of sport. Sport had featured quite strongly in my own time with Marist Brothers Eastwood. Besides playing football, I had swum reasonably well. But cricket was something I was never good at. I could never really see the point of it. Now, as a young teacher, I had been given a cricket team to look after; it was a grade team and, therefore, competitive. They played every Tuesday afternoon against other co-educational high schools scattered far and wide through Sydney.

It was, on a daily basis, becoming apparent to me that my four-year college preparation had very little to do with what I was actually doing. In my course there had been nothing about brass bands and nothing about cricket.

One day, a young boy, who had recently taken up the flugelhorn and had also joined the alto section of the choir, walked into the music room with a book in his hands: a green-covered manual with a cricketer's picture on the front cover. He approached me and said, with all the deference due to an inferior: 'I know you have to coach our team, and I also know that you don't know anything about cricket, so I have brought you this book to read. It contains the rules of cricket. I suggest you borrow it and learn as much as you can.'

I was immediately reminded of my conversation with the young trombonist who had wanted a brass band at school. I also thought of the ancient saying that when you become a teacher, by your pupils you will be taught.

The boy was Kim Williams, and it was the beginning of a friendship that has lasted fifty years, as he has risen to very senior ranks of arts and media management. Kim was passionate about cricket to the point of fanaticism. He wanted me to show enough gumption to learn the rules of the game so many of the kids adored. Well, I never really mastered them, but I umpired anyway, and I did it with flair and theatrical style.

When a kid hit a four I moved my arms in the approved manner, with bold gestures and a strong sense of phrasing. When a kid was called out, I always put my head down, as if deep in thought, for at least fifteen seconds or so, and then I would lift my finger very slowly and solemnly to indicate that he was out. When a bowler had finished an over, I called out 'over' loudly and with more passion than any other school umpire ever did.

Occasionally, I would lose count and either call the over one ball early or one ball late, at which moment both teams would yell at my unforgivable error and blatant stupidity. I recall very distinctly a boy from an opposing team yelling out, 'Can't you count, sir?' to which I offered no reply. From behind me, another member of the opposing team said loudly enough for me to hear, 'Fuckwit'. I turned suddenly towards the boy, who, with great presence of mind, said, 'Not you, sir, him,' pointing to the boy who had cheeked me. The expression 'fuckwit' had just entered the common parlance, not replacing words like 'shithead' and 'arsehole' as terms of abuse, but adding new complexity and richness to the concept of the heartfelt expletive. The kids adored saying it.

My umpiring career was short-lived, as the result of a match in which I caused a major international incident. In my own defence, I felt I was acting in the interest of a boy from Marsden and, consequently, of the team and the school.

It was the cricket competition final, and we were playing away at Frenchs Forest, against Forest High School. The score was tied. The kids were beside themselves with excitement.

I was umpiring at the bowler's end and it was the last ball of the last over. To be perfectly frank, I was hoping it would rain and that the match would be stopped. The Forest High bowler took an almighty run-up and flung the ball down the pitch towards the Marsden batsman. The receiver, jaw clenched and cricket bat held high, smashed the ball with all his might, but had no idea where it had actually gone. I could see that it had travelled a reasonably safe distance through the slips and was heading along the ground towards the edge of the field. The kid didn't move, out of sheer fear. Finding myself caught up in the moment, I yelled out 'Run!' The kid ran, we won the match, and there was the usual shouting and cheering.

We piled on the bus back to school, where I was greeted by the sports master, who ran up to me and said: 'What the fuck happened? I've been on the fucking phone to the fucking school and the fucking sports master at Forest High, and we've been accused of cheating because someone from our side called out for the fucking kid to run.' Naive as ever about the game, I replied: 'I was the one who called out for him to run. I could see that he could get a run, so I called out.' The sports master turned purple and said, 'Jesus Christ, Gilly, are you totally stupid? You're the fucking umpire – you're not supposed to say anything. For fuck's sake.' He walked away, almost in tears. It was the season of superlative 'fucks', obviously, and I had created this maelstrom of hate, made manifest in coarse language and blasphemy on the sports master's part.

I was removed from cricket and put on to house tennis. What an insult! From the heady days of under-fifteen grade cricket to indolent and drowsy afternoons with kids who could barely hit a tree, let alone a tennis ball. I begged to be removed from this indignity and was given grade water polo instead. During winter I had grade basketball, which I took very seriously, and coached on the school courts at the crack of dawn two mornings a week. We had a good team and even managed to win the grade competition at least once, fairly and squarely.

10

The Getting of Wisdom, At Last

In Australia, we are on the verge of a national curriculum. That should be a good thing. I worry, however, about the impact on individual teachers and individual schools. I fear that informed individual contributions will be supplanted by the departmentally-appointed committee, a well-established syndrome in education; and that the search for genuine knowledge will be replaced by sets of bland, dumbed-down documents of learning requirements that have had so much cosmetic work done on them that nobody will be offended. Nobody will be offended, but nobody will really care.

For we live and work in the age of open consultation, in which no individual appears to be ultimately responsible for anything; an age in which committees meet endlessly in sincere but totally misguided attempts to 'reach an understanding with which we're all comfortable', or 'arrive at a bottom line which truly reflects our organisation moving forward'. In the process, we have abdicated our responsibility to education and abused the democratic process beyond recognition.

I have sat on committees recently where I have had to suffer so-called 'experts' pontificating on the music curriculum: people who have no deep knowledge of music and even less of teaching, and who trot out particular party lines in order to cover backsides and protect jobs.

On such occasions I tend to ask them directly what they actually know. This is considered effrontery: it might upset the well-intentioned and very sincere who have, in their own words, 'thought long and hard about these issues'. Rubbish! The emperor has no clothes! I will continue to speak out about the second-rate approaches to education and the creation of sub-standard curriculum while I have the breath and the words to do so.

My principal objection to the current state of Australian education is that children are treated as if they are essentially dumb and incapable of genuine thought. Teachers are undervalued; in the state education systems, they are often perceived as process workers who administer politically correct pap in order to satisfy some national standard of education ending up with meaningless statistics. We are happy in our mediocrity: in fact, we worship, praise and adore the gods at their altars of mediocrity – namely, the god NAPLAN and the demigod MySchool.

I haven't found a single teacher among the hundreds to whom I have spoken who has a good thing to say about standardised testing. I wish they'd all stand up and be counted.

I bang on about these iniquities because I know how positively and powerfully children can respond to genuine teaching: teaching that stimulates their minds, unleashes torrents of creative thinking, promotes vigorous discussion, generates new thoughts and ideas, and causes lives to be examined in all sorts of detail.

Recently, I visited a Melbourne school to talk to a year-twelve class on the theory of knowledge, a subject required for the International Baccalaureate. It was so stimulating to be able to engage these teenagers in conversation with such a strong intellectual base; to listen to their ideas on art, music, dance and drama; to place them in the circumstance of having to defend a particular point of view; to confront them with questions that had the capacity to turn their worlds upside down; and to watch and listen to them deal with these problems. I came away refreshed, mentally and intellectually stimulated, and encouraged to want to do more. In short, I am still learning about teaching, and still being stimulated by the ideas and thoughts of young people.

How wonderful would it be for this country if these young people could be encouraged to go into teaching? And then how disappointing for them to find on entering the profession that they could be severely restricted by aspects of a politically correct document which, in certain circumstances, actively discourages thought in favour of a prescribed way to answer a question.

This topic might seem distant from my experiences as a first-year teacher at Marsden High School, but it is not. In my first year in the classroom the most exciting work was teaching senior students in preparation for the Leaving Certificate examination in music. The syllabus was packed with required material and examined in three distinct parts: a short, but searching, practical examination; an aural examination lasting approximately one and a half hours, and a three-hour written paper, which included composition, harmony, analysis of set works and general essay topics.

I had no idea how to tackle the task I faced; we had had no preparation at college for teaching this syllabus. Perhaps it was delivered on one of the days I had deliberately absented myself, but I do not recall any specific instruction in this regard. I was on my own.

So I took each topic in turn and gave my students as much information as I could, in the only way I knew, which was in the form of notes and information sheets supported by recorded musical examples. The harmony and melody-writing component was less of a challenge, and I found teaching this aspect of the course relatively easy.

In short, I was starting to teach in the way I now despise. The delivery of a syllabus to the specific requirements of an examination, with a view to passing on to the students as much information as possible to pass, does not constitute real teaching, in my view. However, as a young teacher who knew nothing I was perpetuating the sort of teaching I had been subjected to at Marist Brothers Eastwood.

There were only three students in this group, but they were my very first serious students, and I remember them exceptionally well and with great affection. John Grant was a violinist and one of nature's true gentlemen. Graeme McMartin was a cellist, with an especially fine baritone voice. Frances Mortley, also a cellist and a singer, possessed serious intellect.

It was to the eternal credit of the school and Joyce Walsh that music was provided for these three young people as an examination subject. It created a precedent at Marsden for small classes for music, thus enabling children who were serious about studying music to do so knowing that they would be given every chance, and support and encouragement, to realise their ambitions.

My students and I had six forty-minute periods together each week, which I supplemented with extra lessons at my parents' home in Epping during weekends and holidays. In the process I learned much about teaching and learning. In one lesson in rhythmic dictation (in which the student must follow a pattern of rhythm and record it in writing), Fran Mortley burst into tears. She taught me a wonderful lesson in lock-step teaching by saying, through her tears, that if only she was familiar with some of the patterns we might be using, that would at least give her a better chance.

This was a real insight into the concept of teaching sound before musical symbol, a concept that had never been discussed, to my knowledge, in any music method lecture I'd attended. In fact, the more I taught, the more I realised that we had done almost nothing at teachers college that bore any resemblance to what we had to do, or were required to do, in the real world of practical music teaching. Probably a fairer way of saying this is that I had no idea about the teaching of any musical concept in any methodical way and could not recall any lecturer saying, 'This is how you can teach the following concepts in rhythm', or 'This is how fixed pitch can be taught'.

My general classroom lessons were undoubtedly appalling, although I had some idea of giving a music appreciation lesson – that is, presenting recorded music to children – and some little idea of how you teach a song by rote. I survived through pure strength of will, and by being as enthusiastic as I could about music. In this, my first year of teaching, I was afforded a visit by a music adviser, a wonderful man called Alan Curry, who came from the New South Wales Department of Education's Music Branch and who wrote a reasonably encouraging report on my work.

I knew I was floundering but I managed to keep my head above water until Fran Mortley decided she wanted to attempt music honours. She did so to increase her chances of obtaining a Commonwealth scholarship, just as I had once tried to do with French. She was already attempting English honours and was hell-bent on scoring enough marks to enrol in Arts at the University of Sydney on a full scholarship!

The music honours course was entirely historically based, and the subject field changed from year to year. In Fran's year it was devoted to incidental music of the theatre in the nineteenth century. This was a gigantic topic, covering dozens of works, especially ballets, and betraying the bias of the senior examiner towards French theatre music.

Fran and I worked like dogs, to coin a phrase. Near the end of the year, the deputy headmaster, a very kindly man by the name of Frank Taylor, called me into his office to give me some friendly advice. He noticed that I was working from 7.30 am until 5.30 pm each day, as well as working at weekends, and he told me that after two or three years at this frantic pace, I would finally crack under the strain and experience a nervous breakdown. He had seen it happen with young teachers before and I was no different from any other young teacher.

The results were worth it. Fran managed to achieve a good second-class honours, which gave her the necessary marks to attend the University of Sydney on full scholarship. Graeme won a teachers college scholarship to study music. Sadly, John missed out on a pass by a couple of marks. I will always blame myself for that, and have wondered how I could have helped him more effectively.

It is part of teaching to deal with all circumstances associated with public examinations and there is no denying the responsibility, particularly when children depend on achieving the highest possible marks to attend the institution that offers their preferred course. My view has always been, even as a young teacher, that the institutions should set their own entrance examinations and use the school results as a general guide and not a life-determining finality.

At any rate, I survived that first year, and none of what Mr Taylor predicted has yet come to pass. Here I am fifty years later, still working at a cracking pace and still loving it.

Marsden High School had an orchestra, which Joyce Walsh, of course, had established and handed over to me. It was almost a full symphony orchestra, so we decided to try to enter it in the education department's instrumental music festival. I wrote a piece for the ensemble to play, carefully tailored to suit each solo instrument. It consisted of three movements – a march, a tango and a rondo – and was entitled *Fancy Free*. The orchestra was auditioned by members of staff from the department's music branch and was subsequently chosen to appear in the festival, at Sydney Town Hall.

This festival was the responsibility of one Lindsay Aked, adviser on instrumental music at the branch, and a school inspector. He conducted a combined high schools orchestra in which some of our students played, giving them the opportunity to mix with other likeminded musicians and play a wider range of orchestral repertoire with a greater degree of difficulty.

Instrumental music was very much on the rise at this time in New South Wales, thanks in great part to the dedicated leadership of Terence Hunt, who had played a major role at the Music Branch since the late forties. The department had a policy of supplying instruments on permanent loan to schools as encouragement to parents who might later consider purchasing one for their child. It was a very good scheme, from which Marsden High School students benefitted enormously.

Our orchestra was well received at the festival. Lindsay Aked felt my composition needed a piano part to fill out the bass line, and wrote the part himself. Terence Hunt commentated from that I had composed this piece especially for the orchestra and that this was the sort of thing all good music teachers should be able to do. I felt encouraged that I was more or less on the right track.

At the end of my first year I discussed with Joyce Walsh the notion of presenting a public concert, which would include as many examples as possible of the musical activities undertaken in the school, followed by a reduced version of *Oklahoma!*. This concert performance of the musical would be accompanied by friends of mine, orchestral players from the NSW Conservatorium, who were either already teaching or about to be appointed.

I assembled the outline of a concert; an outline that grew in size on a daily basis. The first half was to consist of ensembles: folk groups, the brass band, the school orchestra and some individual class work. We hired the Meadowbank High School hall because Marsden High, as yet, had no hall of its own. I carried out the casting, and rehearsals began in earnest. The kids were enthusiastic, their parents were equally enthusiastic and we had the makings of a reasonable show.

I taught a boy called Ian Freeman my old tap routine, which I could remember perfectly well from my own limited career as a tap dancer at the Lane Cove Musical Society. Freeman performed the dance brilliantly. We walked the students down to the hall for rehearsals when we reached the final stages, and ended up playing to a completely sold-out house of parents and friends.

The father of one of the students in the performance was a journalist for a Sydney newspaper, the *Daily Telegraph*. He was so inspired by what he saw these children doing that he wrote a double-page spread, focusing strongly on how a recently established high school had come of age through music. This was a perceptive article, with far-reaching consequences. What this father had realised was that music had a special power to unite a community, to unite children, to build a sense of teamwork, while, at the same time, promoting the worth of the individual.

He was so right about that. Yet, day to day, I still struggled to interest some of my students, let alone inspire them. One of my non-elective classes, a year-nine group, as it happened, was studying the symphony as one of its topics. The work I had chosen was the first movement of Beethoven's Fifth Symphony in C minor, a relatively well-known piece.

It was a textbook presentation, or so I thought. The themes were on the board for the class to sing; the instruments responsible for playing the themes were also named and beautifully written on the board; Beethoven's birth and death dates and a shortlist of his other works were also prominent. I played a recording of the symphony on the portable gramophone.

The class listened quietly and respectfully to the music, and then I asked: 'What did you think of that?' A boy who was a member of the basketball team I coached, and whose name was David Drennan, called out, 'It's the same old crap over and over again . . . da . . . da . . . da . . . dum . . . da . . . da . . . da . . . dum.' This sentiment seemed to meet with universal approval from the rest of the class, who sided with him, quite rightly as I was able to see later. His answer left me feeling totally isolated. I had failed to convince the class of the beauty and greatness of this immortal work. I had not reached one of them with this extraordinary music.

That was one of the moments in teaching that changed my life forever. The boy's remark set me on a course of thinking that ultimately altered the way I taught. It took me some time to realise that all my assumptions were wrong. I had assumed (incorrectly, as it turned out) that by providing information in a didactic way – that is, telling them everything I felt they needed to know about the music they were to hear – that I was preparing a pathway for their subsequent understanding. This could be classified as an act of overt stupidity.

I assumed further, but again incorrectly, that the class would automatically support and share my views of the work and its extraordinary nature; that they would understand, through osmosis, I supposed, and appreciate the greatness and complexity of the composition in the same way that I did. That could be classified as an act of overt arrogance.

By asking them no specific questions about anything to do with the music, I had taken away any opportunity for their participation, and had consequently implied, albeit obliquely, that I wasn't interested in anything they had to say.

This lesson was underlined for me not much later by Lindsay Aked, who came to observe me giving a lesson on Mozart's Symphony No. 40 in G minor to a senior music class. My official promotion from graduate assistant to teacher was riding on this inspection. After the class, he asked me to go with him into the playground, where we sat on a bench and smoked. His opening words, fixed firmly in my memory, were 'You talk too much'.

That was enough. After that I didn't really hear much of what he said. I was thinking deeply about this remark, and thinking about it in relation to the remark made by David Drennan. Aked's implication was that I was simply directing my students' attention to musical facts and phenomena, which could have been derived from almost any other source.

What I finally learned was that one of my jobs was to lead these children to music through listening, questioning, commenting and discussing, and involving them in a process during which they, through appropriately framed questions, would be able to deduce certain things about the ways in which music behaves; the ways in which music works; the ways in which rhythm, melody and harmony interact and combine to produce a multitude of musical styles, structures and forms, in combination with instrumental and vocal colours. Whether they ended up liking the work was really irrelevant. What was important was that the students would have a chance to appreciate, in the best sense of the word, and end up with a genuine liking for the work.

In order to achieve this, I realised, they required some specific tools. They needed to know something about the reading and writing of music and, therefore, something about composition.

The department offered in-service courses from time to time, often presented by experienced teachers. I attended one given by Pat Quinn, a music teacher at North Sydney Girls' High School. Pat had brought along a class, together with a large collection of percussion instruments known as Orff Schulwerk instruments. The girls played a piece of Carl Orff's called *Einzug und Reigen*, loosely translated as Introduction and Round Dance, and I was hooked in a huge way. I sat there with my mouth wide open as I listened to the sounds of these instruments and the entrancing way in which the layers of sound worked together.

Pat Quinn went on to explain a little more about Schulwerk (a German word, which translates as 'Schoolwork'), and the principles underpinning Orff's approach.

The music was, in this case, essentially pentatonic: that is, constructed out of five notes that have an independent life and do not necessarily belong to a tonal hierarchy such as the major and minor scale system. The pentatonic scale is found in an enormous amount of folk music from a wide representation of musical cultures, including those of China, Arabia, native North American groups, some African cultures, and Celtic and Scottish music. Some musicologists consider it to be the prototype of all scales. It can be easily identified in one of its forms by simply playing in order the black keys found on the piano. It is a scale that has no harmonic foundation, but in which all the notes, even the discords appear to work well with each other.

Hearing this music was another life-changing experience; Pat Quinn's inspirational work opened my ears and eyes. It hit me in an incredibly powerful way that there had to be more to these instruments than simply reproducing the music Orff had composed for them. Surely this approach was an invitation to children to compose their own music.

This approach of Orff's had to contain elements of improvisation: the pentatonic screamed for it. In my own improvising I was, at that time, experimenting with writing songs in pentatonic scales, and was composing, in the loosest sense of the word, a ballet for vegetables. Each vegetable had its own pentatonic scale, which is technically possible, and its own rhythmic identification code. There was 'The Dance of the Cauliflowers' on C pentatonic, 'The Peas Polka' on a G pentatonic, and a 'Corny Can-Can' – pathetic really! This work was not being eagerly sought by the Bolshoi, but it did provide me a vehicle with which to experiment.

Hearing Pat Quinn's group simply confirmed what I had suspected. The reason we teach music, according to Carl Orff, is so that children can make their own music.

This was the next step in the process of revelation and coincided with an extra-special revelation for me, which was coming to grips with the music of Bach.

I WAS A SUBSCRIBER TO A BRITISH ENTERPRISE KNOWN as the World Record Club, which produced inexpensive long-playing records. The quality of its recordings was high and there was a very large classical catalogue, which contained an enormous number of works I didn't know, not that that was surprising, but the catalogue in itself was an education.

One of the discs I ordered was 'The Musical Offering Of Johann Sebastian Bach'. This record remained in its cover for some time after it arrived in the post. At the Con, in the early stages of my interest in playing the music of the baroque and classical composers, Bach had passed me by: I was immature musically and satisfied with everything music had to offer on the surface. All the delights of music were easily obtainable at Woolworths: I had not yet discovered the music equivalent of David Jones' food hall. No amount of being told that caviar is wonderful is going to change the mind of a kid who thinks Weet-Bix is the pinnacle of taste!

But as I struggled to work out ways to teach composition, I remembered a brilliant teacher from the Con called Raymond Hanson, who had encouraged his students to think about relationships in music and the ways in which harmony functioned; harmony being loosely defined as the way in which notes that were piled on top of another made musical sense as a chord when they were sounded together, and then the way in which that pile of notes moved towards the next pile of notes. Hanson believed that tonal music – that is, music in major and minor keys with recognisable melodies – still had a tremendous future as a means for composing. (He was dead right.) He referred constantly to Bach, by way of example.

One evening, arriving home from school, I decided to play the new disc right through. I started to listen more and more intently to a theme Bach had been given by

Frederick the Great of Prussia, as a type of challenge to the composer's ability. Bach had initially improvised a three-part fugue on the theme. The fugue, a term derived from the Latin word meaning to fly or to chase, from which we also get the English word 'refugee', is a musical style in which the parts or voices being played enter one after the other in a relatively strict way. A fugue may be in as many as six parts, or voices, requiring six independent entries, and making life very difficult for the composer. The voices or parts then work their way through a series of keys and key changes known as modulations. Each is characterised with its independent line and has an equally independent life. It is probably the most difficult form of composition in that field of music known as counterpoint.

As the music grew more and more intense, I started to appreciate the complexity of the counterpoint, the originality of the invention, the brilliance of the imagination and the sheer magnitude of the mind that was able to weave this musical magic, bringing fresh life to the theme in each iteration. This music moved me profoundly. I experienced a type of spine-tingling sensation, which made me realise that I was on the verge of understanding how it worked. I was coming to grips with Bach's counterpoint in ways I hadn't done before, and was actually beginning to understand it, and to follow the irrefutable logic of the themes and their respective journeys, their relationships one to the other and their places in the whole work.

I could hardly wait to get my hands on copies of Bach's two- and three-part inventions, and to revisit his preludes and fugues. Even now, from time to time I make it my business to play through all forty-eight preludes and fugues, simply to remind myself that they exist, and to provide myself with endless hours of musical amazement. 'Plough through' is probably more accurate than 'play through', and the only fly that would be on the wall would be a deaf one. The sounds I make on my beautiful Steinway grand piano aren't necessarily pretty, and the language I use is frequently as colourful as the counterpoint, but I find that every time I undertake this exercise, I learn so many things about music in general, about Bach specifically, and about the ways in which notes can be combined one with another in a seemingly infinite variety of ways.

It was this turning point, my seminal experience with 'The Musical Offering', which led me to the decision that, from that moment on, I would teach composition to beginner composers through the music of Bach, and would always include his two-part inventions, using Invention No. 1 as my starting point, or the Suite for Violoncello in C major.

This is the part of teaching that I now most enjoy. I find it utterly irresistible to introduce this music to students, who usually want to compose in any other style. Often, they may have already written quite complex scores, but do not have very strong or accurate perceptions of what they have actually composed.

Some of these students simply want verification from me that they are talented and should be commissioned by all the world's major orchestras. If they are that good, why do they need lessons? Such students barely last the obligatory ten-minute interview. Once I let them know that our first lesson will be on the Two-Part Invention in C major of Bach, you hear their jaws hitting the floor. Or, worse still, if I say that we will begin with the C major cello suite, they frequently look at me as if I should be in some sort of home for the demented. In the end, I teach these students because I want to and not because I have to.

Often a prospective student will say, 'I've done the Inventions', to which I reply, 'Then tell me, how does the first invention begin?'. After the usual 'It's been some time' or 'I don't have a copy handy', I produce my copy and say, 'Go ahead, refresh your memory.' What follows is exactly as you'd expect. 'Well, it's in C major and starts with a motif rising up', at which stage I interrupt and say, 'No, tell me how it begins.' The longest I had to wait for an answer from a student was sixteen minutes, when he finally, on the point of committing murder, said, 'It starts with a semiquaver rest.' 'That is correct; then what happens?'

I try to let them know that the act of composition is exact, as Stravinsky says in his *Poetics of Music*: it is an act of will, it is deliberate. It is not merely or exclusively about chance or inspiration. The old true, tried and tested tradition of composed music, going back to 800 AD or even before, has evolved not because of a series of happy accidents or by some strange chance, but through the workings and musical considerations of some of the world's most brilliant minds.

Those minds include not only those of composers, but also instrument makers, who have had, in many circumstances, profound and lasting effects on the way music is composed for certain instruments, or groups of instruments such as string or wind ones. Makers of keyboard instruments particularly, have had a profound impact on composition and compositional styles.

When teaching composition students I try, from the beginning, to instil in them a love for analysis and for discovery. It is not that analysis is the be-all-and-end-all of composition, but it is a way to show students that there was obviously some sort of plan being employed, or that the composer had an outline of an idea and maybe even a deliberate intention from the start. With Bach, it is so easy to hear how the parts work and how the lines move together when analysing a work by this composer.

It is why the music of Bach is so valuable and why I am eternally grateful for that moment when I listened to 'The Musical Offering', which, incidentally, could be described as a happy accident, to some degree!

While happy accidents do occur, and there are examples of such things happening all the time in any form of industry or business, in the end the composer's genius is actually the hard labour of an individual applying laws of sound and reason, tempered with logic, together with an inherent, or sometimes innate, sense of style. The genuine composer understands how line works in music, and can convince his or her listeners that he or she has written something worth listening to. This is true from Monteverdi to Mahler, Bach to Brubeck, and from Beethoven to Bacharach. While it is true that not all new music is understood immediately on first hearing, with repeated hearings an appreciation of it can be gained.

Then come the statements from many listeners of music: 'Why should it be understood?'; 'Why, if it so good and this composer is so special, don't we get it the first time?' The immediate and appropriate answer to that question is education. One's appreciation or understanding of anything is directly related to education, experience and example. If you have only eaten chicken burgers all your life, beef might taste strange! If you have only worn polyester shirts, cotton shirts will feel different! If you have only cooked with low-fat butter substitutes, then cooking with real butter will blow your brains out!

I have a rule with my composition students: at the end of each lesson I ask them, 'Do you want another lesson?', to which they can say 'yes' or 'no'. I also have the right to let them know that I don't wish to teach them anymore. In this way, every lesson is like a first lesson and a last lesson. Every lesson is truly special, is truly finite without any guarantee of a follow-up one. In this way there is no sense of entitlement from either of us and no expectation of a long-term teacher–pupil relationship. All my composition students work in this way, which removes any sense of dependency, regularity or monotony. I ask them also, 'Why do you have a teacher?' The answer to that question is 'to get rid of the teacher'. My view is that nobody has the corner on truth and nobody can be assumed, reasonably, to know everything that there is to know about all the music in the world. However, we can, in a composition lesson, learn how to look at the music at its face value, and try to assess from the notes themselves just how they might have been put together and, consequently, what artifices the composer has employed to achieve his or her particular effects.

It is through such observation and analysis that a student may have his or her perceptions altered, as may a teacher. Given that we are all capable of perceiving something, it follows that we are all capable of developing this faculty. The silliest thing the Australian Music Examination Board ever did was to ditch the subject known as musical perception.

We can perceive music in two ways. The first is through the sound of the music itself, the prime, and most immediately available way for the majority of the population; and the second is through sight, or by looking at a piece of music and examining it with one's eyes only. Many musicians have the capacity to 'hear' a piece of music from the page. Most practising musicians possess this skill to some degree. I could also add that we perceive music in a very special way when we compose, because when we do so, we are making judgments about all aspects of the composition, about rhythm, pitch, harmony, orchestrations or the instruments we will choose, and above all, the direction our composition will take.

My composition students employ the skills of examining the page both with and without sound when they are observing and analysing. If using sound, they are allowed to refer to the piano only if needed. It is fascinating to me that no matter how often I go through the process of observing and analysing the first Bach Invention, the C major cello suite, or a prelude or fugue, I will always find something new in the music, often due to the perspective of a student. The art, which conceals art, sometimes reveals it and the excitement at this revelation is palpable. I am never happier than when a student shows me a point of view on a work of Bach's I haven't previously discovered, or approaches the process of observation from a brand-new perspective. *Viva la musica!*

♪

By now, as a third-year teacher, I had discovered that many of the minds I was dealing with were sharper than mine. Furthermore, many of these very sharp minds had musical abilities and innate talent, albeit in embryo and quintessentially nascent, which were greater than mine. At first, to be completely truthful, I found this confronting, but I realised very early in the piece that I was not an equal of theirs, nor were they mine. We were not competitors. I was their teacher and my job was to open as many doors as possible and do whatever I could to give them every opportunity to excel.

Once I realised this I really began to relish teaching. It was thrilling to watch young musicians take to their instruments, practise them willingly and, especially, take to the idea that learning music was a necessity to their life. I wish to emphasise the point that the recognition of talents greater than one's own is an essential part of a teacher's responsibility. In doing so the serious and genuine teacher is not underselling himself or herself but recognising that the best reward in the job is to have provided a pathway for someone whose gifts are of a high order.

In essence, a teacher must be able to recognise that, one day, he or she will encounter minds that are smarter, brighter, more switched on and simply more talented. When that day comes, it is to be hoped beyond hope that the teacher has the presence of mind to realise it and deal with it in the appropriate way.

11

A Young Person's Guide to Composition

My revelations about Bach and Orff had a major impact on my students. Music students who undertook HSC studies at their highest level had to complete a major and a minor study, in addition to sitting the routine written exam. They could elect to write a 3000-word thesis on a set topic such as the music of Stravinsky; perform a program of music at a very high level (at least sixth-grade AMEB); or compose some works for selected instrumental or vocal ensembles. I gave my students no choice. Christopher Harrison, Graham Powning and Alan Suthers, all of whom went on to have distinguished careers in music, were the first HSC guinea pigs and all composed major works.

Suddenly, the whole school became alive with burgeoning composers. My general music classes also began to play percussion instruments of the Orff variety, and improvisation became an important part of music making. Now, there was a real reason for teaching music. It was to find within every child the potential creator, the potential composer, irrespective of the level of its individual abilities. It was not about making new Mozarts and uncovering heretofore mute Bachs, but about finding creative life in the Browns, Smiths and Joneses of the world.

My belief was that every child was able to make a creative or original contribution of some sort and add to the overall musical experience of a lesson. It was never truer than in the classes I took that were populated with children who ostensibly had learning difficulties. Music, the great leveller that it is, gave these children unlimited opportunity to invent and improvise their own music. As they made their own music and commented in general terms on what they had composed, it was evident to me that they experienced a very strong sense of accomplishment, and were feeling that they had all made strong and vital contributions. Knowing what I know now, I would happily go back and repeat the whole exercise with renewed vigour.

It was a very happy period for me, professionally and personally. A new headmaster, Jack McCloughin, was appointed. When he took over the school he made it very clear at his first staff meeting that he was only interested in teachers who were prepared to work very hard, who were prepared to go the extra mile, and whose focus and concentration was entirely on the job. My sort of leader! He was strongly disposed towards music and physical education, and his work ethic suited me.

In 1968, something special happened. I met my future wife, Maureen Fryer, as she was then, who had come to Marsden

High School as head of the physical education staff. Both of us were unconventional teachers, and I'm sure some elements of the school community considered us to be slightly mad. Gradually, Maureen and I formed a strong bond, but it could be hardly be described as a conventional courtship – especially as, at the beginning, she was engaged to someone else.

In the late sixties, much of the school became involved in music. We staged a full version of *Oklahoma!*, participated with other schools in the annual choral concerts, and presented music composed by students, as well as two operas I had written for the school. Prior to an afternoon rehearsal of one of these works, something happened that demonstrated how much the school had tilted towards music. A boy named Neil Sharpham was on his way to the assembly hall for opera rehearsal when the sports master raced up to him and called out, 'Hey, Sharpham, where are you going? It's football training now.' The student, who was a principal in the production, turned to him and said, 'Sorry, sir, but I've got opera practice', and proceeded into the hall – as did some other footballers. The sports master turned to me and said, 'Jesus, Gilly' – he frequently addressed me in this way – 'what the hell are you doing to these kids?' I replied that I was looking after their souls, hearts and minds.

The students' interest was bolstered by annual music camps, held immediately after Christmas at the Broken Bay National Fitness campsite. These camps were run by the state education department, and competition for student places was very strong. To be asked to attend as a member of staff was seen as a special privilege. Sometimes you were paid, sometimes not. Terence Hunt, a somewhat eccentric leader, held the view that music camp was a special reward for music teachers who had worked hard all year. The reward was to take ten days out of your Christmas holidays, and work like a dog from 7 am until 10.30 pm. After it ended, I would sleep for two days straight, with minimum intake of any nourishment whatsoever.

There was no doubt that the camp was a collection of highly gifted musicians, students and teachers, assembled under one roof with the universally agreed premise being to make the best music possible. The commonweal that developed as a result of this gathering of like minds was a rare delight. The massed singing, complete with spectacularly improvised harmonies, was extraordinary, and the evening concerts were unfailingly inspiring. I have no doubt that these camps led many young musicians to make career decisions in favour of music.

Attending them was a very special lesson to me in forming my views about the ways in which we foster the exceptionally gifted young person. Whether that talent be for music, sport, art, academic pursuits or, indeed, combinations of those things, students thrive when they are positioned with like minds. It is the strongest possible argument for selectivity in education, and underlines the very severe limitations of a comprehensive system's capacity to offer advanced teaching to the gifted in so many fields of endeavour.

Mediocrity was the last thing on the minds of one group of students from Marsden High. Camp had barely started when this group approached me, complaining that there wasn't enough music going on and that they had come to camp expecting to play it for at least twenty of the twenty-four available hours in a day. They weren't joking. They were obsessed with music, and couldn't get enough.

In fact, this same group of complaining students, essentially a woodwind quintet, had previously built a backyard cubby house of wondrous proportions, specifically for the purpose of advancing the cause of woodwind music. The backyard belonged to the Blackman family, a very musical family. It produced two members of the Adelaide Symphony Orchestra: principal clarinet Greg Blackman, and his brother and contra-bassonist, Paul.

This cubby house, which had been christened 'the orgy house,' was off limits to pianists, string players and percussionists. The quintet were almost universally opposed to all instruments other than wind instruments and felt that the symphony orchestra revolved around the wind section. There would be many professionals in symphony orchestras today who would probably agree with that philosophy.

I once wrote a work for this group called *Scherzo Fantastique*, which they found laughable and simply refused to play. They wanted to arrange their own music for their own purposes, and thought that being involved in anything else was a complete waste of time. Music lessons, unless focusing on wind music, could be a serious trial for this lot. Whenever I played the piano in class, they referred to it as the tinkle-box and agreed among themselves that the piano was not a real musical instrument, or certainly not as real as a flute, oboe, clarinet, bassoon or French horn, the instruments that, to their thinking, ruled the musical world.

In the end, I think I managed to convince them that their positions in the orchestra were only possible because there were string players prepared to sacrifice their lives for the wind section, and that ultimately that was the only reason a string player ever turned up to work: to lay down his or her life for the wind section.

The activity of composition was now strong within the classroom. In order to enhance this activity and provide an outlet for those who were genuine about their compositional ambitions, I established a special class for the school's musical intelligentsia, who flocked to have their works performed and to learn a little more about the act of composing.

There was a theory at the time, coming from the University of Sydney, that effectively propagated the notion that you couldn't really teach composition. I not only taught these gifted students composition, I encouraged them to listen to the very latest in European contemporary orchestral music. It was a challenging experience, which shocked some of them and delighted others. The first time I played the *Chronocromie* of Olivier Messiaen there was practically a riot.

We listened to as much contemporary music as possible, and attended as many concerts at which contemporary music was being played as we could. Then I set them to writing short works in particular styles. The results were interesting. There was no obviously profound influence of any one style, or of any one composer. I certainly didn't say that they had to write like someone else or sound like someone else. I encouraged them to try to find their own voices, as I believed that was one of the hallmarks of the so-called great composers; each one had his own sound and characteristic way of writing music, which typified his style.

My students wrote in a wide variety of styles, which embraced everything from pure tonal music (music in major and minor keys reflecting most of the standard repertoire)

Above: My mother and I. I'm the one in the high chair aged 10 months.

Right: My First Communion, aged 5-plus. Notice my natural smile and the distressed look of the Blessed Virgin Mary in the background.

Heading towards maturity with my Aunt Josephine, my youngest brother, Chris, father Stephen and mother Lydia. Notice the lovely tablecloth made of plastic, a substance adored by my mother.

Tap-dancing my way to Broadway in the role of *Oklahoma!*'s Will Parker. Interestingly and rather surprisingly, I received no phone calls from agents. My friend, Errol, is directly behind Aunt Eller, who is seated in a rocking chair.

At Alexander Mackie Teachers College with fellow students in 1958, having a well-earned smoko. Wearing a tie and a jacket was compulsory... for some of us.

1963 performance by Marsden High School Orchestra at Meadowbank Boys' High School school hall.

Alan Basford, the long-suffering Sports Master, and the under-15s cricket team including Kim Williams, front row third from left, looking distressed at my lack of natural sporting ability.

At Marsden High School in 1968, with my future wife, Maureen Fryer, and student Don Luscombe. The gladdie stem was being used as a weapon.

Settling a scoring dispute during the mini-Olympics on the roof of St Judes, London in 1970. Notice the blue sky; one of the four days of the year in which blue sky actually appeared.

At St Judes with (from left) Leroy and Denley. We had just had 'algebra' and Denley's marks weren't the best but Leroy had done very well.

Rehearsing *Oliver!* at St Judes in 1971. Nancy in conversation with the Artful Dodger, with parents, friends and classmates observing. I survived this production – barely.

This was a truly special occasion, celebrating Carl Orff's 80th birthday in Salzburg. It was followed by a performance of excerpts from *Carmina Burana* in the version for two pianos and percussion.

Maureen and me on our wedding day – the gladdies have been replaced by tulips. Maureen's wedding dress eventually became a christening dress for our three perfect grandchildren.

Conducting a concert at the Sydney Town Hall with the Conservatorium Orchestra in the late ’70s.

Rehearsing barefoot with the Con Singers at St Mary’s Cathedral, Sydney in preparation for a performance of J.S. Bach’s *St John Passion*.

Family shot: Anthony, exhausted in his mother's arms, and Claire, aged 2, rarin' to go. Observe the fashion of the day, and our lovely summer pastels.

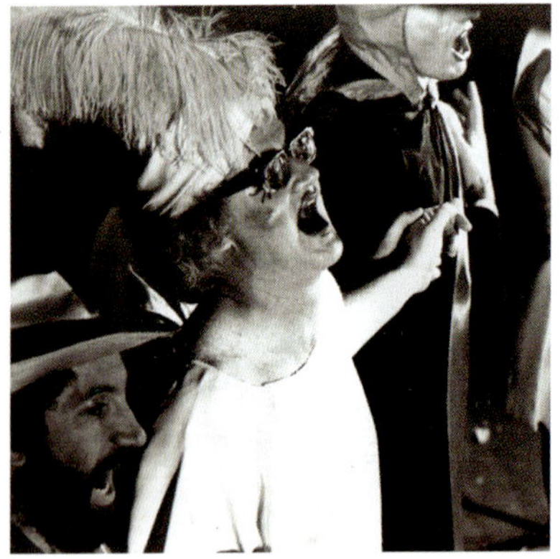

In drag at Rothbury Estate, circa 1979, singing the role of Angelique after the real soprano became suddenly and seriously ill. My performance was described as 'something you would only want to hear and see once in a lifetime.' My portrayal led a close friend to seek voluntary psychotherapy. Music's capacity to change lives!

Back in civvies for an open air concert in Sydney's Martin Place, with the hard-working Sydney Youth Orchestra.

The glorious Professor Jan Rapley and me at California State University, Chico in 1984. A period of great awakenings, pedagogically and musically.

Kevin Johnson persisting with me in a tap dance class during a season of Nick Enright's fabulous play 'On The Wallaby' in Perth, 1986. Still no call from any agents.

Rehearsing with Don Halbert as The Bloke, in George Dreyfus' 'The Sentimental Bloke', based on the C. J. Dennis poems. It is obviously a very intense discussion. The musical instrument, laughably described as a piano, had been in Perth, it seemed, from the day Perth had been founded. No one sounded good playing it, especially me.

Dog, girls and boys. Girls happy, boys a bit grumpy and Louis, who did have eyes, is having the best fun of all.

I was delighted to accept an Honorary Doctorate from the Australian Catholic University because of the great work undertaken by nuns all over Australia in the teaching of practical music. My debt is to Catholic nuns for my first musical experiences.

My brothers Terry and Chris, and my mother, looking as if she was wondering how it all happened. She seems to have a different view on where the camera is.

A rehearsal for OzOpera's *The Magic Flute* in Cobar, in far western New South Wales. The spontaneous standing ovation at the end of the show said it all.

On the road with OzOpera in 1997. I'm feeling very disgruntled and clearly distressed. About what, I have totally forgotten.

Honorary Doctorate from Edith Cowan University, Western Australia. I was genuinely surprised to receive this doctorate and greatly humbled.

Louis, our fabulous French poodle, has been trying to give me a lesson in the subjunctive mood in French. He's disappointed and I'm shattered at my own incompetence.

Photograph by Bernie Heard.

Above: A Schools Concert at the Eugene Goossens Hall, ABC Studios, Sydney with the Sydney Symphony Sinfonia. The jacket I'm wearing in the photograph no longer fits me... regrettably!

Right: With Jonathan Mills outside The Barbican in London in 2002. This was OzOpera's first international tour of Jonathan's and Dorothy Porter's first opera, *The Ghost Wife*. A genuine public and critical success.

Sing-A-Long With Rich. Daughter-in-law Dominique, son Anthony, daughter Claire and a decibel level bordering on dangerous – an occupational health and safety issue.

Anthony's wedding day in 2006.

Young conductor Daniel Carter with me in a rare moment when we are both smiling. We obviously agreed to be nice to each other, just this once.

Sing Your Own Opera at Melbourne's BMW Edge Theatre with a trio of happy newly discovered opera stars.

My best side. Working with and verbally abusing the participants at Sing Your Own Opera. Very happy times with Victorian Opera.

right through to serial music (in which a short series of notes comprises the entire palette of a piece). When we tackled the twelve-tone composers of the Second Viennese School, Berg, Schoenberg and Webern, some of the students resisted mightily, arguing that none of their work made sense. This music relies on the independence of each of the twelve notes, which the composer arranges quite arbitrarily into a 'row' or melody. Many of my students were convinced that unless there was a key centre, something to hang onto, the music made no sense; creating a row was just luck or chance.

As a group we also experimented with avant-garde techniques, aleatoric (or chance) music and, in a small way, electronic music. Two non-elective music students created a machine that made white noise and that we later used in my opera *Jinini.* We covered everything we could in this class, including some of the most wild and chaotic improvisations, which incorporated the simulation of vomiting into open timpani, recording the sound of the vomiter, then playing it back to incorporate it into an improvisation for a solo instrument.

We played pieces called 'mobiles', in which each member of the orchestra was given a specific musical line to play, which they could play at any moment they chose. The musician was encouraged to play the line and interpret the music as freely or as strictly as he or she felt at that moment. In other words the entire performance depended on the will of the individual musician, or the musician's capacity to be moved by the spirit and in any manner the spirit might whimsically dictate.

Teaching colleagues of mine thought I had lost my senses. I hadn't. I knew by then that I was on track. I really did know what I was doing: I could tell when something was working and when students were really involved in learning music. When something didn't work I could eliminate it immediately, and search for another way to explore music.

Among the students, there were divisions, and frequently incredibly heated and angry exchanges. I knew that, in essence, this was good. The students were developing views, were thinking about music, and were expressing opinions, but, in the main, the opinions were based in fact and experience, albeit limited. They were not simply expressing an emotional reaction to something they didn't understand. I was preparing them to be able to say much more than 'I don't know much, but I know what I like'.

This class attracted visitors from other schools from time to time, and one such visitor was a young pianist from Meadowbank Boys' High School, Rick Kefford, now professor of medicine and director of the Westmead Centre for Cancer Research. So many of the brightest and best tossed up between careers in music or medicine, or music or mathematics. Rick would wade into the music debates, all guns firing. With him, Kim Williams and Gavin Gostelow, now an early music expert, the language would fly, tempers would fray and we would try to resolve these issues, with music as the final arbiter.

The glorious leveller in all of this was a wonderful young woman who became director of music at Rose Bay Convent, Sydney. Margaret Wait, as she was then, would simply say, 'Now, boys, we must be calm. I'm sure you all have something to say.' The boys would immediately shut up, and the lessons would proceed. The rest of the group would just sit there, slightly stunned and generally intimidated by the haranguing and yelling.

It was not the usual classroom. I encouraged this type of debate and soon even those who were initially uncertain about what they had to say or how they might be perceived joined in. These students felt free to say what they wished, knowing that they would not be judged or condemned for having a view.

When a student made a wild statement such as 'I think Berg writes rubbish', I was able to stop them dead in their tracks by asking them what work they cited in support of the opinion, and how they defined rubbish. The redoubtable Kim Williams was not going to take this lying down. He would challenge me: 'I hate it when you say that, Gill; you always pull that stunt about repertoire.' But it wasn't a stunt. It was called evidence.

Kim got his revenge. He prepared as a personal test for me – a mix-tape of about seventy examples from the repertoire, covering chunks of symphonic music from Haydn to Messiaen. He had chosen excerpts from the middle of works or from the end of works, lasting in the main no longer than fifteen seconds. Only one work was played from the beginning and that was the first chord, and only the first chord, of the overture to Wagner's *The Mastersingers of Nuremberg*. I stoically agreed to undergo this test publicly.

When I was able to identify something from the examples on the tape, there was general disappointment. When I wasn't able to identify precisely the part of the work played but could identify the composer, that counted as a fail and there was rejoicing at my exposure. Kim inevitably followed this failure with a comment such as 'Well, this is a shock, Gill. Not managing too well here, are we? I would have thought

"Transfigured Night" bar seventy-two would have been as clear as day. It is, after all, a seminal work.' On he went, excerpt after excerpt.

In the end I scored quite highly, considering that there was only about fifteen seconds of music, and sometimes less, for identifying about fifty or so of the seventy excerpts. Kim later said that a teacher who was preparing students for public examinations had a responsibility to the degree of seventy-five per cent for each student, and asked was I aware of that. In other words, it was up to the student to do twenty-five per cent of the work, with the teacher guiding them unfailingly through the other seventy-five per cent.

Where this statistic came from I have no idea, but I have noticed in life that debates are often stopped when someone quotes a statistic that nobody challenges. I have made it my invariable rule to challenge every statistic, and have Kim Williams to thank for that.

♪

I INITIALLY CONCEIVED MY FIRST SCHOOL OPERA, *PIED Piper*, as a project to extend the noble and higher minded of the special composition class. However, that proved too difficult, so I resorted to writing the work myself. I set the complete text of Browning's poem, and composed a score for the school orchestra and a large chorus, with appropriate solo parts.

Its performance was preceded by a program of original music composed by the students in the elective classes. Each composer had to write a short paragraph explaining how their work had evolved, what compositional criteria had been embraced and what they were trying to demonstrate musically in respect to style.

I had invited the inspectorial staff of the Music Branch to the concert. Terence Hunt was beside himself with joy after the first half. He was a great advocate for children being involved in composition and subsequently made a recording of the students' works, for distribution to every high school in New South Wales.

In Sydney at this time, there was a general stirring of interest in opera. There was a plethora of amateur operatic activity being undertaken by local suburban companies such as Rockdale Opera, North Sydney Opera, University of Sydney Opera, University of New South Wales Opera and the New South Wales Con. Opera mania was everywhere, especially with a brand new opera house in the offing, and everyone whatsoever who had any interest in the art form wanted to conduct, direct, design, sing or dance in an opera.

In 1969, I wrote my second and last opera for Marsden High, a work based on two Aboriginal legends, which I had discovered in a book of paintings about the Wandjina. The first dealt with how the Wandjina caused the birth of the seven stars in the southern skies; the second, the legend of Jinini, dealt with the concept of the First Death. Jinini was a young boy whose mother Bima had neglected him in order to be with Japara, her lover. Purukupali, Jinini's father, discovered that the boy had been left in the sun and had perished. The rest of the legend deals with Purukupali's punishment of Bima and Japara. The libretto was written by the emerging young polymath, Gaven Gostelow.

The music for *Jinini* was of a very different order from the music to *Pied Piper.* I was keen to move away from the obvious and simple melodic ideas I had evolved in the first work, not that there was anything intrinsically wrong with simple melodic ideas. I wanted to explore further the concept of orchestral colours, within the obvious confines of the school orchestra and all that implied in respect to the ranges of abilities of the players. I also wanted to examine in more detail the notion of using very obvious dissonances, in an attempt to evoke the harshness of the stories of both legends and, simultaneously, to try to evoke the nature of the country in which they had originated.

In 1965, the Australian composer Peter Sculthorpe had written a work called *Sun Music One.* As I understand it, he was trying to find a sound in his writing that could be characterised as Australian sound. He was very interested in the music to the north of Australia, especially the music of Indonesia. In this he was not alone. There was great interest in the structures and patterns of Indonesian music among musicologists generally.

I bought a score of *Sun Music One* as soon as it became available, and studied it with my senior students. I encouraged them to explore some of the orchestral effects Sculthorpe had included in his work, to copy them and, in their own way, invent new techniques for producing sounds from instruments.

We presented *Jinini* following the pattern established in the *Pied Piper* concert. There was an hour or so of original music and then the opera. It was clear that the music from the students had taken a brand-new turn. It was much more outgoing, in reference to the scope and depth of the musical styles they were exploring. They were taking many more risks with their work and I included some elements of free improvisation in the concert. One of the students, a trumpeter and pianist, Rowley Moore, was a highly gifted improviser. He had a strong flair for jazz and, indeed, by now there was a Dixieland-style jazz group within the school, which loved to play this style of music and, especially, to improvise on jazz standards and twelve-bar melodies.

A music critic from the *Sydney Morning Herald*, Romola Constantino, came to review this concert. She commented very favourably on the work of the students, noting that there was no evidence of imposed stylistic requirements. She commented that there was no reason to suspect the students at Marsden High School were any more or less talented than students anywhere else in the country and, therefore, why wasn't every school in the country operating musically in this way? That a suburban high school was deemed worthy of a review in the *Sydney Morning Herald* was seen as remarkable in its own right. The sports master, who had seen the review, came up to me and said: 'Jesus, Gilly, I've put the paper clipping of the review on the sports notice board.' A great day for music at Marsden.

It was becoming known as a serious music school. Students from Sydney Teachers College were brought out to watch me teach, and we became known as a demonstration school for music. Sometimes the lessons were good, sometimes not. I had experienced a serious falling-out with Joyce Walsh, my co-teacher and technically my senior, and our working relationship had deteriorated quite badly. However, she let me have my head, and I was able to do the things I wanted to do.

♪

THE *JININI* CONCERT WAS MY LAST FORMAL EVENT AT Marsden High School. As usual, there were public examinations at the end of the year, and I had the responsibility of two senior classes to prepare. But otherwise my head was starting to move towards London, where I would soon be going, with the aim of enrolling in a music degree at Durham University. The degree was seen as a prerequisite for promotion.

There had already been suggestions of transferring me, first to Broken Hill High School, then to Epping. But I was now very certain that I wanted to learn how to teach young children, from kindergarten through to second grade, and there was no opportunity to do that in New South Wales. I was also more certain than ever that primary-age children should have the most highly trained musicians teaching them, but that was not the reality generally. I was convinced, after seven years of teaching, that music taught properly and within a wide variety of activities, was a powerful force for good in the life of a child.

As I was approaching the end of my time at Marsden High School, I decided to send my parents on a world trip. I had managed to save quite a bit of money, and knew I probably wouldn't be earning much for quite a while. I went into Qantas and booked a series of flights, which would take them to Ireland via Germany, Austria, France and the UK. My parents had made tremendous sacrifices for their three sons, and for me especially, yet they were quite stunned when I surprised them with a full itinerary of the trip, including accommodation and tours. Lydia wept, and even Steve grew a bit teary.

I was not entirely certain that the world was ready for Lydia, who was never frightened of sharing her views with anyone who was prepared to listen. She had purchased a Stott & Underwood typewriter, and was now pursuing an unpaid career as an author, concentrating her energies on the moral guardianship of the Western world. She began a correspondence with the royal family, the state premiers, goods manufacturers who had any association whatsoever with Japan, and any perpetrator of an advertisement that might contribute obliquely or directly to the decline of western civilisation.

Her correspondence with the British royals included congratulatory letters on births of heirs and spares: 'I do approve of the name Charles for a future British king.' She began to collect truckloads of royal souvenirs. There were royal ashtrays, royal butter dishes, royal jam dishes, royal cereal bowls, royal teaspoons, royal dessert bowls, royal dinner plates, royal tea-towels (you can never have too many), and every other form of kitchen or dining-room equipment that featured the smiling Queen and Prince Philip.

She wrote to a very large cigarette company complaining about the way in which they had used the slow movement of Tchaikovsky's Fifth Symphony to advertise their filthy product. She ripped into them, deploring their lack of originality, detesting their piratical attitude to things cultural, and adding, completely irrelevantly though nonetheless thoughtfully, that although Tchaikovsky was a Russian he was not a Communist and did not subscribe to the idea of communal sharing, especially of his music.

Perched in front of the television set, often with a cat relaxing on her very ample bosom, she would pounce on the typewriter with one turn of the swivel chair from which she ruled her demesne. Whenever she heard or saw something that she found offensive, her fingers would fly over the keyboard, and a letter would be in the post faster than you could say 'disgusting'.

Lydia kept carbon copies of everything; her collected correspondence makes for interesting reading. Her filing system, perfectly arranged, began with 'A' for the current Australian prime minister, followed by a series of sub-files for state leaders. Under 'B' for Buckingham Palace was every article she could muster on the royal family, together with her annotated comments in the margins. The files also contained replies from all these authorities, which she was always confident would come. 'Of course they'll answer – it's rude not to reply to a letter.'

In 1993, her literary skills convinced the State Library of New South Wales to publish a book called *My Town: Sydney in the 1930s*, which described the tram rides in Sydney's main streets. The chapters were headed 'Pitt Street', 'George Street', 'Castlereagh Street', 'Elizabeth Street', 'Thirties Trivia' and finally 'Kings Cross'. A measure of Lydia's style is contained in the following excerpt (notice the homage to Melbourne!):

> There is so much to tell my family, and others, about what Sydney was like in the 1930s that I don't know where to start. The Sydney I knew and loved so much, The Queen City of the South (sorry, Melbourne, though you are a fine Princess City) had a warmth and friendliness that I'm afraid has cooled a little over the years.

Now that my parents have left me and my two brothers orphans, I still find that so many strong and sweet memories of a quiet, deaf, unassuming, gentle, funny man called Steve, and a dominating, powerful, oracular matriarch called Lydia, come into my mind at the weirdest times and on the weirdest occasions.

♪

Before I left for London, I had one mission to complete, which concerned my teaching of the examination classes. It had to do with the way in which I used primary sources: that is, real musical examples, as opposed to the sort of textbook-style examples; the use of scores solely, without cribs or secondary commentaries, and – a style of teaching I never employed – the use of work-sheets.

I had decided, with special regard for a fourth-form class preparing for the School Certificate in music, that I would give them an option for the way in which we worked. I told them that there would be no written essay work, a statement that was greeted by loud cheers, especially from a large group of boys to whom I referred as 'The Grubs'. Further to this, there would be no specific homework of any nature (more and very prolonged cheering), unless anyone especially wanted to do an exercise and then I would be happy to look at it (dead silence!).

There would be no textbooks of any description (loud whistling and banging on the desks), only scores, on which copious notes could be written. All work would be done in class, corrected in class and discussed in class. Anyone who wanted to take extra notes in an exercise book could, but that was discouraged in favour of annotating the margins of scores. Some of the more introverted members of the group found this approach incredibly intimidating and took some time to accustom themselves to it. The boys, especially the Grubs, loved it, as did some of the girls. Discussions on the music set for examination were very open. It wasn't long before most of the class were extremely comfortable with this approach and were able to remember an enormous amount about the music simply from being involved so intensely in the process. Composition and aural training also took on a new lease of life, and the students lapped up everything I could throw at them.

During this period I was inspected for promotion by Terence Hunt. In one lesson with this fourth-form class we were sight-reading a four-part 'Kyrie, Eleison' from a mass by Palestrina. These children were extremely forthright and one of them called out, after I had handed the scores to each student, 'Gill, why are we doing this stuff?'

Hunt raised his head, wondering whether I would check this student, who'd not only called me by my surname (which they all did, actually) but had challenged me giving them this music. I replied to the boy that perhaps an examination of the music itself would reveal the answer. From a simple examination of the score they were able to deduce that the entries were canonic, like a round; that the voices entered in a specific order; that there was climax of some description where all the voices seemed to be working together, which led to a cadence, or end point of some description; and that it didn't sound like anything we had encountered before. They proceeded to sing the music, after which one of them said, 'That music would sound good on brass instruments.' To which I replied, 'A composer called Gabrielli thought so. You might like to search him out.'

The year went on in this manner, with these students growing more and more confident in the ways in which they discussed and analysed music. There was no need to write long essays at this level, as all questions were contained on a paper on which space had been provided for writing any comments or thoughts. There were also questions on score analysis with space provided, music staff lines for composition of melodies, and harmony questions. The examination, as always, was in two parts: an aural paper that required an hour to complete, and a written paper that required two hours.

The students and I were required to attend a neighbouring school for the aural examination, and I was able to observe my charges through a window at the back of the room. I could also hear the tape being played, which had the pre-recorded questions for examination. My lot were ripping through the paper. Once the examination was over I checked the answers with them and, according to my reckoning, they should have all received full marks unless they had said something stupid in the score analysis.

The day of the written paper was a Tuesday, a sports day, and I had responsibilities as a water polo coach. The examination was to be held in Marsden's assembly hall, and was scheduled to start at 2 pm and finish at 4 pm. I knew I'd be back at school before it ended.

I arrived back at school a little before 3.30 and crept quietly into the back of the hall. There was nobody there from my class! There were students from other schools slaving away, but all my charges had gone. The departmentally appointed examination supervisor informed me that all my students had left the examination within an hour and, in one case, after half an hour. I was devastated. The best laid schemes of mice and men often go awry!

All I could do was wait until the students decided to come to school to tell me how they had fared, or until the results came out in January of the new year, and published in the *Sydney Morning Herald* for all the world to see that I had let these children down badly. I was truly crestfallen and was now convinced that my plan had failed.

When the results finally appeared, I could barely open the paper. Thirteen As and one B. The As, I found out later, were all at the top of the state's results, as was the B in that particular category. My way of handling these students, if results meant anything, had been vindicated. Similar results were achieved in the Higher School Certificate, with Marsden High School students fighting it out with the girls from Hornsby High School for the top places.

It was really time to go. I had booked a passage to London on the SS *Ellinis*, a ship of the Chandris line, departing in February 1970. The school's brass band played on the wharf at Walsh Bay as the ship sailed. It was conducted by one of my very first senior students, Graeme McMartin, who had finished his teacher's studies and been appointed to replace me at Marsden.

I was very sad but also very excited. As we steamed towards the Heads, the strangest feeling come over me, a physical conviction that I couldn't get off the boat. I was committed to whatever lay ahead.

12

London, or 'Do You Go 'Ome Evr'y Nigh', Sir?'

APART FROM THE OCCASIONAL FERRY TRIP ON Sydney's magnificent harbour, the idea of spending more than a few hours afloat is now completely repulsive to me. I was cured of any desire ever to travel by ship again by six weeks on the *Ellinis*.

To alleviate the boredom of the long voyage, I taught in the ship's school and played piano in a cocktail bar before dinner – 'Cocktails with Richard in the Caribbean Bar'. I also joined the entertainment crew, to assist with evening concerts, or playing piano or making up the numbers in an item.

There seemed to be a proliferation of folk singers aboard, all keen to appear in concerts. I had brought my guitar with me and, though my playing was never going to threaten John Williams or Andrés Segovia, my profound knowledge of five chords was a boon to those balladeers who needed a little help from their friends.

In fairness, there were some interesting people among the passengers. They included an English gentlewoman, who was a retired headmistress and was making the round trip of nearly eleven weeks. We almost got off on the wrong foot when she said to me, 'Well, air sarpose yar gaing hem, ah yooo?' (I suppose you are going home, are you?) to which I replied, 'Nair, em Orstraylun.' (No, I'm Australian.) 'Eah! Yooo down't sarnd lake one, air marst sair!' (You don't sound like one, I must say.)

Goodness knows what she made of the rest of the company. Many passengers wandered around in an alcoholic haze for six weeks, while others simply sat in the lounges practising elbow-bending until they couldn't walk. Without all the activity I had imposed on myself, life onboard would have driven me insane.

We steamed to our destination via Wellington, Tahiti and the Panama Canal, making stops at Balboa and Cristóbal, then on to New York and across the Atlantic. When the good ship *Ellinis* finally reached New York, we discovered that that great city was in the grip of a longshoremen's strike, which had been called quite suddenly. The captain informed us that we might have to make our berth elsewhere or sail straight on to England. Aggravation! In the end, he decided to take the ship in himself, a feat of seamanship that he accomplished brilliantly.

We docked at about 6 am, and I was first off, jumping into a taxi and heading to Tiffany's on Fifth Avenue, where I found a stall that sold coffee and sweet rolls. I had 'breakfast at Tiffany's', and sang the hit movie's theme song, 'Moon

River', in honour of the occasion, and then walked down Fifth Avenue, taking everything in. New York, to me, was a symbol of everything that was wonderful in the world of music, from world-class opera to jazz. I had just one day in Manhattan and had planned it well in advance: it was going to be all about music.

It was a brisk March morning, so cold that long coats were everywhere. Yet, the sun was out. As I passed a newsstand, I heard the vendor say in a glorious accent, which I took to be a Bronx one, 'Don't tell me the fuckin' sun's goin' to shine in this fuckin' town today.' I hung around for a moment, hoping to hear more such gems. Sadly, none were forthcoming, so it was back to the city's crowded pavements, at 7 am already alive with people walking faster than anywhere else on Earth.

Onboard, I had memorised a map of Manhattan, and knew exactly where I was headed. My objective was Columbus Circle on the Upper West Side, where Broadway runs up to the Lincoln Center, home of the Metropolitan Opera, New York City Opera, Juilliard School of Music and Avery Fisher Hall. At the Juilliard, a security guard armed with a gun stopped me and asked what I wanted. To my explanation that I was a musician from Australia, and was keen to have a look around, he replied that I didn't sound like an Austrian. This confusion of Austria and Australia would follow me wherever I travelled in the US when I worked there in the early 1980s, and in Europe also.

The guard let me pass, after thoroughly examining my bag and warning me to stay in the obviously public areas. I wandered into a room where an orchestra was rehearsing under conductor Leopold Stokowski, by then in his late eighties, but still totally in charge. In the orchestra, I saw a student I had known from Sydney, the violinist Robert Davidowici. This was an extraordinary surprise and a happy coincidence. He motioned me to stay.

The group was playing a contemporary work: the students looked decidedly detached, as did Stokowski, a conductor renowned for being a master of the theatrical gesture. He stopped the rehearsal and asked, 'Where is the composer of this piece?' One of the students called out that he wasn't there. Stokowski said, 'Well then, neither am I. Rehearsal over.' Applause from the students greeted this decision and they left the room in record time.

Robert and I were thus released, to eat ice-cream at a Howard Johnson's parlour nearby. In those days, its '28 flavors' were sheer novelty for an Australian. For me, a passionate devotee of things sweet, it was like arriving in heaven – a pig's paradise. Robert suggested that I take a tour of Avery Fisher Hall and walked me back there, where I joined a small group about to start its tour. We entered the auditorium in time to hear the New York Philharmonic Orchestra rehearsing the Beethoven Violin Concerto with the great Ukrainian Igor Oistrakh as soloist. The conductor was unknown to me but I could not have cared less. To hear this extraordinary music being made by the hands of a master such as Oistrakh was privilege enough.

From there, it was over to New York City Opera, where an orchestral rehearsal was underway for *Louise*, by Charpentier; then on to Carnegie Hall, ending with a visit to Pedelsen's, the legendary music store across the way, where every piece of music ever published seemed to be available. Like many visitors before and after me, I wanted to move to New York.

Tour over, I strolled the streets, and put my head into St Patrick's Cathedral on Fifth Avenue. A mass was in progress. It sent a cold shiver down my back: I had successfully avoided anything to do with the church since leaving school, but now all the old guilt flooded back. I found myself dipping my fingers into the holy water. How effective was the brainwashing!

I made the ship with about ten minutes to spare and we left New York at 6 pm, sailing into some of the worst weather I've ever experienced. I stayed relatively calm until the second afternoon of the crossing, when I was sitting with the captain's wife in the bar, prior to my evening cocktail spectacular. She said quite calmly, 'We've just reached that part of the ocean where the boat nearly rolled last year. Dimitri was wonderful. We stayed on our side for some time before becoming upright. Don't be worried.'

Sometimes the *Ellenis* pitched so badly that meal services had to be suspended and all other activities halted. We finally docked at Southampton on a miserable, cold, foggy day. I passed through Her Majesty's Customs and headed straight for London.

In Stravinsky's opera *The Rake's Progress*, the principal character, Tom Rakewell, unexpectedly inherits a fortune, and is persuaded by a devilish character called Nick Shadow to follow him to London. In spite of his riches and all that the capital has to offer in the way of wine, women and luxury, Tom is deeply disappointed, and sings an aria 'Vary the song, O London, change!'. He asks himself whether the experience was worth leaving home for. Ah yes, indeed.

I arrived, expecting London to be the cultural Mecca I had long dreamed of, and a place of opportunity, its streets metaphorically paved with gold. Wrong on both counts! The streets, especially in the suburbs, were covered with dog excrement, and London itself was filthy. My introduction to dining there was a Wimpy Bar – fried eggs and baked beans with chips on the side. Meat and salad were out of the question, as they were incredibly expensive. That was the beginning of my love–hate relationship with London, which endures to this day. Yet, please notice the word order there – love comes before hate. The year I arrived, 1970, was the Beethoven bicentennial and, fortunately for me, the British capital went Beethoven-mad. So there were compensations.

I needed a flat and a job, pronto! Through the kind auspices of Kim Williams's family, I had an introduction to a friend of theirs, who generously found me a flat for rent in Golders Green. I took it immediately, for £10 a week. It was a third-floor attic with a sloping roof. I could stand erect in the lounge room and in parts of the kitchen, but the bedroom was a different matter. The bathroom and toilet were on the second floor, and were shared with the landlady, who worked as a club manager at nights. She had a son who attended the local comprehensive high school and with whom I had no contact at all.

It was a strange experience; coming from a gregarious family to this almost complete isolation in West Heath Drive, Golders Green. I was required to pay the rent in advance and leave the money in a rent book on the staircase. The landlady signed the book and replaced it on the staircase. Our paths hardly ever crossed; I think I sighted her about five times in the eighteen months I was there.

My first act in getting a job was to buy a copy of the *Times Educational Supplement*, which, it seemed, contained hundreds of advertisements for jobs all over the world. I surmised – quite correctly, as it turned out – that it would be easier to get a position somewhere in the fairly unstable, economically depressed East End than in a more secure area. A job was advertised for an infants mistress at St Judes School, Mildmay Park. This school, in spite of its name, was not attached to a church, but fell wholly within the jurisdiction of the Inner London Education Authority, and was at the lower end of Islington, bordering the East End.

I rang St Judes and said that I was very interested in applying for the job of infants mistress. There was dead silence at the end of the phone. I could hear the headmaster, a Welshman by the name of Ashley Price, wondering what to ask next. He said, very haltingly, 'You don't sound like a woman.' I replied, 'I'm not.' He seemed to gather courage and then asked me, 'Can you stand up?', to which I replied I could. He then asked me, 'Do you have two heads?' I replied in the negative. He then invited me to the school to meet him and, after a glass of sherry, he offered me the job at £17 a week. I was delighted, and agreed to start almost immediately.

I soon found out why I had been so successful so quickly. The pupils, almost eighty per cent of them immigrants from the Caribbean Islands or Africa, and some from India and Pakistan, were the most wilful children I had ever encountered. They did exactly what they wanted to when they wanted to and could only be disciplined through the most violent verbal outbursts from teachers, accompanied by horrifying threats of partial maiming with blunt weapons. They had decided that teachers were their natural enemies, placed on earth to stop them from having a good time; they interrupted their real lives by wasting time with schooling.

Ashley Price was a modern-day saint! He knew it was a difficult place, but he was also smart enough to know that if we could teach the children to read, especially at kindergarten level, we would have a fighting chance of holding their interest during the day. More importantly, reading would save their lives. He was right. I told him that I thought music could also help.

I could easily write a whole book about my London experience; an episode that saw me come as close to a nervous breakdown as I think I ever have. Every day at 7 am, rain, hail or shine, I had to catch the tube train from Golders Green to Euston, where I changed for Highbury and Islington. If luck was running my way, I would connect with a No. 30 bus bound for Hackney Wick, and arrive at Mildmay Park around 7.45.

Along with my responsibilities as infants mistress, I had class four, the equivalent to grade six back home. They were a group of unbelievably unruly eleven- and twelve-year-olds, plus a few thirteen-year-olds who hadn't made it to high school. They were tough, and for a time they had the upper hand. I was fair game: a foreigner. As one of them pointed on my first day, 'Hey, sir, you speak funny!' Fortunately, I knew enough to keep my mouth shut about that.

Should I stay at St Judes? The question exercised me. After some serious soul searching, I realised two significant things. One, the children were incredibly ignorant and nowhere near class four standard. Two, I could choose to walk away, or solve this problem of their astounding ignorance and find ways to engage with them and hold their interest.

At music camp, we had played a game called mini-Olympics. Teams were chosen, and several sites were established for quoits, catching and passing games, jumping games, hopping games and the like. There was a time limit, and each team was scored on how quickly it finished the course. This seemed a good starting point for my class four.

At St Judes, the only space where we could play this game was on the school roof. Out of sheer desperation one day, I took them up there, and introduced them to the concept of mini-Olympics. It was a major hit: they could all take part and succeed to some degree, and there were opportunities to show different skills; they all had a turn; there was no individual winner. Some teams were good at one thing, while others showed skills in another area; everyone felt good at the end.

This was a turning point in my relations with class four. From then, I could use mini-Olympics as a reward. They had a games period, which was their right and was also a complete shambles. It was a wonder there wasn't an extremely high mortality rate during the so-called soccer or netball games, both of which were given over to wreaking vengeance on each other over tribal wars and skin colour. No work, no games was the rule. They adored mini-Olympics and woe betide the child who caused the cancellation of a game through bad behaviour!

I must say, in total fairness to myself, I never held an individual child responsible for bad behaviour, even though there were clear instances of it everywhere. I kept my eyes sturdily on the main issue: how to turn bad behaviour into positive behaviour without killing their spirit. These kids had so little of interest in their lives generally. If we could make school in any way interesting or enjoyable, we would make a difference to them as individuals, and consequently to all those around them. Punitive measures were a waste of time. These children were always being punished.

Maths classes were torture for all of us. The teaching of simple arithmetical procedures of addition and subtraction, multiplication and division, was nearly impossible. The kids knew they were struggling, and were embarrassed by their lack of ability because they knew they should be able to do this very simple work. Their response was aggressive behaviour and downright refusal to engage.

That I was in the circumstance of having to teach arithmetic was laughable, as my own career as a mathematician had been less than stellar. Slowly, it dawned on me that the learning process had to be disguised so that there would be no shame in not knowing.

By now, I had got the kids to be quiet. One day, I recall saying to them that I was about to do something that I had never done with any class before. That was true. I told them that they were going to be treated to a surprise that I had never shared with any other class. Also true. They were special and needed to be prepared for high school, I told them, and so I was going to introduce them to a challenge only high-school children would normally be given, but for which I judged them ready. The reward for accomplishing this task would be an extra mini-Olympic session on the following Friday.

If they did not succeed, there would be no mini-Olympics at all that week. They were all ears.

I had been in early enough to put examples on the blackboard, which I had covered with a map. I revealed the work and there was dead silence. Did silence mean assent? Silence was better than the usual groaning and moaning that greeted anything to do with numbers. Gone were the numbers. Instead, there was a series of letters containing plus and minus symbols, for example:

1.a+b+c=? 2.d+q+y=? 3. a+a+a – a+a+b=?

This was followed by a key at the bottom of the board that had a=4; b=2; c=9 and so on.

The kids looked at the blackboard and then a boy whose name I will never forget, Geoffrey de Moll, put his hand up and said: 'I ge' i' sir. If "a" is like four and youse add vhe "b" what's two, youse'll get six, ain' i'?' (Which translated as: 'I get it, sir. If "a" is equal to four and you add the "b", which is two, to the four, you get six, don't you?') They were off and racing.

I had found a way, which probably every mathematician in the world would say was jiggery-pokery. However, they were adding up and subtracting because they were motivated to do it. They were required to say what was on board aloud as a class before writing it down, which gave the slow ones a chance to hear the right answers (and some of them were unbelievably slow). They had to call out the substitutes, realising that the values of the letters could change every day, so that "a" wasn't always 4; after calling it out, they wrote it down in perfect silence while I worked on the CIC. The CIC was the Class Improvement Chart, a form of hocus-pocus I had invented, and that appeared to be full of coloured lines and diagrams only I could interpret, and which I reviewed for them on a daily basis.

I would say such things as, 'Now, this line here represents your concentration spans and they are improving – see how it goes up! However, this line here represents the people who are talking too much and not working hard enough – see how that is very irregular.'

They loved to look at this chart and pretend that they could understand its every nuance. I certainly couldn't, and I was the one who had made it up. But it served its purpose, and gradually the classroom changed from a battlefield to a place of work. In one sense, I was conning the hell out of these kids but, in another, I was providing an environment in which they could work and achieve.

Not long after the discovery of algebra (that is, my sort of algebra), we had another breakthrough. Essay writing was nearly impossible because of issues with spelling and reading, so I introduced them to what I called 'our special words'. They wouldn't write essays – they'd write poetry. I would simply put up on the board a series of lines such as:

Mind the doors, mind the doors,
Please don't trip,
Stay on the kerb,
Mind your paws, mind your paws,
Fares please, Mister, thank you, Sir.
Over here, Madam, mind the doors.

They could arrange these lines any way they liked, repeating them as often as they wished and adding ideas of their own. The trick was to order them to do it under speed, so they didn't have time to become bored. I believed that if each of the kids could produce a poem, we would have a collection to start reading together, and we could talk about how to improve them. It was a sneaky exercise in literacy.

The line on the CIC for quantity went off the chart. A few students produced work of quality, but W.H. Auden's reputation was safe. What the special words achieved was that the slow kids had been given a start, while the medium-paced kids had been given a good start and could add some extra ideas. For the smartest – a handful – it was an opportunity to do some seriously impressive work.

One day in the middle of an algebra lesson (it being important to call this algebra and not arithmetic), a child asked me, right out of the blue, 'Hey, sir, d'you go 'ome evr'y nigh'?' (Do you go home every night?) I replied that I did, but what exactly did he mean by home? He told me he meant Australia. I asked the class if they thought I could go home to Australia each night and be back in time for school the next morning. Most of them agreed that if I went by plane, I'd be fine but by boat, no way – end of argument.

Here was another clue, which led to some very basic geography. I decided that geography in its own right wouldn't work but if we approached it from the point of view of 'Where do the world's animals live?', we might get somewhere. My approach was always 'We live in London and these animals we are talking about live here', pointing to the appropriate place on the map.

One of the best discussions we ever had was about kangaroos. At that time there was in the United Kingdom an Australian brand of butter known as Kangaroo, readily available at most supermarkets. One child asked me, with considerable concern, whether the kangaroo jumped around too much while it was making butter, would the butter turn into cream. I was ready to explode into gales of laughter but saw instantly that the class respected this point. I cleared up the mystery of the kangaroo, complimented the child on the question, and drew an extra-special line on the CIC graph just for her, to show how well she had thought about things and that thinking was very important for us all.

The only mystery I didn't clear up was that of my own origin. A staff member told me that one of his class two kids had been overheard telling another child that I was an Aboriginal. At that stage I had a huge Afro hairdo, which was incredibly curly. The colour was peppery white, mixed with red and tinges of grey (which I now refer to as champagne mousse). It was therefore a logical deduction that I must be an albino Aboriginal. That was that!

Meantime, in the infants department, we were waging war on two fronts: reading and the chewing of sweets. The matters were not related, but they were wars nonetheless. The reading war was easy. The school was winning simply by spending as much time as possible with children on a one-to-one basis. We did this because we ran a modified version of the integrated day, where groups of children moved from activity to activity, and from the groups we extracted individuals to teach them to read. Reading tuition went on all day and was essentially one-to-one. The classes only met as a unit for a story at the end of the day, or for assembly in the dining hall.

The war on sweets was tougher. It was simpler for parents to buy sweets for children at a local supermarket than to think about nutritious food for morning snacks. I finally invented a character called Sammy Sore-Gum, whose whole diet was sweets. He lived in a nice house but he didn't eat his fruit and vegetables. I turned this into a type of weekly serial, which gradually grew into a hideous gothic tale of Sammy Sore-Gum's teeth falling out in class, his gums bleeding all over the place, his face going red with pain, and his stomach hurting so badly he couldn't stand up. I always performed it with actions, rolling on the floor in pain and shouting out cries of distress.

Some of the other teachers thought I might be overplaying this a little and possibly inflicting psychological damage on the children. I would have none of it, and followed up this story every week with a question and answer session on Sammy's miserable life. It was remarkable how much they remembered; if I left out a detail – say, in respect to which tooth had gone in any particular week – I'd be corrected immediately. Sweets gradually disappeared from the school, until there was not a single one to be seen. What they did at home was their business, but we did make an impact at school. Gradually, fruit started to appear, along with the occasional sandwich.

Many of the children had school lunches (or school dinners, as they were known) provided, and for some, this was the only substantial meal of the day. A few of the children's meals were paid for by a Good Fairy, whose identity remained unknown even to me. I told them that there was a special arrangement we had with the dinner lady and all I had to do was say, 'Everything all right, Mrs Windsor?', to which the reply was, 'Of course, Mr Gill'.

The midday meal was eaten in silence. This wasn't the most socially endearing way to dine, but at least I knew the food was actually being eaten and not thrown around the room. If they talked they finished up yelling, and the noise was deafening. There were no half measures.

Music was not as immediately appealing to these kids as I thought it might be. Singing was a lost cause, at least in the early stages. The school utilised a BBC radio program of dubious value, which played down to the children and was compered by a fakey jolly-sounding announcer, who had a highly evolved North England accent that would have made Pam Ayres sound like the Queen. He began every program with ''Ello, children', to which some of the boys in my class would say under their breath, but loudly enough for me to hear, ''Ello, shithead'. Enough said.

Yet, music found its rightful place in the weekly hymn practice, for which I took the whole school, infants included. The children loved singing hymns and there was a hierarchy of favourites, which sustained us for an entire hour. Afterwards there was a lingering odour in the school hall not of sanctity, but of three hundred small unwashed bodies.

It was during a hymn-singing episode that I conceived the idea of doing a musical. The obvious choice was *Oliver!*, Lionel Bart's work which had recently been turned into a popular film. I had more than the required supply of Fagins, endless numbers of Bill Sykes, a reasonable choice of Nancys, dozens of Dodgers, and any number of Fagin's gang.

We rehearsed this musical endlessly, having cast most of the lead roles from my class, which was, after all, the senior class. The project started off as simply a few choruses from *Oliver!* but grew daily, as the children demonstrated that they could do more and more, and were keen to do so. In the end, we performed the show in the school gym for three nights, and it was a resounding success with parents and friends.

Every day I used to buy two ham rolls for breakfast from the deli opposite the school, and so had become a familiar face there. On the morning after our premiere, I walked into the deli as usual. The owner greeted me with the news that today I would not need to pay for the rolls. She said she had been at *Oliver!* the previous night, and had never seen anything so beautiful; she couldn't believe children could do such work.

It was the sort of genuine compliment that stays with you forever.

♪

Along with teaching at St Judes, I was supposed to be involved in a course of study, leading ultimately to a doctorate in music. The University of Durham offered an undergraduate degree externally, which meant you could work during the day and complete the required university work after hours. Alternatively, there was a program at the University of London's Goldsmiths College, in south-east London which was led by Australian composer and genuine good guy the late Don Banks. I applied for that course and was interviewed by Don in a wonderfully inspiring way. The entry test was extensive and he conducted his own version of the viva voce as part of it, interspersing chit chat about Australia with such requests as, 'Sing two descending minor thirds' or, right out of the blue, 'Would you please sing an ascending major 7th and then a descending minor 7th?'.

After more small talk, he asked, 'Come over here to the piano. This piece has no accompaniment, only chords. Please improvise an accompaniment from the chord symbols on the top.' Don was a jazzman, and I felt grateful for all the time I had spent writing arrangements for the Mark Fours, and filling in on piano in Jimmy Saunders' dance band.

In the end, I was accepted to both universities and decided to go with Goldsmiths. The travel was considerable to and from, and the course covered lectures, three nights a week, which did not finish until 9 pm. It was disappointing to discover it was work I had done before, and that I was the only one in the group who had done it. To enter a doctorate program, I would have to jump through a series of academic hoops over a protracted period of time. I was beginning to have serious doubts about the value of this enterprise, not in its own right but specifically for me.

I spoke to a lecturer and asked for recent examination papers for the Bachelor degree. I spent a weekend completing them: composing a work in the style of Bach, in this case a three-part fugue; writing songs in the styles of Schubert, Brahms and Rachmaninoff, and so on. There were the usual questions on the history of music, and questions on musical form and analysis, which I was familiar with from my days at the NSW Con, and were easy enough. I took the papers back the following Monday. The lecturer corrected them, and said that were I to sit the examination tomorrow, I would pass easily. That was all I needed. I withdrew from the course, making the decision that I would abandon all attempts to extend my qualifications, and concentrate on practical music-making. And that was that.

To this day, I have no formal qualification in music, apart from the Teaching Certificate issued at the end of my four years of study at the New South Wales Conservatorium and the Sydney Teachers College. I was more interested in gaining practical experience, where possible, than trudging out to Goldsmiths three nights a week.

One of the other teachers at St Judes sang in the choir attached to the New Philharmonia Orchestra, of which Otto Klemperer was chief conductor. My colleague suggested I audition for the choir. When I did, I was accepted and was immediately asked if I could stay for rehearsal that night. Klemperer was to conduct Beethoven's Ninth Symphony, as the finale of the cycle of Beethoven symphonies he was presenting at Festival Hall on Southbank. Would I stay? *Would I?*

Wilhelm Pitz, chorusmaster at the Bayreuth Festival, took the rehearsals, flying in from Munich to London each Tuesday night. This choir had a huge sound, and combined the best of the English choral tradition with the power of an operatic chorus. It was a privilege to sing with them, and incredibly humbling.

The day of the orchestral rehearsal arrived and I caught the tube to the studios at Wimbledon where the orchestra was assembled. Klemperer ran through the last movement, which involved the choir. Once it was finished, the rest of the choir left. I was horrified. How could they not want to stay to watch the rest of the rehearsal?

Here was a conductor who had been a friend of Gustav Mahler, and a major figure in music in both his native Germany and his adopted country, the United States, to which he emigrated after Adolf Hitler's rise to power in 1933. Klemperer's recording of Beethoven's *Eroica* symphony was the first long-playing vinyl recording I ever owned, bought from Ashwood's second-hand record shop in Sydney, for a bit over a quid. I played it to death. Klemperer became a demigod in my musical pantheon, so it was the opportunity of a lifetime to watch this extraordinary man work with his orchestra. He began with the first movement – during which he fell asleep! The leader of the orchestra woke him and asked if they should do the repeat in the first movement. He said in an ancient and weary voice, 'Repeat!'.

The concert was an astonishing experience for me. I had never been involved in such an event before, but now I found myself singing in one of the world's great choirs, under one of the world's greatest conductors, with one of England's great orchestras. I remember that the speeds of each movement were incredibly slow, parts of the last movement being almost un-singable for the choir and the soloists. In his later years, Klemperer's speeds had become slower and slower, and this Beethoven Nine was no exception.

We were scheduled for two performances. On the second night, when we arrived at Festival Hall, we were told that Klemperer was ill and the British conductor Colin Davis would take over. The difference was incredible. The speeds were like lightning in comparison with Klemperer's tempi: Davis must have knocked at least ten minutes off the performance.

After this experience with the New Philharmonia, I knew that my decision to find as many possibilities to make music was the right one. In Golders Green, there was a Roman Catholic Church, St Edward the Confessor. I went to mass one Sunday, and discovered that there was a choir that sang late-Renaissance polyphonic music. The choir's sound was beautiful, and it performed music I had sung or at least known since early childhood. At the end of mass I climbed the stairs to the choir loft and introduced myself to Bruno Turner, who was in charge. He suggested that I come along to a choir practice the following Friday night for a try-out. I counted the minutes until then, was accepted and sang the following Sunday, at the High Mass at 10 am.

This was bliss of the first order. We sang the music of Palestrina, Victoria, Anerio, Lassus, Monteverdi, Byrd, Obrecht, Ockeghem and Schutz, along with Gregorian masses and countless other composers from the period. Easter was a musical paradise on earth, from Holy Thursday right through to Easter Sunday. When the church organised concelebrated masses (a number of priests all saying mass at the same time) the music doubled in volume. The church was awash with incense, bells and fabulous sounds. Between the New Philharmonia Chorus and this choir, I felt that I was living in a truly rarefied atmosphere of glorious music.

Bruno Turner was the founding conductor of Pro Cantione Antiqua, an elite group of singers influential in the revival of Renaissance music in Britain. He brought an advanced knowledge of performance practice to early vocal music. I learned a great deal from this man, who very kindly offered to give me lessons in transcription of ancient manuscripts. In everyday life, Bruno was a highly successful businessman, yet his knowledge in his field of music scholarship was, in my opinion, without peer. It is interesting how so much leading research in the field of early music has come from England, from musicians well and truly outside the academy. It demonstrates to me that knowledge is available everywhere, for those who want to find it.

But back to my own quest for musical knowledge. It does not take an advanced mathematical brain to work out that, after deducting rent and train fares from my weekly pay of £17, I was left with very little to spend on food and music. Music won. I relied for sustenance on school dinners, to which I was entitled, and went crazy with the buying of concert and opera tickets. I made the most of that Beethoven anniversary year, hearing the complete symphonies twice, the complete string quartets, the piano and violin sonatas, the piano and violoncello sonatas, and the complete piano sonatas.

I had my own very special seat at the English National Opera, J26 in the Grand Circle, where, for the price of around six shillings I could see operas I had only ever dreamed of attending. Among them was my first Wagner opera, *Twilight of the Gods*, the last work in the *Ring* cycle. The Australian maestro Charles Mackerras conducted, Rita Hunter sang the role of Brünnhilde, and Alberto Remedios was Siegfried. I was unable to shift my gaze from the stage and the pit, and relished every second. In the intervals I eavesdropped in the foyers, listening to the aficionados debate tempi, dynamics and casting. Six hours passed unusually quickly.

I couldn't get enough opera and went to the theatre after school as often as possible, to stand in line for cheap seats. It was not long before I discovered that a former colleague from the Con, Georgetta Psaros, was a resident mezzo-soprano at the English National Opera. I began working with her, helping her prepare to sing Rosina in *The Barber of Seville*, a role she performed to great critical and public acclaim. I also helped her prepare the roles of Semele (from Handel's opera of the same name) and First Norn in *The Ring.* We worked together as often as possible, becoming good friends in the process. Through Georgetta, I was able to develop skills as a vocal coach, suggest ornamentation to her for the Handel, and build my knowledge of the repertoire generally.

For a young, impoverished aficionado of opera, the ENO was really the place to be in those days. If I went to hear the Royal Opera at Covent Garden, I could only afford tickets to the slips, an area of the theatre that had an extremely limited view of the stage. I sat through one average performance of *La traviata*, and a *Boris Godunov* in which half the advertised cast were ill and replaced by understudies. After that, I gave it away.

♪

The word 'career' was alien to me. I felt that other musicians had careers that made sense, and had direction and purpose: careers as opera singers, orchestral musicians, accompanists, teachers and so on. I seemed to be wandering; if not altogether aimlessly, then, equally, not altogether purposefully. The common thread in all I did was music, and if the music was of a practical nature, I felt more or less content. I still think sometimes, 'What will I do when I grow up?' For me, life unfolds and I don't look for an end. The American poet Robert Frost says it perfectly in his poem *The Road Not Taken.* Like him, I am inclined to go by the route less travelled.

My next opportunity came to me via my brilliant friend and colleague Janet Palmer, who had also studied at the NSW Con, and was working in England as a teacher, simultaneously studying for a higher degree. Her brilliant mind and particularly strong powers of observation would eventually take her to the top, as director of the Royal College of Music. Now Dame Janet Ritterman, she was part of the great 'brain drain' of Australian talent in the sixties and seventies, and a huge loss to her country of birth.

Jan introduced me to Margaret Murray, a musician and composer frequently known as the English Carl Orff. Murray was the translator of Carl Orff's major writings, and the editor and arranger of the English edition of the Orff Schulwerk, the music that had so inspired me as a young teacher. Here again was another example of a non-academic leading the way in music education, in this case effectively responsible for introducing Orff Schulwerk to the English-speaking world.

Murray encouraged me to go to Salzburg, to the Orff school, where there was a course delivered in English. The Special Course, as it was known, was available to teachers who already had some teaching experience, together with at least four years' training. It was intense, with a high number of contact hours; designed to give music educators a comprehensive approach to the philosophies and ideas of Carl Orff. I was interested in Orff's approach, and knew that the program would force me to focus, and to work in ways I hadn't really done before. I applied and was accepted to start in the autumn of 1972.

Meantime, I was slowly going broke, having added travel to the list of my personal indulgences. I was fortunate to have in the UK a friend I had known since school, Neil Slarke.

As youths, we had shared the fate of being budding aesthetes trapped by the Marist Brothers. We had appeared together in a high school production of *A Midsummer Night's Dream*, and Neil had kindly introduced me to his favourite piano repertoire.

Without him, my London experience would have been very different. Neil, who was a complete Anglophile, was teaching at a public school named Wrekin College, in Shropshire, and was well established by the time I turned up. With him, I ventured to Paris, and saw *La Bohème* at the Paris Opera. I followed this with a trip to Ireland, land of my fathers, to visit my Uncle Edward and members of my family whom I had only heard of. These adventures left me practically penniless.

Matters came to a head when my landlady asked me to leave. A visit from some Australian friends who had camped in my modest flat had proved too much for her. Fortunately, my brother Christopher, who worked for an airline, arranged a cheap airfare for me to travel home. I left St Judes amid great sadness, boarded a KLM flight at Heathrow, arrived in Sydney on a Tuesday morning and went straight to a new job. I was fourteen kilos lighter than when I first left Australia, and considerably more confused.

13

Sydney–Salzburg–Sydney

RETURNING HOME WAS A CULTURE SHOCK. SPEAKING generally, I had learned that Australia didn't really figure in the world. It was known for its kangaroos, swimmers and tennis players, if it was known at all. Speaking musically, I was a mess. Where did my future lie – in performance or music education? During my time in London, I had heard some extraordinary musicians from all over the world. The result was a sense of self-realisation, in all honesty, and very uncomfortable. Did I have what it took to be a good musician? I felt doubtful. All I knew for sure was that I wanted to do something connected with singing, especially opera.

I had found a job in the music branch of the state Department of Education, as an instrumental adviser to primary and secondary schools. Living at home with my parents, and working at Blackfriars, I saved money like crazy, with a view to returning to Europe as soon as possible. Yet, as the date of my departure for Salzburg drew near, I began to feel an overwhelming sense of responsibility to my job. In retrospect this was a manifestation of fear; of setting off again into new, unknown territory. When I approached Terence Hunt, the head of the branch, with my doubts, he insisted, to his eternal credit, that I take up my opportunity to study in Salzburg. Such a chance would probably never arise again, he said. So I went, and it was one of the best decisions of my life.

Most old European cities have their charm and elegance but Salzburg, birthplace of Wolfgang Amadeus Mozart, and setting of Rodgers and Hammerstein's *Sound of Music*, is altogether extraordinary, especially for the musically inclined. It makes me understand how some people who visit Jerusalem identify with the Holy City so strongly that they succumb to biblical visions and voices. Every time I return to Salzburg, it captivates me, and I gladly surrender to its power. Its physical beauty is inextricably wrapped up with the persuasive and infectious power of music to change lives, to delight and entertain, and to create cohesive communities.

The Orff Institut is located approximately three kilometres from the centre of the Old City of Salzburg, and within sight of the Untersberg, the Alps on the border of Germany and Austria. All the classrooms on one side of the institute have an unobstructed view of these snow-capped mountains. Behind the institute, the Hellbrunner Allee, a beautiful old avenue shaded by huge oaks, and used by walkers and cyclists, connects the district to the city.

I found a place to stay on the Allee, in a suburb called Morzg, about two kilometres from the centre of Salzburg, and a short walk to the Institut. I rented a small room, which had a sink, an electric element for cooking, a bed, a table and a toilet. I asked about a shower and the landlady told me that the Orff Institut had its own. She had three rules: no sex, no drugs, no parties. It cost me 700 Austrian schillings a month, pretty much what I had budgeted for, and there was a supermarket close by. It couldn't have been better.

The Special Course was everything I had dreamed of. It was highly practical, and incredibly intense: we started each day at 7 am, with some sort of movement training; followed by classes in instrumental ensemble, musical improvisation, conducting, recorder, folk dance, historical dance, piano improvisation, percussion, German language, choir, and movement improvisation.

My classmates were a very mixed group. Americans made up the majority, and among the rest were some Canadians, an African from Ghana, an Egyptian, a Thai and two Australians. Because so many were English speakers, it was easy to keep just associating with them. After a while I faced the fact that the way things were going, I would never speak fluent German, so I sought private lessons with the Institut's German teacher, the glorious Frau Weikersheim. She was a direct descendant of a long line of nobles from Baden-Württemberg, and suffered nobody gladly. She told us constantly how appalled she was at the incredibly low standard of English grammar among us native speakers.

I also befriended a group of Germans who became my regular companions. We ate together at lunchtime, a two-hour break in the middle of the day, and went out together socially. I attended many of their classes, as well as my own. Very soon I was dreaming in German, and becoming more and more fluent.

Pedagogy, philosophy, teaching methods, psychology of teaching, and classroom techniques were all integrated into the practical classes, and were treated as essential components of any lesson. The Institut is a division of the Mozarteum, which is itself attached to the Universität für Musik und darstellende Kunst, Salzburg's university for music and allied arts. Yet, any notion that one would study, say, the philosophy of Orff Schulwerk as a purely academic subject was alien to the Institut's approach. Isolating theory from practice was seen as neither necessary nor particularly desirable.

All the teachers who lectured us had to teach children's classes, which took place in the late afternoon. I needed no encouragement to observe as many of those lessons as I could. We made notes about how a lesson had unfolded, what had happened and why; the notes formed the basis of a later discussion with the lecturer. Because I was already an experienced music teacher, I was permitted to teach and be observed by a lecturer. Students were also encouraged to watch other students at work and participate in group-feedback sessions.

There were conflicts, arguments and factions, which didn't bother me. If anything concerned me, I addressed it immediately. I was there for a limited time, and factions and conflicts held no interest for me. The arguments about Schulwerk raged endlessly, because no one would actually define Schulwerk – least of all the school's muse, Carl Orff himself. His visits to Salzburg were a demonstration of his high level of interest in the students who had come from all over the world to study his approach.

I had the distinct pleasure of playing one of the piano parts in a performance, which he conducted, of his famous cantata, *Carmina Burana*. I was even more pleased when he assessed my own composition as being of a very high order and containing strong, original material, which would challenge and inspire children. It was a little bit like God telling you that you had been good; when Papa Orff said 'Gut', all the world sang!

According to the gossip of many of the German and Austrian students at the Institut, Orff had been a Nazi sympathiser. I doubt whether any of these students had ever read the case studies concerning the denazification of composers and other musicians, or understood anything about the classifications the Americans used to describe artists as 'gray unacceptable' to 'gray acceptable'. Orff's case is officially documented: there is, to this day, debate about where his sympathies lay. It is a matter of fact that he was a soldier in the German Imperial Army during World War I. It is also a matter of fact that the Nazis responded powerfully to the driving rhythms of *Carmina Burana* when it was first performed in 1938. That they acclaimed the work says more about the Nazis than it does about Carl Orff: they were aroused by its incantatory form in the simplest way, failing to understand its intellectual and cultural significance. Yet the Nazis' rise to power squashed plans to introduce his Schulwerk to the German public school system in the early thirties. As Orff wrote, it was:

> a political wave sweeping away all of the ideas which we had realised. Whatever was saved from the wreckage was misunderstood and misinterpreted.

My admiration for the man lies in the fact that he came up with an approach to music education that frees the mind, inspires the heart and soul of the child, encourages questions and explores improvisation. One imagines that the Nazis would have found that type of thinking in complete opposition to their own repressive style of thought and, if they had understood Orff properly, they would have seen him as a potential danger to the party.

I was impressed by the composer's sense of calmness, his obvious ease with the company in which he found himself and his complete mastery of his philosophy of music education. His tall, strong physique gave him an imperious quality, which was enhanced by the presence of his co-author, Gunild Keetman, a pleasant, unobtrusive figure, who nodded assent every time Orff spoke on some musical matter.

I came to realise that none of the faculty members at the Institut was ever going to define Orff Schulwerk in a dogmatic or fixed way, a definition so longed for by most of my colleagues. 'But what is Orff Schulwerk?' asked students on a regular basis. There is nothing wrong with asking questions. What you do with the musical information, once you have an answer to a philosophical question, lies at the very heart of pedagogy, and Orff was not going to be led in this matter in any way.

He explained that Schulwerk is like a garden: you plant some things, they grow, they change and then they die. You plant new plants and watch an altogether different garden evolve. Making music with children should be like this. I loved that approach, and warmed very quickly to his concepts of improvisation and exploration in music education. I also loved his explanations concerning the historical basis of his pedagogical ideas, and that he himself grew up interested in composition.

On the question of the Orff Schulwerk approach we were left to make up our own minds. I soon realised that it was exactly what Orff said it was: an approach that, if you took it at face value, gave children an opportunity to make their own music. At the heart of it lies improvisation, the very thing western art music had lost and had been restored to its rightful place with the advent of jazz.

To Orff, rhythm was fundamental to teaching children music. He had the great insight that children have a much better chance to develop as genuine creative musicians when they are provided with opportunities to sing in an improvisatory way, to dance in an improvisatory way and to play percussion instruments in an improvisatory way. Starting off with something as simple as a child's playground chant or a nursery rhyme or folk song, children learned organically how to make sense of rhythm, then of pitch and harmony.

To me there was no argument with this. It reinforced my theory that no syllabus of any prescriptive nature, no matter how brilliantly structured, can replace the well-trained teacher who, through a thorough understanding of the fundamental ingredients that make up music, can inspire and encourage children to create music in an elementary way, leading to an understanding of how music works. My time at Salzburg confirmed this thinking and it is an approach I still use whenever I am asked to teach in the classroom.

♪

My time in Salzburg lasted only one European academic year, but it was a defining period in my life. It helped me to clarify so many thoughts I had about teaching, especially after my stint in London teaching young children. It was also about making music for its own sake. With the fabulously talented American flautist Mary Louise Poor, I presented a program of twentieth-century flute and piano music, including sonatas by Hindemith and Poulenc; Olivier Messiaen's *Le Merle Noir*; and other works by Bruno Maderna and Niccolò Castiglioni. This was a huge program and, for almost the first time in my life, I really dedicated time to practising.

This period had a lasting impact on my personal life. Friendships were formed that I treasure to this day, not least with Werner and Monika Graf, two born and bred Salzburgers, who showed me great hospitality, becoming like family. I met Werner through an English class I taught. He approached me at the end, and said he had never had a lesson like it. He and Monika loved climbing and walking, and we had some wonderful times together, exploring parts of Austria only they seemed to know.

While I was in Salzburg, Maureen came to visit, and the new friends I had made all thought I should marry her immediately. Why had I not proposed already? they demanded to know. I wondered myself. I was thirty now, and realised that I really needed to stabilise my life in some way. The thought of going to Germany and applying for a position as a repetiteur in an opera house occurred to me, but I hadn't really practised any opera scores and had only had intermittent opportunities to work with singers in Salzburg. My work at the Institut had been all-consuming.

The thought of returning to Australia was depressing in the extreme but, faced with the prospect of running out of money, I needed a job. I knew I could go back to Music Branch, so back I went.

I left Salzburg in June 1972, arriving in Sydney in the grip of winter. But winter, spring, summer or autumn, I would have found my home town dreary, given my state of mind. Once again, I was gripped by culture shock. I am pretty certain that I became a real pain in the arse for my family and colleagues, constantly comparing European culture, which I missed dreadfully, with Australia's shortcomings in that regard.

At least I came to a decision about what I really wanted to do: along with teaching, I wanted to work with singers. I soon resigned from Music Branch, thanking them hugely for all they had done for me. Now, I was without a job.

Then, Rex Hobcroft, the director of the NSW Con, telephoned me, and I went around the same day to see him. He asked me to take some choral rehearsals with the Conservatorium Choir and do some part-time coaching in the Conservatorium Opera School. I started work the following day, thus beginning a ten-year association with this great school of music, from which I had departed ten years earlier as a green high-school teacher.

The work was huge fun, and confirmed my feeling that I had been right to leave my job as an administrator. Not long after I started, I was asked to a meeting with David Rumsey, a very gifted organist, and a colleague from student days who had become the Con's head of academic studies. He asked me if I would be interested in taking classes in aural training and harmony. Doing so increased my pay and, more importantly, was an opportunity to go in a new direction. It involved me in the formation of musicianship, as well as in the practicalities of vocal training. I was starting to gather experience in choral work; vocal coaching of opera, oratorio and song forms such as lieder, art song and French *chanson*; taking classes in the academic area; and was starting to make musical connections between different disciplines within music.

Around this time, I also got my start as a conductor, when the Sydney Youth Orchestra Association asked me to take a rehearsal for someone who was absent. The association had two orchestras at that time. The senior orchestra was conducted initially by Robert Pikler, an extraordinary violist and musician, and then by Peter Seymour, the music master at Sydney Grammar School and the devoted music director of the Sydney Philharmonia Choir. I worked with the second orchestra, known as the Evans Orchestra for the Australian pianist and composer Lindley Evans.

We rehearsed Haydn's Symphony No. 104 in D major. To say that I had a good time was an understatement. This was the first occasion I had conducted a large symphony orchestra other than a school orchestra, where the musical responsibility was to shepherd the players through the music with as little incident as possible. The Evans ensemble had many members who already played very proficiently, so the focus was on real music making, not only correction of notes or allied technical matters.

This experience boosted my confidence that I was able to offer useful musical advice to young players. It also provided me with an opportunity to look at and listen to music from a new perspective. After rehearsing intermittently with the group for a period, I was offered a permanent conducting engagement with the orchestra, which required me to attend rehearsals every Saturday afternoon and prepare repertoire for concerts. Gradually, it seemed, I was creating a life in music in Australia.

For all my grumbling about Australian culture, 1973 was not a bad year to be in Sydney, for it was when the Opera House was finally opened. The debates over this building – which ranged from 'Why do we need an opera house when we need more roads?', to this charming comment made by a well-known Sydneysider: 'Who wants an opera house anyway; only a few poofters and a few Jews!' – continued long and loud through the building's sixteen-year gestation. When the Australian Opera finally launched its inaugural season there, they did so with Prokofiev's *War and Peace*. How apt! But the first two operatic performances in the Opera Theatre were actually works by Australians. I vividly recall attending performances of these 'try-outs', which were staged two months before the official season, and conducted by Rex Hobcroft: Larry Sitsky's *Fall of the House of Usher* and James Penberthy's *Dalgerie*.

The people of New South Wales should have been proud. Instead, the fear of spending money on what was perceived to be elitist rubbish permeated the community, and created a hostility, unprecedented in my experience, towards the arts in general and opera in particular. There was a fear of culture, a fear of the unknown and a general feeling that the nation didn't need such a building. At the same time, there were groups with very open agendas, jockeying for position and very keen to have a say in how the building should be used. The politics of culture in this country could do your head in, if you were young and still trying to work out what part you could play in artistic life.

My sanity valve was Maureen, who – against the advice of my mother, and probably hers also – had agreed to marry me. We wed on 10 May 1973, at St Martha's Roman Catholic Church, Strathfield, in a service in some ways more like a concert than a religious ceremony. It was followed by a reception at the local town hall that was something between a well-organised bacchanal and a bush dance. Some (perhaps not all) of the participants described it as the funniest nuptials they had ever attended, more like a really good spontaneous party than a wedding.

I didn't drive and, indeed, still don't. I believe that the road does not need me, a volatile, short-sighted, control freak given to speeding and to yelling abuse at anyone who impedes my progress. Nevertheless, I was determined to drive away from the reception. By constantly turning left, we finally arrived at the Strathfield Travelodge Motel. Being an incurable romantic I had spared no expense in choosing the Travelodge over all other lodging in the district.

Maureen and I changed the life of the member of the housekeeping staff of that worthy establishment, who brought our breakfast in next morning, unannounced, while we were jumping up and down, naked, on the double bed, in an attempt to count how many people we could see on the nearby Strathfield railway station. That is probably a good place to stop.

Without Maureen's contribution to my life, a contribution that has been, in every way, greater than anyone else's, I simply would not be doing what I am doing today, or have come within cooee of achieving anything at all. I daresay that, by now, I would have been installed in some home for the bewildered, being treated for all sorts of neuroses and disorders.

She is an extraordinary woman, adored by her children and grandchildren, loved by her friends, feared by builders, electricians and handymen. She continues to support me and my work, for which my gratitude can never be sufficiently well expressed. I know of no other human being who would have done what she has done and tolerated what she has tolerated. I am truly the most blessed person on Earth, especially when I'm not snoring.

♪

A POSITION DESIGNATED AS LECTURER IN MUSIC WAS advertised at the Con, and I was encouraged to apply. The job description more or less matched what I had been doing, but the rumour mill – in the arts always an active, imaginative and tireless machine – was working overtime with the idea that the Con was going to convert all its courses to degrees, and that jobs as lecturers and senior lecturers would become available as a result of this move. I was concerned that my obvious lack of high academic qualifications would count against me. I put no store in the fact that I was called to an interview, a solemn business with searching questions, which left me feeling well tested.

My appointment meant that I became a salaried staff member with the title of lecturer, responsible for academic subjects such as harmony, aural training and history, along with practical subjects such as choir and vocal coaching. I was also entrusted with the Conservatorium Singers, an ensemble formed by Charles Colman, who had had a major impact on the Australian music scene with his choral group the Leonine Consort. I was stepping into very big shoes indeed.

The Con Singers became central to the musical life of the institution, providing opportunities for young singers to gain experience in solo roles in an environment that was essentially friendly and protective. I believed that the group was exactly what a tertiary institution should provide in the way of pre-professional training for aspiring vocal soloists.

It also provided an opportunity to identify students whose voices had operatic potential, but who had chosen a different musical path. Often these students had been warned off studying music for its own sake ('who'll pay you to sing?'), and diverted into courses, such as teacher education, that more or less guaranteed a job. I know of at least two of them who were 'discovered' in the Con Singers and went on to have careers in opera here and abroad.

I had already had the disappointing realisation that, for an institution for the performing arts, there were an awful lot of non-starters among the student ranks. Once the Bachelor's degree was introduced, the concept of obtaining a degree in music became central to the mindset of some music students, and seemed to overtake music itself. It was always a shock to me that I had to coerce students into attending concerts, even threatening them with failure if they didn't attend the concerts I was conducting at the Con.

I spent many a long hour in classes banging on about concerts, operas, ballets, chamber music and so on, in an effort to encourage students to go and listen to live music. It was very dispiriting to find out that most students had little, or even no, idea what was being played by the Sydney Symphony Orchestra in any given week, or which operas, ballets or chamber music concerts were being performed. It galled me even more when students complained that concerts were too expensive. If they would not take advantage of the generous discounts offered to young audiences, when would they ever experience the music they said they loved?

When the head of opera, Ronal Jackson, decided that the Con should stage Bizet's *Carmen*, to commemorate the opera's centenary in 1975, it fell to me to muster the chorus. The work requires a big chorus – at least fifty voices – so I press-ganged and finally beat into submission a quorum, formed mainly from the education students but with a smattering of voice students. It turned out to be one of the stars of the show.

Georg Tintner, guest conductor with the Australian Opera, was engaged for our production. He wanted to do a special edition of *Carmen* that contained much more of Bizet's original music. I had to organise and prepare dozens of copies of the material for the soloists and the chorus. In those pre-digital days, that meant hundreds of hours of drudgery, standing at a photocopier, but I didn't really mind. I was inspired by Tintner's approach and loved the way he worked. He conducted everything from memory, and was fanatically specific about the way a passage should be played, almost as if he had had a direct revelation from the composer. He insisted on every detail in the score being faithfully realised, and gave explanations as to why it should be so.

Tintner was one of those remarkable European Jews who, fleeing from Nazism, ended up in the Antipodes and stayed, making an outstanding contribution in their new countries. He was a highly evolved eccentric: a vegan, who rode a bicycle to and from the Opera House, and lived and breathed music. His knowledge of the Austrian composer Anton Bruckner was without parallel and he spoke of this composer as if he had a direct line to Bruckner's grave. That sometimes drove musicians mad, especially the Bruckner haters, but I loved the fact that this eccentric man found time away from his work to talk to me about music. He didn't have to do it.

Stephen Hall, a director associated with the AO, had also been engaged for the production, but he withdrew after a short period of time for reasons that weren't at all clear to me. Ron Jackson, who was passionate about the project, stepped into the role. It was a budget production. The set was cobbled together. The costumes were gathered from existing wardrobe stock that had been lying around in trunks for ages, supplemented by whatever the performers could find at home. The result was that the cast really looked like a bunch of dishevelled gypsies. Perhaps there was a specified designer for costumes, set or lighting but, if so, I can't remember this.

For me, the most important things were happening under Tintner's direction. I was captivated by this man and by the music he was able to conjure from the Con's pit. His knowledge of the score was remarkable and he had earned the respect of all the student orchestral players involved, not to mention the singers. They were well served by Verbrugghen Hall, the Con's main auditorium, which was a wonderful theatre for sound. The pit was a series of descending levels, based, in a way, on the Bayreuth model of Wagner's pit; the orchestra's sound was always warm and well balanced with the stage.

The reviews came out, and it is a matter of public record that the production was savaged at every level by the *Sydney Morning Herald*'s Fred Blanks, who wrote his piece in the manner of a Superman commentary – 'Is it an opera? Is it a show? Is it Superman in the pit?' and so on. This critique seemed to us to be very harsh. It devastated the cast, orchestra and crew. Despite it, the show eventually sold out. Here was a lesson for all of us in dealing with the press: a review was one person's opinion and not necessarily a universal truth.

It wasn't the first time one of the Con's productions was savaged by the *Herald*'s reviewers. Roger Covell, the paper's chief music critic, had completely trashed a concert by the Con Singers that I had conducted. We had presented a program of music for Holy Week, concentrating on the music of Tomás Luis de Victoria, a Spanish Jesuit of the late Renaissance, who wrote sparsely, intensely and passionately, in stark contrast to German Protestant music of the time. The concert was very well attended, the choir sang extremely well, and the music was well received. Colleagues whose opinions I greatly respected were effusive. Moreover, I knew enough about music by then to know when a good performance was given and when it wasn't.

In the performance of music, one is rarely if ever satisfied. Valid criticism has a role to play in explaining why. But when a reviewer attacks a performance from a wholly subjective point of view, or uses their review to push their own agenda, then the quality of their criticism is greatly diminished; perhaps their criticism is even rendered utterly useless. I was to be subjected time and time again to that type of review while I was at the Con. The cumulative effect of this sort of commentary on my work was to toughen me up, and teach me how to suffer outrageous slings and arrows.

MOST OF THE TIME, MUSIC MAKING WAS A LOT OF FUN. I was asked to teach Jonathan Mills, who would go on to have a distinguished career as artistic director of the Edinburgh Festival. It was Elaine Mills, Jonathan's mother, who had hunted me down as a potential teacher for her young son. She was like a whaling boat that wasn't going back to shore without a catch – and she succeeded in harpooning me. I wasn't the least bit interested in teaching anyone on a one-to-one basis, but Elaine, a cross between Captain Ahab and Electra when it came to determination, finally persuaded me to at least listen to him play the piano and determine if he had any gifts as a composer.

Jonathan played very well for an eleven-year-old, but improvised even better. I prepared him for piano exams even though I was not, strictly speaking, a piano teacher. The more significant work we did was in composition. There was no doubting his remarkable ability to improvise in given styles, especially classical ones such as sonatas, rondos and sonatinas. This talent was coupled with a highly refined sense of taste, structure and balance that was altogether remarkable in such a young student.

I often forgot to turn up for Jonathan's lessons, simply because they were the last thing on my crowded mind. Finally, Maureen said that she would kill me if I forgot one more time. It was not an idle threat. Jonathan remained my student for about six years, and then entered Sydney University, where he continued his studies with Peter Sculthorpe. I still work with him on his projects and give him what he refers to as 'music lessons'. (Now that he is an international celebrity, I must remember to put up my fees!)

Jonathan's father, the gifted surgeon Frank Mills, was part of a coterie of enlightened Sydney doctors and businessmen who adored fine wine and good food, led by the 'King of Wine', Len Evans. Mills had interests in a winery in the Hunter Valley that was then known as the Rothbury Vineyards, and had been founded by Evans and the winemaker Murray Tyrrell. My wife and I were invited to a lunch at Rothbury, and saw its famous Cask Hall. As soon as I laid eyes on it, I knew that this was a potential venue for performances.

The main feature of this beautifully built hall was the large oak casks stored on elevated racks that ran along the walls. Tables seating twelve or so were arranged in rows down the sides of the room, under the casks, leaving an aisle in the centre and a space at the top of the hall where an improvised stage (inevitably made from wine pallets) could be constructed. This 'stage' accommodated about twenty performers, and was supplemented by a balcony suitable for musicians. With its tiled terracotta floor and friendly gloom, the atmosphere was that of an old baronial hall. Once the tables had been set, the white tablecloths sparkling with silver and glassware, the place looked magnificent.

That was how the Rothbury operas began, in 1975. Our first show was Purcell's *Dido and Aeneas*, performed by the Con Singers with accompaniment from a small chamber orchestra, including harpsichord. The director was David Russell, then choirmaster at St Mary's Cathedral, Sydney. His intense interest in the liturgy, coupled with his outstanding knowledge of Renaissance polyphony and his consummate skills as a choral conductor, had raised St Mary's music to new heights, but he was also a passionate opera lover and a very good stage director.

At wine auctions and specially arranged dinners we performed John Gay's *The Beggar's Opera*; Gilbert and Sullivan's *Trial by Jury*, *HMS Pinafore* and *The Pirates of Penzance*; Ibert's comic opera *Angélique*; and even Rodgers and Hammerstein's *Oklahoma!*. With minimal lighting, and the shortest rehearsal periods known to mankind, these productions played to packed houses, which roared their approval. Each evening ended with the Con Singers serenading the guests' tables with a selection of madrigals, rounds and glees, which became looser in interpretation as the night wore on. These evenings of wine, food and song were not merely hugely enjoyable: for the Con Singers, they were a source of revenue to assist us to do other work of a completely different nature, such as baroque performances of the *St John Passion* of J.S. Bach, and Handel's *Messiah*.

Then there was my teaching work. In addition to my existing responsibilities, I was engaged by the School of Education, which had left the Sydney Teachers College and was now fully established at the Con, to teach kindergarten and primary classes at Camperdown Demonstration School each Monday morning. The school was run by a genuinely enlightened head, Eve Levis, who had around her an equally enlightened staff. I loved this demonstration teaching because it kept me in contact with children in the classroom situation. It was useful to me in helping mount the case for a particular way of teaching, a matter that would eventually lead to a series of fierce philosophical battles and disturbing pedagogical warfare at the Con.

In the meantime, I was approached by the head of music at the Australian Broadcasting Commission, to see if I would be interested in auditioning with the Sydney Symphony Orchestra. (In those days, the state symphony orchestras were all part of the ABC.) It was one of those appointments one looks back on and wonders how it ever came about. I had done some rehearsal work with the ABC Training Orchestra, during which – unbeknown to me – I had been observed by someone from the concerts department.

They asked me to submit a repertoire, from which they would choose a work for the audition. I was also to prepare a concerto for piano and orchestra, the dramatic but parodic *Variations on a Nursery Theme* by Dohnányi. There would also be some sight-reading, which I would be given on the day.

How I passed that audition is beyond me! I can only think that the players were sympathetic towards me, or feeling generous on the day. It was a completely terrifying experience, burned unforgettably in my memory. The work I was asked to present was the first movement of the Bartok Concerto for Orchestra. I stood on the podium, looked across at the double basses and cellos, lifted my arms to give a down-beat, gave the down-beat – and nothing happened. I had no idea why. In the space of several milliseconds I decided that I couldn't stop, I had to go on, so I moved to the second beat.

Just as I did, I heard the first note of the Bartok coming from the section. The music started to unfold. This score requires accelerated playing quite soon after the opening; as I tried to move the orchestra by beating bigger, the music sounded slower, so I started to beat smaller and the music accelerated. I was not only in at the deep end, I was trying to surf giant waves. I felt I had no business being there at all, doubtless a sentiment shared by some of the players.

The Bartok ended and the piano was put in place for the concerto. Again, I was trying to ensure that what I was beating was clear to both the soloist, the gifted pianist Elizabeth Powell, and the orchestra. The concerto ended and there was a slight break in proceedings while the piano was wheeled off, during which one of the players came up to me and said, 'Don't use your left hand too much'. The sight-reading for orchestra came and went without incident. I left the Opera House and went home, knowing I had done a frightful job and was a miserable failure.

Players who had known I was up for this audition had given me all sorts of advice, much of it conflicting. 'Don't, whatever you do, talk too much to the orchestra, and in fact, try to say nothing at all if possible.' 'Make sure you say things very clearly and explain exactly what you want.' 'Just run the pieces through once and then say at the end that they need to watch the intonation or the rhythm, and then let them go.' No wonder I was confused.

Sometime after the audition I received an official communication from the ABC, saying that I had passed and was classified as suitable for schools concerts. I was given a D classification as a local conductor and informed I would be paid a fee of $75 per concert. I had left this audition convinced that I would never stand up in front of an orchestra again. To find that I had actually passed, albeit barely, was more than a shock: it was, in some ways, just as unnerving as the audition itself. I had been offered a real opportunity. Now, I had to do something about it.

Soon after, at Newcastle, I conducted my first schools concert, with the SSO. Whether it was the beginning of some sort of new career was not clear in my mind. Was I, indeed, a conductor? I was well aware that I had received no formal training in this most complex and complicated of musical callings. The audition had sown fresh seeds of doubt. As I privately pondered the issue, I soon discovered there were others only too keen to share my misgivings.

14

Conducting Unbecoming

IT WAS CLEAR TO ME, WITHIN A COUPLE OF YEARS OF my arrival at the Con, that I was not everyone's cup of tea. Many of my colleagues appeared to resent the hours I put in, and to feel that it wasn't necessary for me to work so hard or to make such an intense commitment. I believed in students learning by making music, and thought – not unreasonably, in my view – that the Con was probably the best place to do that. Some staff saw it differently. They believed that making music was not the only reason for being at the Con, and suggested that I was deflecting the students' attention away from other work. I was criticised sharply for scheduling public performances in examination weeks and also for putting on more concerts than just the obligatory annual choral event.

My response was that the students had known about the examination week from day one of semester, so it couldn't have been a surprise. It was more important to me that the students cover as much repertoire as they could. The approach I took was to teach as much as possible about the music from the music itself. That this appealed to them was reflected in growing support for my projects from the student body, which seemed well aware that I had their best interests at heart and was trying to enrich their lives musically.

Inevitably, matters came to a head. The catalyst, oddly enough, was a difference of opinion over the best way to teach pitch. The ability to read and write music can be taught relatively easily, and is something all classically trained professional musicians need to learn. The question was, how was it best taught?

In *The Sound of Music*, when Maria sings to the Von Trapp children 'Doh, a deer', she is using a system for teaching them pitch that is known as moveable doh, or Tonic Sol-fa. It establishes a relationship between intervals that is consistent. Doh, the tonic or key-note, establishes the key. It can be any note. Once the key is set, the intervals can be sung without music, using the sol-fa.

This relative system of pitch was invented by a Victorian Englishwoman, Sarah Anna Glover, and developed to a great extent by her follower John Curwen. The system was embraced by the Hungarian composer Zoltan Kodaly, an influential choral educator, and has had a powerful effect on music education worldwide. It is an extremely useful tool for teaching music and has attracted dedicated and devout followers. At the Con, I wasn't one of them. I believed that tertiary students should be able to cope with fixed, not moveable, pitch; by which I mean they should know the absolute names of the pitch and how to apply it to all forms of music.

In the fixed-doh system, doh is always C, re is D, mi is E, and so on. It's an absolute system that requires a systematic understanding of intervals (especially the smallest intervals, the semitone or half tone). Its advantage is that it enables very precise singing. I led a charge for fixed pitch and, once more, the students followed. Many of them found these classes so helpful that they asked for extra ones, which I gladly provided. The Con was soon divided between fixed and moveable doh.

As previously noted, the students fell into two groups: those studying to become educators (the larger cohort), and those focused on performance. As the battle over fixed doh wore on, a lecturer was brought from Hungary to teach the aural subject to the education students, and also to run the Big Choir, which mainly comprised these students.

I was ostracised by some of my colleagues, and asked to appear before the Conservatorium's academic committee to justify my teaching methods. It was one of the most humiliating episodes of my life: I felt I was on trial for having an idea. One would have thought I was attempting to teach something dangerous!

Looking back, I can see the fault was not all my opponents'. My biggest mistake was that I had adopted the attitude of a crusader, and would brook no resistance. I was behaving as stupidly as they were. So committed to this approach was I, that I couldn't see the wood for the trees. That was an error.

My trouble with the academic committee did not end there. I was asked by the school of education if I would take a subject called choral studies, which was a flash-sounding name for a singing class. So I taught the education students a classroom method of rounds and songs, and gave them suitable repertoire. Again, I was hauled up before the committee, after I corrected a student over a definition of something in music known as binary form. It was my view that a third-year music education student should be equipped to give a more profound explanation than the simple definition of two different tunes, appearing one after the other. The committee took exception. They thought that I had, by implication, criticised another lecturer.

It was becoming clear to me that to present a view different from the party line or accepted thinking put others offside and significantly imperilled one's progress. Obviously I was regarded as a troublemaker who should be dealt with.

By then I had received an invitation to teach at the Orff Institut's annual summer school, held in Salzburg each July, during the Conservatorium's mid-year break. I gladly accepted, returning to the Institut over several Northern summers. The experience opened up a new world to me. It not only led to international contacts, but freed me from the restraints associated with the limited thinking I found at the Con.

In April 1982, I received an invitation from the American Orff Schulwerk Association (AOSA), a powerful organisation of music educators wedded to the propagation of Orff's ideas. I was asked to be the principal presenter at their annual conference in Portland, Oregon, in November that year. I would be required to present a series of workshops around a theme of my choosing, which would demonstrate aspects of Orff's approach to music education.

AOSA is a gigantic organisation: all over America there are chapters consisting of elementary and, sometimes, secondary school teachers. The enthusiasm, energy, knowhow and dedication to music education expressed by this group was without parallel in my experience. In Australia we have enthusiastic teachers but, on an organisational scale, I had never experienced anything like this.

Nevertheless, among many of these teachers there was a view of Orff Schulwerk's pedagogy that seemed to me too narrow and misleading. I thought it actually frightened people away, dictating as it did the ways in which an arrangement of music could be made for specialised instruments: xylophones, glockenspiels, metallophones and masses of ancillary percussion instruments. When I presented my first session I dived in at the deep end and invited the group to think about the Schulwerk in a less contrived way. Throughout my sessions, I heard such comments from teachers as, 'You mean that my idea is OK?', or 'Are you really going to use that?'.

I was giving them new focus, opening new windows and admitting ideas that initially seemed extreme, and beyond the experience many participants. However, the Americans embraced this approach wholeheartedly, and soon I was receiving invitations to teach workshops all over the United States and Canada.

I travelled from November to January with my family, giving workshops and classes that had been planned prior to my visit. Once I had convinced the teachers I met that my ideas were indeed acceptable within the Orff Schulwerk philosophy, it was not hard to persuade them to try them in their own classrooms. I knew from the mail I received, and from the comments in the journals and newsletters produced by each chapter, that I had made an impression on these people, who were willing to try my ideas and judge after that.

How refreshing! I fell in love with the USA; not only with the warmth and generosity of the people I encountered, but their openness, frankness and willingness to explore and take risks.

♪

Not all of my Australian colleagues were unsupportive. One year, while I was away in Salzburg, I received a phone call from a real friend at the Con, Geoff Bailey, a trombonist, great teacher and all-round good guy. He alerted me to the Con's advertisement for a senior lecturer in opera, which entailed being a repetiteur, or vocal coach. I applied, and was promoted to the job, and my appointment killed two birds with one stone. It pleased my supporters in the opera department, who well understood the complexities of teaching singing. It also removed me from delivering syllabus to the education students. (This was not, however, the end of my contact with some of them. At their request, we formed a special chamber choir.)

It was made very clear to me by members of the senior administration that they did not perceive me to be a conductor – especially in my new role. I was directed not to rehearse with the Conservatorium Orchestra, or to recruit orchestral players for any operatic activity I might choose to undertake within the opera school. My job, I was told, was as a repetiteur/accompanist, working exclusively with opera students and helping them to learn their operatic roles. I chose to ignore what they told me.

I was politically naive, gung-ho, independent and, I dare say, a huge pain in the arse to many people. Frankly, I resented the fact that lesser conducting talents were brought in to do operas about which they had not a clue. I learned nothing from them and resented the fact that I had to prepare singers for them.

I set about organising performances of Humperdinck's *Hansel and Gretel*, Flotow's *Martha* and Puccini's *La Bohème*, all with full orchestra and fully staged. I conducted the orchestra, and coached the singers. The students loved playing the operas, hearing the stories, and learning how the music underpinned and enhanced the drama. They played with incredible commitment and concentration.

Once, during a stage and orchestra rehearsal for *La Bohème*, I experienced a moment that will stay with me forever. We came to the point in the third act at which Mimi and Rodolfo agree to part: the singing of lyric soprano Kerry O'Connor was so poignant that most of the orchestra gave way to emotion. There was sobbing from some of the violins, who had a good view of the stage, and could see and hear Kerry sing this glorious music so passionately and with such control.

I found it very moving to watch these young men and women respond so unashamedly and so openly to music. It also served as an excellent demonstration of the fact that our job as musicians immersed so wholeheartedly in a performance is not to cry but to make others cry. We may cry on the inside but we must never betray our emotions publicly while in the business of moving an audience. This is the fine line between professional detachment and complete involvement.

When the reviews for this *Bohème* came out, Roger Covell savaged the production, criticising the string playing particularly. The orchestra had some of the best string players in the Con at the time, many of whom are now in the Sydney Symphony Orchestra or playing professionally in orchestras elsewhere. They were devastated by this report. John Painter, the Con's deputy director, wrote a very special note of congratulations to the orchestra, which was placed on the door to the pit. It was rare for John to be complimentary to such a high degree and the students knew this.

I was well aware that the review was directed towards me. Covell had given me brilliant press while I was still teaching at Marsden High, particularly in a review of a new music concert in 1969, hosted by the International Society for Contemporary Music and mainly featuring music composed by my students. I believe that in his mind, I was a teacher and nothing more.

Interestingly, Covell's own conducting performances at the University of New South Wales, where he lectured, were reviewed glowingly by his colleagues at the *Sydney Morning Herald*. I witnessed some of those performances and will say only that I could not concur with those opinions.

Along with the operas mentioned previously, the opera school, in a genuine stroke of brilliance, invited the celebrated English opera director Anthony Besch to direct a double bill of Stravinsky's *Oedipus Rex* and Ibert's *Angélique*. Robert Pikler, the violist and conductor, was to conduct the Stravinsky with the Con Orchestra, and I was to conduct the Ibert with the ABC Training Orchestra.

My other task was to find sixty men who would be keen to take part in the Stravinsky as the male chorus, when it was one of the most difficult of all choral operas in the repertoire.

I was able to persuade a large cohort of Con students to participate, and they scored a major success with their singing, which was acknowledged critically and publicly.

I learned a lot about the clarity of a good director's vision from watching Besch. At Oxford, he had studied English, but he determinedly made his mark in music theatre and opera, his big break coming when he was appointed assistant general manager at Glyndebourne in the early fifties. He was a tyrant in the best sense of the word, demanding perfection from day one of rehearsal, and pouting or shouting when he didn't immediately get what he wanted.

Watching him rehearse the comedy in the Ibert opera was truly instructive. Every joke was very carefully constructed to the last detail and if a performer felt that he or she would like to change it a little, Besch would be apoplectic with rage. 'Do it the way I showed you,' he would yell fiercely. 'That's funny. What you are doing isn't funny.' He was correct every time. We had in the cast of this opera a group of singers who felt that they had real comic timing. Besch proved them wrong time and time again.

I often look at young directors as they struggle their way through a piece of work and wonder what Besch would have made of them. His motto was that the music tells you what to do. Working with this man was a valuable experience in every way, but he spared nobody. I was conducting a stage and orchestra rehearsal of *Angélique* when I felt him creep up behind me and hiss: 'Last night this tempo was perfect, but today it is a bit slow. Move it like last night.' The venom in the invective was palpable. I rounded on him, and said very loudly, 'I'm not a computer.' The orchestra approved and nothing more was said, but it was a reminder that this director felt a commitment to every detail of the work.

♪

By this time, Maureen and I had two young children. Given my work commitments, I left the lion's share of their care to her. That was really unfair of me, but I was completely driven by music. I did not have a real work–life balance (as they say), and I know I sacrificed time with my own children as a result – a circumstance I regret and am anxious to avoid repeating in relation to my grandchildren. Any other woman would have asked me to leave, but Maureen seemed to understand my need to achieve and always to be busy. It was a crazy time.

Over at the Sydney Youth Orchestra, I had been put in charge of the senior orchestra. Our concert programming was becoming decidedly more adventurous, including symphonic works by Richard Strauss, Sibelius, Brahms, Wagner, Dvořák and Tchaikovsky, among others. The repertoire also included concertos for young soloists and some new music especially commissioned by the Youth Orchestra Association.

My Saturdays were now very full, especially as I involved the SYO in a novel program of weekend concerts for very young children and their parents and grandparents, known as the Babies Proms. These concerts had grown out of something I'd seen: Dean Dixon, erstwhile chief conductor of the Sydney Symphony Orchestra, inviting a group of kids to a rehearsal and letting them wander among the orchestra to observe the players at work. It planted a seed, and I convinced the Opera House and the Youth Orchestra Association to introduce interactive children's concerts.

They were an enduring success. In Sydney, they have been in operation for well over thirty years, and have been replicated all over the country. It is to the eternal credit of the Opera House leadership that the idea was fostered and has continued to this day. The concerts I conceived and conducted were full of opportunities for singing and dancing to the orchestra's accompaniment. The children were also invited to have a go at playing real orchestral instruments. But the music was treated seriously: I didn't dumb down musical examples, or trivialise the work of the musicians.

It may seem counter-intuitive, but serious orchestral players see the value of this approach at once and realise their power in informing parents of the efficacy of music. The children need no persuading: they are engaged wholeheartedly from the moment they enter the hall. The parents, on the other hand, are the ones who will make decisions about the role of music in the lives of their children. It is imperative that they hear and see the music presented in the best circumstances possible.

It was with respect to parents, their children and the music played in the home that a recording project evolved that was initiated by a great friend and colleague, the late and deeply missed Clare Scott-Mitchell, a lecturer in early childhood literature at the then Sydney Kindergarten Teachers' Training College. She approached me, with her friend and colleague Rod Bowie, lecturer in drama at the same college, asking if I would arrange some traditional nursery rhymes for voices and instruments for a recording. The point was to demonstrate as much variety in the sounds as possible, while keeping the playing time of each example well under two minutes to accommodate the concentration span of a young child.

From this discussion two albums emerged, *Three Bags Full* and *Have You Any Wool?* I arranged the rhymes for a string quartet, a woodwind quartet, and a group of Orff instruments, including a spoken chorus and vocal solos. Later on, I published some of the arrangements with the illustrious firm of Schott Music Germany, Carl Orff's own publishers. I still receive a royalty cheque each year. The amount of money does not run to the cost of a good bottle of wine – but it is enough to afford a more economically priced high-class wine of the most recent vintage!

The Sydney Youth Orchestra was flourishing and, in my view, playing well. An invitation from the Singapore Youth Orchestra to undertake a ten-day tour, in January 1980, could hardly be refused. We played a very fine concert at the Australian High Commission, which included the overture to *Hansel and Gretel*; Bruch's Concerto for Violin No. 1, with the orchestra's leader, Thomas Jones, as soloist; and Sibelius's First Symphony, albeit without harp.

It was a euphoric experience for the young players, and the euphoria remained with them as we played more repertoire at other venues, including the International School and Singaporean high schools. Our soloists were two brilliant young pianists, Corey McVicar and Michael Harvey (now better known as Michael Kieran Harvey).

We returned home to a season that I anticipated would, in essence, be no different from any other: more repertoire, more concerts, and plans to celebrate the tenth anniversary of the Sydney Youth Orchestra Association. I was soon made aware that Sir Charles Mackerras had been invited to conduct Mahler's Third Symphony, and that I was to prepare it for him. I was also asked if I might prepare something to open the concert. Who was I to argue with the choice of Mackerras? Nevertheless, I was surprised and upset that this plan was presented to me as a fait accompli.

After ten years of hard work with the SYO I sensed, not unreasonably, that my days with that organisation were coming to an end. I also sensed, and this instinct proved to be correct, that members of the SYO's board were unhappy with me, for some unknown reason. When I spoke to Tim O'Leary, the chairman, he confirmed it. I had previously been told by a number of SYO staff that my lack of experience as a string player would hold me back as a conductor. Now those views were coming home to roost.

I asked the chairman why, if the board had been unhappy, he had waited so long to speak about it. He agreed that was probably unfair. I could immediately think of instances in which aspiring conductors, musical directors and singers had been sent away for further specialist study, at the behest of the organisation with which they were associated. I should be so lucky! I was desperate to learn, desperate to study with someone and desperate to be shown things, but apparently that was not an option.

Not long afterwards, I was rehearsing the Bartók's *Concerto for Orchestra* when Sir Charles came to hear the orchestra. He said, 'Many, many congratulations', then left to conduct a performance of *Tristan und Isolde*. The writing was on the wall for me. I felt that, in the eyes of the board,

I had been weighed in the balance and found wanting. The following Monday, the association's music director, Joy Lee, came to a class I was teaching, to let me know my services would no longer be required. I told her that I had resigned the Saturday before.

There were seemingly endless meetings with concerned parents and orchestral members. I found out very quickly that I had next to no friends within the association at the administrative level, which was a terrible surprise. Apparently, my shortcomings as a conductor had been highlighted in great detail at the organisation's meetings; yet, at no stage were any of these alleged deficiencies ever addressed directly to me.

I was very aware of my shortcomings as a conductor, but the way I was treated at the SYO was a massive shock. To be honest, I still feel nothing but contempt for some of the people who were involved in this move to get rid of me.

Sometimes in the middle of a busy career, it feels like it's not raining but pouring. At the Con, I had made significant inroads in the field of early music, which at this time was becoming much better understood by musicologists and European musicians. Each year I organised a performance of Bach's *St John Passion* that explored some particular aspect of baroque performance practice. Two staff members, who were thrilled to be involved in this project and to whom I owe an incredible debt, were the fearless flautist Margaret Crawford and the erudite recorder player Howard Oberg. These musicians, who truly understood early music, backed the idea unreservedly. I was able to go to them on a daily basis and ask them all sorts of questions.

Howard had a copy of Carl Philipp Emanuel Bach's 'An essay on the true art of playing keyboard instruments', as well as Johan Joachim Quantz's *On Playing the Flute* and Leopold Mozart's *On Playing the violin.* He had read these books a million times and committed them to memory, especially the Bach, which for him was tantamount to a bible, if more holy and less fictitious. He would recite from it chapter and verse on aspects of style including ornamentation, note values, articulation and any number of musical matters about which I was abundantly ignorant. For her part, Margaret was totally approachable, but uncompromising in exposing ignorance.

The nature of the project meant, however, that my work on early music was essentially carried out in isolation. I needed encouragement, not discouragement; or, at least, critical and helpful evaluation of what I was doing. I was completely open about my own lack of knowledge, which is why I approached so many staff members to assist me. I knew the questions to ask and the people to whom I should turn for help. I knew we were taking steps but they were small steps.

A wonderfully generous violin maker, John Godschall Johnson, organised a huge number of violins and violas, many of them French and Italian instruments from the seventeenth and eighteenth centuries, to be used on permanent loan. In light of developments in Europe at that time, especially with regard to early music and performance practice, Australian musicians were living in a cultural backwater. The only local string players then who came close to being involved in this work were John Gray, who played double bass and violone, and his wife, Catherine Finnis, who played violoncello and viola da gamba. From this pair of wonderful musicians I learned much about string playing and their approach to early music. Other musicians who participated in our early concerts included Paul Dyer, Roger Brooke, Susan Reppion, Rita Fin, Nicholas Parle, Nicholas Petrou and the now internationally acclaimed baroque and classical oboist Geoffrey Burgess.

When we introduced students to the concept of playing with baroque bows on gut strings, we encouraged them to reduce the amount of left-hand vibrato. Vibrato is often a contentious issue among string players. The *Harvard Dictionary of Music* calls it 'a slight fluctuation of the pitch produced on sustained notes by an oscillating movement of the left hand'. Vibrato can be produced on all string instruments, to my knowledge, without altering pitch, and it is generally used to warm the sound or to heighten the expressive quality of the sound and can be a wonderfully rich effect. It is often less appropriate in baroque music.

I knew it did not bode well when I found out that certain string players among the student body had been warned off working with me. Some string teachers at the Con had told their students that playing early music would ruin their technique for life. Involvement in early music was seen as being a little subversive and only for those who couldn't play Brahms. Their overwhelming instinct was to prevent any of the students from being involved in this experimentation.

The case for early music at the Con probably wasn't helped by a review written by music critic Laurie Strachan for *The Australian*, in which he referred to one of our early concerts of the *St John Passion* as one of the most excruciating moments of his life. I understood this reaction, as we were on the brink of learning about this style of playing, a style that is now second nature to musicians who perform early music. However, what Laurie failed to see was that this was a performance generated by teachers and students from within a teaching institution, and was breaking new ground.

For years, it seemed to me, there had been a tradition in the recording of early music (a term that in Australia in the 1970s meant baroque music), that everything sacred was slow and everything secular wasn't much faster. The awakening of interest in early music, its performance practice and stylistic traditions, provided all musicians with new insights at a great many levels. Almost overnight, the speeds or tempi at which music was played were being reconsidered; the dynamics, or relative intensity of music in respect to loudness or softness, were being re-examined in light of the instruments for which the music had been written; and the vexed question of vibrato.

The idea that instruments that belonged to the period were required to execute the music properly might seem obvious now, but at the time it was completely revelatory. On early instruments, the music sounded fresh and alive. The articulation, phrasing, harmonic and rhythmic language rendered a vitality and cleanness that were totally new to me.

All over the world, musicologists continued to unearth new insights about so many aspects of playing techniques and sound production. This research also revealed much about the compositional techniques used, thus providing contemporary composers with fresh insights into modern music and its composition. In short, it was an examination of the tradition of composition, and any young composer worthy of the name would need to spend time looking at this early music with fresh ears and fresh eyes in order to discover how the tradition in which they found themselves evolved.

The resurgence in early music also made people more aware of performance practice in other periods: the Rococo, Classical and Romantic. Some resisted this new information, which was in fact old information, saying that adopting playing techniques from these periods would ruin one's abilities to play instruments properly. The implication was that the baroque musicians weren't really proper musicians and that the modern instrumentalist was an improvement in every way on his earlier counterpart. It was an unenlightened view. We were hearing much of this early music as if for the first time, and I certainly felt encouraged to continue to find out as much as I could. I still do. Even as I write, I'm preparing for a performance of Mozart's *Marriage of Figaro* in just that way.

I was a willing learner and always have been, and I was well aware that I had started something quite significant at the Con. Why were there such feelings of resentment and such suspicion regarding what I was doing? Staff members who should have known better, who should have fostered a sense of enquiry and should have encouraged real research, resisted my efforts to bring a new approach to the performance of this music. Even if they had all arrived at the opinion that what I was doing was so far off the mark as not to warrant any further expenditure of time, that would have been something, as it would have required a serious evaluation of the undertaking. Instead, my work was dismissed out of hand by many people who should have known more about the concept of academic freedom and the dissemination of knowledge.

Early one morning in 1983, the telephone rang. It was 2 am. Janice Rapley, a professor at California State University and who was co-chair of the AOSA, was on the line, asking me if I'd like to come to work in the United States. I recall asking Maureen if we should go. She said yes, which was all I, too, could really say when offered an international job at that hour.

That day, I went into the Con, and said I was leaving for the United States and would be gone at least a year. I think the administration was glad to see the back of me. It was a very good decision and one I didn't ever regret. I had many opportunities at the Con and, in most cases, I had created them myself. I had made my own bed and was very happy to lie in it. I had assessed very quickly the number of staff members who would be helpful with projects and, in every case, they were totally forthcoming. The pity was that the number was so small. The occasion of a staff member telling me that the piano was an improvement on the harpsichord, and the harpsichord should be abandoned as a serious instrument, more or less suggested to me that the time was not yet ripe for intense work in early music.

In the main, I wasn't actively hindered in the early years, but it soon became evident to me that, as I was in the habit of ruffling feathers and was also politically naive, I did not endear myself to those in charge of the Con. Even my work at the Conservatorium High School came under threat when I was challenged over the way I was teaching harmony. It really was time to go.

I'm basically a peg for which no appropriate hole has been found. That is not a disappointment. It is simply a fact.

Nonetheless, I can truly say that I regret very little about this time at the New South Wales State Conservatorium of Music. I was naive in thinking that everyone would find my ideas irresistible and this naiveté provided me with a protective shell, which, over ten years at the Con, copped a considerable amount of flak. It was, however, a time for making and creating opportunities. For my failures I have only myself to blame. However, in the case of the small number of successes, I am happy to share the credit with all those with whom I worked so happily and with such pleasure, and who contributed directly or obliquely to my knowledge.

Quite recently, I was invited to give classes to some of the Con's composition students, an invitation I happily accepted. Sometime later I was telephoned to say that the invitation had been withdrawn because my ideas might conflict with the ideas being propounded at the Conservatorium! This type of thinking was coming from a university, a place that, one could be forgiven for thinking, might encourage diversity of thought, a quest for the truth and differences of opinion. A university should be a place where the expression of ideas is encouraged; a place where enquiring minds can seek argument and discussion with those most qualified to engage in these activities.

As I struggle with trying to be a musician, I'm constantly reminded of Tennyson's lines from his dramatic monologue *Ulysses*, which opens: 'Come, my friends. 'Tis not too late to seek a newer world. Push off, and sitting well in order smite the sounding furrows.' This poem has kept me focused more times than I care to recall.

Since my resignation from the Sydney Youth Orchestra I have worked with the SYO again, and have been able to focus on the music rather than the past. Yet, there are some things that have happened in my life I simply don't forget. It is not a harbouring of an idea or an emotion but, quite simply, a memory in which hurt remains. It is impossible to pretend it is not so. The popular idea of 'closure' is rubbish, in my view. Every experience forms us as human beings, whether for better or worse. Closure, to me, indicates an end, a finality; it sounds like a politically correct way of shutting the door on painful experience and avoiding reality.

What I try to focus on is that music is bigger than all of us and, in my view, time should not be lost in regret. I have never given up and have never let distressing circumstances deter me. Whinge and bitch a bit, have a good moan, and then look onwards and upwards.

While some people around us may choose to thwart us or prevent us from achieving what we wish to, there are always those who are actually with us, and who are forces for good. For me, America was a good example of this. It turned out to be home to some of the most generous people on Earth, prepared to give me an opportunity to show my wares and challenge their thinking. It was an invigorating period of my life, giving me new insights into education and teaching, and introducing me to the notion of independent thought. I was so ready for this.

15

From Sea to Shining Sea

My new job was at the California State University in Chico, in northern California. Set in a rich food bowl in the foothills of the Sierra Nevada, Chico was the home of the most glorious almond orchards; it was the home also of Velveeta Cheese and, subsequently, often referred to as Velveeta Ville. Last but not least, it was home to quite possibly the biggest party campus in the whole USA, as I would soon discover.

Maureen, the kids and I found rented accommodation and began a time in our lives known as our cardboard period. We had almost no furniture, except for what we had received in some care packages sent to us very generously from friends in the Orff Schulwerk movement. We were almost broke, as we had spent a considerable amount travelling to the USA and it was going to be at least a fortnight before I received a pay cheque. Some friends in San Francisco, Margaret and Tom

Lopez, helped in every way possible. Margaret, an Australian, knew exactly what we wouldn't know about our new home, and was an expert local reference.

Finding a school for the children was one of our main concerns. We had visited the local Catholic school out of interest and the children were frightened by the appearance of the nuns. Once we met the Mother Superior I was frightened too, and that was that. At Parkview Elementary, a school on the edge of town, we found three of the world's best teachers, in Judy Jacobsen for Anthony, and Peg Rhielmann and Mrs Oxley for Claire. These women were extraordinary teachers, who would now be considered old-fashioned, in light of contemporary educational claptrap.

The children went ahead in leaps and bounds, with every opportunity provided for them to think, imagine, be creative, and to learn to read, write, spell, and to dive into the wonders of arithmetic, geography and history. They also learned to sing all the patriotic American songs, including, 'O beautiful for spacious skies, for amber waves of grain', which has a line in which the word America is articulated twice. I'm sure our children have not been the only aliens who thought the song was called 'I'm Erica, I'm Erica'.

My new job was as a lecturer in music education to students who were going to be elementary-school teachers. I couldn't imagine that Parkview Elementary's wonderful teachers had ever been anything like the students I encountered at the local university. It was difficult to believe that, just a few years hence, they would be unleashed on the world of children.

Cal State Chico's busiest day on campus was Wednesday. Being a party town, the student body liked to prepare on

Thursdays and Fridays for the Friday night celebrations, which continued well into Saturday and Sunday. Monday was recovery day, but on Tuesdays some students would creep back to campus and attend a couple of classes. By Wednesday, the place was alive and kicking.

I taught a huge range of classes, including music appreciation, music method, choir and opera. For the formal classes where students had to be assessed for a grade, I convinced the university authorities that it was a waste of time to give these students written examinations. I certainly had no interest in reading what they had to say, which, judging from their answers to questions in class, was precious little. Nor did I want to spend weekends grading papers, for the same reason.

I decided that the semester's work would be examined in a viva voce lasting no more than five minutes per student. Immediately afterwards, the two examiners would give the student their result, to assure that fair play was in operation. If they wished to, students could appeal the result on the spot.

My very dear friend and colleague Professor Janice Rapley was my co-examiner. I had suggested to her that we would be shocked at how little the students really knew and how difficult they would find it to answer our questions. Others on the faculty thought that the students would romp through this examination and there would be too many As awarded, with the result that our glorious bell curve of As, Bs, Cs, Ds and Fs would be skewed. (My next book, devoted to education, will be called *Bugger the Bell Curve*.)

These future teachers needed to be able to express ideas succinctly, explain factual information clearly, sing some simple songs and play some simple tunes on a recorder. From the first minute of questioning, you could tell how each candidate would fare. American students tend to be highly articulate and socially very much at ease, with opinions on almost everything. That quality diminished very quickly in the viva voce, when they had to craft a response to an open-ended question or exercise imaginative thought.

As it turned out, the average grade was, indeed, a C. There was only one A+, and a small sprinkling of grades from A– through to B–. The herd of Cs was followed by a tail of Ds and even a few Fs. Some appealed, but the grades I had awarded held. The results were a revelation to my colleagues.

These students were the most hilarious people I have ever worked with. I loved the fact that they could become distressed about the way in which they had applied their make-up for the day. I vividly recall one madam, at the beginning of a class, saying to anyone who'd listen: 'Well, Professor Gill, the jeans I've got on today are not really the right colour or the right style, because I went to a colour consultant and she said that I was definitely not an autumn person, no way, and that I was really more like a well, like, you know, like a spring person and I should be doing pastels, for Crissakes. So where do I get fucking pastel jeans from, I ask you?' I wasn't able to help her.

There were some wonderful students, who could not get enough tuition and who begged for extra work, but they were few and far between. For most, my class was simply an interruption to lives that consisted principally of parties and fashion. The movie *Clueless* says it all.

Far more stimulating were the workshops I staged at weekends for the Orff Schulwerk chapters, running courses that teachers took for credit at their local universities. Among the people who attended were some terrific musicians, teachers and composers. The experience made me feel genuinely liberated as an educator. It was while engaged in this activity that I made the less than startling observation that Orff Schulwerk in America was pretty much a one-way street, with an accepted pattern of behaviours and outcomes. It generated its own music and was feeding off itself. Like any club, it was inward-looking and concerned with protecting established rules and mores.

Having observed some American teachers at work, it was very clear to me that they had turned Orff Schulwerk into an activity that not only fed entirely on itself, but also kept on dividing itself and multiplying itself in its own image. As a parallel, if you teach a child to read only Dick and Jane books, and then keep on inventing a succession of stories about Dick and Jane in which neither the vocabulary nor the characters ever change or develop, then real literature is ignored and no real learning is taking place. In the US, Schulwerk was not related to any music outside its own Orff-style music. I was also concerned that it dealt so cursorily with improvisation, even though improvisation was at the heart of Orff's philosophy.

Jane Frazee, an outstanding music educator who taught at Hamline University in St Paul, Minnesota, was sufficiently interested in these views to discuss them with me in great detail. She asked me to teach at the Hamline summer schools, which were attended by some of the most experienced Orff teachers in the country. My job would be to enrich the groups with all the things I believed to be important: concentrating on improvisation, and connecting the Schulwerk to wider repertoire. Frazee had given me my head.

I continued to drive the idea that we were still not relating this approach of Orff's to real music, particularly historically, and question how we should remedy this. It seemed to me that the organisation of the Schulwerk materials, the actual musical examples compiled by Orff and his co-author, Keetman, which drew their inspiration from and were founded in real music, implied a strong historical approach to the teaching of music and improvisation generally.

Frazee finally gave in and threw down the gauntlet. She said, not without a certain amount of exasperation, that she would be prepared to invite to Hamline about thirty or so of the very best music teachers from around the US; leaders in their fields, teachers who were in high demand as clinicians or workshop leaders, teachers who had long years of service and nothing to prove. They could be my test case.

If I could convince them of my ideas, she would buy them, and would, as a result of being convinced, have a suggestion for me regarding the future. If I couldn't convince them, that would be my last summer at Hamline University. I was asked to teach six hours a day for five days, without any extra help – no assistant teacher, and no scribe to take notes. It was a one-man show.

I had to be able to justify my approach every day and with every activity I presented. At the end of the day I was required to present a summary of the activities associated with the musical examples I had chosen. It was up to me to demonstrate as clearly as I could the real relevance to music and music education of these examples. Furthermore, I had to place them contextually within the philosophy of Orff Schulwerk and, finally, demonstrate their usefulness in generating in the children a desire to make more music and to improvise on this material.

It was a tough call but I had more or less dictated the terms myself. I began each class with a three-part vocal canon that I had composed for the day, based on the material we were about to study. The canon always exemplified repertoire sourced from one of the best books I know: the *Historical Anthology of Music* by Davison and Apel, a goldmine of musical ideas. Day one ended with a participant coming up to me to say that I had scored ten out of ten for that day, but she wasn't sure I could keep that up.

That these teachers were responding was clear. That they saw the connection between the historically based music and the Orff principles was just as clear. The proof of the pudding would be if one of them were to volunteer that they would find this activity useful in the classroom – if they pronounced they would actually use this approach with children. In the middle of the improvisations, which were of the highest quality, one of the participants volunteered the notion that she felt she could do this with her grade six class and that they would be able to achieve a number of genuine musical outcomes. I couldn't have been happier.

The participant who had given me ten out of ten on the first day said nothing on the remaining days, which I found slightly unnerving. On the Friday afternoon, she finally approached me and said that every day had been a ten but she had just wanted to see how I'd cope without knowing that. I was put through my paces in no uncertain terms and, likewise, I put them through hoops they didn't even know existed. In the end, this tough, very experienced and extremely wise group of educators were convinced that there was, indeed, a real point in engaging children in music outside the confines of the narrow repertoire normally associated with Orff Schulwerk.

Frazee was as good as her word and discussed with me the idea that I might accept a position as a Professor at the University of Hamline, in charge of postgraduate education studies. The salary was extremely attractive and, in light of the home-grown talent in these classes, the suggestion that I might be just the person to do this work was the highest compliment. The confidence Jane showed in my ability was also reassuring.

I thought seriously about it but, in the end, declined the offer, as I also did offers from other American universities. Even though I loved working in the States, I was not really keen to relocate holus-bolus. I knew that once I was on the treadmill of American academic life, with its all-pervasive imperative to publish or perish, my capacity to make music would be very restricted. I was also aware that the musical life of academics in the United States seemed to bear no relationship to the professional music world. There was the academic music world and there was the professional music world, and never the twain shall meet. My time teaching in American universities had made me realise that I still wanted to explore opportunities to conduct. So, home we had to go.

I took the family to New York, where I was to run more classes for some local chapters. Around this we fitted a family holiday, with Broadway musicals almost every night, opera at the Met on non-Broadway nights, and every gallery we could manage with two young children in tow. They adored the experience.

It was while we were in New York that I received a phone call from someone in Western Australia: a gifted pedagogue, enlightened arranger of music, and general force for good, by the name of Alan Bonds. I knew Alan, though not well, from the national music camp. He told me that the West Australian Conservatorium of Music would be launched in 1985, and asked if I would consider putting in an application for the position of dean.

This was a bolt from the blue. Maureen and I discussed the idea with the children: the clincher was that if I was successful and we had to move to Western Australia, they could have a dog of their choice. We said so long, but not goodbye, to the USA and headed home.

I have never lost my respect or affection for the United States and the people associated with our time there. It was such a positive experience of working in music education that it stands in stark contrast to much of my Australian experience. I cherish the memories and the fact that we were so warmly welcomed wherever we went. 'I'm Erica' is very much part of my life.

♪

WE FLEW TO SYDNEY VIA SAN FRANCISCO, AND THEN crossed the continent to Perth in short order. This series of rapid relocations was a shock to all our systems. As we landed at Perth Airport, the first words that came out of Maureen's mouth were 'What have we done?' She spoke with an undertone of pain.

Meanwhile, I was utterly absorbed with the idea that I was now in charge of my own music school. After years of bitching and whingeing about educational matters, I finally had my chance to change the record. The responsibility was huge and, quite simply, caused me to neglect the family.

Our time in Perth was the closest Maureen came to having a nervous breakdown, no doubt brought about by my neglect in the early part of our time there. She was isolated in a community that was strange in every way. What was worse was that I was unaware of her circumstances because of my, by now, obsessive-compulsive nature, which drove me to achieve in this new job to the exclusion of much else. It was a poor effort on my part, and one of those experiences that stand in the memory: a painful reminder that I have a tendency to lose sight of everything besides music and work, and that what happened then must never happen again.

The WA Conservatorium's campus was in a leafy inner suburb, where we decided also to live. The first school the children went to turned out to be a disaster. Claire's teacher – and here I use the word 'teacher' in its loosest sense – had a cruel and vindictive nature. From the very first week, she was determined to change our daughter's handwriting, which distressed Claire to the point she hated going to school. Anthony did not fare as badly, but there was no doubt that moving from the United States to Perth had an effect on the children.

In week two, we found a Catholic school quite near the Con, with a group of teachers who actually cared. I never thought that I would be grateful to the Catholic system, yet its enlightened principal, Roberta Chapman, ensured that the children had relatively uninterrupted schooling.

Once we had moved into our house, we had to find the dog that was part of the Perth package. The kids finally lighted on

Louis, their unanimous choice from a litter of seven or eight jet-black Standard Poodle puppies, who bounced and jumped around the room in uncontrollable excitement. Anthony came up with Louis' name and he was, in many ways, Anthony's dog – to the extent that he belonged to anyone in particular.

In truth, he was his own dog, and clearly gifted in so many ways that any person who couldn't see that at first meeting would have to be described as unobservant. His bark was rich and sonorous, and capable of conveying information in fluent French or English, and he had impeccable table manners, sitting comfortably on a stool at the table at family mealtimes. Yet, he could scare the hell out of strangers, and so was a perfect watchdog.

To say that the family was obsessed with this animal is an understatement. Like all Standards, he was a brilliant jumper, and bounced with excitement when any of us returned home. He would not hesitate to put his front paws on your shoulders and plant his face fairly and squarely in front of yours, as a sign of acceptance of your friendship and of his great love – well, for that moment. Sometimes Maureen brought him into the conservatorium, whereupon he would go berserk and run all over the building. The students loved him and he was spoiled rotten.

Although the WA Con had only just been established, it came with a readymade set of problems arising from its complex organisational structure. It was one of two schools within the West Australian Academy of Performing Arts, or WAAPA, which, in turn, was part of the Western Australian College of Advanced Education, or WACAE – more commonly, and quite accurately, known as WACKY.

This monolithic organisation had come into being through the amalgamation of separate teachers colleges, as part of the national reforms to post-secondary education in the early 1980s. (Those amalgamations were, in my view, the beginning of the end of sensible tertiary music education in this country, of which more later.) I reported to a board and director of WAAPA, but was ultimately responsible to the executive of WACAE, who tended to regard the academy as upstarts and spoiled brats.

The cumbersome structure was definitely a case of too many chiefs and not enough Indians. To complicate matters further, there was another dean within WAAPA, Geoff Gibbs, who had been one of the driving forces behind the academy's success. He headed up the School of Dramatic Art, which sat parallel to the Con. Geoff was an actor, and enormous fun. We would get on well, even though we didn't always see eye to eye.

The conservatorium was already blessed with a small core of talented staff, and had its own string quartet. The quartet consisted of Paul Wright and Alan Bonds (violin), Berian Evans (viola) and Gregory Baron (cellist). The Con had a small piano, vocal and theory staff, which included Robert Curry (now principal of the Conservatorium High School in Sydney) who was responsible for history of music, and Jean Farrant, who taught theory and aural training. The pianists at the Con included Stephanie Colman, Wallace Tate, Stephen Dornan, Kenneth Weir and Jenny Warren, together with her wonderful flautist husband, Brian. Other staff included New Zealand soprano Pettine-Ann Croul and the virtuosic horn player Darryl Poulsen. With the invaluable support of my second-in-charge, the gifted and imaginative composer Dr Brian Howard, I set about building a school of music that would attract the best students and staff to one of the most remote capital cities in the world.

One of the more subtle tasks was to establish a guiding philosophy. There was a notion, generally accepted, that the Con and the School of Dramatic Art would work together in an interdisciplinary way; moreover, that there would be natural synergies between the departments. This seemed fundamentally wrong to me. The music student's ultimate objective is to work as a musician. In that sense, a conservatorium is more akin to a trades school or TAFE college than to a liberal arts college. Students receive tuition directly related to the career they want to pursue.

In a successful conservatorium, there are enough students to provide the necessary competition for them to vie with each other, and discover, sooner rather than later, whether they are good enough to have a chance professionally. If they are, the competition within the Con also helps them develop the sharp elbows needed to thrive in the professional world.

I am well aware that this thinking is old-fashioned but I don't know of a better way of teaching a crack violinist than to give her as many lessons as possible, then lock her up in order for her to practise as much as she can every day. Substitute any instrument or any player, the scenario is the same. From day one of my tenure, I was determined to prove the notion of cosy interdisciplinary interdependence wrong. The trick was to go about it in a positive way.

Very early on, I organised a string group from within the Con to record Warlock's *Capriol Suite* as an enticement to the academy's dance department. Alan Alder and Lucette Aldous, who ran the department, loved the recording but weren't sure how they could use it. That was dance solved.

I invited the students in the music theatre department, then run by an Australian Opera director Michael Beauchamp, to audition for a special chamber choir or become members of the Con's Big Choir. Music theatre solved.

The drama students could also sing in Big Choir, I suggested to Geoff Gibbs. That was the extent of the integration and the cross-pollination. As far as I was concerned, if they were all doing music, that was fine by me. I just didn't want to be involved in the spurious practice of cross-fertilisation and have the music students wasting their time doing unrelated activities.

But Geoff, who had been principal of the academy before the creation of the conservatorium, and was influential in the development of the curriculum, was absolutely wedded to the notion of foundation studies. When I arrived, all students enrolled in the associate diploma of performing arts, a state-funded course, had to undertake three hours a week of foundation studies. These classes involved creating a project in which all the disciplines were meant to share ideas, in order to devise a performance. I watched one group try to develop something based on the story of the Pied Piper of Hamelin. Its opening line was 'The rats, the rats, we've got to get rid of the rats'. The result was desultory, a flaccid piece of work that would embarrass most grade-five children.

I knew I had to find a way out, and the answer lay in establishing a degree. I needed to design a bachelor's degree in music, inextricably linked to the Con, a stand-alone qualification, with no direct connection to any other department within WAAPA.

Meanwhile, the inevitable leadership tensions emerged. The director of WAAPA, Lionel Lawrence, a Canadian with a very diverse background, had accepted his position in the belief that he had been hired to run an autonomous institution. The scales fell from his eyes when he attended his first meeting at Churchlands, the seat of power for WACKY.

Its director was Dr Douglas Jecks. I didn't mind Jecks, despite his 'my way or the highway' style of leadership. It gave life a certain frisson. One day, Geoff Gibbs was in my office when Jecks telephoned. Geoff, not quite believing who was on the phone, was fooling around, screaming like a banshee. In sonorous and threatening tones, Jecks told me: 'And don't bother aligning yourself with Gibbs because that'll get ya nowhere.'

One day, Lawrence came back from a meeting with Jecks, whom he described as a character one might meet in Chicago. His inference was clear. Shortly after that seminal meeting ('seminal' being one of Jecks's favourite words), Lionel resigned and accepted a position as director of the Victorian College of the Arts. The chairman of the board of management approached me and asked if I would assume the reins. I declined. I was not interested in becoming purely an administrator: I wanted to be in charge and involved as well!

Lionel asked me to apply for the position of dean of music at the Victorian College of the Arts. I did, and gave the most appalling interview of my life. *I* would not have appointed me. Around that time, the New South Wales Con was also looking for a director. It was a position I'd always wanted, so I didn't hesitate when I was asked to apply to head up an institution to which I had already given ten years of my career. In the end, it came down to John Hopkins or me. John won.

Truthfully, I must say that I found Perth itself to be less than inspiring. At that time, it was a small, isolated city with a chip on its shoulder. I know that lots of people feel just as indifferent to Sydney, but Sydney is home to me. Perth, on the other hand, was the shock of the new. *Everything* was unknown! New house, new schools, new job, new people, new friends to make and, above all, new professional hurdles for me to jump, with lots of onlookers wondering if I would fall flat on my face. Even the time of day felt wrong. It was strange to get to one's desk in the morning and remember that colleagues in Sydney or Melbourne had already been at their desks for three hours. It only increased my sense of insecurity, of being always on the back foot and trying to catch up.

Nevertheless, after the unsettled nature of that first year, I decided, in the words of the poet W. H. Auden, to end my self-indulgent intermezzo. I resolved that I would make the West Australian Conservatorium of Music the place to be and set out with my staff to do just that.

The bachelor's degree I wanted to introduce would, for the sake of excellence, comprise four years of intensely practical study. I was well aware of what was already happening to the bachelor's degree at the NSW Con, as hours devoted to practical music making and individual instruction were whittled away in the service of economic rationalism.

Once academic work starts to supersede the practical component of the work, and a student's progress as a practical musician is hampered because of academic requirements, then the student is not being served. Prodigiously gifted musicians with outstanding executant ability were being unfairly penalised. Similarly, academically gifted students with a bare modicum of practical talent were beginning to graduate as performing musicians.

I encouraged the staff to submit ideas for the establishment of a degree, and good, strong constructive debates were held. I was not looking for consensus. My job was to take their best ideas and fashion them into something that would make sense as a course of study for a student to follow over four years. I also encouraged Pat Crichton, our head of jazz, to come up with a four-year jazz degree, which would be a national first.

For my money, we developed the best bachelor of music program in the country. The students had two one-hour lessons a week in their major practical studies, such as piano, violin and cello, and one hour a week in their second study, which was either voice or an instrument of their choice. Each day they had an hour of aural training, history, harmony, orchestration and language. With participation in chamber music, concert class, and choir or orchestra, this made a total of about nineteen contact hours a week, fourteen of which were completely practice-based. The timetable dictated that academic subjects were always run between 11 am and 3 pm, to allow students to practise in the early mornings and after class.

The degree was launched in 1987, and soon started to attract students. It was then that I became sharply aware of the second major problem confronting the Con: Perth was really not big enough to have two competing tertiary music institutions. On the one hand, I needed more staff. On the other, the long established University of Western Australia was concerned we were starting to become a serious magnet for students. Its music department had been well looked after for over thirty years by the musician and scholar Sir Frank Callaway, who had built up its teaching staff and music library. Its leadership had recently passed into the hands of Professor David Tunley, a specialist in French music, and a renowned and gifted scholar.

There was suspicion from the university about the activities we were offering at the Con, and many music students who normally would, and without a second thought, have nominated the University of Western Australia as their preference now chose us. The university was concerned and this led to a dialogue, which I instigated with David Tunley.

I spoke to him about amalgamation, and he pointed out that the university had a long and honourable tradition while we were a brand-new, unproven institution. He then asked me who I was, implying that I had no serious track record as an academic or leader of a tertiary institution. I was not offended by this as I was suggesting that a mere puppy should join forces with a well-established greyhound, and he clearly knew nothing about me and why should he have? The conversation amounted to nothing.

Yet I believe I had planted a seed in Professor Tunley's mind. I could see the writing on the wall for Perth, in spite of my lack of experience as a leader of a tertiary institution. While it was undeniably a good thing for Western Australia to have its own conservatorium, there simply was not the required critical mass of students to provide a full symphony orchestra or to run effective chamber music classes with a diversity of instrumental combinations.

In this situation, one can reach an impasse. Without enough students, it is hard to attract staff. Without enough excellent staff, it is hard to draw good students to an institution. I wanted to establish the jazz department by increasing the number of full-time staff, an idea welcomed by Pat Crichton who always cheerfully referred to his department with the words, 'It's World War Three over there'. I wanted to increase the staff on the classical side and set about establishing a wind quintet. Darryl Poulsen was as determined this would happen as I was, and so I trotted off one fine day to meet the minister for education, who was responsible for our state funding.

We got off to a brilliant start. He said: 'So, you're the Wise Man from the East who thinks he knows everything. Well, let me tell you something, mister, we are sick of Wise Men from the East telling us what to do.' I explained as calmly as I could that I had no intention of telling him what to do. I informed him that I was trying to establish a school of music for Western Australia, a brand-new school of music into which he, as the minister, might have significant input and possibly be remembered for his enlightened contribution in this area of education. It was a tough battle, but I won.

We got the funding for a wind quintet, which we established from within the Con. Its members set about giving concerts and attracting talented new students. We appointed musicians who all went on to have distinguished careers: Wendy Clarke, Catherine McCorkill, Anne Gilby, and Peter Moore.

I also made some more staff appointments. The wonderful pianist Pauline Belviso joined us as head of the keyboard department. Tony Maydwell, a spectacular harpist, joined us as lecturer in charge of aural training. The musical tornado Gary France became a percussion teacher, and had an almost immediate impact on percussion nationally. Janice

Taylor-Warne and Megan Sutton joined the singing staff and, together with Pettine-Ann Croul, were an imposing group. I dubbed them 'The Divas', a name embraced by the entire academy, and I believed they enjoyed that special tribute. To have a strong vocal department completed my notion of the Con as a properly functioning and serious music school.

My own management style was emerging. I believed in surrounding myself with the best people possible, I would let them do their jobs, support them where needed, and thank them as often as possible for their contributions and achievements. In my view, most people truly appreciate being properly and specifically thanked. If there was a problem, my door was open. The only time I couldn't be interrupted was when I was teaching. That rule was sacrosanct.

I held regular staff meetings at which ideas about teaching were discussed, where philosophies of music education could be shared, where staff members were free to offer thoughts and ideas, and where course structures were discussed. The bachelor's degree had been approved, the associate diploma had been approved, and that wise and highly intelligent luminary, Sister Veronica Brady, spoke in glowing terms about our course structures, suggesting that they should be used as a template around the country.

We programmed an opera as soon as we could, choosing Brian Howard's *Metamorphosis.* Lyndon Terraccini sang the lead role of Gregor, a role he had created at the premiere of the opera, and I coached the remaining singers in my studio at the Con as often as I could. John Milson directed, in his thoroughly theatrical way. I conducted an ensemble of staff musicians who played this incredibly difficult score spectacularly well. (In the process, I received a conducting lesson from the percussionist David Pye, who asked me to make sure that in a particularly difficult entry for the percussion, I gave the up-beat perfectly in time!)

By now, the conservatorium of music was a thriving hub of musical activity. The West Australian Youth Orchestra had set up offices within the Con and rehearsed all its orchestral ensembles there every Saturday morning. The West Australian Youth Jazz Orchestra was also in residence.

Towards the end of 1987, I received a phone call from Margaret Seares, a truly great academic (and a superb harpsichord player), who lectured at the University of WA and was blessed with buckets of common sense. She indicated to me that were we at the Con to offer another course, the university might have to think twice about what it was doing. Discussions were held again, this time with University of WA staff, with a view to amalgamation. I was well aware that I was on very dangerous ground. As far as WAAPA was concerned, any move to relocate the Con or associate it more closely with the university would be anathema. I held these talks privately, without consulting my superiors, but at that stage nothing came of them. The idea of amalgamation was too hard to digest!

As the nation headed towards the bicentennial year, 1988, Roger Smalley, an Englishman who had spent a great deal of his working life in Australia, was commissioned by the Western Australian Youth Orchestra to write a large-scale work. *The Southland*, as it was entitled, was a massive undertaking for symphony orchestra, large chorus and soloists. The Big Choir slaved over the work and produced a very good result, not only as singers but as imitators of Australian bush birds and animals. It was a huge success for Smalley personally and a great unifying act for WAAPA. The orchestra played superbly and Big Choir, which consisted of acting students, music theatre students, production students and the like, rose to new heights of commitment and performance standards.

In 1988, I also conducted three world premiere ballets for the West Australian Ballet Company. This was a big deal. Three composers, three designers and three choreographers were appointed to create a triple bill associated with an Australian theme. Brian Howard's *Celestial Mirror* was choreographed by Barry Moreland and designed by Charles Blackman; Graham Koehne's *Voyage Within* was choreographed by Garth Welch and designed by John Olsen; Carl Vine's *Night of the Full Moon* was choreographed by Jacqui Carroll and designed by the Western Australian artist Robert Juniper. The West Australian Symphony Orchestra was assigned to the pit, and rehearsals went ahead.

The orchestra loathed Brian's work from day one: 'very contemporary!', 'very modern indeed', and, worst of all, 'where are the tunes?'. At every performance they expressed their loathing by placing on my stand, on top of Brian's score, an instrument or tool, such as you might find in a motor mechanic's workshop. This procession of tools started with a small screw-driver on opening night, and by closing night had worked its way through to a jemmy, big enough to be used in the changing of a tyre on a large aircraft. I used to hold these articles up for all to see, and then we would proceed with the ballet.

The orchestral techniques that Brian employed almost drove some of the players insane, particularly the strings, who had to play a series of sounds that required them to place their hands in very awkward, uncomfortable positions. Nevertheless, the orchestra gradually came to prefer playing his work. It wasn't that the scores by Koehne and Vine weren't well constructed; it was that Brian Howard's piece was infinitely more complicated rhythmically, melodically and harmonically, and the orchestra had to concentrate extremely hard in order to even come close to bringing it off. It was very encouraging to hear a number of players say after the last night of the season that they had come right around to Brian's work and were really beginning to enjoy playing it.

My relationship with the state symphony orchestra was not as strong as my relationship with the other orchestra in town, the Arts Orchestra, whose role it was then to accompany ballet and opera. It was seen as the second orchestra, from the musicians' point of view, in that it used a number of students along with professionals, although players from the WASO were not averse to coming in and making up the numbers if they happened to be free.

My most significant concert with the Arts Orchestra involved the return of David Helfgott to the concert platform as a soloist in Greig's Piano Concerto. Helfgott, who became a household name with the release of the movie *Shine*, had been brought to my office by his wife Gillian with a view to seeing if David could be helpful as a teacher in the piano department. I listened to him play and was impressed by his prodigious memory, his ability to recall works in an instant and his phenomenal technique. At that time there were no vacancies in the department, so we left it at that.

David was playing at a restaurant in Perth known as Riccardo's. It had been suggested that he had made considerable progress after his illness and was ready to perform in public again. I was never party to the folklore and mystique that surrounded Helfgott, but I took him for what he was, a fine pianist, and was full of admiration for his gifts.

I was approached by the Arts Orchestra's management to conduct his return concert, an invitation I gladly accepted. It opened with Puccini's youthful *Messa di Gloria* for chorus, orchestra and soloists, which was followed by the Grieg Piano Concerto and, after interval, Borodin's *Polovtsian Dances* for chorus and orchestra (better known as the theme of 'Stranger in Paradise' from *Kismet*).

Rehearsals with David were spectacularly unpredictable. That he knew the music was not in question. That he could play every note was not in doubt. Rather, it was the fact that once he got an idea in his head about a tempo he was virtually unshakeable, and this was never more true than when we came to the third movement of the Grieg, which he liked to play like the wind. In rehearsals, he would frequently set new land-speed records with it.

When he walked out on to the stage at the Perth Concert Hall on that historic evening, the house went mad. Perth welcomed back one of its most prodigious and well-liked sons. The concerto opens with a timpani roll followed by a mighty series of descending chords leading to a short cadenza, or showy section for the piano, before the orchestra enters with the main theme. It is accurate to report that the mighty chords attracted several bonus notes as they descended to the bottom of the piano. The cadenza had a certain freshness and improvisatory nature, possibly even bordering on the inventive. My heart was racing at a dangerously high level.

I smiled reassuringly at the orchestra, who looked back at me in disbelief. After the first orchestra theme the piano restates it: Helfgott looked at me as much as to say, 'Now, I'm going to be very good, so don't worry.' He played the first two movements like an angel. The orchestra relaxed and started to enjoy his playing. I was hoping above hope that he would take the third movement at a reasonable pace and not get carried away. He played the introductory transition to the third movement slower than he ever had and I was greatly relieved. Then, as if inspired by some demonic force, he took off faster than he ever had before. We simply had to keep up. I will never forget the smile that crossed the face of Joan Wright, the wonderful double bass player, who looked over at me as if to say, 'He got ya!'.

To the eternal credit of the orchestra, they kept up – after a fashion. Most of the time we were, give or take a crotchet, in the same bar as Helfgott. We arrived at the last bar of the concerto together, which was no small achievement, and the house exploded with screaming and cheering for Helfgott. I think I lost fifteen kilos that night through sheer nervous energy.

♪

I FIRST STARTED TEACHING CONDUCTING REALLY SERIously while I was in Perth. I encouraged a young man called

Tom Woods to be a conductor and then, later, another young man called Philip Griffin. Both these men are now making vital contributions to music, in spite of the fact that, during this time, I was openly criticised for daring to teach undergraduates how to conduct. The great and good, who obviously knew more about it than I did, believed that conducting was a post-graduate exercise and absolutely not something that should be dallied with by undergraduates or, in two cases, schoolchildren!

Needless to say, I listened most attentively and respectfully to the advice, and then proceeded to go about my business. The great and the good were simply wrong. I knew exactly what I was doing. Moreover, I gave these students genuine experiences of music making. They had access to orchestral players and choirs, and were given opportunities I would have given my left leg for at the same stage in my student life.

What business do students have standing up in front of a student orchestra and choir? Every bit of business in the world, is the answer. Given appropriate supervision of the student conductor, all parties can learn about music, the ways in which it might be made, and the ways in which musical ideas might be transferred from one musician to another.

Only in teaching conducting does one sometimes enter, unwittingly or unwillingly, into competition with a student. Perhaps it is better to rephrase that statement. When I teach conducting, I am often very aware that my student sees himself as a competitor and that I, the teacher, have to be conquered or eliminated from the competition. A young conductor is like a young bull: anxious to conquer, determined to succeed at any cost, to be king of the herd and, above all, to get rid of the old bull as fast as possible.

Young conductors are also very keen to let the world know that their highly evolved views on Beethoven, Mozart, Brahms or anyone else you care to name, are revelatory, especially as they have been studying, for example, the Beethoven Fifth symphony for at least three hours. Their views also have special emphases on the notion that every other conductor up to now has either been slack, or not had the faintest idea how to conduct a Beethoven symphony, especially the fifth; so, watch out world, here I come.

I have taught a number of young conductors, most of whom are working professionally somewhere in the world and most of whom would answer to these descriptions. In fact, it is imperative that they fit them, as otherwise they wouldn't survive. A tame, meek, colourless personality is not the sort of requirement you are likely to read in a job advertisement for a music director.

After Lionel Lawrence left WAAPA, Bill Woods had acted as director. When he retired, Robert Vickery, the former director-general of education and chair of the board of management, was appointed to the post. Although Vickery and I had maintained a good relationship early in the piece, once he became director, things changed for the worse. One day when I walked into his office, he actually said to me: 'Every time you walk in here, I feel sick.'

That was late in my tenure, after John Dawkins had taken the reins as federal minister for employment, education and training, intent on bringing efficiency to the higher education sector. His agenda spelled the end of the separate university and CAE systems, and ushered in the concept of mass higher education through the provision of more student places, the introduction of fees, and the reduction of teaching costs.

I sensed that economic rationalism was about to take over at the WA Con, and I wasn't wrong. Questions were being asked about expenditures regarding individual lessons. The Con's one-to-one teaching (one teacher to one student, two hours a week) was costly, but it was producing fantastic musicians. In my view, it was the lifeblood of the institution. So, when it was suggested that it be replaced with class tuition, I saw red.

I immediately informed the staff, who all said that they would resist any effort to erode the teaching hours. When Dr Vickery was informed of this reaction, he said it was no good telling him that my staff supported my view – he knew I had convinced them to follow me to hell if required.

That was the beginning of the end, both for me at the Con, and for the delivery of tertiary music education as I approved of it. It is very noble and worthy to talk of liberal education, but if that is what one wants, then go to a university. If you want to be a professional musician, then a vocational institution such as a conservatorium is for you. The trouble nowadays is that the conservatoria in Australia are all linked to universities, which, quite reasonably, demand a modicum of academic work not necessarily related to music. Were the preparatory system in Australia of a better standard, we might be able to afford the luxury of liberal arts degrees, but the standards within the schools generally are so low that tertiary time is taken up with making up lost ground.

At Perth, we had experienced five fabulous years and now people wanted to change things. I was well aware by then that, given the Con's achievements and its public profile, I could ruffle feathers and cause a lot of trouble if I chose to. In the meantime, I kept trying to find opportunities for students to perform as groups without the pressure of a full recital.

I established a series called Wednesdays at Eleven, so that primary-school groups could visit the Con and learn something about music and instruments. I used groups of students who were free to play a work or works of their choice as practice for an upcoming recital or concert. This series was hugely popular with local schools, and it meant that we were reaching the community at a very early level and informing them of our existence.

At Alan Bonds' suggestion, we also began a pre-tertiary program called Exhibitioners for gifted school children, which operated from 4 pm to 7 pm on Fridays. When most children were celebrating the end of a week at school, these youngsters flocked to classes in analysis, singing and chamber music and concert class. The legacy of this program was profound. It helped produce a long line of musicians, including notable professionals such as composer Iain Grandage and conductors Ollie Cuneo and Tom Woods.

The Perth years provided me with an opportunity I will never forget. I had always wanted to run my own school, and Western Australia gave me that chance. I remain thankful to all those staff and students who had faith in me to lead the charge, in spite of what appeared, at times, to be insurmountable difficulties, coupled with the frustrations associated with working in a monolithic institution. While the outcomes may not have always been to their taste or satisfaction, they nonetheless stood with me, knowing that they were completely free to air their views. No matter the circumstance and no matter the issue, they would be listened to and taken seriously.

During these years, I grew enormously as a musician, simply because I was surrounded by better musicians. Know thyself! These musicians helped me to know myself even better.

As opera is one of my passions, it won't seem strange that I encouraged fully staged performances of Purcell's *Dido and Aeneas*, Puccini's *Suor Angelica* and *Gianni Schicchi* and, finally, Janáček's *Cunning Little Vixen*, all directed by John Milson. This was when the breadth of WAAPA came into its own. We could cast the operas from music theatre students as well as students of the Con, and we had the resources of the production and stage management students to assist us, and this helped prepare them for the profession. As I listened to Tom Woods conduct the final performance of the *Vixen*, I was sure that Kathryn McCusker, in the title role, would end up at the Australian Opera, along with a girl Emma Lysons, now Emma Matthews, who sang one of the fox cubs. And so it proved.

I would again meet and work with many of these young talents from the WA Con, after I left Perth and took up a job in Sydney with the national opera company.

16

'Il coro è meglio che l'orchestra'

VERDI'S *IL TROVATORE* IS ONE OF THE BEST-KNOWN works in the operatic repertoire, partly because of its famous choruses. One day, soon after my arrival at Opera Australia, I was backstage at the Sydney Opera House, conducting the gents' chorus. It had just finished singing the 'Miserere', which is sung offstage in the final act of the opera. The formidable, ever-passionate, ever-energetic baritone Michael Lewis was waiting for his next entry and, when he complimented the chorus on their singing, I added 'Thank you, gentlemen', at which point they left the stage faster than a collection of speeding bullets and with the agility of people who could leap tall buildings at a single bound.

Maestro Vladimir Kamirski was in the pit, directing this general rehearsal, and at the end of the run-through he called for the gents' chorus to return. A stage manager walked onto the empty stage and told Kamirski that the chorus had been released. Kamirski was apoplectic. He spoke English with a strong Polish accent, which somehow made his angry exclamations even more dramatic: 'Never before, in twenty years, did this ever happen to me. How can this happen? Who did this terrible thing? Why is this allowed?'

Someone had to confess, so I did, publicly, even though, technically, I had not let the chorus go. I had merely said 'thank you', which, I learned later, is as good as a release. Kamirski looked at me as if I had suddenly contracted bubonic plague, then released the orchestra and repeated his litany of 'How did this happen to me? After twenty years never such a thing so horrible', and so on.

I felt that my operatic career, brief and uncertain, was coming to an end quite swiftly. I was a neophyte, in the best sense of the word. It was expected that I would know all that there was to know about the operation of the company, including the protocols and procedures, all of which had to be followed meticulously. There was no manual available, or any sort of reference; I had to learn the ropes by myself. To mix my metaphors completely, it was a baptism of fire.

I was there because of a phone call from the Australian Opera to my then agent, Virginia Braden, enquiring whether I would be interested in working as a temporary chorusmaster for the summer season, and then travelling with the company to Melbourne for the autumn season. I had recently renewed my contract as dean of the WA Con, agreeing to stay another four years. But this short-term work at the national opera company was an opportunity I knew would probably never come again. I would have been completely crazy to turn it down. My answer was a resounding, unhesitating 'yes'.

I had arrived at the Australian Opera studios in Surry Hills to take my first chorus rehearsals for *Il trovatore* one Tuesday morning in late December 1990. I loved going to work there. The ground floor of the Elizabeth Street building, which consisted of the wardrobe department and scenery shop, was the most theatrical part of the premises. You could watch the brilliant shoemakers at work, observe the costumes being sewn, or marvel at the ingenuity of the scenery makers, as they translated highly technical designs into working sets. It was the true foundation of the company's enterprise.

The rehearsal studios and paint docks were upstairs. To reach them, you passed the first floor, home of the administrative offices and library, and of the other Joan – Joan Hopkins, for years the glorious voice of the AO's switchboard. On the second floor were the large, airy studios: huge rooms with lots of natural light, in which an opera set could be installed, an orchestra could be rehearsed and all sorts of production calls could take place.

The call that first day was for 10.30 am, so I made sure that I was there half an hour before the allotted time. I was instructed to go to Studio 2, where, I was told, there was a stop-work meeting with the chorus in progress, which would continue for at least another forty-five minutes. That was a sign of things to come, though I didn't know it then.

We were to rehearse Elijah Moshinsky's production of *Il trovatore*, a celebrated version that had been designed by Sidney Nolan, and had originally starred the great contralto Lauris Elms as Azucena, the gypsy. In this iteration, the role was sung by the fiery and very experienced Jolanta Nagajek, a Polish-born Australian mezzo; Leonora was sung by Nicola Ferner-Waite, a creamy soprano with beautiful limpidity in the voice that reminded me very much of Sutherland's sound; Manrico, by Kenneth Collins, whose wonderfully full and rich dramatic tenor I adored; and Count di Luna by the redoubtable Michael Lewis. It was a great cast.

While Kamirski was rehearsing the orchestra I was expected to conduct the production calls, in which the chorus comes together with the principal singers and takes instructions from the director. In charge was Elke Neidhardt, a very fine resident director who completely understood musical intention. This was work that made me very happy. Here I was at the age of fifty, doing what I had wanted to do for a very long time. But there was much to learn.

It was part of my job during the run of a show to do the backstage conducting, some of the most nerve-wracking work that there is in the theatre. The advantage was that it gave me time to observe other rehearsals and other conductors at work. I also had to play the anvil during the Anvil chorus. Was I good enough? After opening night I called Robert Mitchell, a chorister with the company whom I had known since the 1960s, when he was a student at the Broken Bay music camp. I asked him if he had noticed anything untoward with the anvils, and he replied in the negative. I was still, at that stage, in a new job where, unless everything went perfectly, it was a disaster.

I had a meeting with Moffatt Oxenbould, the company's artistic director. Moffatt – as I can now, with my experience at Victorian Opera, appreciate – had both the best and worst job in the world. Choosing operas for presentation, casting them with the best singers available and selecting the teams to direct, design and light the works is one of the plum roles in opera. The tough part is letting all those who have not been cast know why, should they actually ask, or enduring their scorn if they believe you have miscast. It's a bitch of a job when it's not going well, and when it's not going well it is entirely the fault of the artistic director. When it goes well, it's because some external factors have come into play!

Moffatt had trained at the prestigious National Institute of Dramatic Art. There is no doubt that his passion for all things theatrical, which would have been fired up at NIDA, found a ready home in opera. He worked his way up through the opera company from stage manager to artistic director. He brought to the top job an encyclopaedic knowledge of the company's history – of its artists, artisans and repertoire, and its place in Australia's cultural landscape.

He was, in every sense, a good shepherd, with the interests of the company completely at heart. Although I disagreed with him from time to time, and he with me, I believe that there was a mutual respect and admiration for each other's work. I found him to be completely fair. He was not a trained musician and was mindful of this; if he was sometimes inappropriately advised on musical matters, his heart and soul were nevertheless wedded entirely to the company.

In this early, brief conversation, he asked me whether I would be interested in taking over the role of chorusmaster in a full-time capacity. I agreed, on the condition that I would have a chance to conduct from time to time. A deal was struck. I returned to Western Australia to formalise my resignation. Maureen and I sold the house, and we moved back to Sydney.

There was in the company at that time a buoyancy and liveliness from many of the artists and orchestral players alike. This ethos of enthusiasm for work permeated the company, from the stage management and production staff, right through to the workshop. Donald McDonald, the chief executive officer, was an enthusiastic manager who knew all of his employees well: not just the administrators, but the artists and artisans equally. In his management style, he was an optimistic positivist. I believe one of his aims – absolutely appropriately – was to keep the company on an even keel, as far as possible. He sought to present a strong public persona, one suggesting that everyone in the organisation had a common goal.

It was a very strong style, which was suited to the company at that time. If it had a downside, it was that bad news was treated as unwelcome and unsettling. My perception was that it was regarded as better to stifle the circumstances that had created the bad news than bring them to the foreground. I may be wrong about that: I am content to be challenged on it. Yet, although this was my first professional experience in an opera company, I had worked in many situations where there had been opportunities to observe management styles.

During my time at the Australian Opera, life within the company's music staff was far from a bed of roses. Many members of the staff and many artists lived their professional lives in fear of bullying and harassment. Yet, the source of the bullying and harassment was allowed to continue unchecked. There are many repetiteurs, former members of the music staff, ex-vocal coaches and artists who can testify that this type of behaviour was entrenched and pervasive. I dealt with it in my own way, at great personal and professional cost.

Notwithstanding the company's failure to manage this problem, McDonald was quintessentially supportive of his staff and artists, and generous in his thanks and support. He was the master of the post-performance speech, able to find something positive to say even when an opera had not gone particularly well. He was an accomplished public relations man, and wooed sponsors and patrons with his charm and powerfully persuasive manner. As with Moffatt, the Australian Opera was fortunate to have him.

On the musical side, numerous artists will remain forever in my memory, but Carlo Felice Cillario will always have the number one position. Carlo was a truly great conductor, an Italian born in Argentina, who had made his opera career in Europe, and whose name was linked professionally with such stars as Maria Callas and Montserrat Caballé. He first conducted in Australia in the late sixties and, for a few years, was the AO's principal conductor. As a guest conductor, he was a presence in the company all the time I was there.

Carlo was eccentric, imaginative, fiery, prickly, rude, cheerful, blustery and a musician par excellence. When it came to the Italian repertoire, especially Verdi and Puccini, he had no equal. Richard Bonynge, another favourite of mine for totally different reasons, was able to produce extraordinary sounds from the orchestra in the bel canto repertoire, the Rossini, Bellini, Donizetti operas of which he was the consummate master, but even he couldn't excite me as much.

No one could start Verdi's *Otello* the way Carlo did. And no one was better at turning an orchestra around. If the ensemble had played indifferently from the *sitzprobe** through to the stage rehearsals, you could pretty much count on Carlo to conjure from them a sparkling opening night performance that would be beyond all recognition.

I remember vividly a general rehearsal of *Falstaff* in which there were some serious ensemble issues in the pit. The orchestra was simply not playing together but it didn't seem to bother Carlo. On opening night, the offending passage was perfect. Later, I overheard Moffatt Oxenbould say admiringly of the conductor, 'He's a wily old fox'. He most certainly was. He knew every trick in the book and used them to the best musical advantage. In my view, we have not seen his like on these shores since, and are unlikely to ever again. He was a breed apart, a law unto himself, a leader of spectacular confidence, and you had to be good to keep up with him.

Working with him in my capacity as backstage conductor could be a nightmare. Following him on the television monitors, which relayed his beat backstage, was never easy at the best of times. I once asked him to do a bar in a clear four for me and he conducted it 'at' me on the screen, as if I were a three-year-old having a first lesson in counting.

He used to call me Maestro Jill, with a soft G, a title which annoyed particular people. He would yell out in his husky voice, 'Eh! Maestro Jill, come here.' He could also be extremely rude when irritated by errors – which happen quite often backstage when one is trying to achieve balances, and

* *Sitzprobe* is a German word, meaning to sit and practise. It is the first rehearsal at which the orchestra and cast come together.

doing the backstage conducting in the theatre for the first time. One time, he yelled out at me during a stage orchestral rehearsal, 'Eh! Stupidino', which loosely translates as 'Hey, little stupid one'. It actually doesn't get much ruder than that.

Moffatt Oxenbould had formed a group of artistic associates to examine the goals of the company, and discuss audience development, the rate of repertoire turnover, the commissioning of new work, and other considerations that had an impact on the company's artistic well-being. The group was made up of artists, conductors, directors, board members and senior management and invited international guests. Carlo, by then a visiting guest conductor, had been invited to attend one of these meetings.

His tolerance for such gatherings was very low. There was a discussion in progress about the chorus and the orchestra, the detail of which I have completely forgotten, but it is safe to say that none of these discussions ever entered the territory of passionate debate. I was sitting next to Carlo and noticed that he was writing on a small piece of paper. His lack of interest was obvious. Soon, he slid off his seat onto the floor, and crawled around the table on his hands and knees to a phone, which was in the corner of the room, and began dialling a number.

Moffatt was genuinely amused at this, as I was, but some of those at the meeting who were not used to Carlo's individual approach to life were not sure how to react. I am assuming the number he dialled remained unanswered, as there was no evidence of any sort of conversation taking place. He replaced the receiver and crawled back to his seat, following the same route. I loved this sort of behaviour from him: he was the only one who could have got away with it.

He sat down next to me again and handed me the piece of paper on which he had been writing. The words on it were '*Il coro è meglio che l'orchestra*' – in Italian, 'the chorus is better than the orchestra'. I knew exactly what he meant, and have kept that piece of paper as a memento of a genuine compliment from a great man.

Later in the meeting, as the group took a short break, Carlo called me over to one side and said: 'You know, maestro, you have an enemy in the orchestra, a big one. You must be careful – he doesn't like your hands.' I thanked him sincerely for telling me. I knew exactly to whom he referred. The truth is that none of the news about the existence of enemies was a surprise: we all have enemies at some time in our lives.

Nevertheless, Carlo's comment that someone in the orchestra didn't like my hands came as an unpleasant surprise. I took it to mean that someone didn't like my conducting. It was the first indication of the trouble that lay ahead.

Carlo Felice Cillario was a kind of godfather to me, and symbolically still is, even since his death a few years ago. He was the real thing in a world where real things were few and far between. I know that people suffered under Carlo because of his often blunt and pungent remarks, and his infamous gesture of flushing a toilet when he found the singing not to his taste, but I feel compelled to say how I found him to be in the five years in which I worked within his ambit.

To Carlo's name as a formative influence on me, I would add the director John Copley, whose seamless and magical productions for the Australian Opera were derived from a complete and thorough understanding of the score. I consider myself fortunate indeed to have joined the company in time to see this great artist work. Some small measure of an opera director's competence can be gauged by how they treat the chorus, and, in turn, by the chorus's response. I have seen some directors die a thousand deaths in front of the chorus, but in Copley's case, there was plain and simple old-fashioned mutual respect.

♪

When Geoffrey Arnold was Chorusmaster of the Australian Opera, from the company's inception until 1978, the chorus was one of the most brilliant jewels in the opera's crown. I remember going to performances and being blown away by its rich, powerful sound. I saw it as my job to restore that quality, and to try to recapture that sound that had so impressed me. My work with the chorus gradually became noticed throughout the company and, indeed, in the press. More important was that the chorus itself noticed a difference, and visiting conductors and regular guest conductors also commented favourably. I tried to prepare the choristers particularly well in the fields of memory and language, so that by their first production calls they would be ready to go straight to the floor. Generally, I succeeded.

However, when the company presented Rossini's *L'italiana in Algeri* in 1992, I had seriously underestimated the time it would require to prepare the chorus adequately. It was a hideous feeling. I felt I had the entire company on my back, and I worried about singlehandedly bringing the company into musical disrepute. On opening night, the chorus got there by the skin of its teeth. It was a great lesson to me. Looking back on a quarter-century of professional engagements, it stands out to me how the disasters and near disasters occupy so much of one's thinking. During that episode, certain quarters within the company made me feel as if I had no business to be alive. No surprises there!

I was tough on the chorus and expected nothing but the best at all times. When I suggested that they might do some homework on a particular passage they were finding difficult, I was told, in no uncertain terms, that if it wasn't learned in the rehearsal it wasn't going to be learned at home. I was also told, during one particularly stressful rehearsal in which I insisted on detail after detail, that it seemed I wouldn't be happy until I could see the blood trickling down the sides of their chins. I replied that I needed the blood to be trickling down both sides to make me really happy.

I actually loved working with the chorus and when they were on fire they were spectacular. Nevertheless, there were many difficult decisions about chorus membership, which I made in consultation with senior management. In the end, the final decisions were mine and mine alone. They were not always popular, but I figured that I hadn't been employed to be popular.

I could see my time coming to an end when the company decided to form joint consultative committees. The chorus had such a committee, to which I had no access whatsoever. It was not seen as pertinent to have the person in charge of the chorus present at the meetings. In my view, this committee became a forum for bitching and griping about everything from the condition of the wash basin in the ladies' dressing rooms at the Opera House, to milk containers never being put back in the fridge in the green room.

The day came when it was recommended that there should be no language coach at first rehearsals. Once the committee started to tell me indirectly how to run a rehearsal, I knew I had to go. The problem with these committees was that the membership actually believed they had real power when, in fact, they didn't. Consultation and employee inclusivity is one thing; the patients running the hospital is another. With the amount of time I have spent with consultants, advisers, work analysts, time and motion study experts, consultative committees and the generally uninformed practitioners of 'how to succeed in your business about which we do not understand the first thing', I sometimes feel I could have reconstructed the pyramids of ancient Egypt with one hand tied behind my back.

On the conducting side of things, Moffatt was as good as his word. I was given some wonderful assignments, for which I am eternally grateful. I conducted *Turandot* in the Sydney Domain, as part of the Australian Opera's enlightened policy to bring opera to as many people as possible, and I also conducted it in the Opera Theatre. On the main stage I conducted *Fidelio*, *Rigoletto*, *Il trovatore*, *La forza del destino*, *The Pearlfishers*, *La perichole*, *The Merry Widow*, *Lucia di Lammermoor*, *The Gondoliers*, *Faust*, *Orpheus in the Underworld*, *Julius Caesar*, *The Love for Three Oranges*, *The Eighth Wonder*, *Lindy*, and the Verdi *Requiem*. I also conducted several works for OzOpera.

The most terrifying circumstance I ever experienced as a conductor occurred quite early in my time at the Australian Opera, during a performance of *Turandot*. We had arrived at the moment in the second act when Princess Turandot sings the very testing aria 'In questa reggia', which gives an insight into her psychic pain and explains her icy contempt for men.

It is a spectacular showpiece requiring unbelievable vocal control and not inconsiderable power, and on the occasion I write of, it was being sung by the American soprano Leona Mitchell. It was a role that she had already sung at the Met, to rave reviews. She was a big star.

At the podium, I turned the page to the aria and looked down into the score. No aria. I turned another page of the score and still no aria. The entire aria had been very neatly removed from my score. Yet, before the show, my score had been intact. I knew this with certainty, because I have a habit before I begin a performance of turning every page I am about to conduct, to check on any passages that have proven difficult. Then I go back through the score, to rehearse tricky joins or difficult passages. I do this without fail.

I could feel the sweat pouring down my back. What could I do? I realised that if I reached for the leader's violin copy I would have panicked and distracted the orchestra. I decided not to betray my feelings to anyone, but to focus exclusively on Leona Mitchell as she sang. I knew the aria and the orchestration, knew the chorus entries and just kept smiling at Leona, who needed lots of encouragement and who had asked me to watch her like a hawk in this aria, in case she went flat. I also managed to smile at the orchestra from time to time, as if to say, 'Isn't this all lovely?'

All these contingencies travelled through my mind in a microsecond. As the aria progressed, and was going well, a dreadful thought occurred to me: what other pages might be missing? As I finally arrived at that part of the music where my score dovetailed with what was unfolding on stage, I felt relieved, but still shaken internally. It was not an accident or a case of a page or two falling out. I still believe it was an attempt to sabotage the performance. If so, it was an incredibly stupid act, which could have resulted in catastrophe. Yet, I thank the anonymous saboteur for providing me with the most precipitant moment of challenge of my life in the pit.

Next day, I related the episode to Moffatt, who looked at me as if I had made the whole thing up. I assured him I was telling him the truth. I had my suspicions, but no witnesses, so the matter rested there. From that day to this, I have always taken my own scores into the pit and taken them out with me during interval.

THE MOST CHALLENGING TIME I EVER HAD AS A conductor at the Australian Opera was the rehearsal period and subsequent performances of Alan John and Denis Watkin's *Eighth Wonder*, followed by the conception, gestation and forceps delivery of *Lindy*, by Moya Henderson and Judith Rodriguez.

Both of these operas had been workshopped some time before, in Canberra at the National Opera Workshop curated by the lavishly talented Robyn Archer. The subject matter of the operas was equally strong: *The Eighth Wonder* was about the controversial creation of the Sydney Opera House, *Lindy* about the Azaria Chamberlain case. Among the pundits, the word was that *Lindy* was the better work and that *The Eighth Wonder* had some way to go. Better or not, John's work was chosen first for performance and received its premiere in 1995.

On the Sunday night before we began rehearsals I received a telephone call from Moffatt to tell me that, for personal reasons, Jim Sharman, who was to direct the opera, was withdrawing. The Monday morning meeting was an incredibly black affair, with Moffatt being badgered from all sides about an appropriate replacement for Sharman.

It was clear that Moffatt was under considerable duress. The thrusting and parrying taking place, often waspish and demeaning, was inappropriate in the extreme. The only people in the room who actually knew the work and what was required were Alan John, Denis Watkins and I. After a long series of decidedly unpleasant exchanges, it was finally agreed that Neil Armfield would direct.

He was in Melbourne doing *Hamlet*, so Moffatt's assistant, David Crooks, was given the job of relaying Neil's instructions to the *Eighth Wonder* ensemble for the early rehearsals, which were then filmed, sent to Melbourne for Neil to examine overnight, and returned first thing next morning with his corrections. Just to add to this mis-starred set of circumstances, Clare Gormley, the soprano who had been cast in the main female role, arrived seriously jet-lagged and unable to sing at the initial music rehearsals. (She went on to sing the role of Alexandra Mason, with incredible beauty of tone and dramatic certainty.)

Neil Armfield finally arrived in person and, in a remarkably short time, the production was put together. The *sitzprobe* took place and we finished the opera with three seconds to spare. This rehearsal was greeted with spontaneous applause from the chorus, orchestra and soloists.

Alan John is an exceptionally gifted theatre composer, whose knowledge of the repertoire, in my less than humble opinion, is only equalled by Brian Howard. Both of them have the rare ability to sum up the theatricality of a scene in very few notes. It is the hallmark of a genuine composer of the theatre, and follows in the great tradition of Monteverdi, Gluck, Rossini, Bellini, Donizetti, Weber, Mozart, Verdi, Wagner, Puccini and Stravinsky.

The opening night of *The Eighth Wonder* was a huge success. ABC-TV decided to telecast the opera live from the Sydney Opera House, an event compered by the journalist David Marr. On the final night of the season and, coincidentally, my fifty-fourth birthday, we were greeted with a standing ovation. It was such a great privilege to work with artists of the calibre of Heather Begg, Donald Shanks, John Pringle, David Hobson, Clare Gormley, Emma Lysons (now Emma Matthews), Geoffrey Chard, Roger Lemke and other distinguished soloists. I felt that I had reached a new level of musical understanding and had made a small but significant contribution to this new work. *Lindy* would be a consideration at a later date; for the time being I was content.

It was during this time of working on a new Australian repertoire that I approached Rita Fin, then music master at Sydney Grammar School, with the idea of writing an opera for the senior school boys. The opera was to be based on the Greek legend of Oedipus. Clare Scott-Mitchell, with whom I had worked previously making records of nursery rhymes for young children, would write the libretto. The school's music department, under Rita's leadership, turned themselves inside out to make the opera happen. The work the boys produced was extraordinary, right from the orchestral playing and singing to the stage-managing.

Oedipus was followed by *Beowulf*, a similar experience in every way. To me, it was yet another persuasive argument for having like minds together in one school. While the operas might never again see the light of day, they provided some boys with an opportunity to experience a different aspect of learning and to extend their imaginations.

Sometime during 1995, Moffatt Oxenbould had the brilliant idea of establishing a small touring company, one that could travel the country fairly easily, bringing opera to people who otherwise might not see it, particularly Australians who lived in remote places. Moffatt's concept was that the staged works would be reduced in scale as far as the orchestra and cast sizes were concerned, but would be complete in form, so that audiences would have the chance to experience the full power of opera as music theatre.

The company was to be known as OzOpera. At the meeting at which Moffatt announced its formation, someone asked who would curate this new arm. Moffatt replied that he had somebody in mind, but gave nothing more away. Sometime later I was asked if I would be interested in being in charge of the new venture. I leapt at the chance. I could hardly wait to present the first production, which was to be *The Magic Flute.* It would open at the 1996 Adelaide Festival, during Barrie Kosky's reign as festival director, and then go on tour.

Because of its magical qualities, the *Flute* can absolutely captivate audiences who have never seen opera before. Yet parts of it are arcane, to say the least. Greg McLean, a young man who has gone on to find fame as the writer-director of the

2005 film *Wolf Creek*, was chosen both to direct the OzOpera production and to present a new version of the dialogue. We had many meetings about the nature of this dialogue and the earthy flavour of the original language. I suggested to Greg that a pantomime style of dialogue might be appropriate and he came up with some lines, many of which were corkers. Papageno, the birdman, vowed that he was so hungry 'he could eat the crutch out of a low-flying duck'. When his future wife Papagena, in her magic disguise of an old crone, bent over in front of Papageno, his line was: 'Her bum's so big it should have its own postcode.'

The script underwent several revisions because some of the artists complained about the language, but Greg was determined to maintain the flavour of the dialogue as slightly ocker Australian. There is no doubt that the punters loved the lines and lapped up his irreverent approach. But he copped criticism from some artists and from management, an eventuality for which I hold myself in large part responsible, simply because I was the one who initially encouraged him to go down that path. I'd love to do another opera with him one day. I have the perfect one in mind; that is, if he were interested.

For the tour that followed, I prepared a reduction of the score, to accommodate a string quintet; a standard wind quintet, consisting of flute, oboe, clarinet, bassoon and French horn; together with a trumpet and a trombone. We added an electronic keyboard, which had all sorts of effects, such as bells and timpani, played by my dear friend Simon Kenway, who followed me as chorusmaster at Opera Australia.

In New South Wales, we played in conventional venues, such as school halls and gymnasia, and less conventional ones, including the betting ring at Orange Racecourse, the Circus Oz tent on the Cobar Primary School oval, and a sheep shed in Wagga Wagga. In Victoria we played in an army drill hall in Queenscliff; and in Tasmania, a hall in Cygnet, which was a small miracle, blessed with some of the best acoustics I've heard anywhere in the world.

These touring productions were designed to be erected in as short a time as possible. When the truck pulled up at a venue, the set, costumes, props, orchestral paraphernalia and lighting gear all had to be unpacked and placed perfectly in a space that was usually unfamiliar to the crew. Once the cast and orchestra arrived at the venue, the rehearsal started immediately. I gave music notes and the resident director gave the production notes, a process that in any company often produces some hilarious excuses for unwitting stuff-ups:

'I missed that entry in the sextet because I was certain that I heard the bassoon and then I didn't hear the bassoon so I didn't sing and then I did hear the bassoon and then it was too late; it won't ever happen again, promise.' It would be too heart-breaking to explain that the bassoon isn't even in the sextet, so one accepts the explanation in the spirit in which it is offered.

Or, one of my favourites, after about fifteen performances of a show: 'Am I supposed to sing at that point, because I haven't been, and it hasn't felt right and I know you've given me the note before and I'll sing it tonight. If you can give me a really big cue, that would be good, thanks.' Groan!

It was fortunate that we could rely on our audiences for perfection in timing and brilliance in repartee. When we played the betting ring at Orange, the audience had been at a lavish dinner before the show, and arrived feeling no pain.

There was an undercurrent of merriment and an overtone of jubilation.

The overture – which is, of course, wonderful – was greeted with even more than the usual rapturous applause. In the opening scene when Prince Tamino awakes and utters the line 'Where am I?', from somewhere in the bowels of the theatre came the obvious retort, 'You're in Orange, sport!'. The audience rocked with laughter at this remark, and found everything thereafter funny, from the suicide scene to the deeply spiritual and uplifting finale.

I thought the cast would all require therapy. At the end of Act One, I called them together to tell them that the audience members were enjoying the show in their special way; and that it would all be over soon, and we could disperse to our motels. It was cold comfort. If anything, the second act was even more boisterous. The final curtain was greeted with thunderous applause and wild cheering.

We were blissfully unaware that, in Sydney, trouble was stirring. Unbeknown to most operatic earthlings, the machinery that was to bring about the demise of the Victoria State Opera, and its so-called amalgamation with the Australian Opera, was already well in place.

Moffatt Oxenbould had an enviable track record of being available to talk to his artists when they needed an ear into which to pour their troubles. He was also able to withstand most crises with fortitude and calm. However, I do not think I have ever seen a man more shaken than he was at the fateful meeting one morning in October 1996, at which he gave senior staff the bad news about the national company's merger with the VSO.

I am not privy, for obvious reasons, to what transpired at board level either at the Australian Opera or the VSO: the announcement of an amalgamation between the two companies came as a complete surprise to me and, I imagine, all my colleagues.

Nine years later, Moffatt described in his memoir the 'anger, hurt, outrage, [and] sadness' he felt over the amalgamation. 'It appeared that the idea of a merger had been conceived and developed in Melbourne in response to an uncomfortable financial predicament and the uncertain future that then faced the Victoria State Opera,' he wrote.

What was clear to me was that the word amalgamation was a sham. The Australian Opera was a full-time company with a complement of full-time singers, a full-time chorus, and a complete administrative infrastructure, which included every aspect of opera production from wardrobe through to scenery. It was a complete unit.

The Victoria State Opera had a small full-time administration, a small music staff and support staff, but no full-time chorus, no permanent ensemble of artists outside of the Young Artists Program, and limited scenery and wardrobe facilities. So, this was never going to be an amalgamation of like-sized companies.

Equally, it was never going to be supported by the old brigade of the VSO, who, quite rightly, adored their state company. I know! I have heard it almost daily in my role as music director of the Victorian Opera. The so-called amalgamation was perceived by many Melburnians as a takeover, and a cruel assault by the greedy marauders of the north on the virtuous citizens of the south.

To those of us in Sydney, it also felt very painful. For one thing, we lost the name of our company. It took forty years to make the world aware of the Australian Opera, and forty seconds to screw it up!

For some time, I had been contemplating leaving the company, in favour of embarking on a freelance career. I would turn fifty-five in November that year, and many caring and considerate friends advised me not to go, believing that I would be better off staying in a secure job until I retired. The concepts of safety and security were anathema to me, as attentive readers will have gathered by now. Also, other opportunities that interested me greatly had come up during the year. After a discussion with my long-suffering wife, who supported my decision, I left Opera Australia about a week after the merger was announced, and did so with what I believe to have been impeccable timing. Clearly, it would take months, if not years, for the changes there to settle.

I would continue to work for the national opera company, but as a freelance conductor.

17

Making My Own Fun

AFTER THE MERGER, MOFFATT OXENBOULD CONTINUED in Sydney as artistic director. Lindy Hume, who had been his equivalent at the VSO, went to OzOpera. She made an attentive and vitally imaginative artistic director of OzOpera, and it was a pleasure to work for her.

Lindy and I have had more fun rehearsing operas together than is really fair. This was never more so than during the production of *The Barber of Seville*, in which she convinced me to lisp my way through an introduction to the opera in broken Spanish, translated by a chorister, Max Naguit, who looked far more Spanish than I did. It was all downhill from there!

I probably appreciated the experience even more because it was only one of many enjoyable things I did as a freelance. Without doubt, my decision to go out on my own was one of the best calls I ever made. It meant that I was completely in charge of my own life, at a stage of my career where I had the contacts to generate sufficient quality work. I gloried in the variety, combining conducting with music education and even television appearances, and working all over the country. I particularly enjoyed the freedom to say yes to offers that genuinely interested me, and no to work that had little or no appeal.

In 1992, at the request of Mary Vallentine, general manager of the Sydney Symphony Orchestra, I had accepted the position of artistic director of the Sydney Symphony education program, and this now became a larger focus of my work. My job was to devise appropriate programs for the SSO to play for schoolchildren aged between five and eighteen. I also devised and ran workshops for teachers, extending the concert repertoire into pre- and post-concert activities that made direct connections with the music and provided a context for the lessons.

I had, from time to time, conducted schools concerts for the Sydney Symphony Orchestra, but was unsatisfied with their effectiveness and general presentation. I imagined how a child attending their first symphony concert would feel on discovering that they had been allocated a seat in the very back row of the Concert Hall of the Sydney Opera House: it was, as far as I could see, a guaranteed way of alienating youngsters who, in other circumstances, might have been potential music lovers.

My idea was that the concerts should be played in a smaller venue, where every child had a clear view of the orchestra, and the presenter or conductor had the opportunity to communicate with every child. The Eugene Goossens Hall at the ABC Studios in Ultimo proved to be the perfect venue. I agreed to conduct the concerts there and their nature changed, in my view, for the better. Then the orchestra's chief conductor, Edo de Waart, decided that, from 1996 onwards, the full orchestra would no longer be available for schools concerts, due to recording and touring commitments. We needed to find a solution quickly.

I suggested to Mary that there had to be some players who, by virtue of the roster system, would be available to form a small chamber orchestra with some advanced students from the NSW Conservatorium to play the school concerts. The point was to create a small orchestra in which emerging professionals could work in a relatively safe environment. The demands in respect to the concert repertoire would be less stressful and intense than if the students were trying them out in a full-size symphony orchestra, and the experienced professionals would act as mentors. The students would be paid a fee, as the concerts were professional engagements.

To my way of thinking, this would kill two birds with one stone. The pathway of an orchestral musician, from their first instrumental lesson to fully fledged membership of a symphony orchestra, is not always straightforward. Completing a tertiary course in orchestral studies is no guarantee of employment, and enrolment in a higher degree can actually reduce the chances of gaining employment as a hands-on musician.

The window of opportunity is narrow. Instrumental talent will tend to identify itself early in life, and needs immediate advanced pedagogical nourishment. Again, I say that is why attaching conservatoria to universities makes no sense. The study of music performance is, by definition, practical.

To her eternal credit, Mary Vallentine approved my idea of blending experienced players and students. We agreed to approach the conservatorium to ascertain the students' interest in the concept of such an orchestral experience. A notice was pinned to some out-of-the-way noticeboard at the conservatorium and three students applied.

I visited the Con with Margaret Moore, the SSO education manager. The day that we addressed the students, eighty-five of them applied. Thus, the Sydney Sinfonia was born. Now in its eighteenth year, the ensemble has become a tried and tested nexus between studentship and the profession, succeeding largely because of the gradual development of the orchestral members' interest in continuing the program.

The Sinfonia now has a one-year full-time fellowship program of mentorship and workshops. There is also an associated Sinfonietta program, a national program for schoolchildren who have special talents in the composition of music. Having live musicians on tap to evaluate and criticise the students' work is, without doubt, the most useful thing about the program. The students receive instant feedback and can correct errors immediately. My role is to offer suggestions in all areas of the compositional process, with a view to finding the strengths and weaknesses within each student's work. The environment is quintessentially supportive, students are not afraid to make mistakes and have them exposed, knowing that it is through the analysis of error that one learns.

Three special talents have emerged from this program: Andrew Howes and Philip Jameson, who so impressed me that I asked them to prepare works for the Sinfonia Discovery series, and Daniel Carter, who is now concentrating on conducting.

To promise anyone a career in music is a ridiculous thing to do. However, if talent, commitment, outstanding musical skills, and a highly developed sense of imagination have anything to do with it, all the signs point to these young men succeeding as composers and conductors.

In addition to my development work at the Sinfonia, I helped Musica Viva convince its musicians to change the way they presented music to children, in order to involve their young audience in active enquiry about the way music works. Musica Viva offered children an astonishing menu of musical experiences, from string quartets to brass groups, percussion ensembles to a cappella vocal groups and jazz ensembles, and folk groups from almost every country on Earth.

Some of the players were, naturally, more interested in performing than in facilitating the children's engagement with their music. They strongly resisted the idea of having to plan more complex strategies, but their resistance soon faded when they witnessed how the children's attention spans increased, along with their capacity to listen, to observe and to analyse the music developed.

Before I climb down from this bandwagon, allow me to say that Musica Viva and the Sydney Symphony Orchestra are exemplary in the way they deliver education programs: in realising that the programs are worthwhile, regardless of commercial outcomes for audience development; that children deserve to have intense experiences with live music, whether or not they go on to become regular concert-goers as adults.

Children have a fundamental right to the best music education possible, but in most places in Australia it is not possible. The Sinfonia and Musica Viva programs may be the only contact some youngsters ever have with any sort of live music, and on that basis alone they are justified.

It is not only children who respond to music education opportunities. At the SSO, we followed the success of the Sinfonia with programs pitched at adult audiences, during which I introduced aspects of the standard repertoire, by talking about the music and using the players to demonstrate particular musical points. In New South Wales, this program first ran under the title of Adult Themes – which seemed brilliant, until we realised internet filters were preventing audiences from finding out more about it. (The title was the brainchild of Tim Calnin, then the SSO's artistic administrator.) We had to find another name! I suggested 'Ears Wide Open', a play on Stanley Kubrick's *Eyes Wide Shut*, but the brilliance of this was more apparent to me than to my SSO colleagues. They ended up branding their program Discovery, but the Melbourne Symphony Orchestra kindly attached my preferred title to a similar series of programs I now run for them.

One day, we might get it right with music education in this benighted land! Educational activity should be seen as an ever-evolving function of performing arts organisations. Too often, especially at Budget time, this function is discounted or overlooked. Symphony orchestras and other musical ensembles are written off as high culture, and not for all, when in fact they are a vital part of community life.

♪

In 2001, Simone Young was appointed music director of Opera Australia, an appointment heralded both inside and outside the company. There was no doubt that she brought a new energy to OA, and with this energy she was determined to play hardball with everyone: singers, artisans and musicians alike.

Moffatt Oxenbould announced Simone's appointment in 1999, at the same time that he announced his own plans to retire. She made it very clear at the start of her reign that she would revisit musical standards, which was her right, of course, even though the way this was expressed seemed something of a slight on Moffatt's era. In my view, she tried to do too much too quickly, and fell victim to the considerable hype that surrounded her appointment. At any rate, her contract was not renewed after 2003.

I had known Simone from her student days at the NSW Conservatorium of Music, and was well aware of her talent and capabilities as a conductor, even though she had been overseas during most of my time with the company. We had a short meeting in 1999, not long after her appointment. Her revelation to me was that the Australian Opera and Ballet Orchestra, which accompanied OA performances in Sydney, found my conducting unsatisfactory. As she put it, they did not like my hands. The good news was that Orchestra Victoria had no such problem.

Her comments immediately brought to mind Carlo Felice Cillario's warning to me: 'You have an enemy in the orchestra.' I had recently conducted a well-received *Rigoletto* for Opera Australia, and felt I was being shafted on the basis of an observation from a player. The experience was like falling off the back of a truck as it turned the corner to change direction.

It was the beginning of a hideous period. I received the news that I was not to be used as a conductor during Young's tenure. The message was delivered to me in a phone call the morning of the dress rehearsal of the world premiere of Dorothy Porter and Jonathan Mills' opera *The Ghost Wife*, for which I was music director.

Based on a short story by Barbara Baynton, *The Ghost Wife* was a gothic tale of murder in the outback, starring Dimity Shepherd as the Wife, Grant Smith as the Husband, and Kanen Breen as the Swaggie. It had been commissioned for the 1999 Melbourne Festival, and was produced by OzOpera. Despite my inauspicious news, the Melbourne season proved a success, and was followed by performances at the Sydney and Adelaide Festivals. In 2002, we were invited to London by the Barbican to take part in its program of international theatre events. The opera was a critical and public success, receiving positive reviews, including a glowing one in the *Guardian*. I had been this project's godfather, welcomed by Jonathan and Dorothy to help them scrutinise the work from every possible musical and dramatic angle so that we would arrive at the finest possible result.

Around this time, I also became chief conductor of the Canberra Symphony Orchestra. Strange as it may seem, it was in the national capital – generally speaking, that most well-resourced of cities – that I witnessed first-hand just how vigilant orchestras need to be to protect their futures.

In 2001, the CSO's principal oboist, David Nuttall, asked me whether I would consider taking over the reins as chief conductor. I was glad to accept the position. Part of my brief, as I understood it, was to plan some imaginative programs, which would bring more of the public into its home at Llewellyn Hall, reawaken an interest in the orchestra, and – in a perfect world – have a positive effect on its cash flow.

The orchestra, which had begun life way back in 1950, was a part-time operation drawn mainly from staff and students of the Australian National University's music school. It was partly government funded but, as the 2005 review of the nation's orchestras would note, it deserved more financial assistance. The CSO had a very special determination to maintain its rightful place as Canberra's professional orchestra. Its members worked incredibly diligently and tenaciously to maintain this hold, and I enjoyed working with them during the six years of my involvement.

I was thrilled to be able to offer Max McBride some conducting engagements from time to time. Max was the orchestra's principal double bass, and, in my view, the eminent Haydn scholar in Australia. The orchestra's leader, Tor Fromyhr, was wonderfully supportive, as was Barbara Jane Gilby, who occasionally led for me. Both players had refreshing things to say about music, and were highly respected by the orchestra.

My experience with the CSO, helping foster audiences and sponsorship, and programming on a modest budget, proved an excellent preparation for my years at Victorian Opera. While there were tough times, I would like to think that the positive experiences outweighed them by a million to one. I'd also like to think that my programming made a difference to the bank balance. One of my guiding principles was to offer work to many local performers. I will always cherish my memories of our performances of the cantata *St Nicolas*, a work Britten wrote for a large ensemble, but one that required only a small number of professional musicians. We used community and children's choirs, marshalled and schooled by the hugely talented Judith Clingan.

Meanwhile, despite Simone Young's original edict, I found my way back onto the conducting roster of Opera Australia. Now she insisted that if I didn't conduct Moya Henderson's new opera, *Lindy*, it would not go ahead.

This was one of those new works I had been associated with for a number of years, going well back into Moffatt's stewardship. I have been castigated roundly in scholarly publications and learned tomes, by people whom I doubt ever saw the production, for making cuts to *Lindy.* Contrary to the received wisdom and popular opinion, I was a champion of Moya's opera from day one. I was the one who pushed for its inclusion in the Opera Australia repertoire, and who battled my way through the labyrinth of directors until Stuart Maunder, the company's new artistic director, finally agreed to accept the directorial role.

It was clear to me that the score, beautifully prepared and immaculately presented, was overlong and contained much superfluous information. Moya Henderson, a composer who by then had won many plaudits, would never agree with that idea, and I wouldn't expect her to. It was not her job to agree. It was her job to hand over the score and let the team bring it to life. Three directors walked away from the project, for all sorts of reasons. These were Brian Fitzgerald, a polymath, fine director, gifted linguist and, until my arrival, the Australian Opera's resident pedant; Elke Neidhardt, who refused it, based on pre-existing commitments; and Ros

Horin, who graciously and generously tried but was unable to find a way through.

There was a meeting at Opera Australia with a negotiator who had been engaged to try to smooth the waters between Moya and me.

My attitude has always been to provide the composer with as much assistance as possible, offer suggestions, try solutions, and arrive at a place where all parties feel the best musical result is being achieved, as far as possible. Nothing is ever done in this regard without the composer's consent.

Moya had seemed to forget that I was the only active champion inside the company of the work at this point, and it was close to being jettisoned. I was advised, independently, to walk away but I felt that the work needed to be heard.

As I mentioned, Simone Young made it perfectly clear that if I walked away, *Lindy* would not be staged. Stuart Maunder, with whom I had had extensive conversations, made some brilliant suggestions for cuts, each of which had my full support, so that the work ran as an uninterrupted sequence of events and made very good sense as a drama.

Judith Rodriguez, the librettist, also tried to be accommodating. In her eternal wisdom, she could see that Stuart and I were completely committed to the work, and very keen to produce a dramatic realisation of a story that had absorbed an entire nation and evoked passionate debate and stimulated great controversy.

Joanna Cole, the Australian soprano, had been cast as Lindy and she was miraculous. David Hobson, equally well cast as Michael Chamberlain, was a perfect foil to Barry Ryan and Elizabeth Campbell, both of whom played legal eagles from opposing sides. The opera attracted a barrage of national publicity, the type that opera companies usually only ever dream about. Miriam Cosic, a well-schooled and exceptionally perceptive journalist, began writing a feature article about it for *The Australian*. A photograph of Joanna Cole as Lindy was to appear on the cover of the paper's weekend magazine.

During the interview I had reason to point out to Cosic how brilliantly Cole was singing in one of the courtroom scenes. Cosic then asked Moya Henderson her thoughts about what I was doing with the music. Moya replied: 'He's fucking it'. It's there on the record, for all to read.

On 25 October 2002, Stuart Maunder and I gave Henderson and Rodriguez a powerful premiere of their opera. It was certainly not how the composer had conceived it, but it was an exciting evening in the theatre. The performances sold out and an ABC recording was made for posterity.

I had pushed like a madman to have this opera performed, and stood firmly by the principle that the OA had given Henderson an undertaking to stage the work. In doing this I am reminded of the maxim 'No good deed goes unpunished'. In spite of all this, I still believe quite firmly that the opera deserves another outing. Four performances of a new work are hardly enough to assess potential longevity and I would happily go into the pit to conduct it, although, I dare say, Moya Henderson wouldn't want me to fuck the music again!

♪

IN 2003, LINDY HUME ACCEPTED AN APPOINTMENT AS director of the Perth International Festival, and I was approached to take over the reins of OzOpera, which I did gladly. This was, in essence, a part-time appointment, requiring me to spend some time in Melbourne, in residence at Opera Australia's Melbourne headquarters in Southbank. The OzOpera in Schools program was run alongside the OzOpera national touring program. I instituted the OzOpera Youth Opera project in conjunction with the Victorian College of the Arts, the idea being that the project would provide on-the-job experience for emerging production managers, stage managers, and set, costume and lighting designers, and also provide opportunities for pre-professional orchestral musicians to play in an opera orchestra.

It was a very good model, and worked well up until 2006, when the rationalisation process started within the Victorian College of the Arts and the University of Melbourne. In the end, it just became too hard to continue, but that circumstance has since been corrected, with the joint venture now being conducted between the University of Melbourne and Victorian Opera.

In that period we presented Benjamin Britten's *The Little Sweep*, John Gay's *The Beggar's Opera*, Hans Krasa's *Brundibar*, and Malcolm Williamson's *The Happy Prince*. Many of the students we worked with in that time are now employed by Victorian Opera.

It was nearly the tenth anniversary of the collapse of the Victoria State Opera when I received a telephone call from Arts Victoria's director, Penny Hutchinson. She asked me if I was interested in becoming a broker for opera in Victoria. The idea was to try to unite all the disparate companies, in an attempt to have them work together as one big happy family.

There are still a number of so-called opera lovers who actually have no idea how opera companies work, and who feel that all the opera companies in Melbourne should be one. Try to suggest to these do-gooders, who may be brilliant pathologists, lawyers or dentists, that all the pathologists, lawyers and dentists in Melbourne should be in one big happy company: they'll tell you not to be stupid.

Penny Hutchinson's idea was finally realised in a program known as the Winter Opera Workshop, presented at BMW Edge, a relatively recently established performing venue within the site known as Federation Square. The aim was to put on four contrasting programs of operatic excerpts or related works, over a series of Sunday afternoons. The workshop would showcase some of Melbourne's well-known singers, of whom there were many, and many of whom had not really worked professionally in opera since the demise of the state company.

After 1996, the old VSO had more or less disappeared into the national opera company. The result in Melbourne was that professional opportunities to sing were severely reduced, and the serious study of voice had suffered massively. The collapse of the old VSO had left a vacuum, something abhorred by nature, especially when amateur musicians rush into the breach. Melbourne saw the rise of a number of small opera companies, either amateur or pro-am. While they deserved credit for trying to meet a need, these companies faced great challenges in presenting opera (and, in my opinion, they still do). Nevertheless, they were a practical demonstration of Melbourne's strong desire to re-establish a state opera company.

The winter opera workshops took place and were reasonably well received, but were followed by a deathly hush. There was some sort of expectation that a political announcement would be made about the formation of a new company: instead, silence. A firm of global business consulting strategists was employed to investigate the need for a new opera company, while another investigative committee, led by Jonathan Mills, spoke to as many interested parties – locally, nationally and internationally – as possible, in order to examine the viability of a new ensemble. At that stage, there was no commitment from the government to establish any sort of replacement for the VSO. All this information was to be presented to the Victorian premier, Steve Bracks.

Other forces were at work in Melbourne, vying for the premier's attention. These forces had very clear designs on how a new company should be formed, where the potential funding should go and, ultimately, who should direct it. It is to the eternal credit of the Bracks government and Arts Victoria that their views were rejected.

What was important was that the government was persuaded to put up just over $7 million over four years to fund a state company to be known as Victorian Opera. From most quarters, there was general rejoicing as Mary Delahunty, the Minister for the Arts, announced the news in late 2005. But some stakeholders expressed disappointment at the news, and bitter spite at the announcement that I would be the inaugural music director.

In the eyes of some Melburnians, mine was the worst possible appointment. One former Sydneysider who now resides in Melbourne described me in an interview as a spy from Opera Australia and a plant from the north! I had barely relinquished my job at OzOpera to take on this new role, and the knives were out for me. Some former colleagues from Opera Australia predicted that I wouldn't last more than six months and the company would collapse.

None of their forebodings came to pass. Steve Bracks was undoubtedly supportive of the new company. As far as I am concerned, he has earned immortality by giving his wholehearted imprimatur to the venture, and supporting it financially. It was not the biggest grant in the world, as dozens of my colleagues in opera reminded me on a daily basis. But I was determined to make it work artistically and to publish surpluses every year. Henceforth, I was to be known as FRR: Fiscally Responsible Richard.

♪

ALMOST AT THE SAME TIME AS I ACCEPTED THE POSITION at Victorian Opera, I received an invitation from ABC Television to be lead judge on *OperatunityOz*, a show that would search for a new Australian operatic voice. The winner's prize was to take some part in an Opera Australia production.

With such a prize, thousands of people in Brisbane, Sydney, Adelaide and Perth auditioned. Only twenty were selected to go into the finals at Opera Australia's studios in Sydney. The audition trail was strewn with broken hearts.

That we would find a talent was never the issue for me. My major concern was that, in the interests of making good television, there would be a desire to concentrate on the bizarre or the freakish, with voice coming second. From the start,

I put my foot down about this process, and said that singing had to be first and foremost, and that it would be unfair to promote people to the final twenty who really didn't have a chance.

My fellow judges were the soprano Antoinette Halloran; one of Australia's great singing teachers, Anna Connolly; the highly experienced and musically gifted opera director Elke Neidhardt; and, for the final section of the competition, Yvonne Kenny, the doyen of Australian sopranos, who brought a very strong international perspective to the contest.

The competition revealed that an obvious lack of training and basic music education had handicapped some wonderful talents – how sad! I remember a plumber from Brisbane who had one of the most beautiful raw talents I had ever heard. His voice was a glorious natural instrument, and he had a strong instinct for drama. In the final stages of the competition, Yvonne Kenny worked tirelessly with him. It was not his voice that held him back, but his lack of basic knowledge about music and musicianship. I blame an inadequate education system for this. All over the country, we heard raw talent that, with some elementary training, might have had careers in opera.

I had to work reasonably hard to convince everyone at the ABC that a single winner would not reflect a true picture of the process. I believe that the rest of the panel was with me in this. In the end, the powers that be agreed to accept three winners. They were David Parkin, bass; Roy Best, tenor; and Emily Burke, soprano. Roy, who was going to play the Duke in the final act of *Rigoletto*, had no experience working with female co-stars. Fortunately for him, the great Australian mezzo-soprano Roxane Hislop was playing opposite him as Maddalena, the 'beautiful daughter of love'. Roy relished his romp with Roxane and remained completely focused throughout the scene. Emily, who sang the role of Gilda on the final night, and David, who sang the role of Sparafucile, were also standouts for me. In fact, when I first heard Parkin, very early in the proceedings, I noted that he would probably win.

This television program demonstrated very clearly a depth of genuine interest in opera in Australia that I had not previously suspected. It was very heartening. The show screened over four Sunday nights, its ratings swelling with each instalment, and many viewers channel-surfing between *OperatunityOz* and *Australian Idol.*

Afterwards, I received an invitation to appear on ABC-TV's *Spicks and Specks.* Both my television involvements have been positive experiences for me and, I believe, positive for music and for opera. Alan Brough, Myf Warhurst and Adam Hills were enormous fun to work with, and I always felt welcome on every episode. I was gobsmacked by the musical knowledge of Myf and Alan, and Adam was no slacker in that department either. *Spicks and Specks* is sorely missed now that it is gone from our screens.

As an irrepressible show-off since birth, I enjoyed my brush with television, even at the expense of the inevitable teasing from family and friends. Simon Target, the producer of *OperatunityOz*, said that the only reasons I succeeded on a show like *Spicks and Specks* were: one, that I didn't wear product in my hair; two, I was the oldest person in the room; and three, I looked as if I'd been found sitting on a park bench somewhere. Simon has such a lovely turn of phrase and is especially gifted in the art of bestowing praise.

18

The Paris of the South

EVER SINCE I MOVED TO MELBOURNE SEVEN YEARS ago, I have been asked if I prefer it over Sydney, the clear implication being that the only rational answer is yes. Well, any Australian city that refers to the top end of one of its main streets as 'the Paris end' has serious identity issues, in my view, and probably suffers a bad case of parochialism tinctured with petit-cringe.

The truth is that, while I have gradually come to love and appreciate Melbourne – its heritage architecture; its theatrical laneways and arcades; its endless obsession with creating new restaurants and making the best coffee – my heart belongs to Sydney. My family is there, and Sydney Harbour is there, along with some of the world's most glorious beaches right near the city. Sydney is my home – end of story.

Yet, I will never forget that Victoria has provided me with the musical opportunity of a lifetime: for this, it has my eternal gratitude. The chance to start an opera company with committed recurrent government funding comes but rarely. I have had opportunities to do things I had only ever been able to dream about before taking on the job. I have relished, adored and appreciated those opportunities more than I can ever really express in mere words. Frankly, it delights me when successive arts ministers express their feelings about the company's work as 'having exceeded all their expectations'.

The position of founding music director of Victorian Opera was never advertised. The recruitment search involved a process that included the input of two especially constituted committees that interviewed a number of candidates from Australia and overseas. These interviews were by invitation. In the eyes of some critics, this was a scandalous circumstance. That I, from the north, was chosen for the job was anathema. And that I had been recently employed by Opera Australia was a disgrace in the eyes of some of the Melbourne establishment.

The Victorian government, Arts Victoria and the newly constituted board of Victorian Opera, under its chairman, Michael Roux, all expected that I would move to Melbourne from Sydney. In the world of opera and symphony, however, the circumstance of a music director taking up permanent residence in the city of his or her appointment is extremely rare. The Australian symphony orchestras, for example, are fortunate to secure twelve to fourteen weeks a year from their chief conductors, and those weeks will certainly not be consecutive. I was being asked to take on a position for fifty-two weeks of the year, which I did in spite of the fact that there was no precedent for such terms. I sometimes feel that I am given little credit for this.

It is easy to dwell on the negative in any circumstance, but from the beginning of the company's history, the negativity and downright hostility expressed towards me and the company were astonishing; the like of which I had never previously encountered.

I knew it wouldn't be easy. The term 'poison chalice' was bandied around in the press and the phrase 'doomed to fail' also mentioned regularly. My task, daunting as it was, would have been considerably easier if the naysayers had decided to get onboard at the beginning, or had simply shut up; equally, it would have been much easier if one or two of Melbourne's so-called society types had not dwelled on the fact that I was from Sydney and therefore less qualified for the job than several Melburnians they could think of. (Apparently they had forgotten that the last artistic director of the old Victoria State Opera was originally from Sydney!)

It might have been easier, too, if there had not been a group of people who persisted in attacking the company, by going behind my back to the federal and state governments to complain about me and my choice of operatic works. I wasted time on vain attempts to win them over; I should have remembered my sainted mother's words: 'Arguing with a fool shows there's two.'

There was also the matter of the Victorian government's funding, which attracted criticism from all sorts of quarters. Some of my friends in Europe told me that I had been funded to fail. Others who lived here advised me to kick and scream about the level of funding, saying that we couldn't do the job for the money provided. At the time, I found these comments damaging and personally hurtful. I already knew that I faced a major challenge: negativity was unhelpful.

The company set up temporary offices in an annexe to the kitchen of Arts Victoria. Anne Frankenberg, who had worked with me at OzOpera, was appointed as the company's first managing director, and we were away. Within months, Kylie McRae had joined our team as artistic administrator and Lucy Evans became our finance officer. I also persuaded Jane Millett to join us as director of operations, completing a senior management team you would not want to meet on a dark night after a budget meeting. I had women telling me what to do all day long, women I had chosen and in whom I had faith.

I knew nothing substantial about the old Victoria State Opera; a good thing, as I started without preconceptions. The only solid information I had was a collection of the company's old programs and brochures, which had been donated to us to form part of an archive. I read them closely.

I deduced that the VSO had become more and more ambitious, with an ever-increasing accent on the size and scope of the works, including outdoor events and spectaculars. It was also clear that significant effort had been put into developing local artists, and that a coterie of local professional singers had been established. At some time in its past, the company had obviously been very successful. Over a period approaching that fatal day in 1996, it had struggled financially, requiring bail-out at a time when Victoria was still recovering from the severe recession of the early nineties.

The old company was long lamented. Were I to set about recreating it in a new guise, I would have raised false expectations in the hearts and minds of the Victoria State Opera community. It was time to move in a completely new direction.

While there had been pressure placed on me by a number of external forces to create a company that presented only standard nineteenth-century repertoire – Verdi, Puccini, Rossini, Bizet, Gounod, Weber, Wagner and so on – I knew that any one of those big operas, properly staged, could entirely swallow our small budget. We had to be more resourceful than that, understanding full well that we had no venue of our own and were therefore dependent on hiring. Our programming also had to be different from Opera Australia's work, as the national company visited Melbourne twice a year, generally presenting standard repertoire with production values that were impossible within our budget.

I very clearly articulated my programming platform to the panel that interviewed me for the job in 2005. My philosophy would be one of community inclusion, achieved within a repertoire both broad and deep, underpinned by a strong education program with a Youth Opera component, and featuring new commissions and regional touring, as well as main-stage events.

I examined what we had, and what we lacked. We had hundreds of singers wanting work, not to mention directors, lighting and costume designers, and technicians. The State Theatre, where Opera Australia played, was beyond our budget as a venue. We could not afford to do big chorus operas, and still can't. We could not afford big orchestras, lavish sets and lavish costumes.

Faced with these limitations, the repertoire began to self-select. I could program any number of baroque operas, and four of Mozart's works, including *Così fan tutte*, *Don Giovanni*, *The Magic Flute* and *Le nozze di Figaro*. The eighteenth-century Gluck operas, such as *Orphée* or *Iphigénie*, were not out of the question but the nineteenth-century ones looked much more unlikely, though it occurred to me that we could stage some of the bel canto repertoire, if we did so very simply in a small theatre. The twentieth century, with its plethora of chamber works, was a beacon of possibility. Finally, the commissioning of new work would be a sure-fire way of creating operas that were essentially in one act, with small vocal and instrumental forces.

Arts Victoria had indicated that we should not feel any pressure to stage a production in our first year. I appreciated their consideration, but disagreed. I wanted to start work immediately. In late January and early February of 2006, Anne Frankenberg and I auditioned over 350 singers. From this group I selected a chorus, many of whom still sing with the company today, and a small group of young artists to work with the company over a two-year period.

As my programming model began to take shape, I did not consult anyone or examine any existing model. I wanted to arrive at my own decisions and was well aware that everyone in the company was an artistic director! Many singers who auditioned in that period found it necessary to tell me how to run the company. I heard all about the direction the company should take with repertoire, and how to cast it.

As I had just left OzOpera, I was seen by some singers as being very much in the Opera Australia camp, and therefore unlikely to give them a fair go. It was a perception that I couldn't change, and could only deny. The rumour had been viciously spread by VSO camp-followers, and was to become just one of many unkind and inaccurate characterisations of the new company and my worthiness to be its artistic leader.

'But, of course, you are really just a teacher,' one old biddy levelled at me. As if being a teacher were a bad thing!

I programmed 2006 and went to the board of directors with my ideas. The inaugural board was, in fact, a board of management, which worked tirelessly to help establish the company. With the exception of the soprano Merlyn Quaife, its membership had no experience managing an opera company. They were overwhelmingly guided by business principles and the notion that we had to be fiscally sustainable. Fiscal sustainability was not an issue for me. I supported it wholeheartedly, and said so at the company's launch. The VSO's demise, and its financial issues, hung like the sword of Damocles over all our heads.

Some board members were of the view that we should be doing popular repertoire, in order to put bums on seats. I understood that view completely, but didn't agree. Not only were we unable to compete with Opera Australia on that front, but Melbourne's amateur and pro-am companies were also venturing into that repertoire, with enthusiasm and energy.

I was aware that the variety of views aired at board meetings about repertoire and artistic direction were expressed with the company's best interests at heart. Nevertheless, I maintained my independent view, programmed as I saw fit, and in that year established a blueprint for programming that I followed meticulously thereafter. The works I chose for performance in 2006 were *Noye's Fludde* by Benjamin Britten; a gala concert at Hamer Hall; Mozart's comic opera *Così fan tutte*; J.S. Bach's *St John Passion*; and *Metamorphosis* by Brian Howard.

This program clearly enunciated my philosophy: we would present something from the standard repertoire with a small chorus, which could potentially tour; something from the baroque or early classical repertoire that called for a smaller orchestra but a potentially larger singing cast; something for our Victorian Youth Opera, with implications for education; and something local from a composer and librettist who were still breathing.

Noye's Fludde, the Old Testament story of Noah's Ark, opened our first season. While sceptics criticised me for launching an opera company with a children's production, a criticism I understood, I had little choice in the matter. The decision was based on the fact that, at such short notice, we could not get into an established theatre to perform a fully staged opera. A performance space at the Victorian College of the Arts, suitable for children's opera, was all that was available in late June or early July.

I was determined to turn this circumstance into an advantage, because I had to make every post a winner. Over 140 children auditioned for a singing role, and I accepted every one of them. I based this decision on the idea that parents and teachers would immediately see that we were inclusive and encouraging of young singers of all ages. We had rewarded these youngsters simply for auditioning. Nevertheless, they were all able to see that some had been chosen for big roles and others for much smaller ones.

The work calls for a congregation to sing a number of hymns, a role I assigned to this very large chorus. They were costumed in plastic poncho-style raincoats, and a sea of blue umbrellas. Our youngest chorister was seven, and our oldest was twenty-two. The entire work was cast from students. Chorus, principals, orchestral players, conductor, director, set designer, costume designer, lighting designer, stage managers, assistant stage managers and front of house were all students, from prep school through to university level. The orchestral players came from Melbourne High School and Blackburn High School. The VCA provided all the artisans, whose participation was assessed as a component of their coursework.

Several considerable talents emerged from that first production. Nicole Car, who sang the role of Mrs Noah, became a resident soprano with Opera Australia. Daniel Todd, who sang one of Noah's sons, Shem, and Olivia Cranwell, who played the role of God, became Developing Artists with Victorian Opera. Nicholas Carter, who conducted the performances, became an assistant conductor at Hamburg State Opera.

The arguments for identifying talent early are powerful and persuasive. It is paramount, in order to preserve those aspects of the talent that make it special. Often, raw young singers receive bad or indifferent teaching at the hands of rank amateurs, during which time bad vocal habits become ingrained and damage is done. I have first-hand evidence of this sort of damage from auditioning hundreds upon hundreds of young singers. It disturbs me that very young voices are being taught to emulate the sort of adult singers we see on popular TV programs like *Idol*, placing incredible strain on the young vocal folds and creating serious vocal damage. These kids are encouraged to shout, using a style known as 'belt', without understanding how to use the technique properly. Belt is a perfectly acceptable way of singing but needs to be taught by teachers who really know how to sing in that way.

The damage sustained is not only physical: musical damage in the form of out-of-tune singing is frequently observed. It is why youth opera was such an important part of my remit at Victorian Opera, and why the company also runs classes for teachers of singing and for classroom teachers who find themselves in the position of having to offer singing instruction to young children.

The gala concert at Hamer Hall in July, shortly after *Noye's Fludde*, was a huge success, launching the company in an official capacity. At the behest of the chairman, Premier Bracks spoke and stamped his personal imprimatur firmly and appropriately on the company. In this concert, we made the most of our limited access to Orchestra Victoria. The orchestra, which also plays for Opera Australia and the Australian Ballet, was allocated a number of calls to us as part of its funding. A thousand orchestral calls can be gobbled up surprisingly quickly: once the allocation was used up, we had to find money within our own budget for any extra calls, and oftentimes for our own musicians.

For *Così fan tutte*, we moved to Her Majesty's Theatre, in my view, a perfect venue for a company of our size and mission. The Grand Old Lady of Exhibition Street stands as a living reminder of the great days when every theatre had red plush seats, a glorious house curtain, boxes, a circle and grand circle, and dozens of rooms behind a very serviceable stage to accommodate wardrobe, sets, costumes and dressing rooms.

Così, directed by Jean-Pierre Mignon, was a great success, surprising the critics and charming audiences. Just as well, as it was the first instalment of four in a projected cycle of Mozart operas. For me, these works, together with the eighteenth-century Italian arias, are the lifeblood and foundation of good operatic singing. Where possible, I encourage all voice students to sing examples of both styles.

We moved on to St Michael's in Collins Street for a performance of the *St John Passion*, and then to Melba Hall, at the University of Melbourne, for the final performance of the year, a concert version of *Metamorphosis*. I had chosen this work as a salute to the Victoria State Opera, which had commissioned it in 1983.

The same nemesis who had told me that I was a good teacher had a view about *Metamorphosis*, exclaiming: 'People don't want to see operas about cockroaches!' She interfered sufficiently in my programming to cause a senior federal politician to suggest to me that I might try to program *Traviata* or *Bohème* from time to time, just to keep everyone happy: 'You know how it is, Richard, if ya know what I mean . . . wink wink, nudge nudge.' Yes, minister, I know exactly what you mean, and I am appalled that you even listened to her and shocked, that you, a senior federal minister, would dare try to impose your unwelcome influence on the running of a state opera company.

As the reader may interpret, I was (and still am) very sensitive about the first year of the company's life, when the attackers were out in force, ready to damn me at a moment's notice. We ended the year defiantly, posting a very healthy surplus, and planning a series of seasons up until 2009. The future was looking bright and the naysayers were gnashing their teeth. One Opera Australia staff member, who had blabbed all over that company that we wouldn't last six months, was proved quite wrong.

Arts Victoria had believed that once a state opera company was up and running, the various small companies that had sprung up post-VSO would disappear: this was naive, in my view. It did not come to pass. Victoria should have its own state opera company, but there should be as many opera companies as people want. The amateur companies have a place, and will forever remain amateur. The pro-am companies also have a place, and will tend to be more 'am' than 'pro', based on my most recent observations. This doesn't stop them from criticising!

We had won the first round of the battle for the hearts and minds of Victorian opera-goers, but would we win the war? The next couple of years were critical to our success. I opened the 2007 season with a concert that was a Stravinsky double bill: *Les noces* (The Wedding), a work scored for four pianos, six percussionists, mixed chorus and soloists, was coupled with *Oedipus Rex*, an opera-oratorio based on the tragedy by Sophocles. This concert provided an opportunity to present the Victorian Opera Chorus to general music lovers, in a major concert hall, with a larger orchestra on stage. It launched the company's season by demonstrating its commitment to a wide variety of programming.

Gluck's *Orphée*, a version of the Orpheus and Eurydice legend in the Berlioz arrangement, followed. We returned to Her Majesty's, hoping for the same success we had had there with *Così*. The Gluck was directed by Bangarra Dance Company's Stephen Page, ably assisted by Talya Masel, designed by the very gifted Peter England, and conducted by Matthew Coorey. It was a great piece of programming, which, very sadly, had a mixed critical reception.

I should begin by saying that I blame myself entirely for this circumstance. On reflection, I had all the right ingredients but was following the wrong musical recipe. While all the individual talents were intrinsically strong, I had created a combination of experienced artists and artisans and complete newcomers, which needed a catalyst in the room capable of combining these strengths into a unified whole. It was an error on my part. Whereas I thought I was doing the right thing by all involved, I was in fact asking people to do things they had never done before, without providing them with the necessary safety net.

It was grist to the mill for the naysayers. However, I learned much from the experience, during which I was reminded of the wonderful French proverb '*un chat echaudée craint même l'eau froid*': a scalded cat fears even cold water!

Our next show, a co-production of Richard Mills' and Timberlake Wertenbaker's *The Love of the Nightingale*, was a huge critical success, but widely misunderstood by the public. I conducted the premieres in Melbourne and Brisbane, and shocked Mr Mills with some of my tempi, which, he later came to realise, were actually his own. Two bulls in the paddock – not a good idea! Like most new works, this one would have benefited from some substantial cutting, but there simply was not time.

By now, we had started to attract flak. It was becoming clear that the company was not simply going to be a purveyor of standard fare. While we toured *Così* through regional Victoria to great acclaim, in town our critics were baying for blood over the poorly received *Orphée*, and the Stravinsky, which had apparently proved so 'contemporary' that it had Melbourne matrons reaching for their intravenous valium.

I also became accustomed to receiving hate emails about my casting, from people with highly unlikely names, such as Friedrich Morgenstern, who wrote some of the vilest things about my choices of singers. Such correspondence comes with the job. After the first thirty or forty, you start to ignore them completely. (Let me just say, however, that though the source of some of the hate emails is well known to me, their identity is something I would never *dream* of betraying.)

You could hear the sighs of relief all over Melbourne when I announced that a Puccini gala would open 2008, and that the season would include a production of Donizetti's *Elixir of Love.* Between the two, we mounted a new production of Monteverdi's *L'incoronazione di Poppea* (The Coronation of Poppea), directed by Kate Cherry, then of Melbourne Theatre Company fame.

The staging of this opera was a critical point in my musical development. Written in 1642, it represented a turning point in the development of opera, which was one of my reasons for presenting it. Yet, faced with the challenge of producing *Poppea*, I found myself losing confidence in my capacity to work with early music. I knew I had fallen out of touch with what was happening in this field in Europe, and with recent developments in the treatment of Monteverdi's work.

I saw the Belgian conductor René Jacobs as a model of performance practice for baroque music. He had long been one of my sources of inspiration. But when I purchased his recording of the opera, what I heard shocked me. It was nothing like the score I knew. All the music had been filled out with accompaniments arranged by Jacobs. He argued that it was what Monteverdi himself would have done.

I grabbed music manuscript and pencil, and sketched and copied about twenty examples of my own. If it was good enough for Jacobs, it was good enough for me. Yet, writing these accompaniments felt terribly like I was transgressing. In desperation, I finally contacted the editor of the edition I was using, the incredibly wise Alan Curtis, one of the most gifted musciologists working in the field today. He said, and I bend my knee before him, that, in spite of what his learned European colleagues were doing, there was no shred of evidence to suggest they were correct. There was absolutely no evidence that the work was played in any way other than he had presented it in his edition of the score. When I learned this, I felt as if a heavy load had been lifted from my shoulders. I had sweated blood over the decision to rewrite chunks of Monteverdi, all the time feeling like a complete fraud.

The result of all this musical angst was spectacular: I played the harpsichord and directed the music. Stefan Cassamenos played second harpsichord. Under the leadership of Paul Wright and Howard Penny, string students from the Australian National Academy of Music joined us to present the work, which was played in an ancient tuning.

This opera, about an emperor who wouldn't listen to wise counsel, could not have gone down better with Victorians, who love a dash of politics with their arts. We turned the South Melbourne Town Hall back to front for the production, to avoid using the high proscenium stage: with Richard Roberts' elegant screened set and John Busby's transcendent lighting, the illusion was complete. Kate Cherry's scenic transitions, a source of amazement, will remain with me forever. Soprano Tiffany Speight, as Poppea, and the young counter-tenor

David Hansen, as Nero, were pure magic; Tiffany won a Helpmann Award for her performance. Sally Wilson's Ottavia was just as powerful.

Unlikely as it might seem, our *Poppea* proved to be a triumph. From this experience, I learned to have the courage of my convictions, and to stay with them, in good times and bad. I felt that this was the moment at which many Melburnians began to connect with what I was doing, to see the point of me pushing and pulling them towards unfamiliar repertoire.

It was a shame, therefore, that our *Elixir*, which followed closely on *Poppea*'s heels, turned out to be a less than magic draft. If I had my time again and were able to redesign 2008, I would cut *Elixir* altogether and do a new *Barber of Seville* instead. I had huge problems with the production, and knew it was a bad choice when enemies suddenly became friends and said such things as: 'Now the company is finally on track with this repertoire.'

The flaws in this production had nothing to do with either of the casts, although I received a considerable number of hate emails about the singers. Many external forces were operating in respect to programming. I was manoeuvred into staging a Romantic Italian opera, to see if some vestigial incarnation of the old Victoria State Opera was still alive and kicking. The experiment proved emphatically that it continued to be a corpse. Having been persuaded against my wishes to present this particular work, it was the last time I allowed any interference or committee approach to programming.

THE ELIXIR HAD BEEN INCLUDED IN THE 2008 SEASON at a time when I was under pressure, at many different levels and from all sorts of people, to be more cautious about programming. This pressure came from both inside and outside the company. I dare say all the suggestions I received were made out of interest and kindness, but I do not, on such occasions, play well in the sandpit with the other children. It is my firm belief that an artistic policy does not allow everyone to have a say. One ship, one captain, thank you very much. If only those to whom I reported would agree!

Not only did the board of directors feel free to comment on programming, but I had to face an artistic advisory board, which made comments on every event we presented. Their responses were collated and sent on to Arts Victoria, the funding body. While some members of this committee were incredibly generous with their time, and made strong constructive comments and justifiably fair criticisms of my work, others used their presence to undermine the programming, and saw themselves as righteous adjudicators who could judge, sentence and execute. These were some of the most difficult meetings I ever had to sit through, but it was my own fault, as I had actually initiated this group in order to demonstrate to the board my skills as a team player. Wrong!

Nevertheless, boosted by the success of *Poppea*, I looked to 2009 as an artistic turning point. The opening of the Melbourne Recital Centre that year provided us with a perfect venue for baroque opera, acoustically speaking, though its auditorium, Elisabeth Murdoch Hall, was not a theatre in the conventional sense of the word.

Dame Elisabeth's generosity had enabled the hall to be built; it would be wrong of me to tell the story of that 2009 season without reflecting on her extraordinary contribution to opera. Not only was she a founding patron of Victorian Opera, she was a generous donor to the company. Her support has been invaluable to me as music director, and essential to the company's morale. I doubt that I could ever thank her sufficiently for the difference she has made.

In light of the welcome addition of the Melbourne Recital Centre to the city's cultural life, the concept of presenting Handel's *Xerxes* was irresistible to me. The casting of the fabulous Australian counter-tenor Tobias (Bobes) Cole in the title role was the icing on the cake. There was, of course, predictable controversy in the opera world when I announced his casting. The role had been sung by a mezzo-soprano for the last century or two, and nobody other than myself thought it should be sung any other way. The wise, the good, the noble and the strong tried to dissuade me from this apparent act of madness, as did most of Australia's mezzos. This time, though, I had learned my lesson, and I stuck to my guns.

When the show opened in August 2009, Cole had a brilliant success in the role of yet another arrogant young king, as brilliant as the success achieved by David Hansen in *Poppea.* Toby's voice is thrillingly accurate in intonation and, in addition to its remarkable flexibility, has just a little bit of the right sort of theatrical madness, which makes him a performer par excellence. I knew Toby would sing this role spectacularly, and I was correct.

The opera was conducted by the prodigiously knowledgeable John O'Donnell and directed by one of this country's special stage directors, Roger Hodgman, a genuine genius if ever I have seen one. New Zealand Opera had joined us in this adventure and we finished up with a terrific co-production that suited both companies very well indeed, enhanced by Trelise Cooper's lush, imaginative and voluptuously realised designs.

I believed we had now demonstrated strongly that there was an appetite for this type of opera in Melbourne, along with an appetite for new music: the ground was shifting slowly but surely in our direction. By now, I was completely confident of my work, and had stopped listening to all the kind, caring and helpful programming advice I was being offered – especially from board members.

The Victorian Opera board was a collection of very helpful people who had only the best interests of the company at heart. They also had to act as a board of management from time to time, and there is no doubt that I clashed with them on many issues. In the past, I had often left their meetings feeling that I had failed at every level. Their role was to oversee the financial and managerial aspects of the company, and to help facilitate our work. It was out of order for them to tell me how and what to program. I would not have walked into their places of business to tell them how to run them, but they often felt that they could give me programming advice. I was hired to be music director and artistic leader. I was not hired to follow simple instructions for programming or to do menial tasks.

I also decided to change the function and title of the artistic advisory committee to artistic *assessment* committee, altering the role from one of providing artistic advice to one of giving feedback. I wasn't the slightest bit interested in hearing anyone else's artistic views on programming or receiving any advice. I do not mean this arrogantly. One cannot serve two masters, let alone three.

I also rejected advice from people who had ideas about programming based on their individual likes and dislikes. I held myself up to the same measure. Though I detest the operatic music of Benjamin Britten (his writing is too anti-romantic and clinical for me), I have programmed four of his works, with good reason. An artistic director's job is identify work for as many people as possible to enjoy, while at the same time developing audiences' tastes and appreciation for operatic fare outside the Top Ten.

It was a sign of the company's burgeoning maturity that I took this independent stance and got away with it. But that didn't mean I could avoid the assessment that the board undertakes to examine the financial risks associated with any given season. To assign composers a rating out of one to five for risk is hilarious, in my view. Mozart is a one – low risk. Janáček is a five – high risk. A colour-coded chart let me know just how risky I was as a programmer. (Lots of green, and the risk was very low; lots of red, and it was high. Guess my colour!) Faced with such an evaluation, it was no wonder that I was beginning to make profound decisions about my future. Our differences over programming would continue right up until I handed in my notice.

By late 2009, the press had started to notice the company in a way that was quite remarkably different from their first observations of our work. Reviews from that season were overwhelmingly positive: and the young company was starting to find its musical and dramatic feet in a strong way. Moving to

Horti Hall in Victoria Street was a boon, providing us with a fine rehearsal hall and some offices. As we grew, we displaced the Melbourne Chorale, with whom we had been sharing premises. They were willingly embraced by the Melbourne Symphony Orchestra and renamed the Melbourne Symphony Orchestra Chorus.

Our funding was starting to restrict our natural growth. In 2010, the Victorian government announced a boost to our funding of $1.4 million. I have no doubt that it was the astute and active work of several board members, under Michael Roux's leadership, which secured this extra money.

Victorian Opera's artistic success is measured in several ways, including feedback we receive from audience members. Every work we present, no matter where we perform it, comes with an opportunity for audience members to provide a written response to the performance they have just seen. I make it my business to read all this feedback, as it is sometimes very informative. A single event might draw both extremes, from 'The worst night I have spent in a theatre' to 'Please keep doing this sort of work, my friends and I love this company'.

These responses provide me with a fairly reliable insight into the way our work is perceived and the effectiveness of our programming, especially for new audiences. The best sort of feedback – for *Xerxes*, for example – comes with comments such as: 'I had no idea about baroque opera, but I came to see this piece and loved it. More please.' On *Rembrandt's Wife*, a commission we entrusted to composer Andrew Ford and librettist Sue Smith: 'I thought modern music was supposed to be awful but I was really surprised. There were some good tunes.' Or of Handel's *Julius Caesar*, which we presented in 2010: 'Without doubt, this could have been presented anywhere in the world.'

I am well aware that my programming is not to everyone's taste, but it is mine, and I stand and fall by it. By the time I have left the company I will have seen seven out of seven surpluses published. I have watched negatives turned to positives; I have had subscribers admit that they have come around to our style of work, albeit slowly; I have watched patronage grow based on the nature of the programming and the support of the team at VO.

I have also lost some battles when the board felt that my programming was so far of the mark that audiences would find the temptation not to come overwhelming. One such program, for instance, consisted of three works by Schoenberg, to do with the concept of man's inhumanity to man on a massive scale, followed after interval by Mahler's *Song of the Earth*. The Schoenberg works were *Peace on Earth*; *A Survivor from Warsaw*; and *Kol Nidrei*, an Aramaic chant intoned in the synagogue on the eve of Yom Kippur.

The overtones in the programming were powerful. Mahler, a Jew who converted to Catholicism and whose music was later banned by the Nazis, bridged a gap between the music of the late Romantic style and the Second Viennese School, centred on Berg, Schoenberg and Webern. But my program completely nonplussed the board, and I was left shattered. One day, I know, I will do this program, as it is an absolute corker.

19

You Can't Stop the Music!

THE VICTORIAN GOVERNMENT MADE IT VERY CLEAR to me from the outset of my appointment that the state's artists had to be served extremely well by the new company. The collapse of the VSO had, of course, done massive collateral damage to local talent. Overnight, employment dried up for many opera professionals: singers, directors, designers and freelance orchestral musicians. It was a personal disaster for many.

I was very mindful of their situation when I started my new role. There was no doubt in my mind that Victoria had a rich operatic resource, with singers such as David Hobson, Roger Lemke, Suzanne Johnston, Roxane Hislop, Tiffany Speight, Dimity Shepherd and Gary Rowley. Victorian Opera has been able to offer all these singers work. I hope that, at the same time, I have been able to offer them a source of encouragement to continue singing.

From the start I made it my business to speak on a one-to-one basis with as many of the senior Victorian artists as I could. I did this during especially arranged interviews with them, which enabled me to spend a serious amount of time learning of their aspirations: for the roles they wished to sing, and for their place within the new company, if such a place existed. I encouraged them to talk frankly about themselves, but also told them that I would not make false promises.

I was aware of the pain that had been experienced by these singers, and set about trying to heal some of the wounds, even though I had not inflicted them. In most cases, I have been able to find something for these singers, even if it has only been a concert. Sometimes, however, there has been a dry year, simply because the repertoire has not allowed for them to be cast.

Among all the conversations I had with senior artists, I recall one with the mezzo-soprano Roxane Hislop, whom I had taught as a Diploma of Opera student at the NSW Conservatorium in the early 1980s. As a student she exhibited great promise, which I believe she has realised: she has made a great contribution to opera in this country.

Roxane indicated to me that she would be willing to support the company in any way she could. She further indicated that she also understood that it might be difficult to cast her, as our programming fell almost completely outside her usual repertoire. For example, she had sung a fabulous Maddalena in performances of *Rigoletto* I had conducted for Opera Australia in Sydney and such productions were never going to be within our limited budget, so we both knew that casting her would be a challenge. Roxane indicated that she was philosophical about this and would be prepared to roll with the punches.

Her case interested and challenged me. In her personal life, Roxane was established, with a family, in Melbourne. Yet, here was a mezzo-soprano with a very special dramatic quality beginning to emerge in her voice, left suddenly without work in her home state.

Some singers were only interested in principal roles, feeling that anything else, such as a role in an ensemble, was beneath them. That attitude cut no mustard with me. Here we had a company that was starting from scratch on a tiny budget. I was not interested in playing 'spot the diva', and needed singers who were prepared to come with me, irrespective of the territory. Roxane Hislop was never a diva of this type. Cast as Juno, a member of the ensemble in *The Love of the Nightingale*, she demonstrated that she wanted to sing and was prepared to be a team player.

I started to cast her against type, and put her into roles that would normally be played by a different sort of mezzo-soprano. I also cast her with directors who I knew would demand the highest acting standards from their casts; who would not be afraid to direct firmly, without fear or favour, and would extend even the most experienced of singers.

A turning point came in 2009, when I cast her in *Rembrandt's Wife*, in the role of Geertje Dircx. Here, she was teamed with director Talya Masel, who pushed Roxane well and truly out of her comfort zone. The result was thrilling. While it was clear that Roxane had acting skills, it was the chemistry that fired between her and Talya that brought out the best in this singer. As mutual respect for each other's talents grew, so did Roxane's portrayal of Geertje, and in an amazing way. She became completely committed to the theatre of the work, using her voice as an expression of the drama and the text in ways I had never seen or heard before. As a result, she had a huge success with this role, and was nominated for a Green Room Award, Melbourne's awards for excellence in the performing arts.

Casting Roxane in the role of Amastre in Handel's *Xerxes* was a no-brainer for me. However, I received a lot of negative feedback about the fact that she and some of the other cast were not typical 'early music singers'. To me there are two types of singer – good and not so good. Roxane ate this role for breakfast, silencing the 'pure-voiced', who had to eat a little slice of humble pie. She responded brilliantly to Roger Hodgman's exacting direction and made the role her own.

In 2012's programming I threw down the gauntlet to this singer, casting her against type in three out of four of her assignments. In the pantomime *Cinderella*, I cast her as the wicked stepmother, mean and nasty and a real villainess. We gave her a gorgeous costume, which compensated a little for the horrible role. In Stravinsky's *The Rake's Progress* I cast her as the freak from St Giles' Fair, a character called Baba the Turk. She had to wear a full beard and a moustache, together with multi-coloured pedal-pushers. No lovely skirt as compensation here.

In Gordon Kerry's and Louis Nowra's *Midnight Son* she played multiple roles, including a swinger called Feral Meryl. By comparison, her last outing, as Marcellina in *The Marriage of Figaro*, was a walk in the park.

While Roxane's story, in one sense, is not unique, it demonstrates an opera singer's tenacity to remain involved in the profession, to take risks, to face up to tough directors, to maintain a sense of purpose and to approach uncharted waters with courage and determination, while watching rising young stars gradually entering her territory.

Just as the Victorian government wanted me to engage experienced local singers, it was part of my charter to select new operatic talent for development. Throughout the massive set of auditions I conducted in early 2006, I made it my business to welcome each singer into the room, introduce them to the team, ask them to sing and then speak with them after their audition had finished. I am well aware that this type of practice is often seen as unwise, as some singers feel that if they talk to an auditioning panel after trying out, it signals the beginning of a relationship and possible work. My philosophy has been to let the singer know then and there how they fared and, if they are interested in hearing feedback, give them any suggestions I think might be pertinent to improving their work. I am also careful to remind them that my view is, obviously, just one view. I then usher them out of the room and thank them for coming. Many people find auditioning a nightmare. Every singer who turns up is important, and I always start off the audition believing that this is the best voice I'm going to hear today. In other words, I want them to do their best.

In my time at Victorian Opera, I have made a point of personally hearing every voice, whether adult, adolescent or child. Whenever my staff kindly encouraged me to let someone else do an initial 'cattle call', I thanked them and explained that I needed to build the idea in the community that the VO genuinely cared about singers. I was also terrified that I might miss out on hearing that special voice, or hearing a voice that had been wrongly categorised and was singing inappropriate repertoire.

When I sat down in 2006 and listened to more than 350 singers, the last cab off the rank – the absolute last cab – was a young man by the name of Samuel Dundas. He came in and sang splendidly. I recognised his talent immediately and, as was my habit, asked him to have a chat with me about his aspirations. It was very clear that he had a huge natural talent and a highly evolved instinct for singing. He simply opened his mouth and out came this beautiful sound.

In the course of the conversation he revealed that he thought he was a bass and, indeed, had been told so by several people who knew about voices, so it must be right. Without wishing to shatter his illusions about his range or to disagree with him immediately, I suggested to him that he might have a tendency towards the top of the vocal range, and that he should not discount the possibility that one day he might actually become a baritone. What I was saying, in the nicest possible way, was: 'Sam, forget being a bass, you are a lyric baritone if ever I have heard one.'

I offered him a position in our developing artists' program, and he accepted gratefully. It would be wonderful to say at this point that the rest is history, now that he is a full-time artist with Opera Australia, but it isn't so. There was not the slightest shred of doubt in my mind that this boy could sing and act. He had a great instinct for the stage and loved an audience. The issues with Sammy were twofold: his doubts about having a career as a singer and a curious lack of confidence in his own abilities. Curious in the sense that many young singers, when auditioning, believe that they are truly ready to go straight on the stage in a leading role, and are a little taken aback when you suggest that you might like to hear them sing again in a year's time.

The incredibly dangerous philosophy espoused by some schools, associated with dreaming the dream, leads inevitably to the idea that if you have a dream you can be anything you want to be. It misleads some young singers into thinking that they are much more talented than they really are. In Sammy's case, this couldn't have been further from the truth.

In 2006, I asked him to cover the baritone role of Guglielmo in *Così fan tutte*, in preparation for the 2007 tour, along with singing the bass aria in Bach's *St John Passion*, a one-night engagement. This was a contradiction in casting, but it provided Sam with the evidence about his voice type that he ultimately needed. When Bach writes for a bass voice, the type of bass required is rarely specified. Although Sam managed his aria reasonably well in rehearsals, the performance had a few slippery moments. It was the beginning of an extended period of self-realisation, during which Sam often asked the question 'Do I really want to sing?'

My attitude to young singers has always been to support them to the hilt, but promise them nothing in the way of a career. It is morally indefensible to promise anyone a career in opera, simply because we have no idea how things are going to change in an incredibly fluid world. The only promises I make to the young singers and, indeed, to experienced artists, is the promise of a contract for a role in a specific season.

I was acutely aware of Sam's dilemma. We spent time talking about it, but in the end I realised that the only way he would solve his problems would be to tackle the situation head-on and simply make the decision that he was going to sing. No one else could do this for him. I reassured him that he would have my full support, whatever his decision. It is a perfectly reasonable thing for a young singer in a developing artists' program to say, 'Hey, this is not for me'.

I really believe that my casting of Sam in the title role of *Don Giovanni* in 2009 was a significant stepping stone for him. Launching a young, unknown baritone into one of opera's greatest roles entailed risk on a significant scale. Giovanni is on stage most of the night, and the demands on the singer are gigantic.

I put Sam up against the wonderfully ebullient and highly experienced Andrew Collis, who played Don Giovanni's servant, Leporello. My bet was that the experience of working with an artist like Collis would either immediately rub off on Sam, or he would miss the boat completely. An added complication was the fact that I was sharing the conducting with my student, Nicholas Carter, of which more later. The singers playing the parts of Zerlina and Masetto were also making debuts in their roles, and the Masetto, Anthony Mackey, was making his professional debut with the company.

Sam took to the role of Don Giovanni in a spectacular way. All the chemistry I had hoped would coalesce and bubble between him and Andrew Collis not only bubbled but caught fire. Sam's instinct was unerring and, in the hands of Jean-Pierre Mignon, a highly experienced director, he was challenged to scale new heights. I watched the element of risk gradually disappear as Sam's certainty in the role evolved. He also responded to his ladies in a very mature way. The glorious soprano Caroline Wenbourne, singing the role of Donna

Anna, and the equally glorious Tiffany Speight, making her role debut as Elvira, gave Sam no leeway at all. He had to rise to their levels and prove himself worthy of this part.

As usual, doubts and concerns were heard from the Negative Nevilles and Nasty Nancys. How can a young man create this role? By now I was heartily sick of the negativity, and chose to ignore it completely. Sam had an amazing personal success with *Giovanni*. When the opera toured, he grew in the role even more. I did know what I was doing!

A major setback to Sam's development occurred when he suffered an injury and was unable to perform the role of Boniface in Ibert's *Angélique*. But he recovered, and by the time I cast him as Papageno in our 2011 season of *The Magic Flute*, he had been offered a position with Opera Australia as a young artist, along with another VO graduand, Nicole Car.

His portrayal of Papageno, one of Mozart's most endearingly realised characters, was strong, vital, musically convincing and an especially mature performance. I watched Sammy work every night from my position in the pit, and frequently thought back to our first meeting in 2006 and the huge transformation that had taken place in him.

At every stage in his development I made myself available to listen – as I do for all artists. I was determined, unknown to anyone else, that this major talent would not be lost to the operatic world. I knew if I pushed him, he'd go. I knew also that if I showed no interest in him, he'd go. By keeping my distance, but also maintaining a close eye and ready ear, I hope I helped him along the road.

Sam's story is not unique. I try, as far as I possibly can, to do as much as I can for the artists in the company. I am also very well aware of the support team behind me, knowing every day that they can never be thanked enough for their work. Watching artists like Samuel Dundas emerge and blossom is an experience unmatched by anything else we do in the course of our work. Indeed, every time an artist has a success, it is a source of pleasure for me as much as it is for them.

♪

These days, people are less likely to ask me whether I prefer Melbourne to Sydney, and more likely to ask me why I'm leaving. I'm leaving Victorian Opera because enough is enough. I mean this in the best way possible. I feel that the company is very much at the top of its game and that it is a good time to hand it over. Melbourne, much and all as I love it, is not my home. I need to be with my family, my children and grandchildren in Sydney. I have given this company seven years of my life, twenty-four hours a day, seven days a week, by living in the place in which I work.

I was given an opportunity to start a company from scratch. That is a rare and special opportunity.

From its start, right up to the time of writing, the adventure has been challenging, fulfilling, thrilling, devastating, uplifting, exhausting and exhilarating, all the while providing me with opportunities to take risks, explore new horizons, break the operatic mould, confound the sceptics (I always think how close that word is to septic), delight the supporters, challenge audiences with new work, and promote debate and discussion about opera. It has also been a thrill to deal with our operatic neighbours in Sydney, even if only to let them know that we are here to stay.

I wish the company, and all who sail in her, every good wish possible. I hope that the legacy of a functioning Youth Opera and vibrant education program, a healthy commissioning program, a community and regional outreach program, a widely diverse main-stage program, and a strong developing artists' program will continue to flourish and grow. It may not have escaped observant fans of opera that my final staged operatic work is Elliott Carter's *What Next?*. What next, indeed? Back to freelance again? Certainly. Start another opera company? Now, there's an idea!

♪

THERE IS ONE MORE STORY I WOULD LIKE TO TELL, about encouraging young people in music. Encouraging the young is vital to ensure that the supply of talent continues. Finding the right talent is hard, and sometimes you miss the mark. I would rather take a chance and miss the mark occasionally, than not have identified the talent in the first place. Better to have sung and lost than not to have sung at all.

I can say quite truthfully that almost all the students whom I have taught on a one-to-one basis, either as composers or conductors, have been essentially much more innately gifted than I am. My joy has been to teach them things about music they had not had the opportunity to perceive, or of which they were entirely unaware. Through this new and heightened perception of music, we can find opportunities to enhance their innate gifts and facilitate their development of a higher level of understanding.

I am also a great believer in giving talented students real experiences in which they can achieve musical results, and succeed, not necessarily painlessly, through hard work and constant supervision. Watching the face of a young conductor as they stand up in front of a group for the first time is one of the great wonders of the musical world. Watching a young composer listen to his notes come alive in the course of a rehearsal is also a musical wonder. I know my work is nearing completion when I experience the first signs of resentment from a student at a suggestion I make; when a young conductor looks at me as if I dwell in some primeval swamp from which I have recently emerged, covered in slime. Therein lies a tale!

When Sam Dundas was going through his experience with *Don Giovanni*, I was challenged by the board because I allocated some performances to a young conductor, Nicholas Carter. Five years had passed since he had begun his studies with me, but the board was concerned that on the occasion of Nicholas's first performance I was scheduled to be away working with another orchestra. If something were to go wrong in my absence, I wouldn't be around to save the situation. Little did the board know that young Mr Carter, not inappropriately, was hoping that I might meet an errant bus or runaway tram and that he'd get to conduct all the performances. So confident was he of his ability that he walked into the communal gentlemen's dressing room on opening night and said, 'Well, best wishes for the next three general rehearsals. The real opening will be next Tuesday, when I take over.'

Had something gone wrong, Nicholas would have been placed in the position of having to fix it himself. Things go wrong during the performance of opera more often than the general public ever know. Nicholas was cracking his neck to conduct these performances and was also trying to crack mine – in the nicest possible way! We were sharing the rehearsals in the studio for *Don Giovanni*, in itself a difficult way of working, but I wanted him to have the best preparation possible. There was undoubtedly tension between us, as he had views differing from mine for all sorts of reasons, but in the end he did conduct three very good performances.

The analogy of the young bull wanting to kill the old bull is deadly accurate! What the board hadn't understood was that in this process of letting a young conductor embark on his first major performance, the teacher has to remove himself entirely from the circumstance. There is no turning back; there is no jumping in and saving the situation.

Sam appeared to lack confidence; Nicholas had it in spades. That a student has such self-assurance after several years of study is probably a sign that he or she has been well taught, and is ready for the next step and completely dedicated to the idea of meeting the challenge. This confidence is also a signal to all teachers of highly gifted students: a signal we all have to be able to recognise, and then be willing to admit to ourselves that there comes a time when things have to change in the relationship between teacher and taught; when the student has to move out of the path of the teachers' influence. It is a moment to be reckoned with, but a positive one. In most cases, that moment is generated by the student and is very clear: there is a reluctance on the part of the young conductor to ask questions, a desire to be totally in charge and a strong resistance to accepting anything that reeks of a suggestion. The moment comes when they say, 'Will you be in the room for the next rehearsal?' The very strong suggestion is 'Get out of my way!'

My way of working is not to everyone's taste. But it is my way, which has evolved over fifty years in professional music and is still evolving. I know what I need to know; I know the questions I need to ask and I know where to go to ask those questions.

I love to ask questions. I have so much to catch up on that I can hardly wait to ask questions. I will frequently call people out of the blue if I have a question that is worrying me and to which I cannot find the answer in one of the great treatises. I love working with artists like Eddie Perfect, Paul Capsis, Melissa Langton, Christa Hughes, Erkki Veltheim, Casey Bennetto and Paul Wright, all of whom have inspired me with their dedication and their particular brand of artistry. Our production of *The Threepenny Opera,* a collaboration for which I invited Michael Kantor, then artistic director of the Malthouse Theatre, to the operatic table, was roundly criticised by our well-meaning artistic advisory committee. An opera company has no business doing this sort of repertoire, one of the more pompous members of the committee opined. The production took the company to new heights and introduced a range of artists to our ever-widening circle of people performing on the lyric stage. The Sydney Theatre Company thought well enough of it to include it in their 2011 season, so something must have struck a chord.

For me, the next fifty years promise to be very challenging indeed: there is still so much to do and so much to catch up on. To ward off the symptoms of old age – and I assure you that I don't feel a bit old and can still run rings around the youth in the company – I have taken a membership at the local gymnasium, where I have a regime of training. Sadly, the effects of this regime are usually negated by my mouth, a ready receptor for all things edible, especially bread and butter. Indeed, anything essentially containing carbohydrates and fat with a sprinkling of sugar is good. A student asked me recently, 'When I'm fat and old like you, will I have as much energy as you?' That he still lives is based on the fact that the principal idea implied in his statement is hope. Hope is all we have.

I hope one day every child in this land will be able to have a music teacher who can teach them music properly. I hope one day we will all find the courage to tell the bureaucrats exactly what we think of their stupid ideas. I learned in London the value of a direct response and was delighted to find that the sentiment of this direct response was, in fact, universal. A young child – let's call her Joyce – was coming to school in the middle of winter in cotton skirts and bobby socks. A well-meaning school aid, by the name of Mrs Windsor, said in her beautifully expressive Cockney accent, 'Joyce, you mus' go 'ome and tell your muvva vat you 'ave to 'ave a win'er coa'.' Joyce returned the next day and was asked by Mrs Windsor: 'Well, Joyce, did you ask your muvva abou' a coa'?' To which Joyce (who was from the West Indies) replied, 'Yes, ah did, Miss Winsah, an' mah mudder sez dat you can kiss her ass!'

Thank you, Joyce (who by now must be about fifty years old). The message was clear.

I trust that my message to those who have it in their power to change things for the better in this country musically is equally clear and direct. Had any of those who have the power to change things at a government level been at our recent performances of the medieval miracle play *The Play of Daniel*, they would have seen why music study should be mandatory across the land. This show was a collaboration between the Victorian Youth Opera and a classical Turkish music group, the Nefes Ensemble. As the show opened with a Turkish flute melody that led into the first chorus of young voices, an unlikely community of singers, instrumentalists and audience members were united by this uplifting and intensely spiritual music.

After fifty years in music I found myself learning about Turkish classical music and having new musical doors opening for me. How lucky am I? Very!

If music be the food of love, play on, give me excess of it.

Notes on the Text

Although this book is primarily a memoir of my experience, these works by others were consulted in the research, and some are also quoted in the text:

Anthony Besch obituary (*The Guardian*, 2 January 2003)

'The Dawkins Reconstruction of Australian Higher Education' / Grant Harman (paper presented at the American Education Research Association's annual meeting, San Francisco, CA, 27–31 March 1989)

'Dingoes and Divas: The Making of an Opera Called *Lindy*' / Miriam Cosic (*The Australian Magazine*, 19 October 2002)

'The Schulwerk – Its Origin and Aims'/ Carl Orff, transl. by Arnold Walter (*Music Educators Journal,* April–May 1963)

Timing is Everything: A Life Backstage at the Opera / Moffatt Oxenbould (ABC Books, 2005)

Acknowledgements

In editing this book, the vigilant and astute Sybil Nolan indicated, in an early series of edits, that I had spent considerable time talking about our poodle, Louis, and almost no time in mentioning my family, the people I love more than anything else in the whole world and for whom I have only immeasurable respect and admiration.

My family, consisting of my wife Maureen, to whom this memoir is dedicated, and my children, Claire and Anthony, have been a source of inspiration to me always. It is very testing living in a household in which the other three members have always held views, opinions, ideas and suggestions especially for me and the running of my life.

Claire once confronted me with this gem prior to a music examination, which was: 'I need to know the answers to these questions and don't give me any of your free-range teaching … I just want the answers.' Anthony, on the other hand, arrived in the kitchen one morning in Perth with: 'How do you see the world in a grain of sand?'

Maureen, blessed with an abundance of that rare commodity known as common sense, has always been able to help me see things in a more measured way, reducing my oftentimes homicidal reaction to some situations, (referred to by Claire as frontal lobe disinhibition) to a considered and rational view.

My family is now increased and enhanced by Dominique, Anthony's wife, and mother of the three most perfect grandchildren the world has ever been lucky enough to see, Camille (Poupsie), Elise (Schmoo) and Antoinette (Toutsie).

I also want to acknowledge my brothers and their wives, Terry and Evelyn Gill, Chris and Dot Gill, and their families for their love and support.

In every chapter of this book there are many people whose names have been omitted. Their names may not be in this book but they are absolutely in my memory, from my first friend at St Anthony's Clovelly in 1946, a boy called Jimmy Bolton, to my most recent work colleagues and friends, Lucy Shorrocks, Managing Director of Victorian Opera and David McSkimming, Victorian Opera's fabulous Head of Music.

It is not possible to mention all of the activities that I have been engaged with both professionally and privately, no matter how stimulating or engaging they have been. Likewise it is impossible to acknowledge all those who have been part of my life, or who have influenced me in the many facets mentioned in my memoir. The risk of giving offence, through omission, led me to believe that a general acknowledgement would be the way to go.

Finally to Tom Gilliatt, I hope that your decision to invite this memoir from listening to one impassioned TEDx talk is justified … thank you.

Index